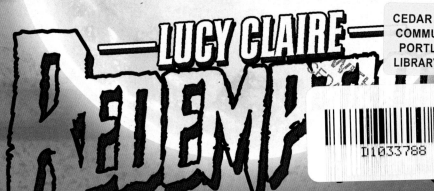

LUCY CLAIRE
REDEMPTION

VOLUME ONE

Shadowline

image

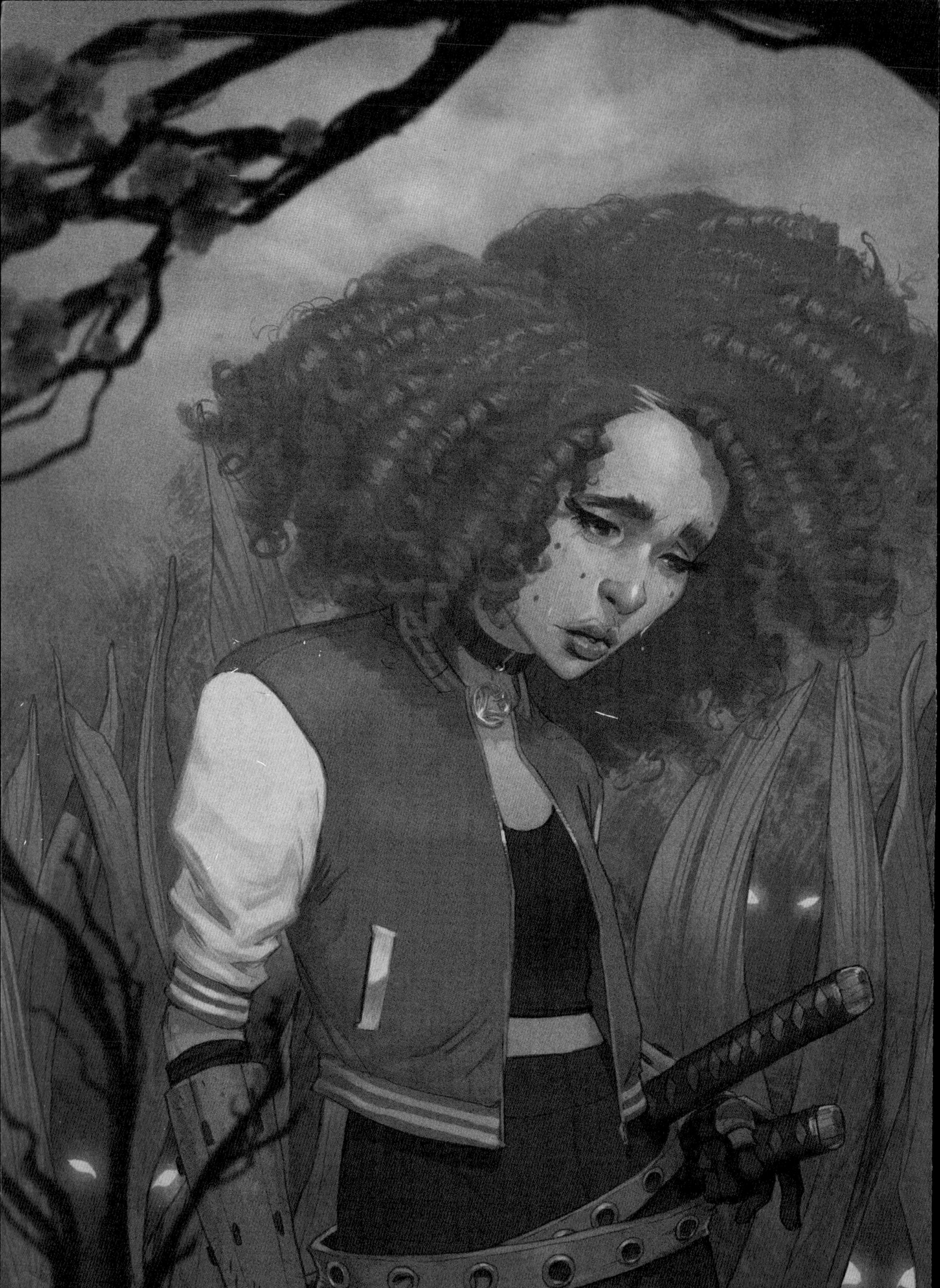

LUCY CLAIRE: REDEMPTION, VOLUME ONE

FIRST PRINTING: SEPTEMBER 2020 ISBN: 978-1-5343-1616-4

Published by Image Comics, Inc. Office of publication: 2701 NW Vaughn St., Suite 780, Portland, OR 97210.

CREATED, WRITTEN, ILLUSTRATED
and LETTERED by
JOHN UPCHURCH

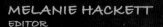

MELANIE HACKETT
EDITOR

TIM DANIEL
LOGO DESIGN

MARC LOMBARDI
COMMUNICATIONS

JIM VALENTINO
PUBLISHER/BOOK DESIGN

IMAGE COMICS, INC.
Robert Kirkman—Chief Operating Officer
Erik Larsen—Chief Financial Officer
Todd McFarlane—President
Marc Silvestri—Chief Executive Officer
Jim Valentino—Vice President
Eric Stephenson—Publisher/Chief Creative Officer
Jeff Boison—Director of Sales & Publishing Planning
Jeff Stang—Director of Direct Market Sales
Kat Salazar—Director of PR & Marketing
Drew Gill—Cover Editor
Heather Doornink—Production Director
Nicole Lapalme—Controller
IMAGECOMICS.COM

FOR MY CHILDREN

YOU ARE MY HAPPINESS,
YOU ARE MY HEART,
YOU ARE THE LOVES OF MY LIFE.
THE THREE OF YOU MEAN MORE
TO ME THAN ANYTHING THIS
WORLD CAN OFFER.
YOU BEING MY CHILDREN
AND I YOUR FATHER
HAS CREATED THE GREATEST MOMENTS
I WILL EVER KNOW.
YOU ARE BRILLIANT,
YOU ARE BEAUTIFUL,
YOU ARE MY ALL.

I LOVE YOU.

CHAPTER ONE

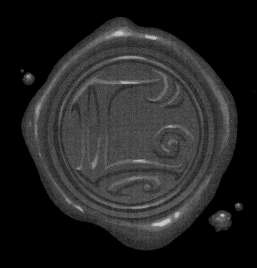

"EVERY DAY WITHOUT YOU
IS UNIMAGINABLE PAIN.

AND WITH EVERY DAY THAT PASSES
THE PAIN ONLY GROWS WORSE."

ISSUE #1 COVER A

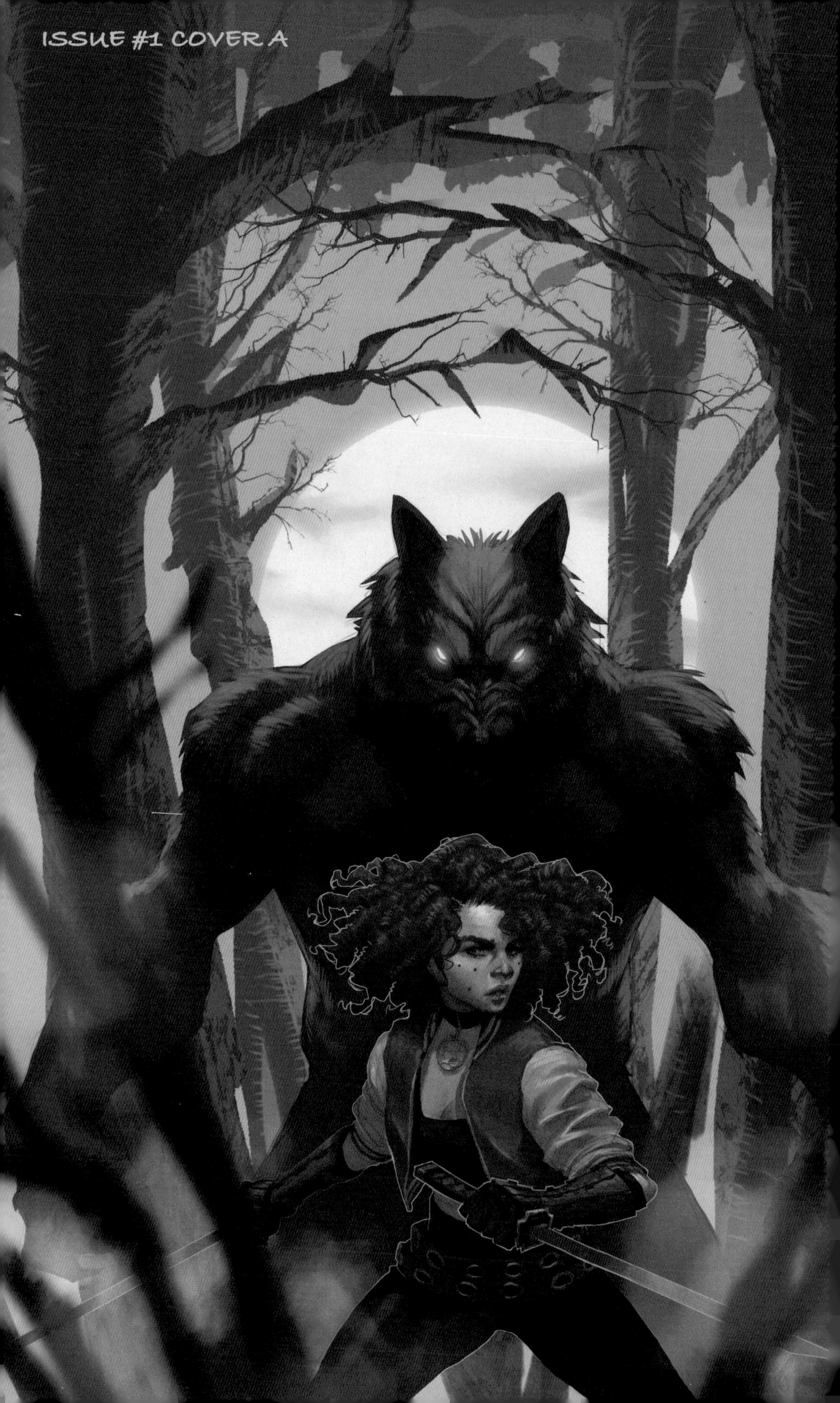

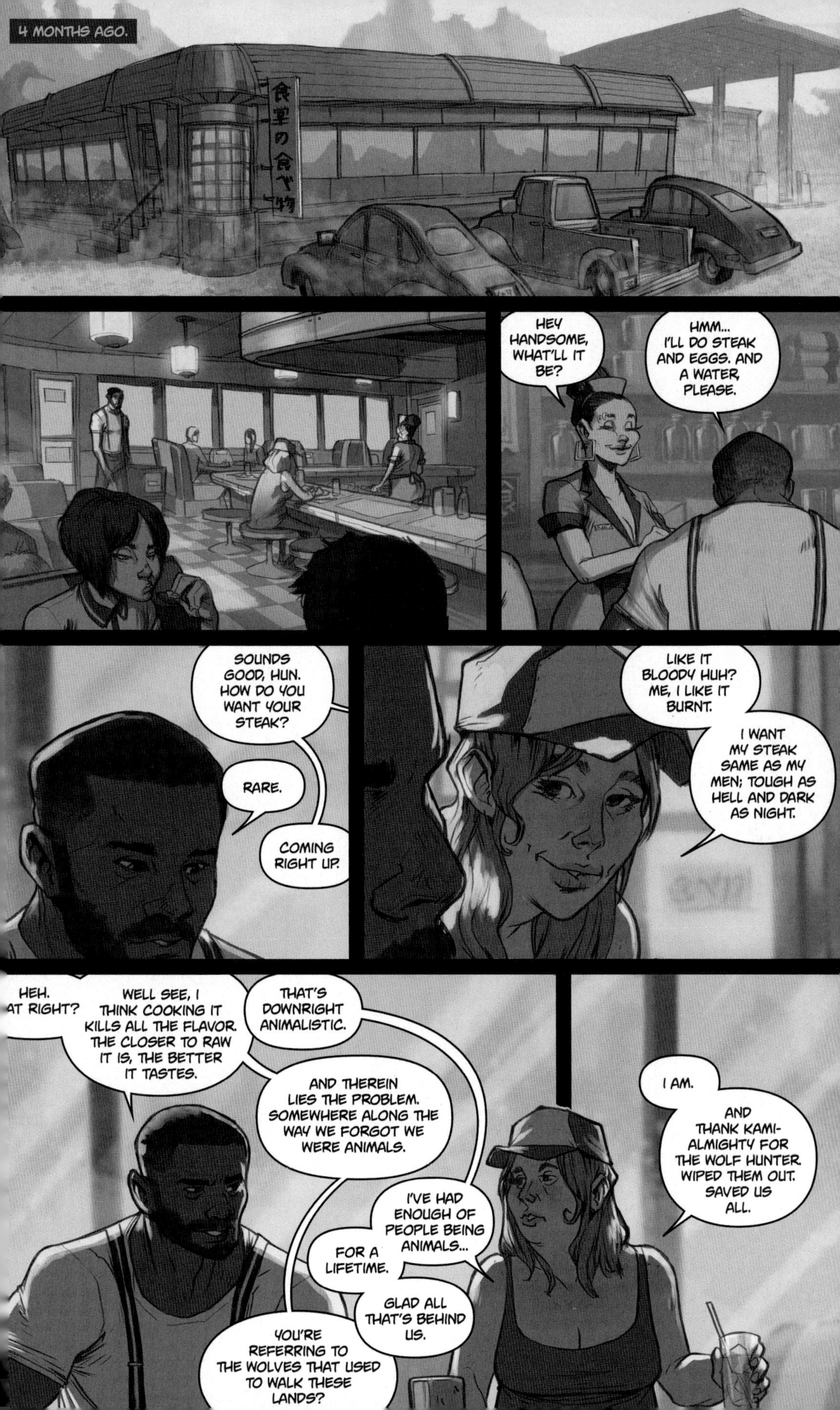
4 MONTHS AGO.
食堂の食べ物
HEY HANDSOME, WHAT'LL IT BE?
HMM... I'LL DO STEAK AND EGGS. AND A WATER, PLEASE.
SOUNDS GOOD, HUN. HOW DO YOU WANT YOUR STEAK?
RARE.
COMING RIGHT UP.
LIKE IT BLOODY HUH? ME, I LIKE IT BURNT.
I WANT MY STEAK SAME AS MY MEN; TOUGH AS HELL AND DARK AS NIGHT.
HEH. AT RIGHT?
WELL SEE, I THINK COOKING IT KILLS ALL THE FLAVOR. THE CLOSER TO RAW IT IS, THE BETTER IT TASTES.
THAT'S DOWNRIGHT ANIMALISTIC.
AND THEREIN LIES THE PROBLEM. SOMEWHERE ALONG THE WAY WE FORGOT WE WERE ANIMALS.
YOU'RE REFERRING TO THE WOLVES THAT USED TO WALK THESE LANDS?
I AM.
AND THANK KAMI-ALMIGHTY FOR THE WOLF HUNTER. WIPED THEM OUT. SAVED US ALL.
I'VE HAD ENOUGH OF PEOPLE BEING ANIMALS...
FOR A LIFETIME.
GLAD ALL THAT'S BEHIND US.

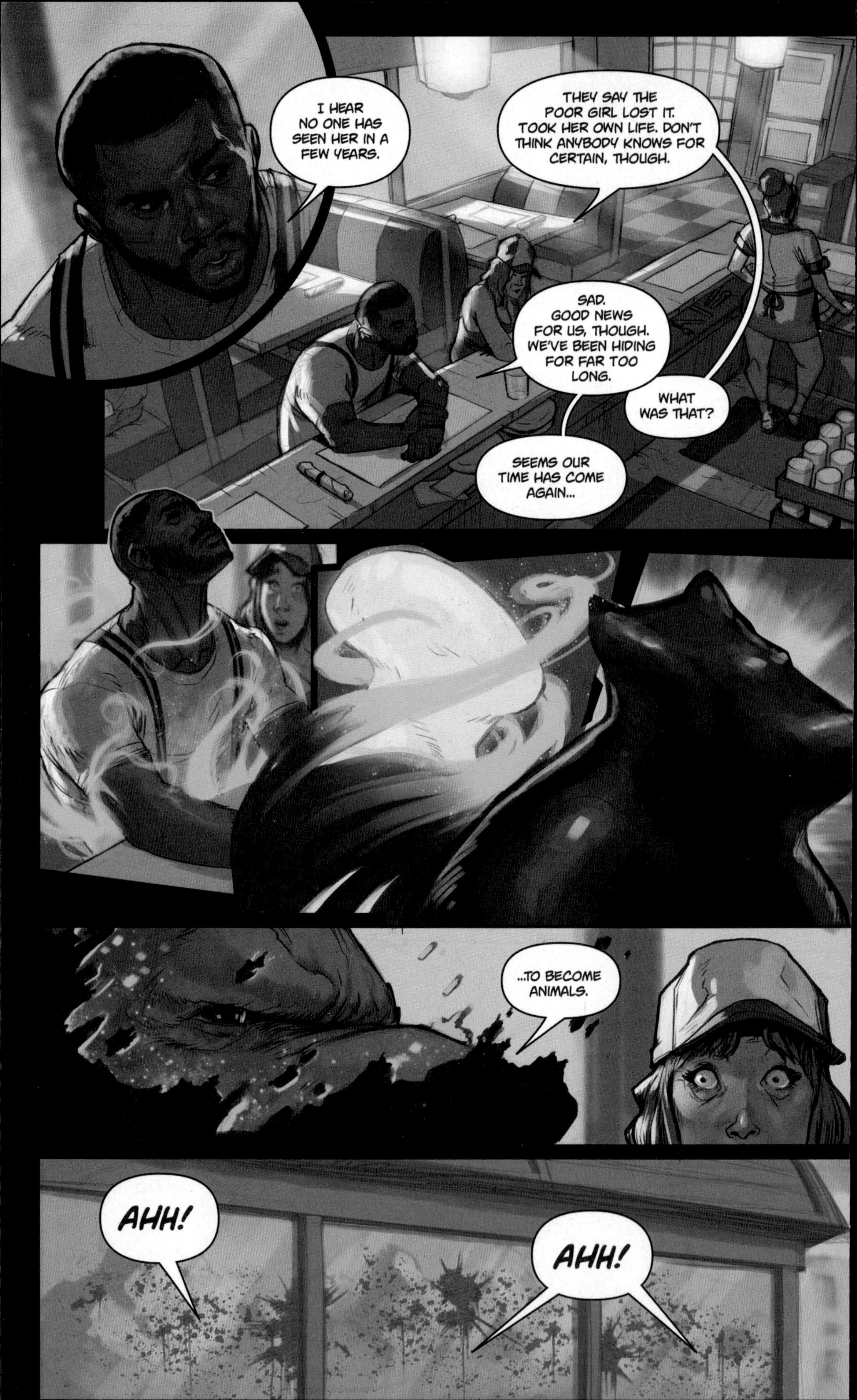
I HEAR NO ONE HAS SEEN HER IN A FEW YEARS.
THEY SAY THE POOR GIRL LOST IT. TOOK HER OWN LIFE. DON'T THINK ANYBODY KNOWS FOR CERTAIN, THOUGH.
SAD. GOOD NEWS FOR US, THOUGH. WE'VE BEEN HIDING FOR FAR TOO LONG.
WHAT WAS THAT?
SEEMS OUR TIME HAS COME AGAIN...
...TO BECOME ANIMALS.
AHH!
AHH!

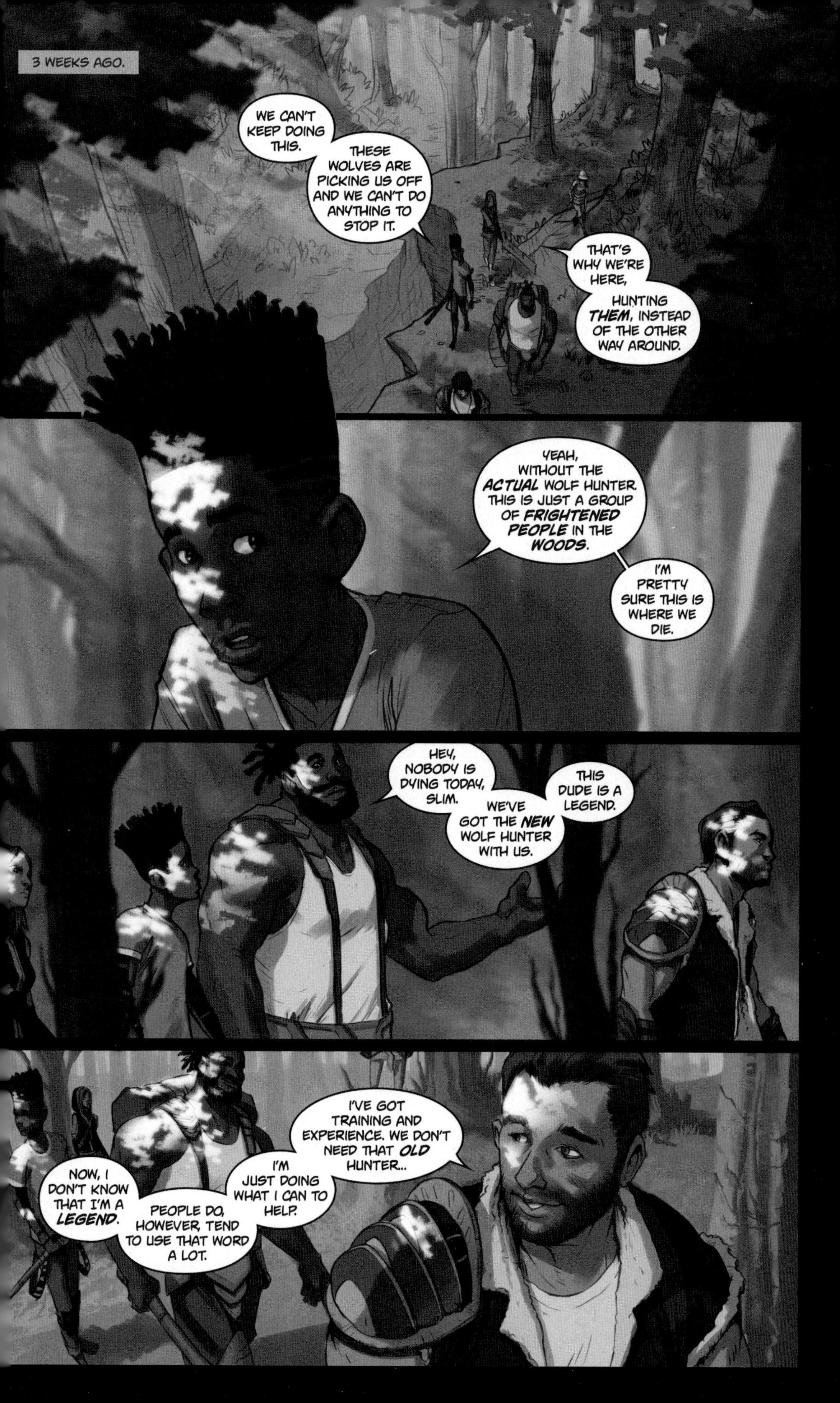
3 WEEKS AGO.
WE CAN'T KEEP DOING THIS.
THESE WOLVES ARE PICKING US OFF AND WE CAN'T DO ANYTHING TO STOP IT.
THAT'S WHY WE'RE HERE,
HUNTING THEM, INSTEAD OF THE OTHER WAY AROUND.
YEAH, WITHOUT THE ACTUAL WOLF HUNTER THIS IS JUST A GROUP OF FRIGHTENED PEOPLE IN THE WOODS.
I'M PRETTY SURE THIS IS WHERE WE DIE.
HEY, NOBODY IS DYING TODAY, SLIM.
WE'VE GOT THE NEW WOLF HUNTER WITH US.
THIS DUDE IS A LEGEND.
NOW, I DON'T KNOW THAT I'M A LEGEND.
PEOPLE DO, HOWEVER, TEND TO USE THAT WORD A LOT.
I'M JUST DOING WHAT I CAN TO HELP.
I'VE GOT TRAINING AND EXPERIENCE. WE DON'T NEED THAT OLD HUNTER...

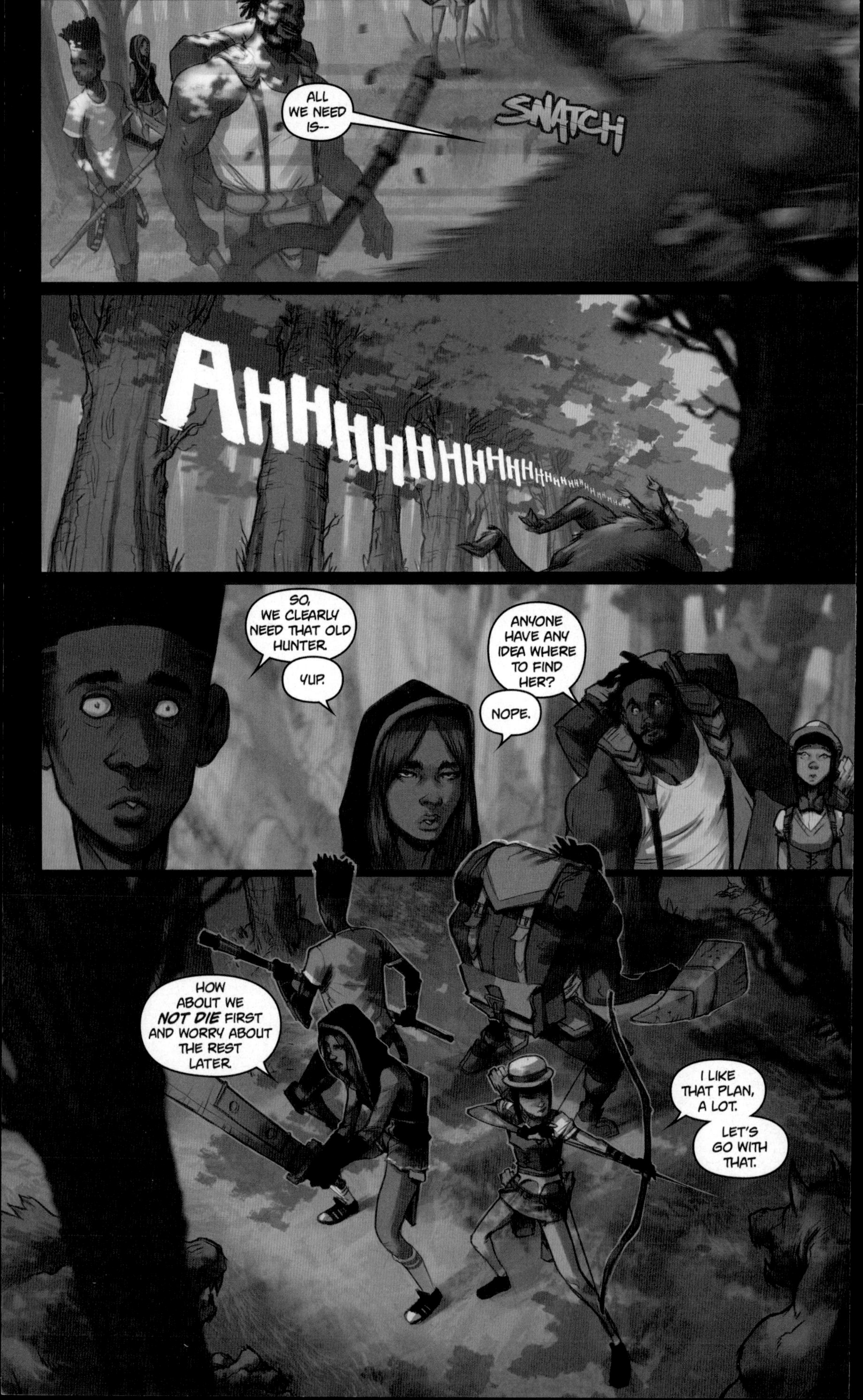
ALL WE NEED IS--
SNATCH
AHHHHHHHHHHHHHHHHHHHH...
SO, WE CLEARLY NEED THAT OLD HUNTER.
YUP.
ANYONE HAVE ANY IDEA WHERE TO FIND HER?
NOPE.
HOW ABOUT WE NOT DIE FIRST AND WORRY ABOUT THE REST LATER.
I LIKE THAT PLAN, A LOT.
LET'S GO WITH THAT.

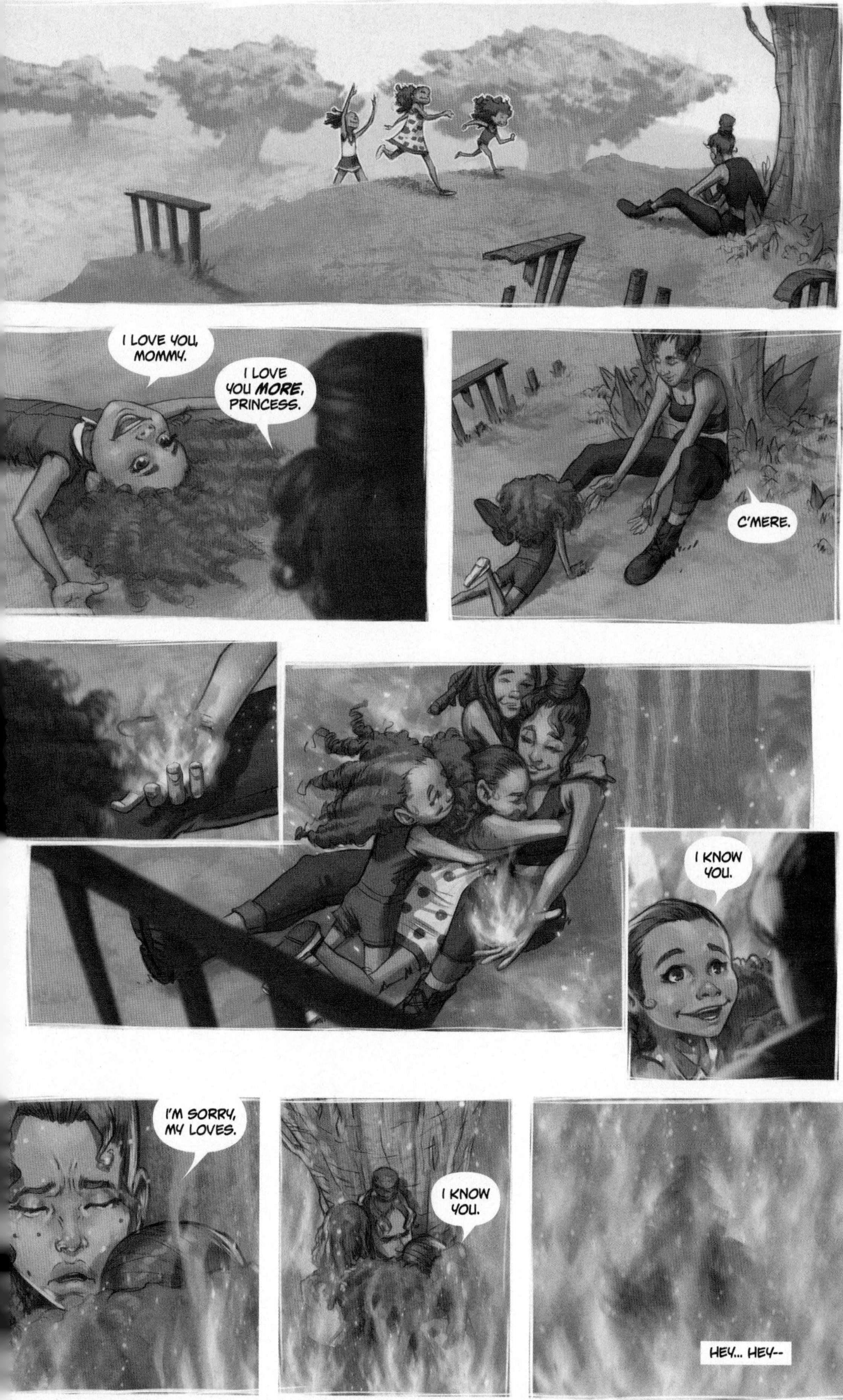
I LOVE YOU, MOMMY.
I LOVE YOU MORE, PRINCESS.
C'MERE.
I KNOW YOU.
I'M SORRY, MY LOVES.
I KNOW YOU.
HEY... HEY--

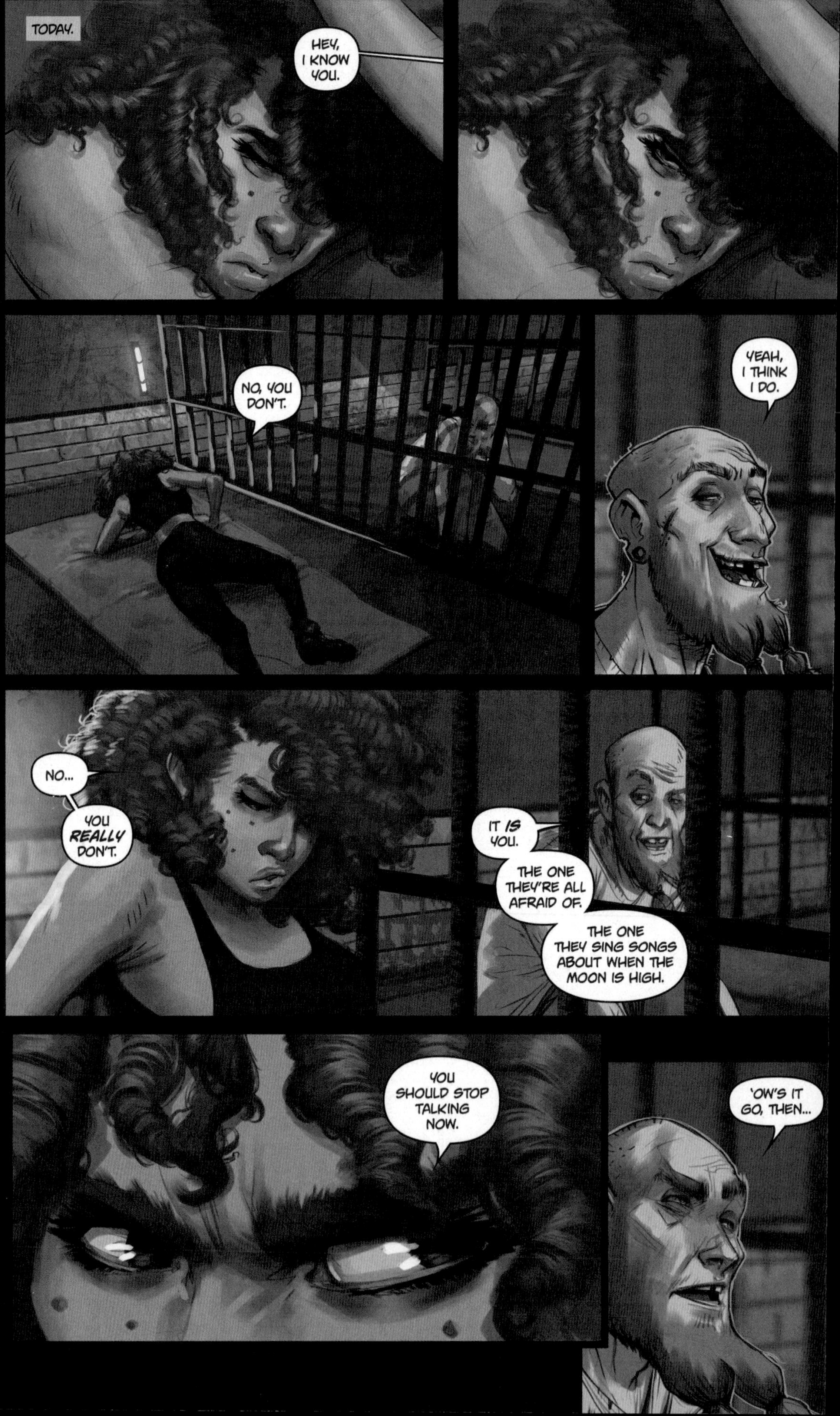
TODAY.
HEY, I KNOW YOU.
NO, YOU DON'T.
YEAH, I THINK I DO.
NO...
YOU REALLY DON'T.
IT IS YOU.
THE ONE THEY'RE ALL AFRAID OF.
THE ONE THEY SING SONGS ABOUT WHEN THE MOON IS HIGH.
YOU SHOULD STOP TALKING NOW.
'OW'S IT GO, THEN...

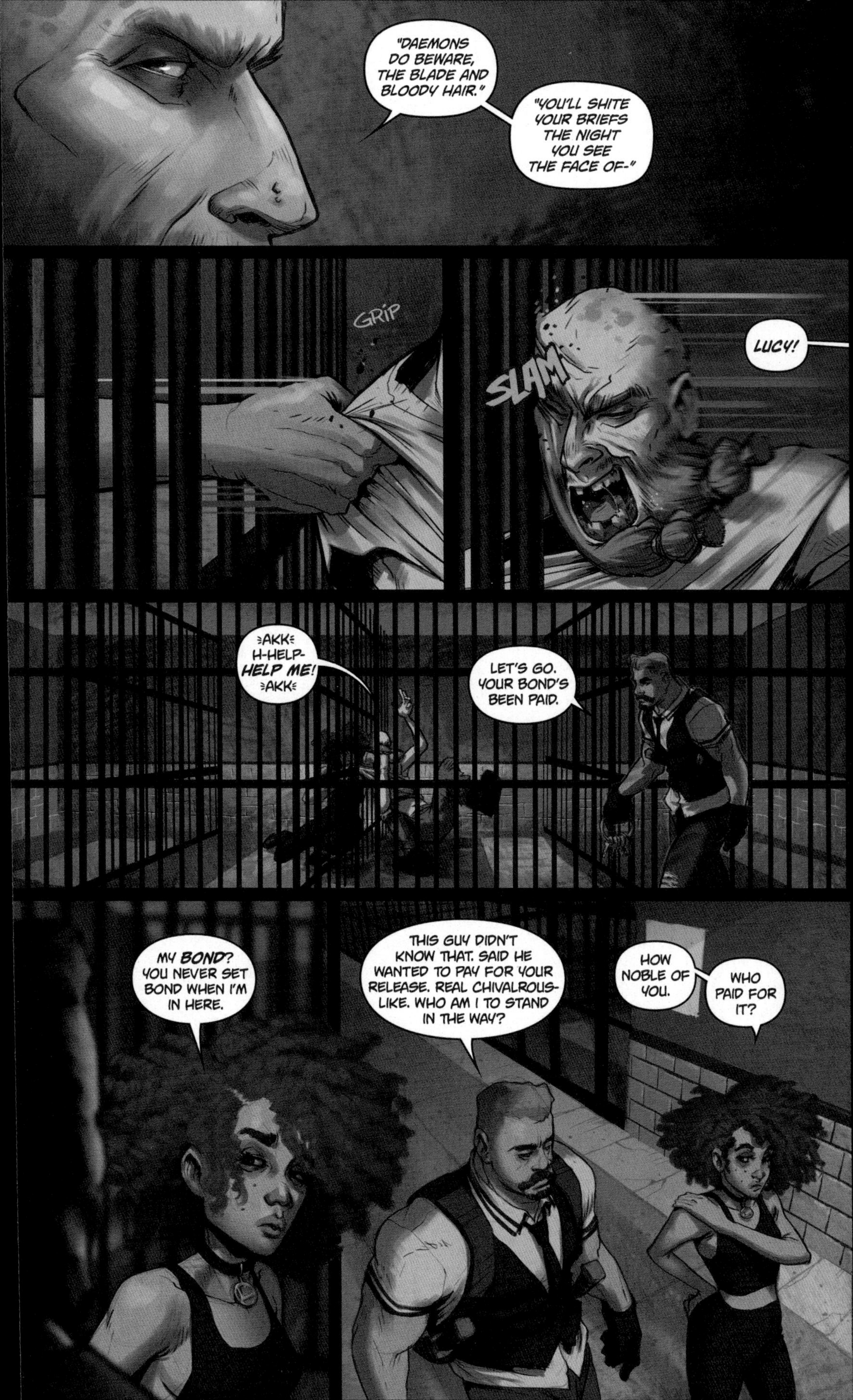
"DAEMONS DO BEWARE, THE BLADE AND BLOODY HAIR."
"YOU'LL SHITE YOUR BRIEFS THE NIGHT YOU SEE THE FACE OF-"
GRIP
SLAM
LUCY!
AKK H-HELP- HELP ME! AKK
LET'S GO. YOUR BOND'S BEEN PAID.
MY BOND? YOU NEVER SET BOND WHEN I'M IN HERE.
THIS GUY DIDN'T KNOW THAT. SAID HE WANTED TO PAY FOR YOUR RELEASE. REAL CHIVALROUS-LIKE. WHO AM I TO STAND IN THE WAY?
HOW NOBLE OF YOU.
WHO PAID FOR IT?

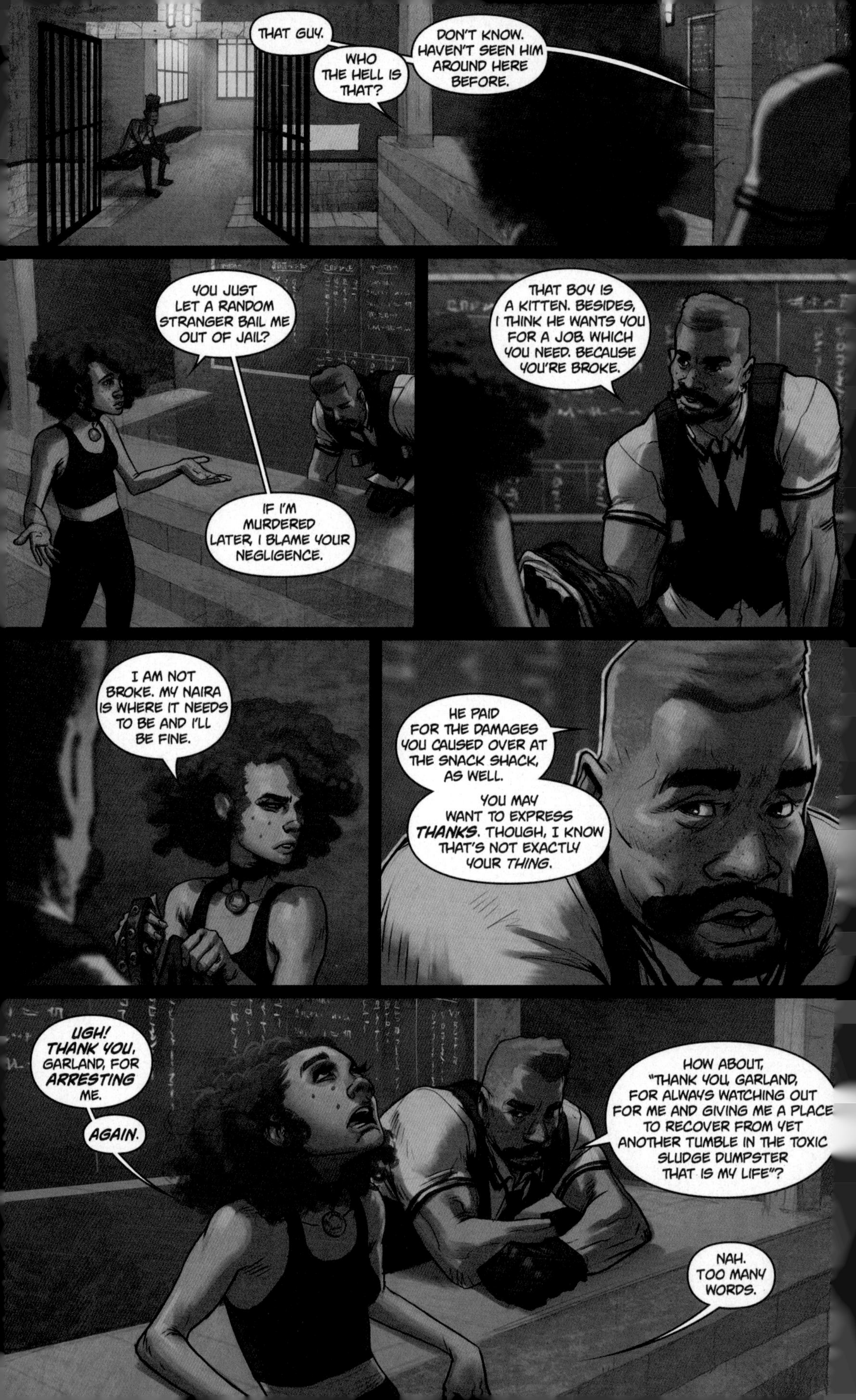
THAT GUY.
WHO THE HELL IS THAT?
DON'T KNOW. HAVEN'T SEEN HIM AROUND HERE BEFORE.
YOU JUST LET A RANDOM STRANGER BAIL ME OUT OF JAIL?
IF I'M MURDERED LATER, I BLAME YOUR NEGLIGENCE.
THAT BOY IS A KITTEN. BESIDES, I THINK HE WANTS YOU FOR A JOB. WHICH YOU NEED. BECAUSE YOU'RE BROKE.
I AM NOT BROKE. MY NAIRA IS WHERE IT NEEDS TO BE AND I'LL BE FINE.
HE PAID FOR THE DAMAGES YOU CAUSED OVER AT THE SNACK SHACK, AS WELL.
YOU MAY WANT TO EXPRESS ***THANKS***. THOUGH, I KNOW THAT'S NOT EXACTLY YOUR *THING*.
UGH! THANK YOU, GARLAND, FOR ***ARRESTING*** ME.
AGAIN.
HOW ABOUT, "THANK YOU, GARLAND, FOR ALWAYS WATCHING OUT FOR ME AND GIVING ME A PLACE TO RECOVER FROM YET ANOTHER TUMBLE IN THE TOXIC SLUDGE DUMPSTER THAT IS MY LIFE"?
NAH. TOO MANY WORDS.

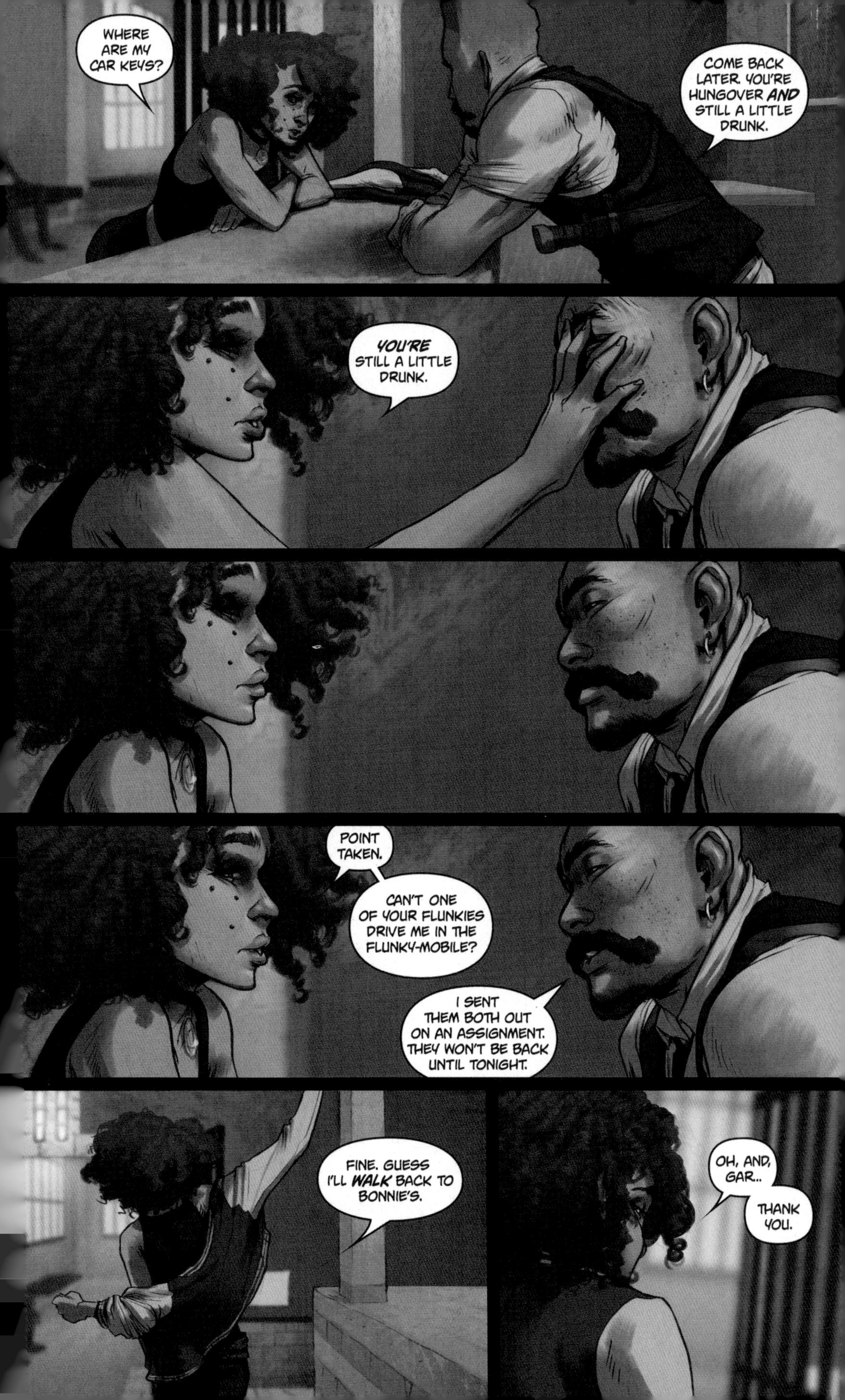

WHERE ARE MY CAR KEYS?
COME BACK LATER. YOU'RE HUNGOVER **AND** STILL A LITTLE DRUNK.
YOU'RE STILL A LITTLE DRUNK.
POINT TAKEN.
CAN'T ONE OF YOUR FLUNKIES DRIVE ME IN THE FLUNKY-MOBILE?
I SENT THEM BOTH OUT ON AN ASSIGNMENT. THEY WON'T BE BACK UNTIL TONIGHT.
FINE. GUESS I'LL ***WALK*** BACK TO BONNIE'S.
OH, AND, GAR...
THANK YOU.

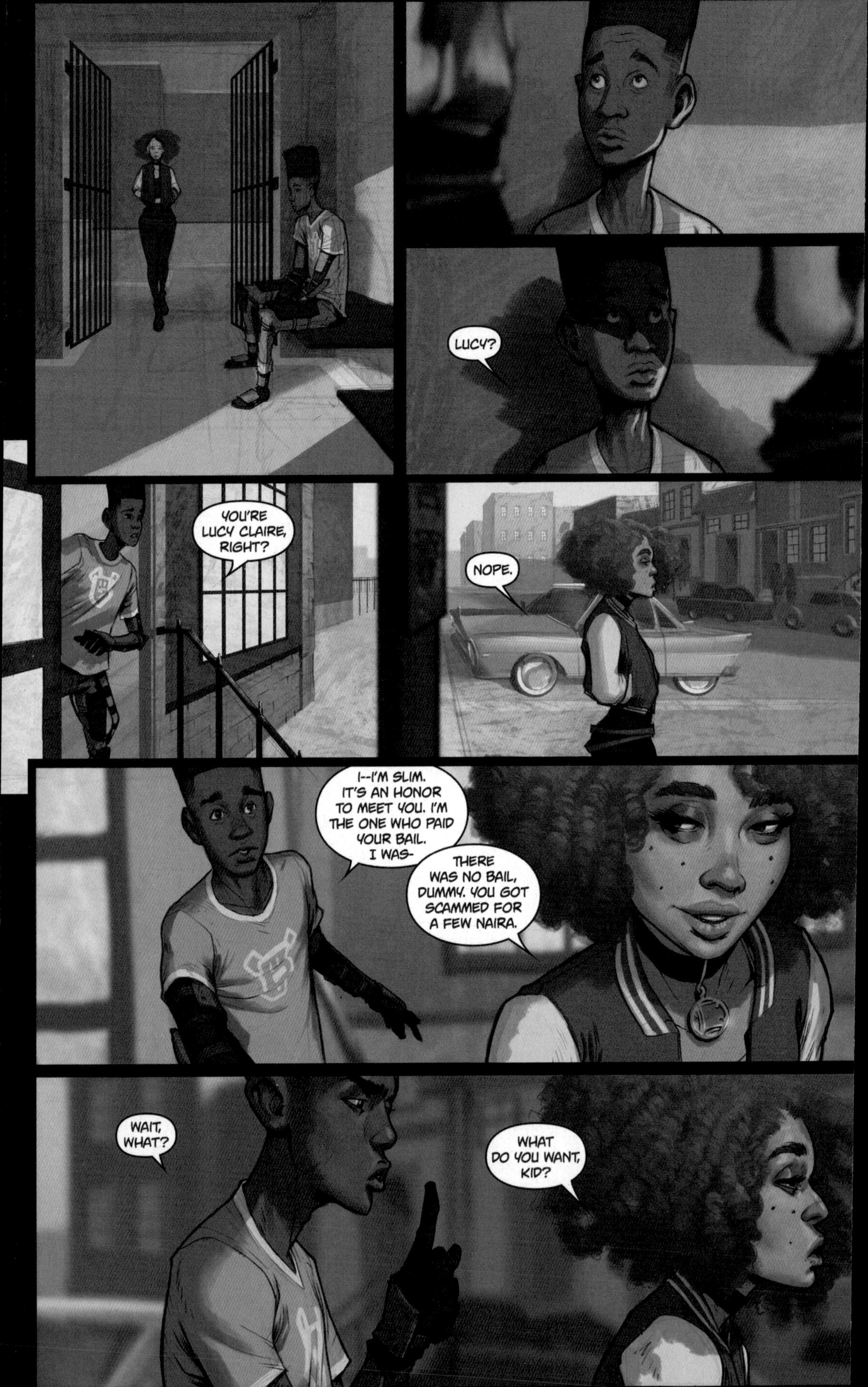
LUCY?
YOU'RE LUCY CLAIRE, RIGHT?
NOPE.
I--I'M SLIM. IT'S AN HONOR TO MEET YOU. I'M THE ONE WHO PAID YOUR BAIL. I WAS-
THERE WAS NO BAIL, DUMMY. YOU GOT SCAMMED FOR A FEW NAIRA.
WAIT, WHAT?
WHAT DO YOU WANT, KID?

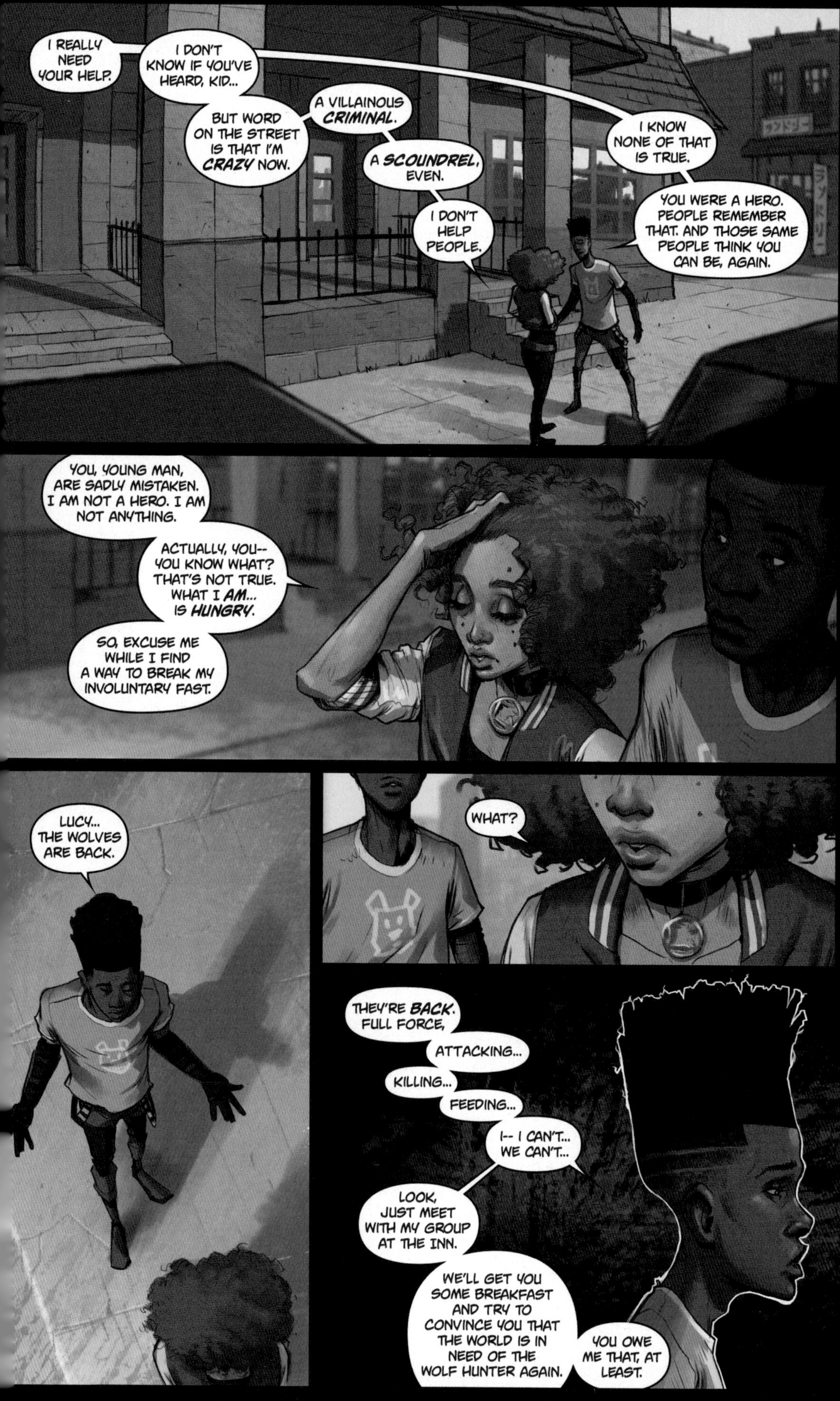

I REALLY NEED YOUR HELP.
I DON'T KNOW IF YOU'VE HEARD, KID...
BUT WORD ON THE STREET IS THAT I'M CRAZY NOW.
A VILLAINOUS CRIMINAL.
A SCOUNDREL, EVEN.
I DON'T HELP PEOPLE.
I KNOW NONE OF THAT IS TRUE.
YOU WERE A HERO. PEOPLE REMEMBER THAT. AND THOSE SAME PEOPLE THINK YOU CAN BE, AGAIN.
YOU, YOUNG MAN, ARE SADLY MISTAKEN. I AM NOT A HERO. I AM NOT ANYTHING.
ACTUALLY, YOU-- YOU KNOW WHAT? THAT'S NOT TRUE. WHAT I AM... IS HUNGRY.
SO, EXCUSE ME WHILE I FIND A WAY TO BREAK MY INVOLUNTARY FAST.
LUCY... THE WOLVES ARE BACK.
WHAT?
THEY'RE BACK. FULL FORCE,
ATTACKING...
KILLING...
FEEDING...
I-- I CAN'T... WE CAN'T...
LOOK, JUST MEET WITH MY GROUP AT THE INN.
WE'LL GET YOU SOME BREAKFAST AND TRY TO CONVINCE YOU THAT THE WORLD IS IN NEED OF THE WOLF HUNTER AGAIN.
YOU OWE ME THAT, AT LEAST.

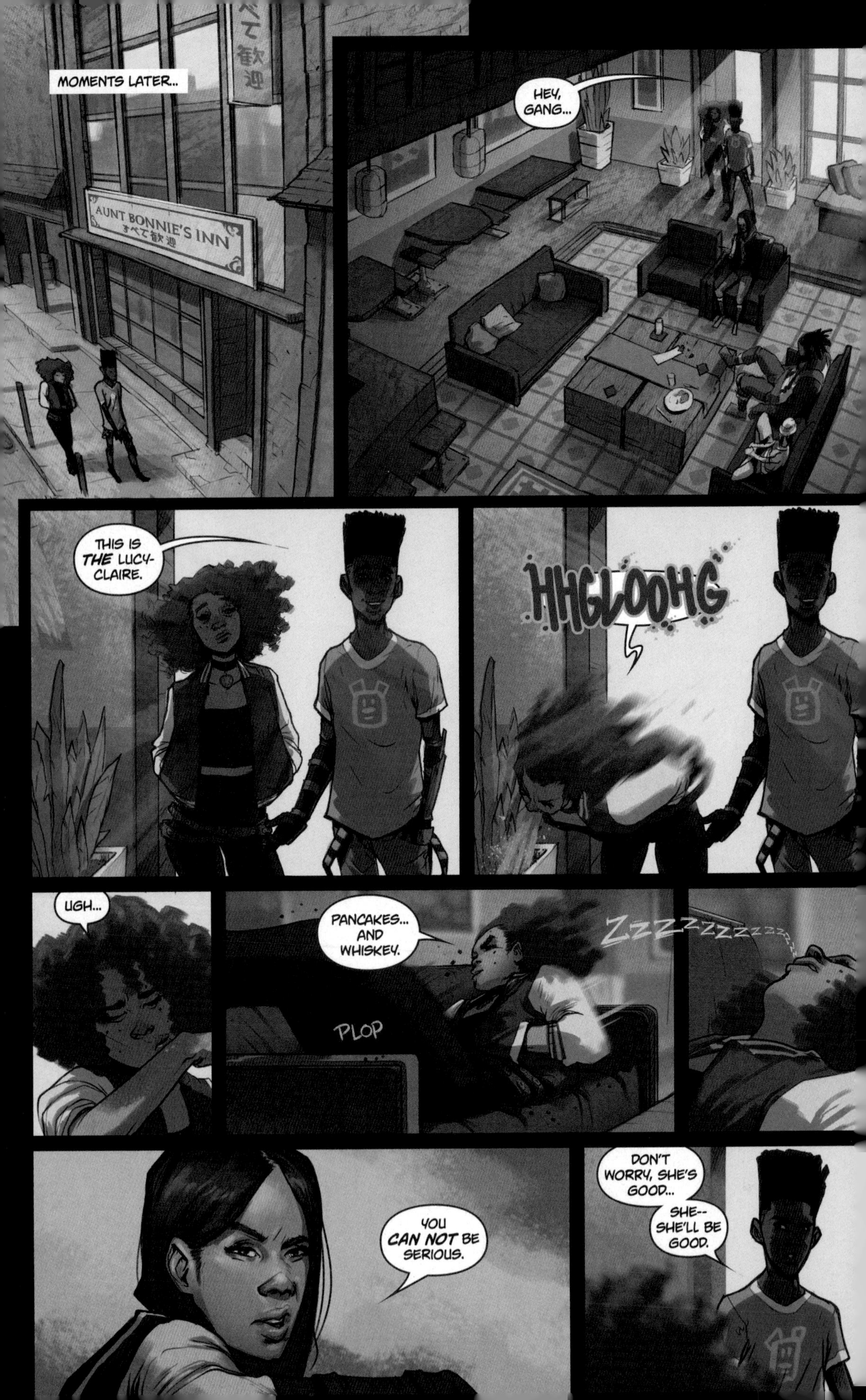
MOMENTS LATER...
AUNT BONNIE'S INN
すべて歓迎
HEY, GANG...
THIS IS THE LUCY-CLAIRE.
HHGLOOHG
UGH...
PANCAKES... AND WHISKEY.
PLOP
ZZZZZZZZZ
YOU CAN NOT BE SERIOUS.
DON'T WORRY, SHE'S GOOD...
SHE-- SHE'LL BE GOOD.

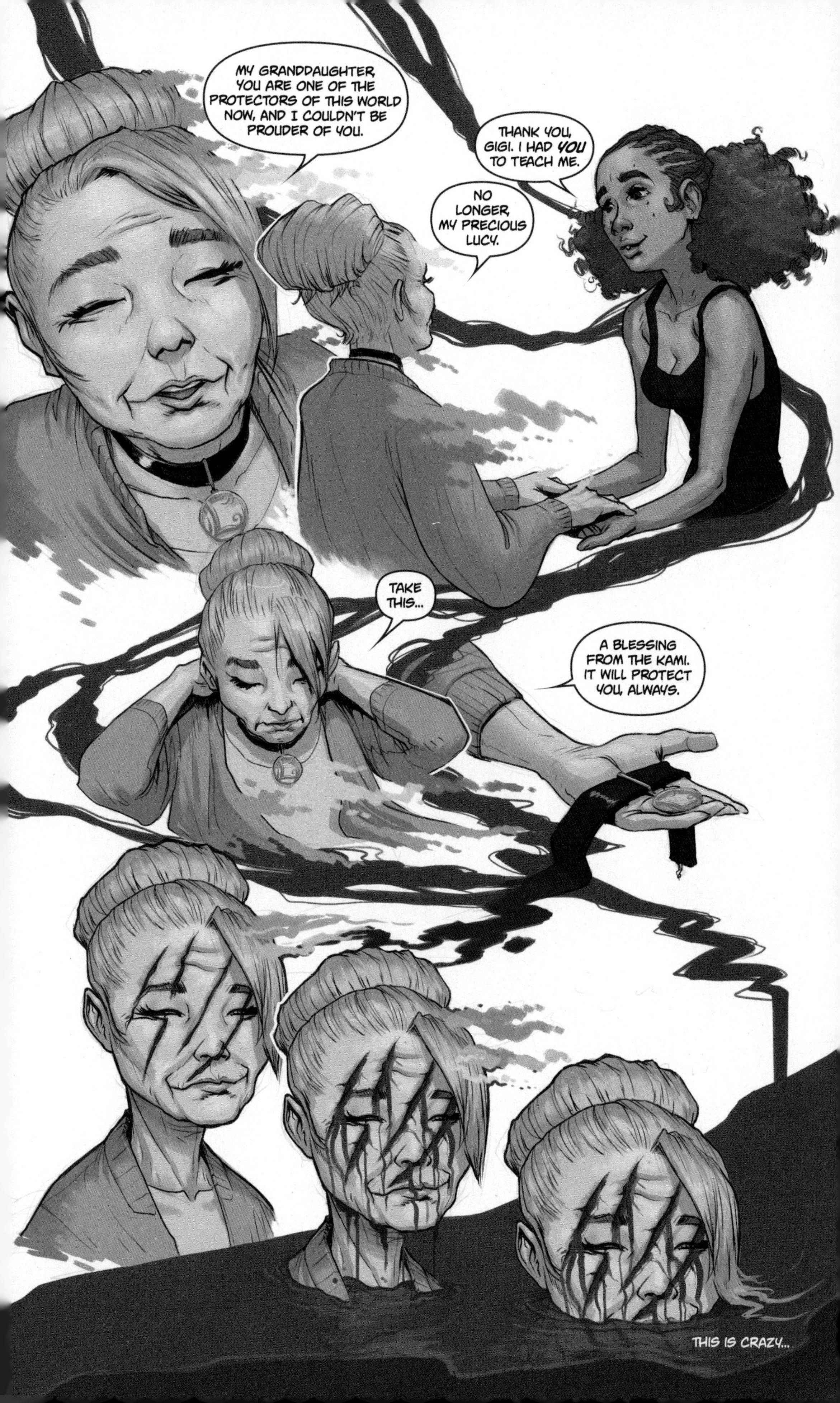
MY GRANDDAUGHTER, YOU ARE ONE OF THE PROTECTORS OF THIS WORLD NOW, AND I COULDN'T BE PROUDER OF YOU.
THANK YOU, GIGI. I HAD *YOU* TO TEACH ME.
NO LONGER, MY PRECIOUS LUCY.
TAKE THIS...
A BLESSING FROM THE KAMI. IT WILL PROTECT YOU, ALWAYS.
THIS IS CRAZY...

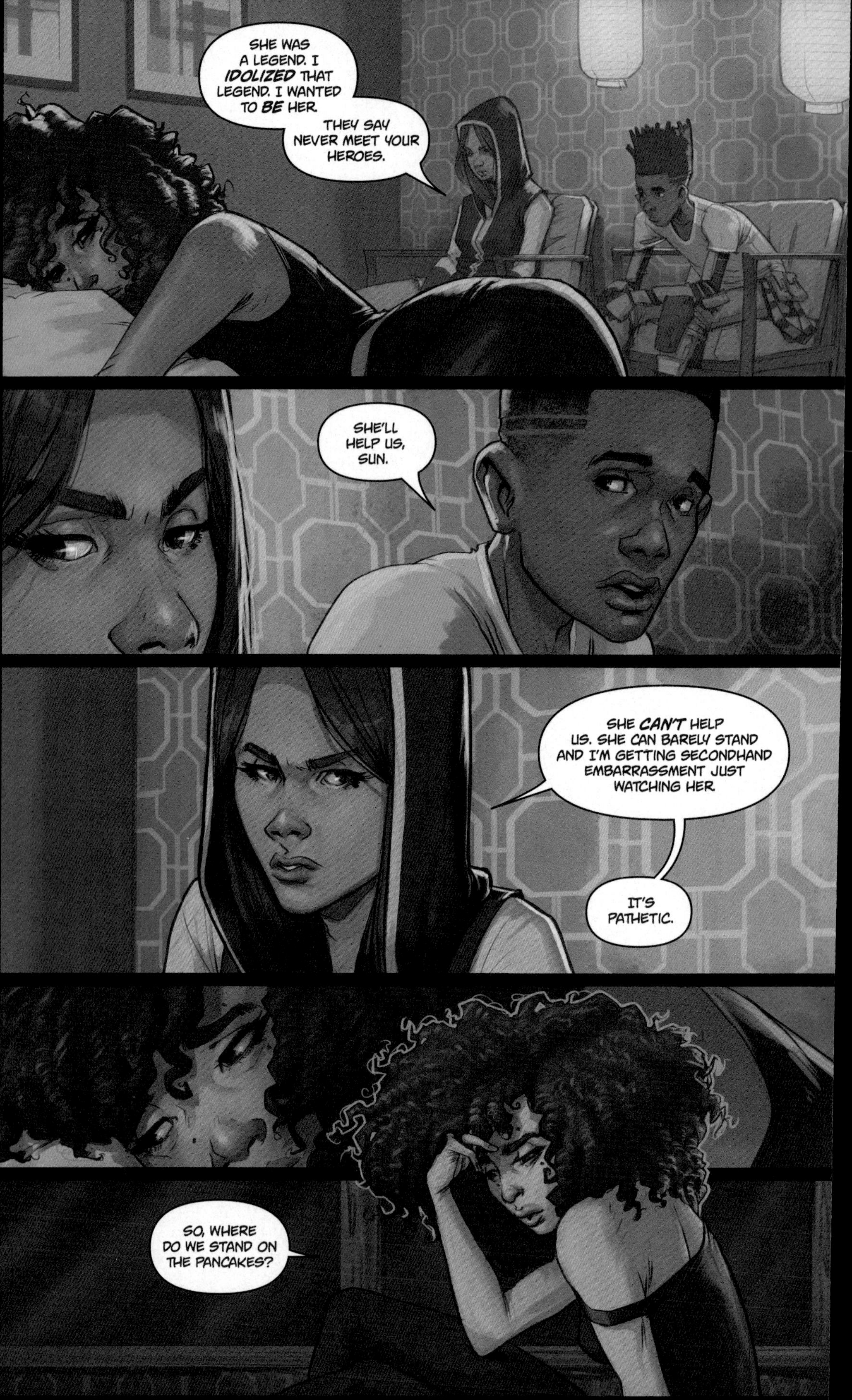

SHE WAS A LEGEND. I IDOLIZED THAT LEGEND. I WANTED TO BE HER.
THEY SAY NEVER MEET YOUR HEROES.
SHE'LL HELP US, SUN.
SHE CAN'T HELP US. SHE CAN BARELY STAND AND I'M GETTING SECONDHAND EMBARRASSMENT JUST WATCHING HER.
IT'S PATHETIC.
SO, WHERE DO WE STAND ON THE PANCAKES?

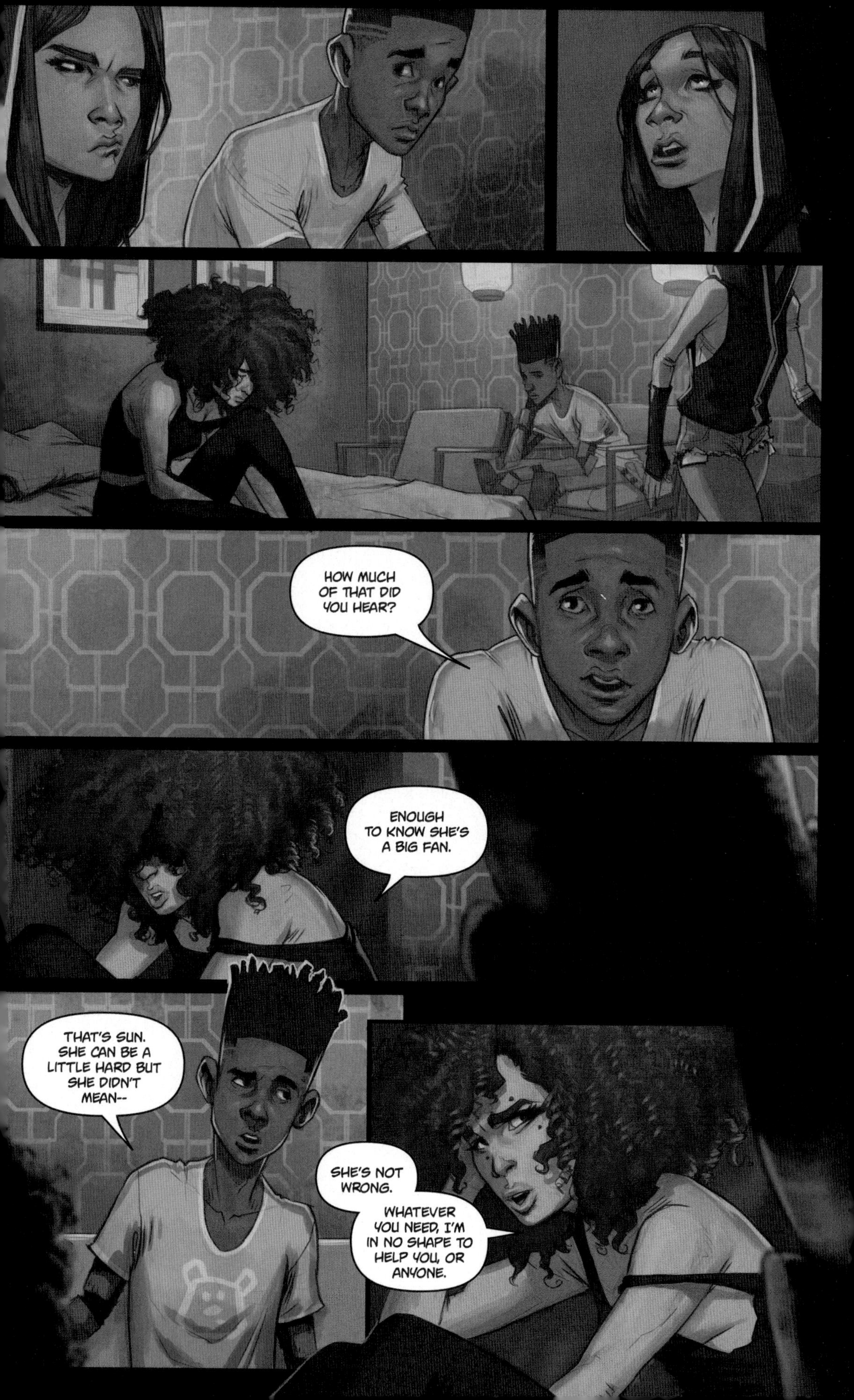
HOW MUCH OF THAT DID YOU HEAR?
ENOUGH TO KNOW SHE'S A BIG FAN.
THAT'S SUN. SHE CAN BE A LITTLE HARD BUT SHE DIDN'T MEAN--
SHE'S NOT WRONG.
WHATEVER YOU NEED, I'M IN NO SHAPE TO HELP YOU, OR ANYONE.

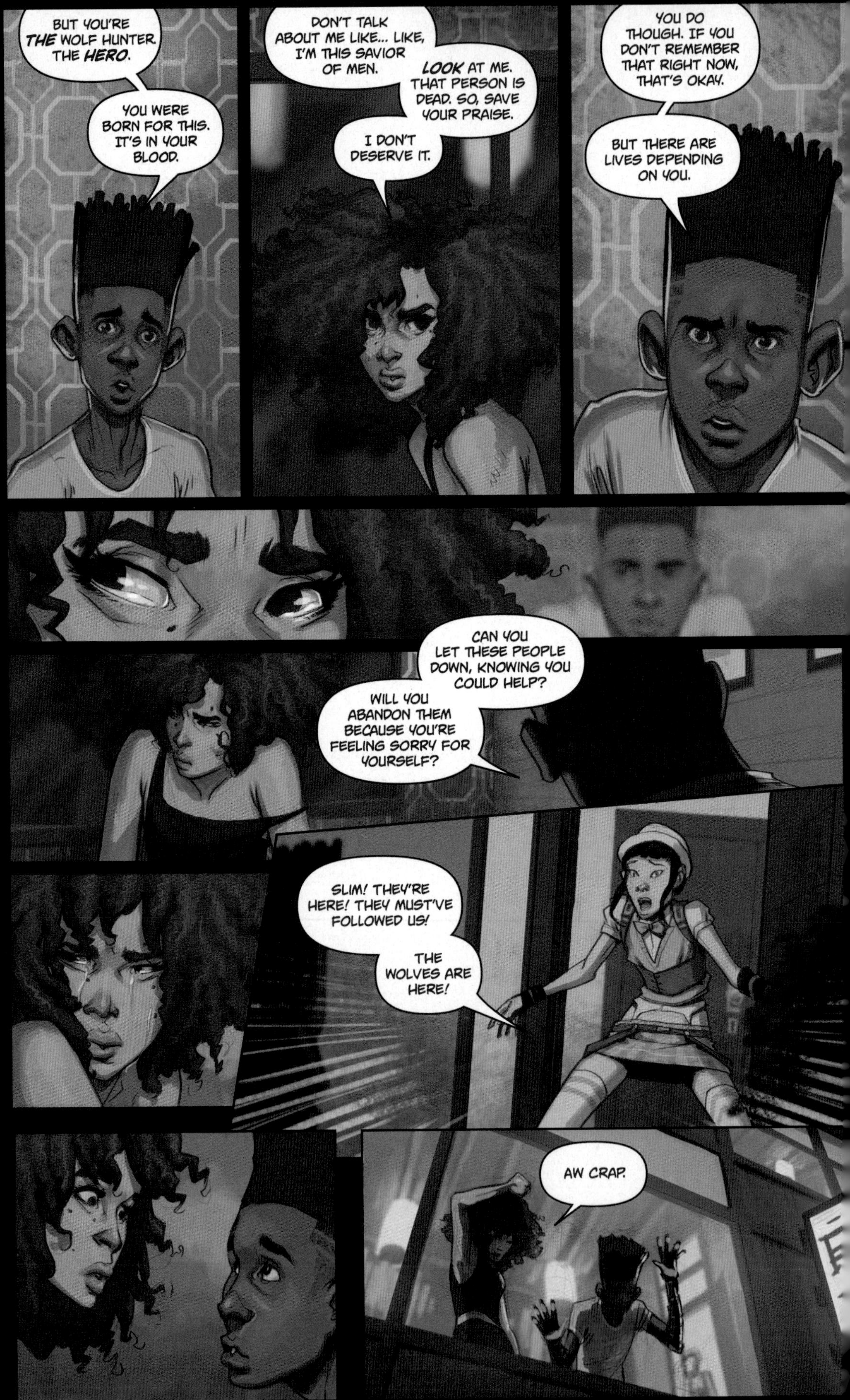
BUT YOU'RE THE WOLF HUNTER. THE HERO.
YOU WERE BORN FOR THIS. IT'S IN YOUR BLOOD.
DON'T TALK ABOUT ME LIKE... LIKE, I'M THIS SAVIOR OF MEN.
LOOK AT ME. THAT PERSON IS DEAD. SO, SAVE YOUR PRAISE.
I DON'T DESERVE IT.
YOU DO THOUGH. IF YOU DON'T REMEMBER THAT RIGHT NOW, THAT'S OKAY.
BUT THERE ARE LIVES DEPENDING ON YOU.
CAN YOU LET THESE PEOPLE DOWN, KNOWING YOU COULD HELP?
WILL YOU ABANDON THEM BECAUSE YOU'RE FEELING SORRY FOR YOURSELF?
SLIM! THEY'RE HERE! THEY MUST'VE FOLLOWED US!
THE WOLVES ARE HERE!
AW CRAP.

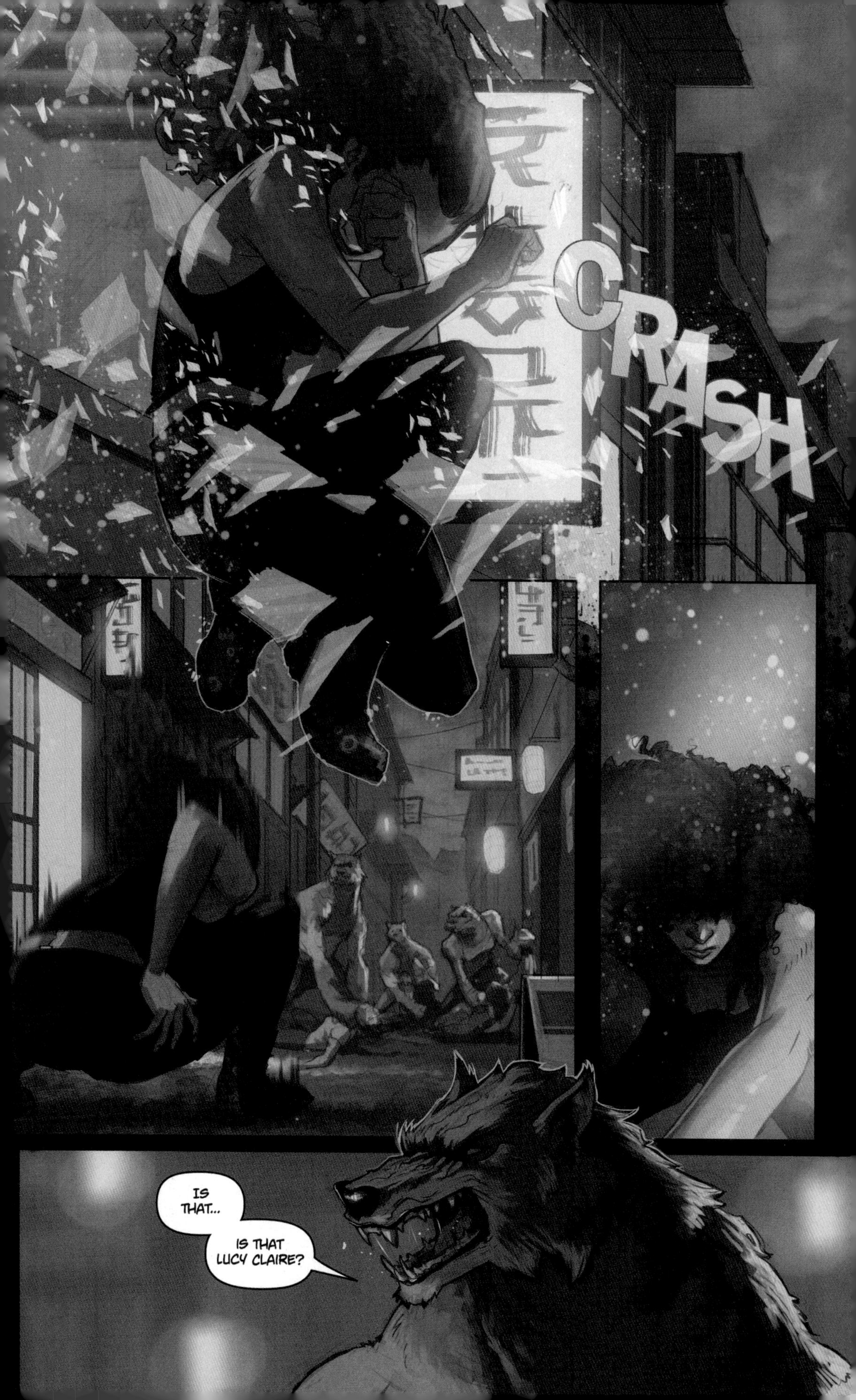
CRASH
IS THAT...
IS THAT LUCY CLAIRE?

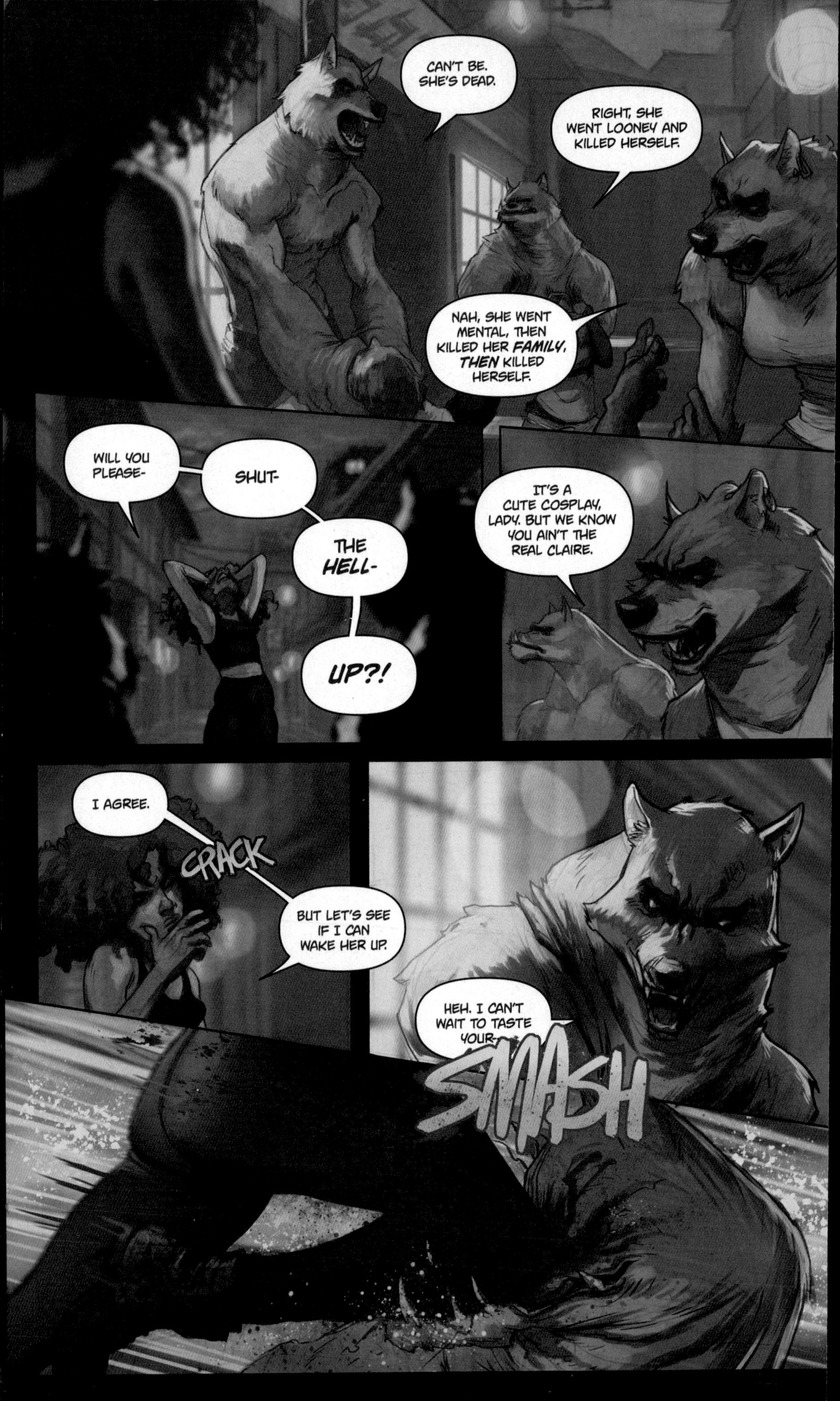
CAN'T BE. SHE'S DEAD.
RIGHT, SHE WENT LOONEY AND KILLED HERSELF.
NAH, SHE WENT MENTAL, THEN KILLED HER *FAMILY*, *THEN* KILLED HERSELF.
WILL YOU PLEASE-
SHUT-
THE *HELL*-
UP?!
IT'S A CUTE COSPLAY, LADY. BUT WE KNOW YOU AIN'T THE REAL CLAIRE.
I AGREE.
CRACK
BUT LET'S SEE IF I CAN WAKE HER UP.
HEH. I CAN'T WAIT TO TASTE YOUR-
SMASH

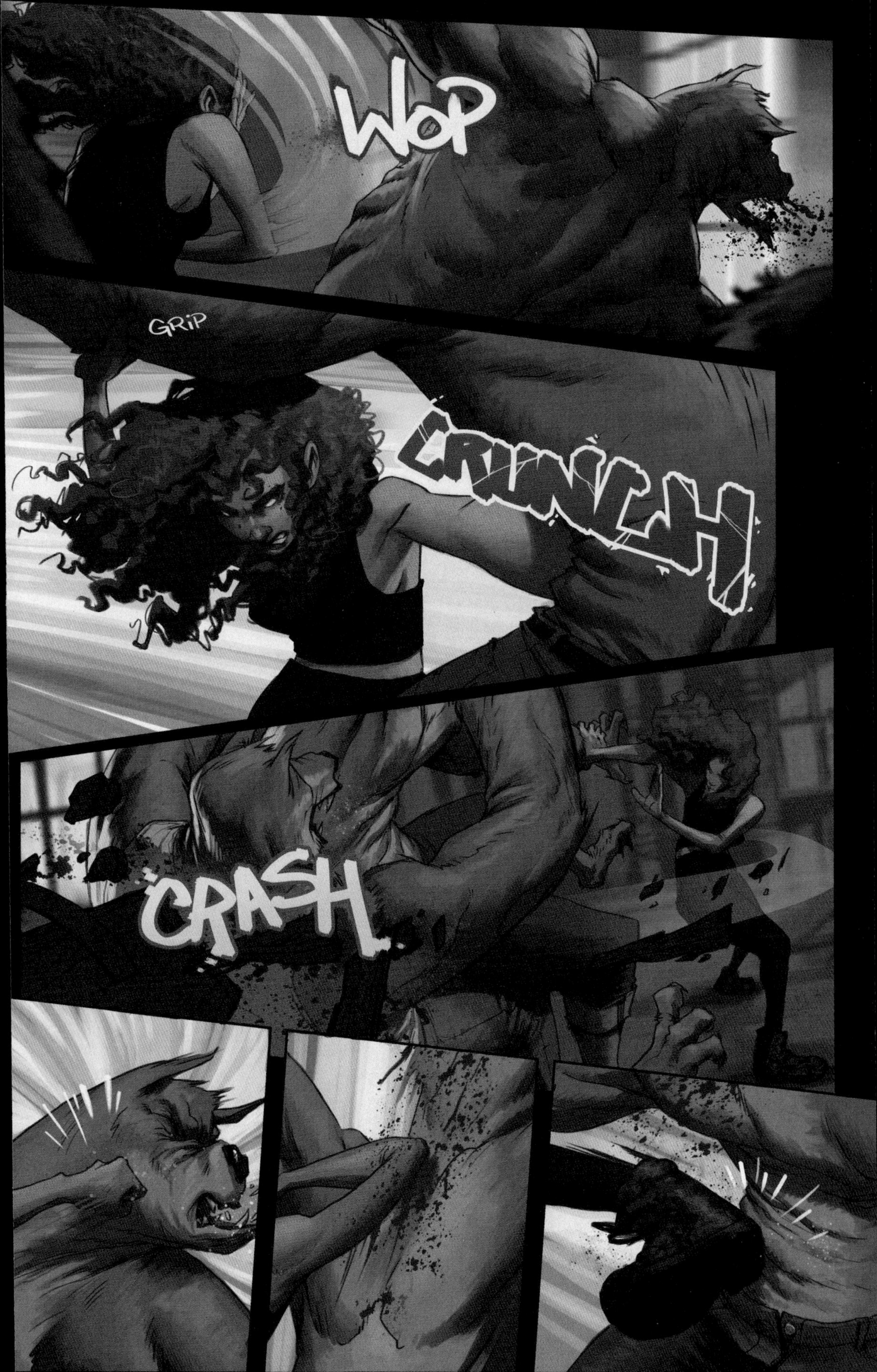
WOP
GRIP
CRUNCH
CRASH

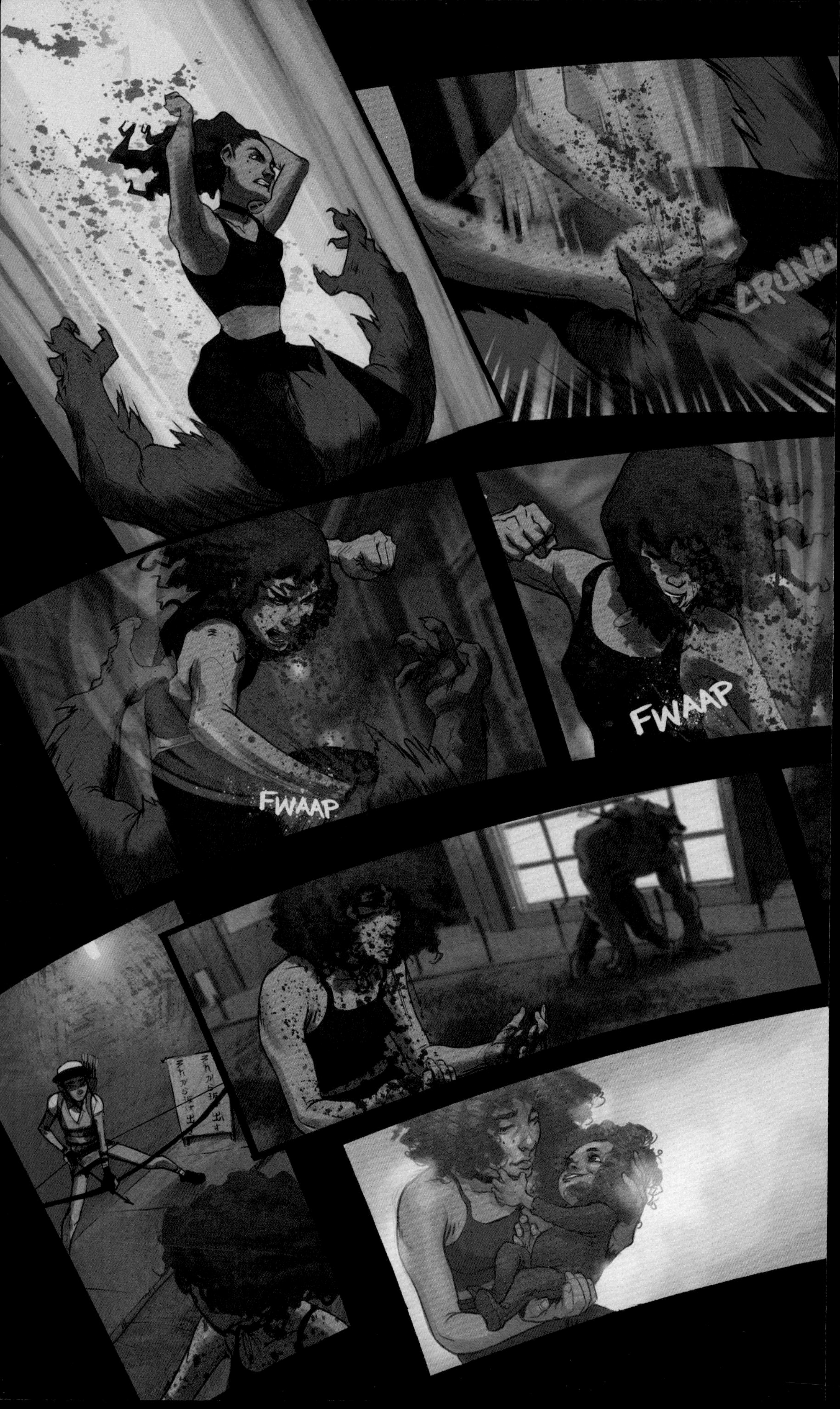
CRUNC
FWAAP
FWAAP

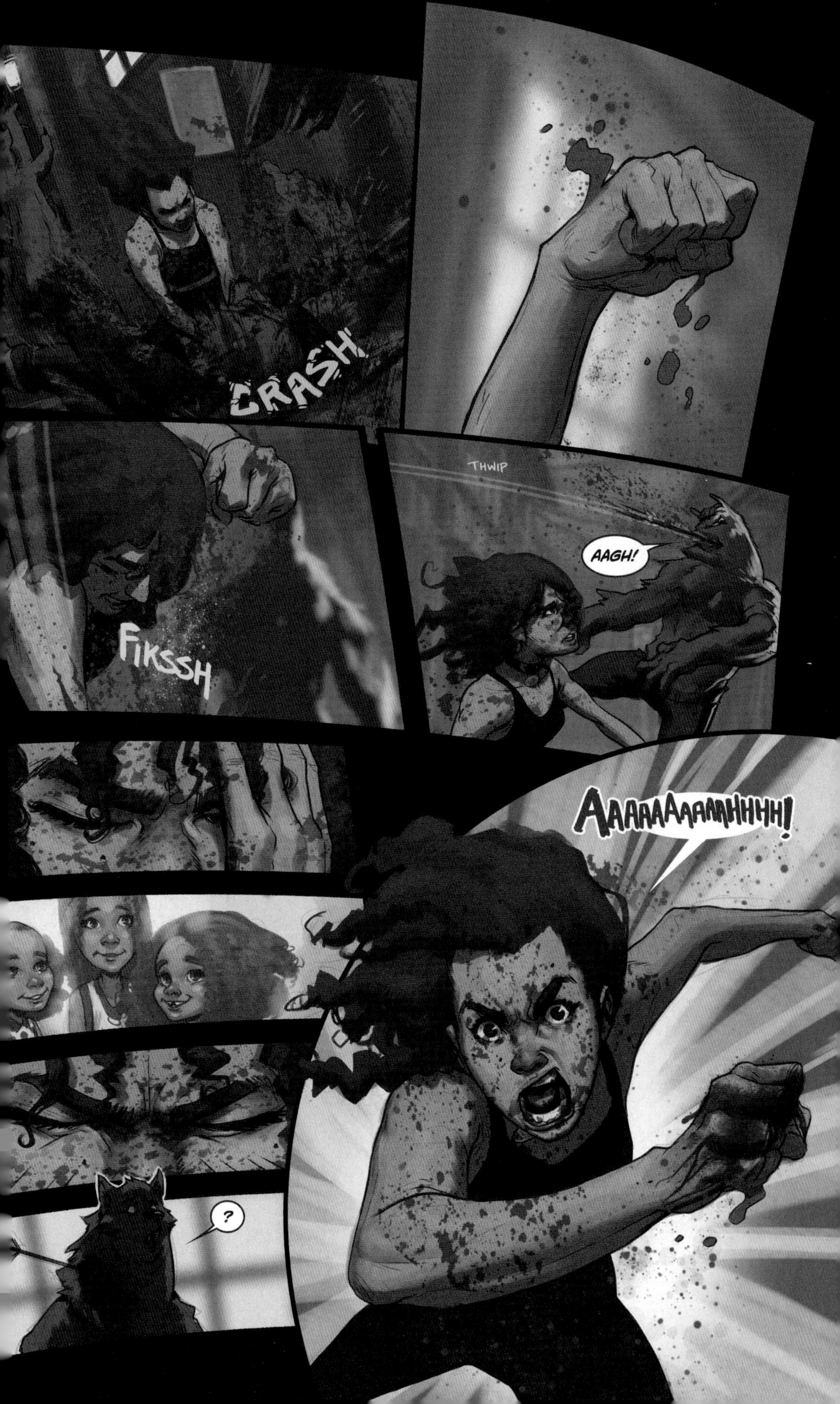
CRASH
FIKSSH
THWIP
AAGH!
?
AAAAAAAAAHHHH!

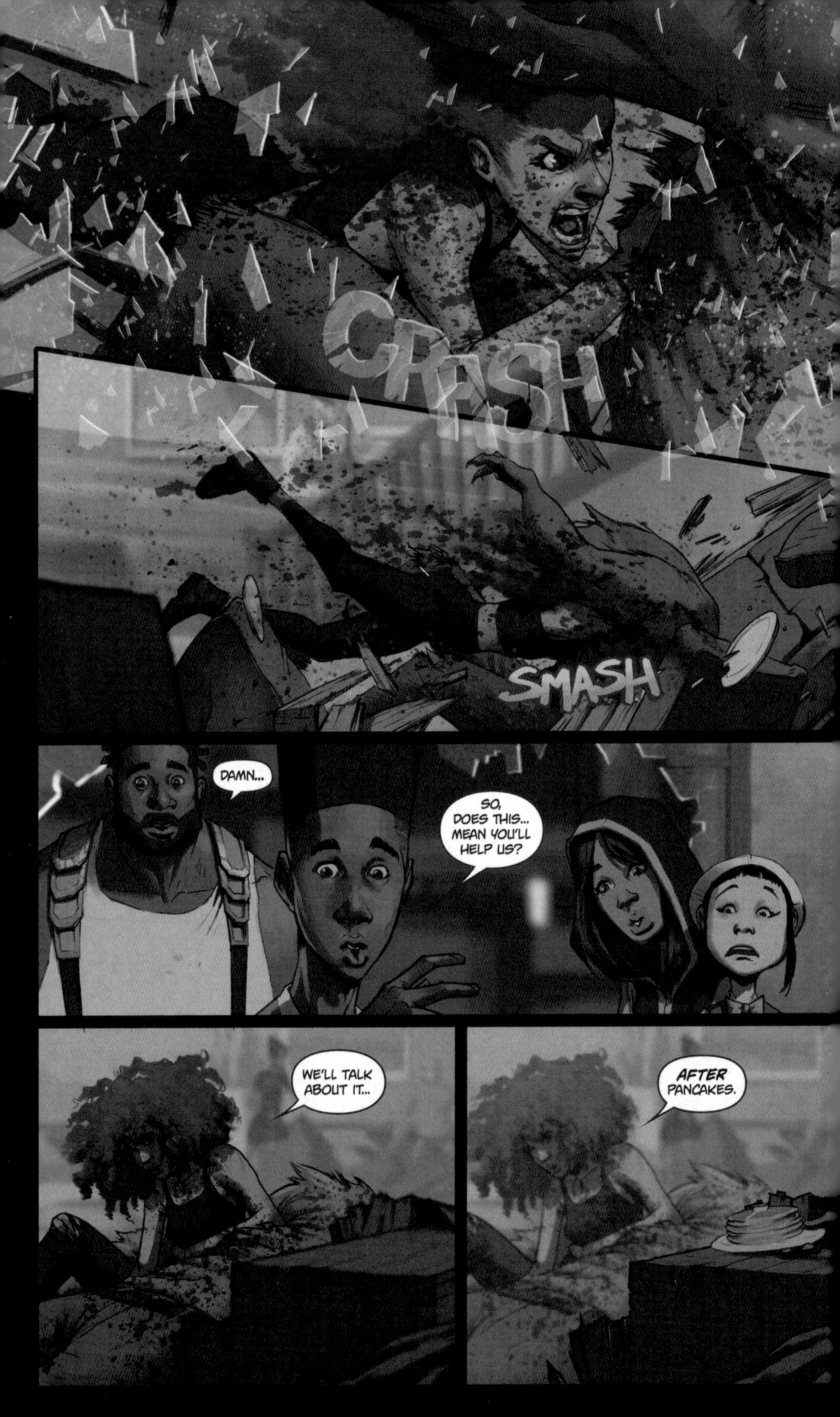
CRASH
SMASH
DAMN...
SO, DOES THIS... MEAN YOU'LL HELP US?
WE'LL TALK ABOUT IT...
AFTER PANCAKES.

CHAPTER TWO

"MY LIFE IS NOW EMPTY.
NOTHING CAN BE WHAT YOU WERE,
WHAT YOU ARE.

MY EVERYTHING,
MY ALL."

ISSUE #2 COVER A

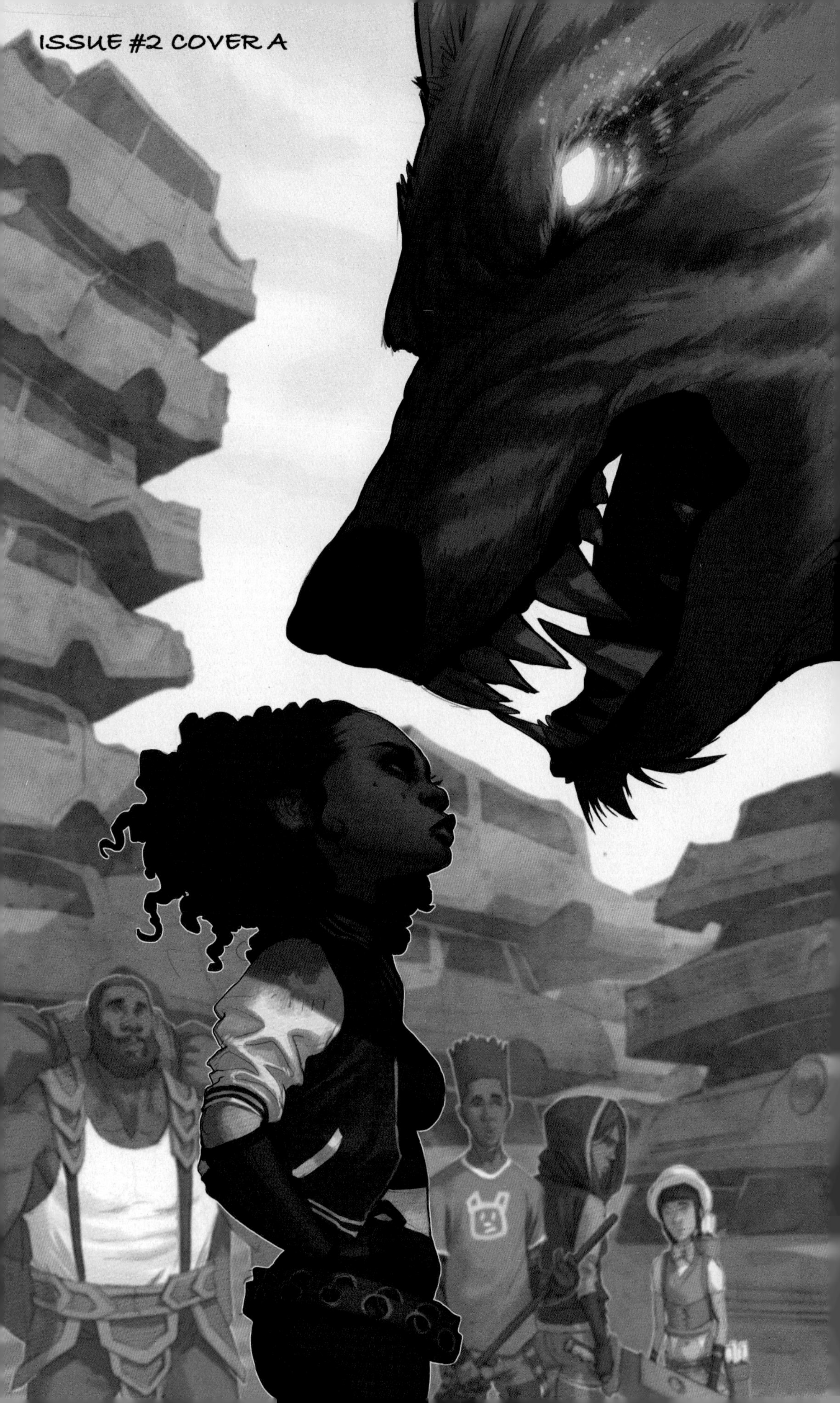

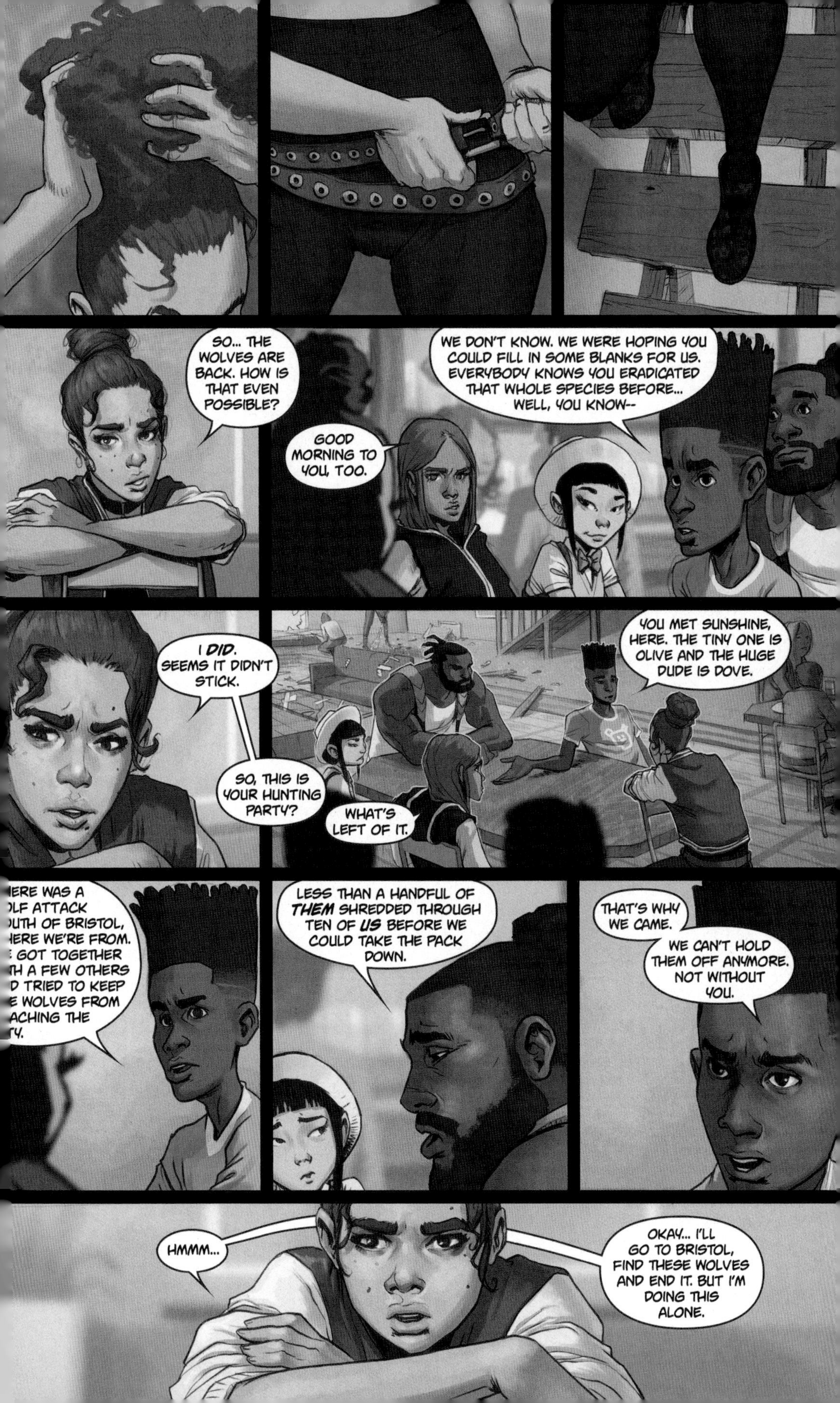
SO... THE WOLVES ARE BACK. HOW IS THAT EVEN POSSIBLE?
GOOD MORNING TO YOU, TOO.
WE DON'T KNOW. WE WERE HOPING YOU COULD FILL IN SOME BLANKS FOR US. EVERYBODY KNOWS YOU ERADICATED THAT WHOLE SPECIES BEFORE... WELL, YOU KNOW--
I *DID*. SEEMS IT DIDN'T STICK.
SO, THIS IS YOUR HUNTING PARTY?
WHAT'S LEFT OF IT.
YOU MET SUNSHINE, HERE. THE TINY ONE IS OLIVE AND THE HUGE DUDE IS DOVE.
HERE WAS A OLF ATTACK OUTH OF BRISTOL, HERE WE'RE FROM. GOT TOGETHER TH A FEW OTHERS D TRIED TO KEEP WOLVES FROM ACHING THE TY.
LESS THAN A HANDFUL OF ***THEM*** SHREDDED THROUGH TEN OF ***US*** BEFORE WE COULD TAKE THE PACK DOWN.
THAT'S WHY WE CAME.
WE CAN'T HOLD THEM OFF ANYMORE. NOT WITHOUT YOU.
HMMM...
OKAY... I'LL GO TO BRISTOL, FIND THESE WOLVES AND END IT. BUT I'M DOING THIS ALONE.

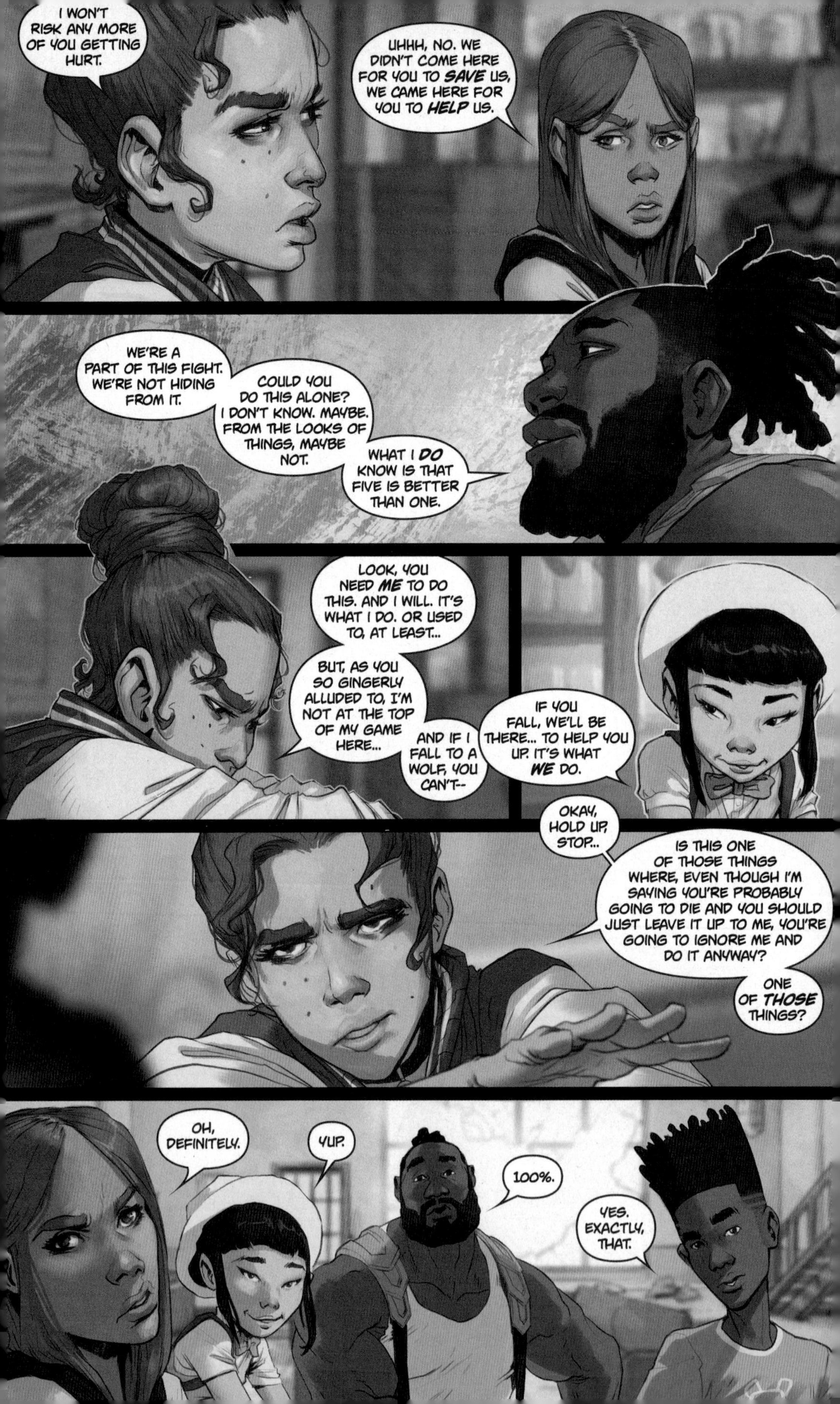
I WON'T RISK ANY MORE OF YOU GETTING HURT.
UHHH, NO. WE DIDN'T COME HERE FOR YOU TO *SAVE* US, WE CAME HERE FOR YOU TO *HELP* US.
WE'RE A PART OF THIS FIGHT. WE'RE NOT HIDING FROM IT.
COULD YOU DO THIS ALONE? I DON'T KNOW. MAYBE. FROM THE LOOKS OF THINGS, MAYBE NOT.
WHAT I *DO* KNOW IS THAT FIVE IS BETTER THAN ONE.
LOOK, YOU NEED *ME* TO DO THIS. AND I WILL. IT'S WHAT I DO. OR USED TO, AT LEAST...
BUT, AS YOU SO GINGERLY ALLUDED TO, I'M NOT AT THE TOP OF MY GAME HERE...
AND IF I FALL TO A WOLF, YOU CAN'T--
IF YOU FALL, WE'LL BE THERE... TO HELP YOU UP. IT'S WHAT *WE* DO.
OKAY, HOLD UP, STOP...
IS THIS ONE OF THOSE THINGS WHERE, EVEN THOUGH I'M SAYING YOU'RE PROBABLY GOING TO DIE AND YOU SHOULD JUST LEAVE IT UP TO ME, YOU'RE GOING TO IGNORE ME AND DO IT ANYWAY?
ONE OF *THOSE* THINGS?
OH, DEFINITELY.
YUP.
100%.
YES. EXACTLY, THAT.

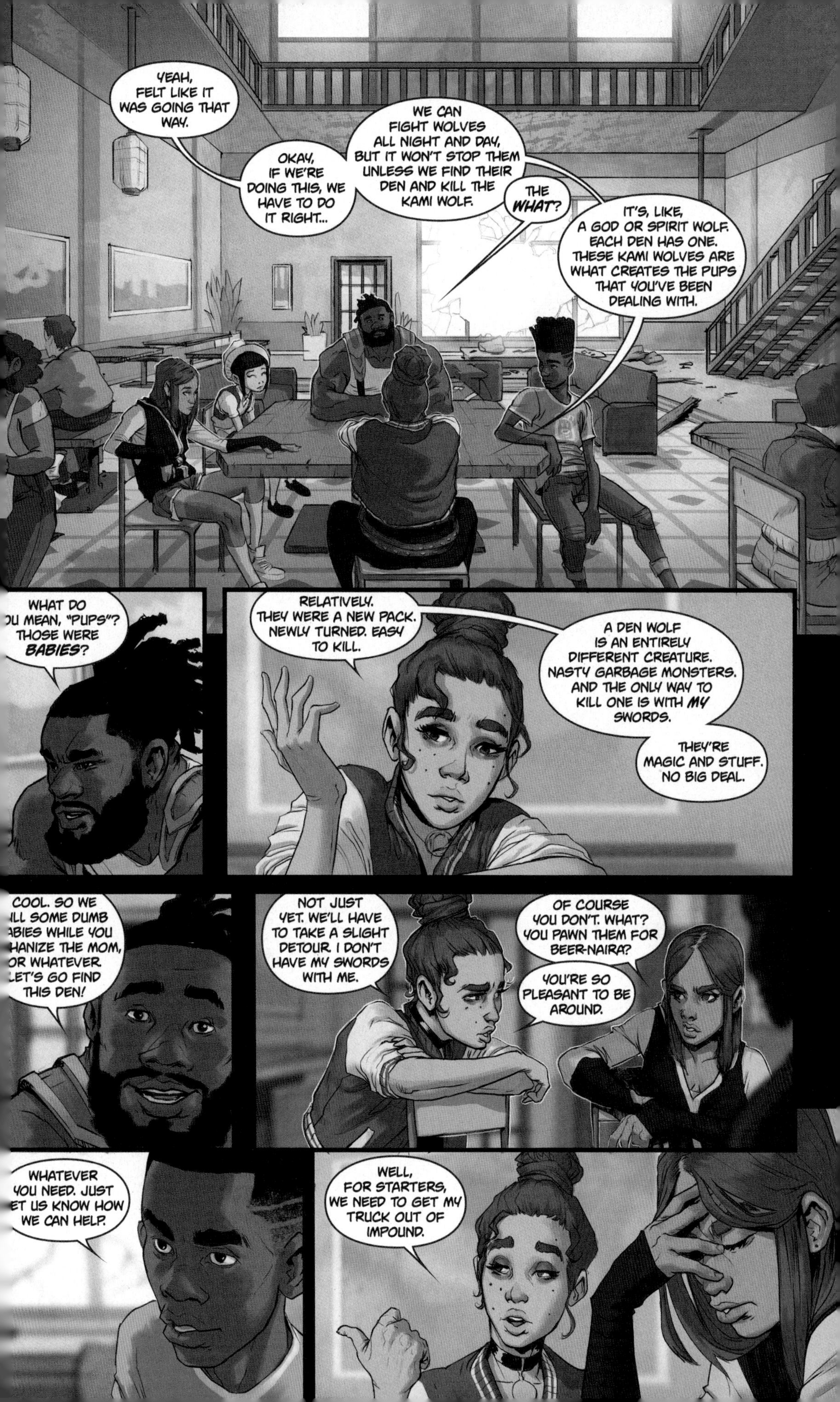

YEAH, FELT LIKE IT WAS GOING THAT WAY.
OKAY, IF WE'RE DOING THIS, WE HAVE TO DO IT RIGHT...
WE CAN FIGHT WOLVES ALL NIGHT AND DAY, BUT IT WON'T STOP THEM UNLESS WE FIND THEIR DEN AND KILL THE KAMI WOLF.
THE *WHAT*?
IT'S, LIKE, A GOD OR SPIRIT WOLF. EACH DEN HAS ONE. THESE KAMI WOLVES ARE WHAT CREATES THE PUPS THAT YOU'VE BEEN DEALING WITH.
WHAT DO OU MEAN, "PUPS"? THOSE WERE *BABIES*?
RELATIVELY. THEY WERE A NEW PACK. NEWLY TURNED. EASY TO KILL.
A DEN WOLF IS AN ENTIRELY DIFFERENT CREATURE. NASTY GARBAGE MONSTERS. AND THE ONLY WAY TO KILL ONE IS WITH *MY* SWORDS.
THEY'RE MAGIC AND STUFF. NO BIG DEAL.
COOL. SO WE ILL SOME DUMB ABIES WHILE YOU HANIZE THE MOM, OR WHATEVER. LET'S GO FIND THIS DEN!
NOT JUST YET. WE'LL HAVE TO TAKE A SLIGHT DETOUR. I DON'T HAVE MY SWORDS WITH ME.
OF COURSE YOU DON'T. WHAT? YOU PAWN THEM FOR BEER-NAIRA?
YOU'RE SO PLEASANT TO BE AROUND.
WHATEVER YOU NEED. JUST ET US KNOW HOW WE CAN HELP.
WELL, FOR STARTERS, WE NEED TO GET MY TRUCK OUT OF IMPOUND.

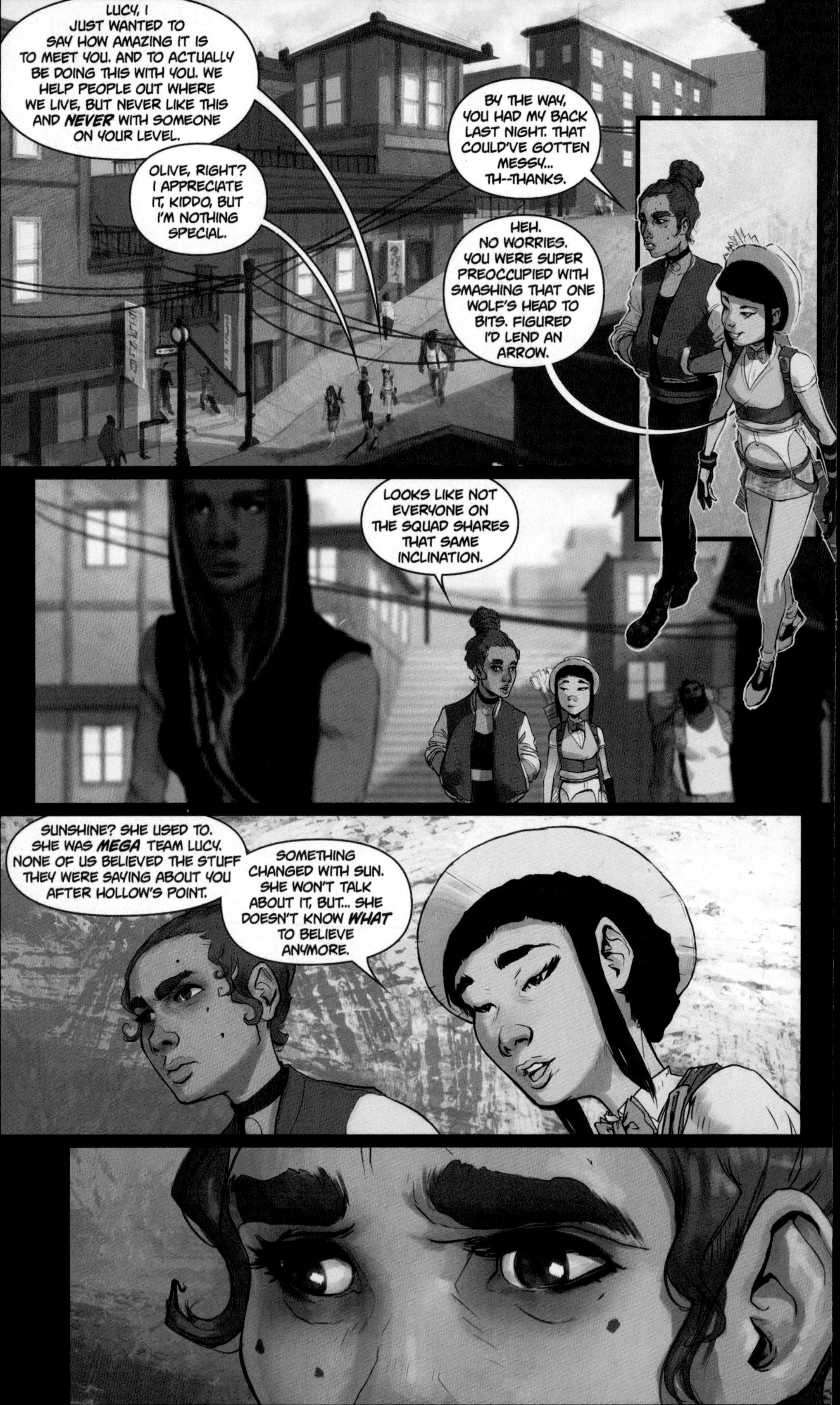
LUCY, I JUST WANTED TO SAY HOW AMAZING IT IS TO MEET YOU. AND TO ACTUALLY BE DOING THIS WITH YOU. WE HELP PEOPLE OUT WHERE WE LIVE, BUT NEVER LIKE THIS AND **NEVER** WITH SOMEONE ON YOUR LEVEL.
OLIVE, RIGHT? I APPRECIATE IT, KIDDO, BUT I'M NOTHING SPECIAL.
BY THE WAY, YOU HAD MY BACK LAST NIGHT. THAT COULD'VE GOTTEN MESSY... TH--THANKS.
HEH. NO WORRIES. YOU WERE SUPER PREOCCUPIED WITH SMASHING THAT ONE WOLF'S HEAD TO BITS. FIGURED I'D LEND AN ARROW.
LOOKS LIKE NOT EVERYONE ON THE SQUAD SHARES THAT SAME INCLINATION.
SUNSHINE? SHE USED TO. SHE WAS **MEGA** TEAM LUCY. NONE OF US BELIEVED THE STUFF THEY WERE SAYING ABOUT YOU AFTER HOLLOW'S POINT.
SOMETHING CHANGED WITH SUN. SHE WON'T TALK ABOUT IT, BUT... SHE DOESN'T KNOW **WHAT** TO BELIEVE ANYMORE.

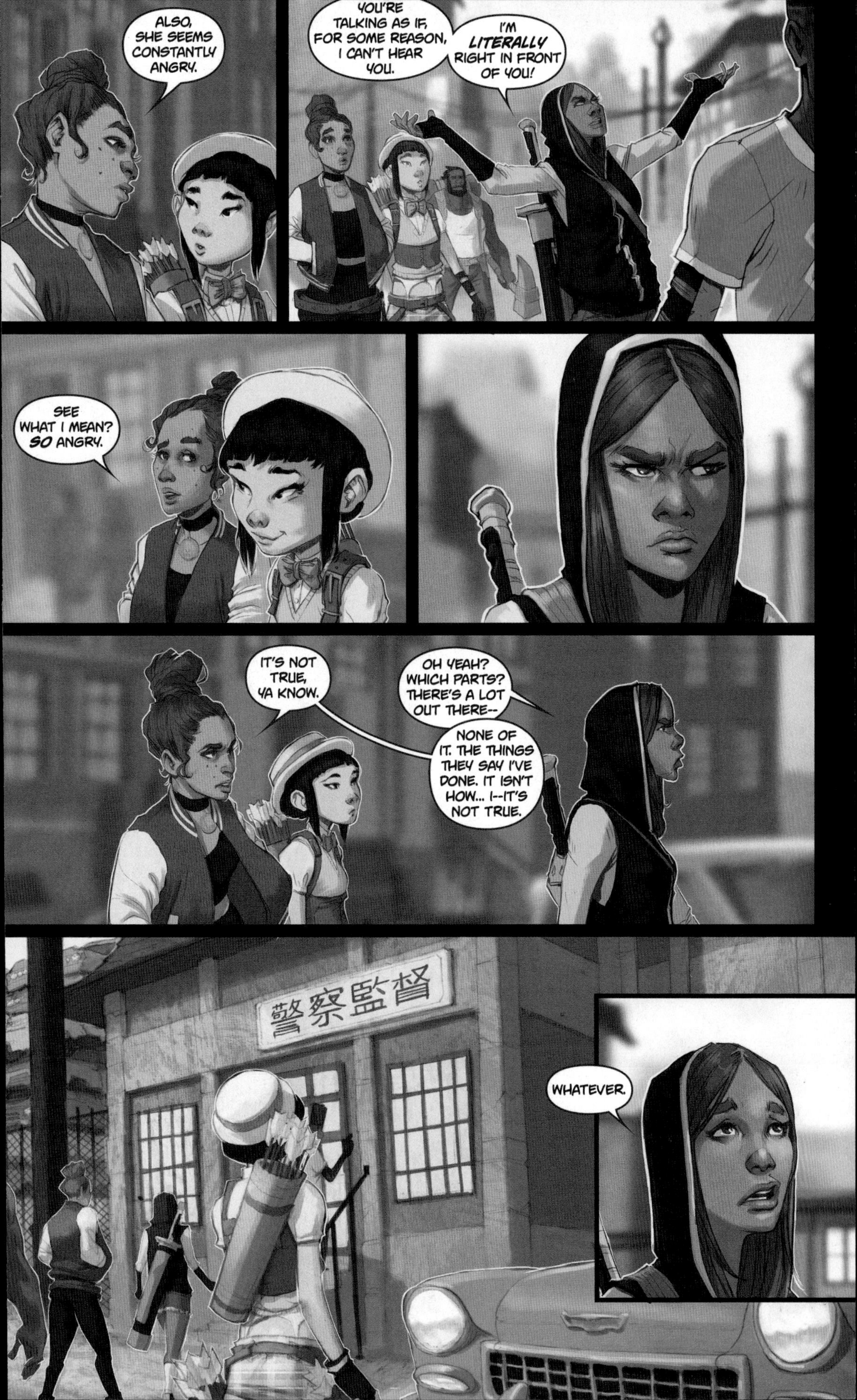
ALSO, SHE SEEMS CONSTANTLY ANGRY.
YOU'RE TALKING AS IF, FOR SOME REASON, I CAN'T HEAR YOU.
I'M *LITERALLY* RIGHT IN FRONT OF YOU!
SEE WHAT I MEAN? *SO* ANGRY.
IT'S NOT TRUE, YA KNOW.
OH YEAH? WHICH PARTS? THERE'S A LOT OUT THERE--
NONE OF IT. THE THINGS THEY SAY I'VE DONE. IT ISN'T HOW... I--IT'S NOT TRUE.
警察監督
WHATEVER.

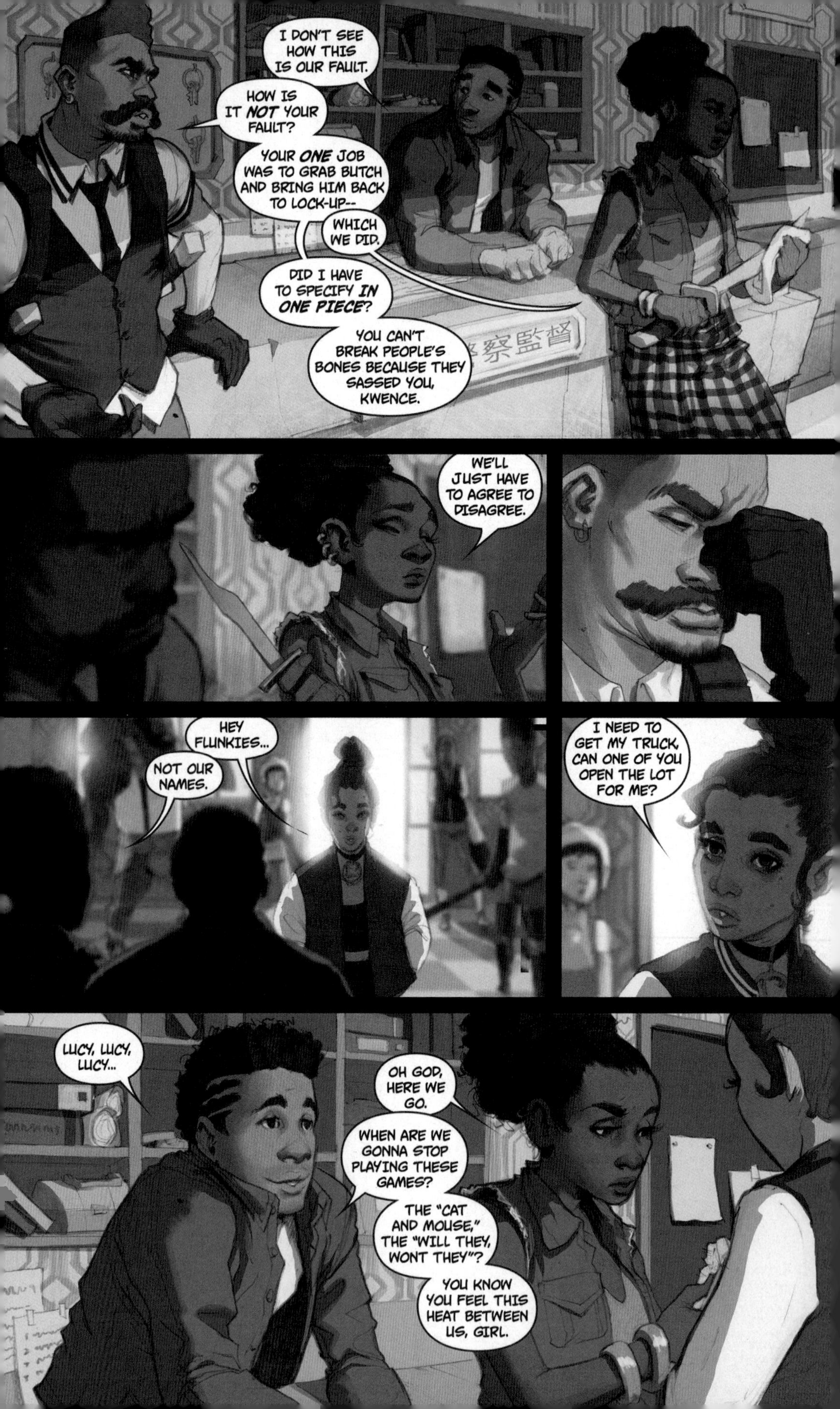
I DON'T SEE HOW THIS IS OUR FAULT.
HOW IS IT *NOT* YOUR FAULT?
YOUR *ONE* JOB WAS TO GRAB BUTCH AND BRING HIM BACK TO LOCK-UP--
WHICH WE DID.
DID I HAVE TO SPECIFY *IN ONE PIECE*?
YOU CAN'T BREAK PEOPLE'S BONES BECAUSE THEY SASSED YOU, KWENCE.
察監督
WE'LL JUST HAVE TO AGREE TO DISAGREE.
HEY FLUNKIES...
NOT OUR NAMES.
I NEED TO GET MY TRUCK, CAN ONE OF YOU OPEN THE LOT FOR ME?
LUCY, LUCY, LUCY...
OH GOD, HERE WE GO.
WHEN ARE WE GONNA STOP PLAYING THESE GAMES?
THE "CAT AND MOUSE," THE "WILL THEY, WONT THEY"?
YOU KNOW YOU FEEL THIS HEAT BETWEEN US, GIRL.

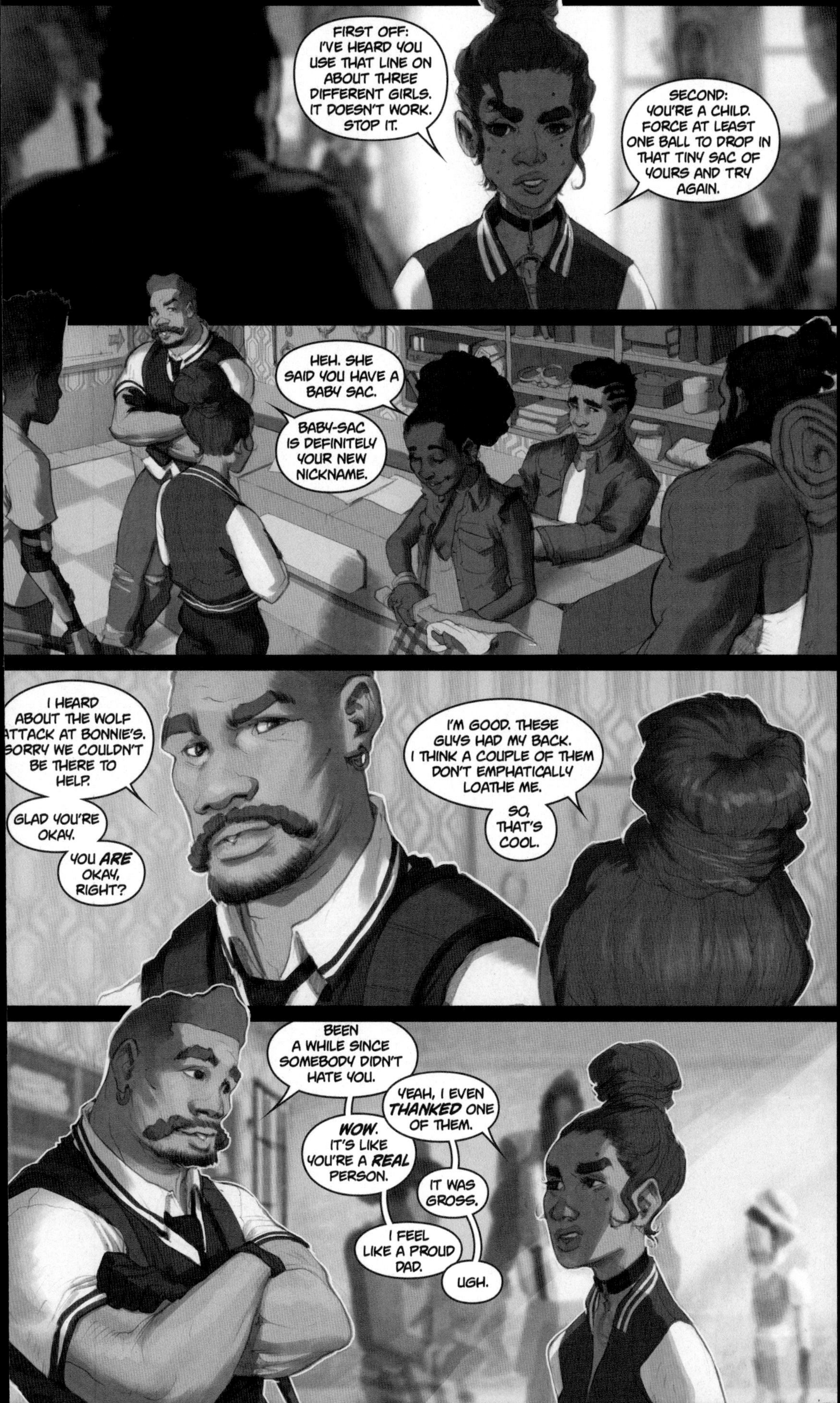
FIRST OFF: I'VE HEARD YOU USE THAT LINE ON ABOUT THREE DIFFERENT GIRLS. IT DOESN'T WORK. STOP IT.
SECOND: YOU'RE A CHILD. FORCE AT LEAST ONE BALL TO DROP IN THAT TINY SAC OF YOURS AND TRY AGAIN.
HEH. SHE SAID YOU HAVE A BABY SAC.
BABY-SAC IS DEFINITELY YOUR NEW NICKNAME.
I HEARD ABOUT THE WOLF ATTACK AT BONNIE'S. SORRY WE COULDN'T BE THERE TO HELP.
GLAD YOU'RE OKAY.
YOU ARE OKAY, RIGHT?
I'M GOOD. THESE GUYS HAD MY BACK. I THINK A COUPLE OF THEM DON'T EMPHATICALLY LOATHE ME.
SO, THAT'S COOL.
BEEN A WHILE SINCE SOMEBODY DIDN'T HATE YOU.
YEAH, I EVEN THANKED ONE OF THEM.
WOW. IT'S LIKE YOU'RE A REAL PERSON.
IT WAS GROSS.
I FEEL LIKE A PROUD DAD.
UGH.

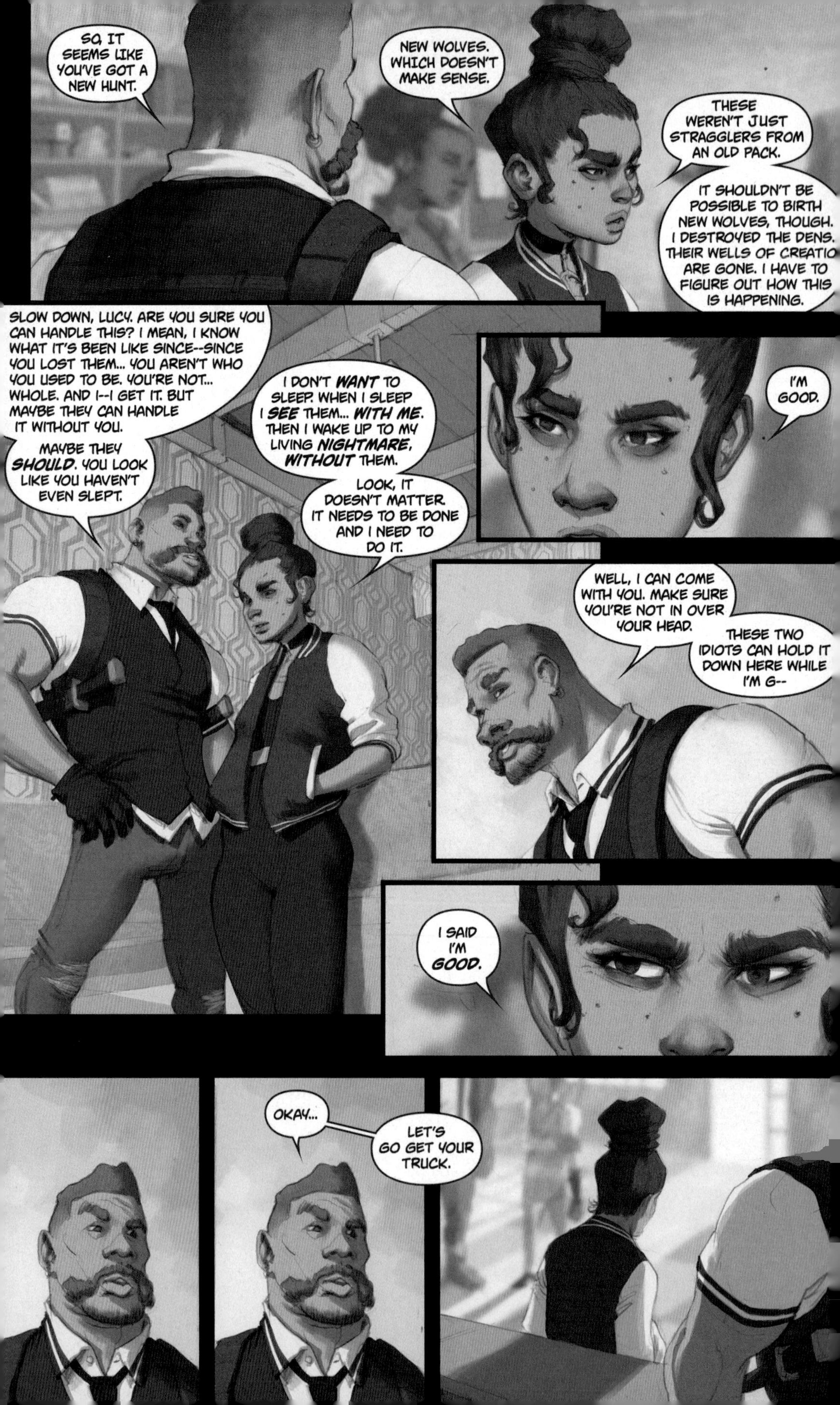

SO, IT SEEMS LIKE YOU'VE GOT A NEW HUNT.
NEW WOLVES. WHICH DOESN'T MAKE SENSE.
THESE WEREN'T JUST STRAGGLERS FROM AN OLD PACK.
IT SHOULDN'T BE POSSIBLE TO BIRTH NEW WOLVES, THOUGH. I DESTROYED THE DENS. THEIR WELLS OF CREATIO ARE GONE. I HAVE TO FIGURE OUT HOW THIS IS HAPPENING.
SLOW DOWN, LUCY. ARE YOU SURE YOU CAN HANDLE THIS? I MEAN, I KNOW WHAT IT'S BEEN LIKE SINCE--SINCE YOU LOST THEM... YOU AREN'T WHO YOU USED TO BE. YOU'RE NOT... WHOLE. AND I--I GET IT. BUT MAYBE THEY CAN HANDLE IT WITHOUT YOU.
MAYBE THEY **SHOULD**. YOU LOOK LIKE YOU HAVEN'T EVEN SLEPT.
I DON'T **WANT** TO SLEEP. WHEN I SLEEP I **SEE** THEM... **WITH ME**. THEN I WAKE UP TO MY LIVING **NIGHTMARE**, **WITHOUT** THEM.
LOOK, IT DOESN'T MATTER. IT NEEDS TO BE DONE AND I NEED TO DO IT.
I'M GOOD.
WELL, I CAN COME WITH YOU. MAKE SURE YOU'RE NOT IN OVER YOUR HEAD.
THESE TWO IDIOTS CAN HOLD IT DOWN HERE WHILE I'M G--
I SAID I'M **GOOD.**
OKAY...
LET'S GO GET YOUR TRUCK.

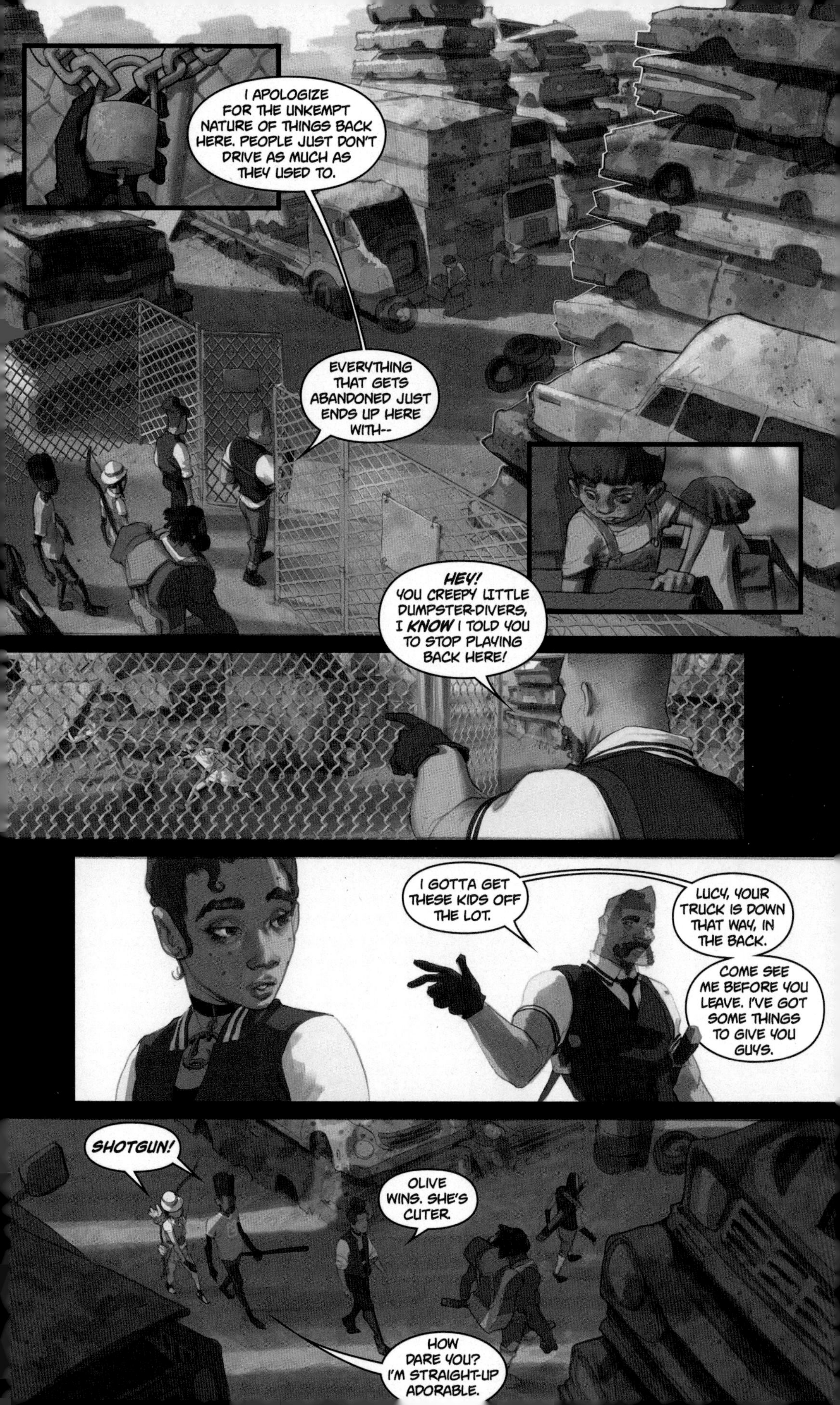

I APOLOGIZE FOR THE UNKEMPT NATURE OF THINGS BACK HERE. PEOPLE JUST DON'T DRIVE AS MUCH AS THEY USED TO.
EVERYTHING THAT GETS ABANDONED JUST ENDS UP HERE WITH--
HEY! YOU CREEPY LITTLE DUMPSTER-DIVERS, I KNOW I TOLD YOU TO STOP PLAYING BACK HERE!
I GOTTA GET THESE KIDS OFF THE LOT.
LUCY, YOUR TRUCK IS DOWN THAT WAY, IN THE BACK.
COME SEE ME BEFORE YOU LEAVE. I'VE GOT SOME THINGS TO GIVE YOU GUYS.
SHOTGUN!
OLIVE WINS. SHE'S CUTER.
HOW DARE YOU? I'M STRAIGHT-UP ADORABLE.

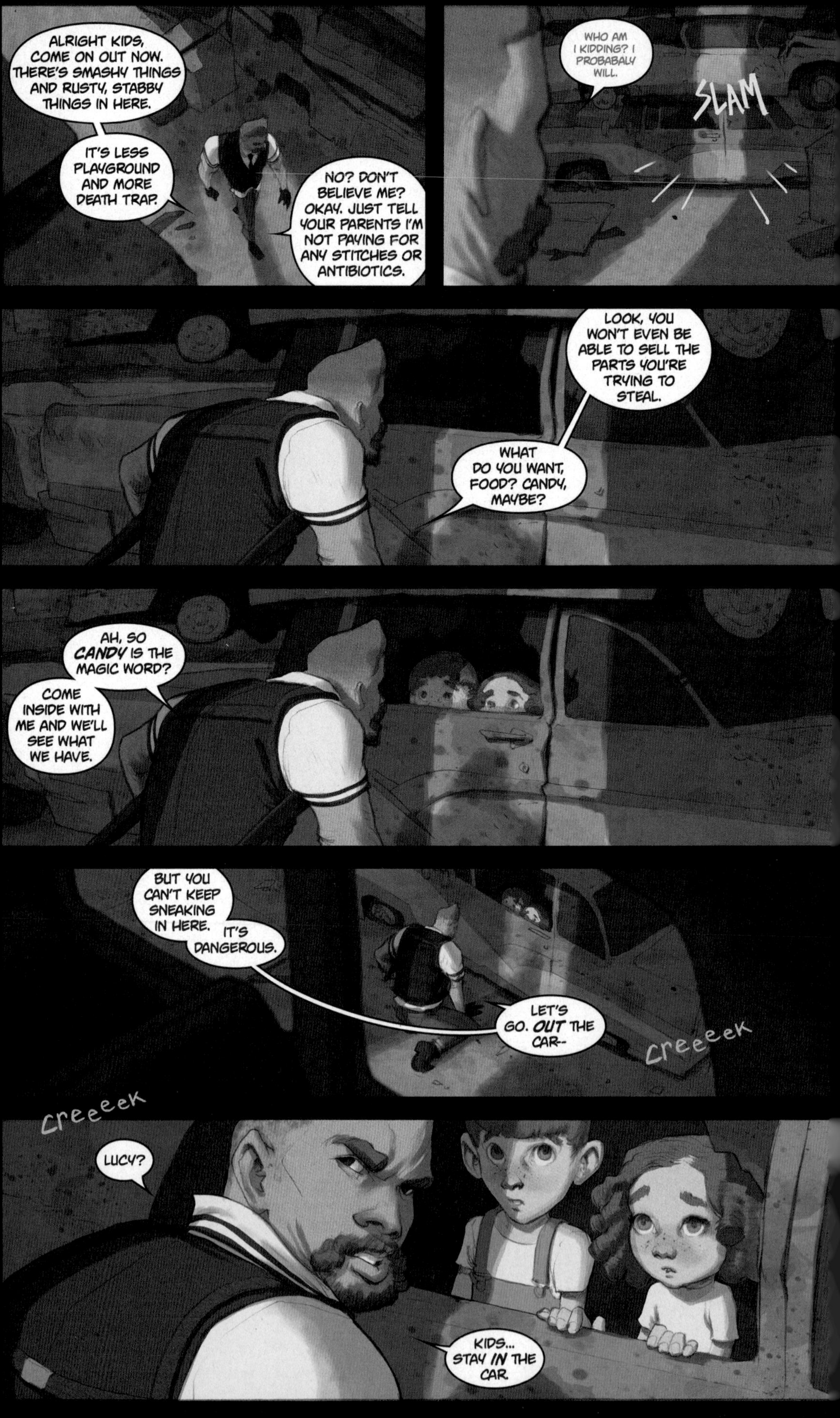
ALRIGHT KIDS, COME ON OUT NOW. THERE'S SMASHY THINGS AND RUSTY, STABBY THINGS IN HERE.
IT'S LESS PLAYGROUND AND MORE DEATH TRAP.
NO? DON'T BELIEVE ME? OKAY. JUST TELL YOUR PARENTS I'M NOT PAYING FOR ANY STITCHES OR ANTIBIOTICS.
WHO AM I KIDDING? I PROBABALY WILL.
SLAM
LOOK, YOU WON'T EVEN BE ABLE TO SELL THE PARTS YOU'RE TRYING TO STEAL.
WHAT DO YOU WANT, FOOD? CANDY, MAYBE?
AH, SO CANDY IS THE MAGIC WORD?
COME INSIDE WITH ME AND WE'LL SEE WHAT WE HAVE.
BUT YOU CAN'T KEEP SNEAKING IN HERE.
IT'S DANGEROUS.
LET'S GO. OUT THE CAR--
Creeeek
Creeeek
LUCY?
KIDS... STAY IN THE CAR.

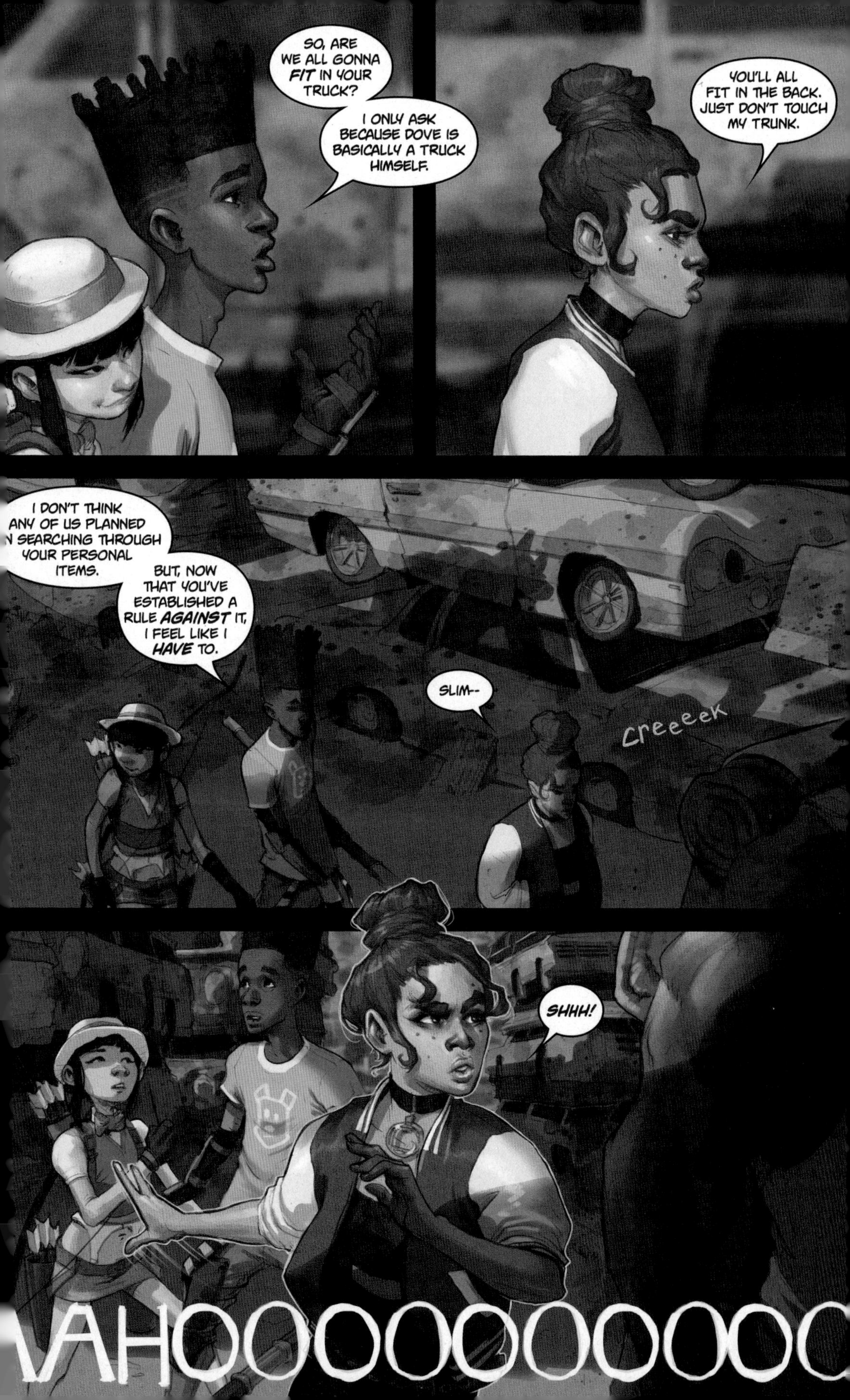

SO, ARE WE ALL GONNA *FIT* IN YOUR TRUCK?
I ONLY ASK BECAUSE DOVE IS BASICALLY A TRUCK HIMSELF.
YOU'LL ALL FIT IN THE BACK. JUST DON'T TOUCH MY TRUNK.
I DON'T THINK ANY OF US PLANNED ON SEARCHING THROUGH YOUR PERSONAL ITEMS.
BUT, NOW THAT YOU'VE ESTABLISHED A RULE *AGAINST* IT, I FEEL LIKE I *HAVE* TO.
SLIM--
Creeeek
SHHH!
AHOOOOOOOOOOO

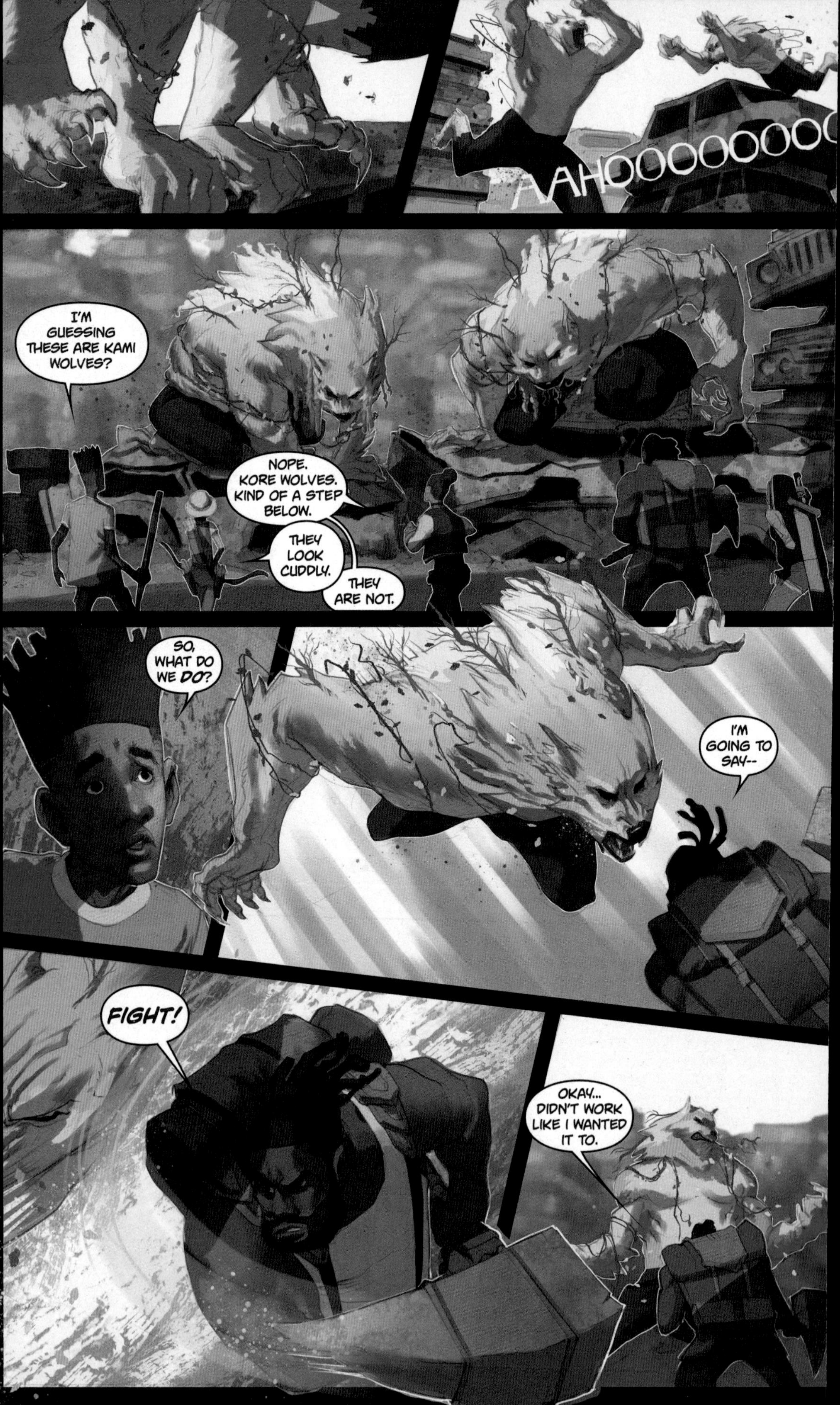
AAHOOOOOOOOO
I'M GUESSING THESE ARE KAMI WOLVES?
NOPE. KORE WOLVES. KIND OF A STEP BELOW.
THEY LOOK CUDDLY.
THEY ARE NOT.
SO, WHAT DO WE *DO*?
I'M GOING TO SAY--
FIGHT!
OKAY... DIDN'T WORK LIKE I WANTED IT TO.

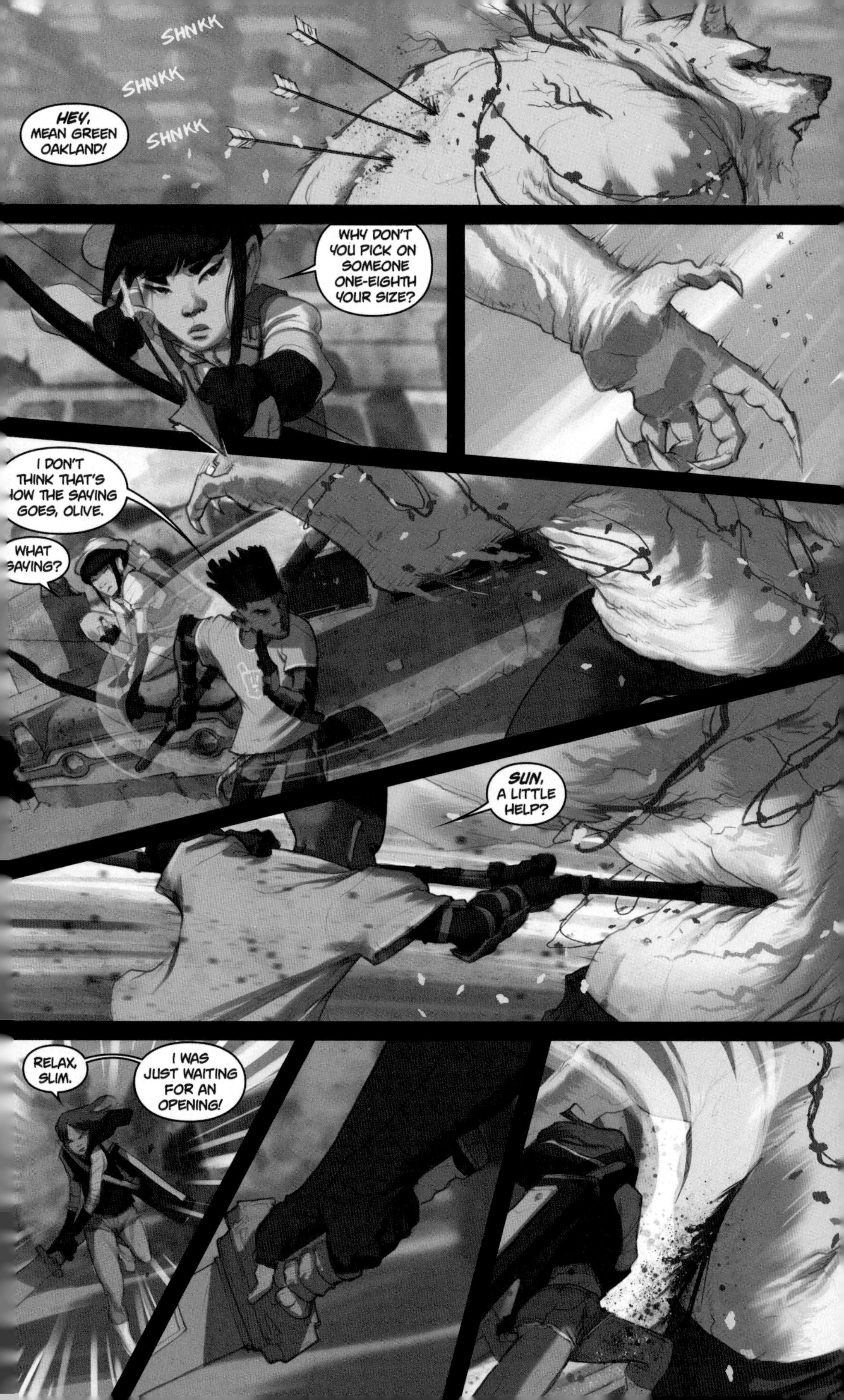
SHNKK
SHNKK
SHNKK
HEY, MEAN GREEN OAKLAND!
WHY DON'T YOU PICK ON SOMEONE ONE-EIGHTH YOUR SIZE?
I DON'T THINK THAT'S HOW THE SAYING GOES, OLIVE.
WHAT SAYING?
SUN, A LITTLE HELP?
RELAX, SLIM.
I WAS JUST WAITING FOR AN OPENING!

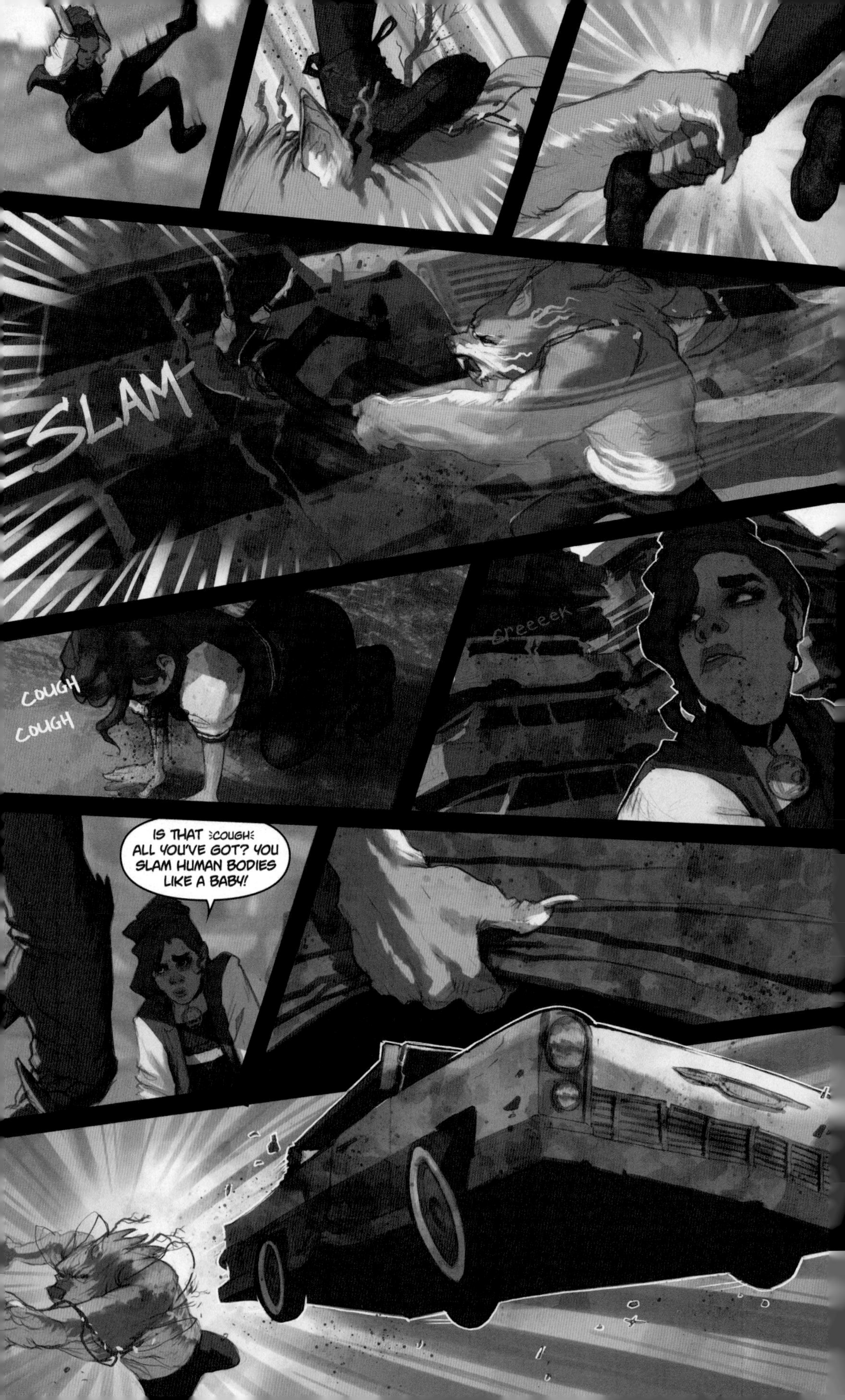
SLAM
COUGH
COUGH
Creeeek
IS THAT ≈COUGH≈ ALL YOU'VE GOT? YOU SLAM HUMAN BODIES LIKE A BABY!

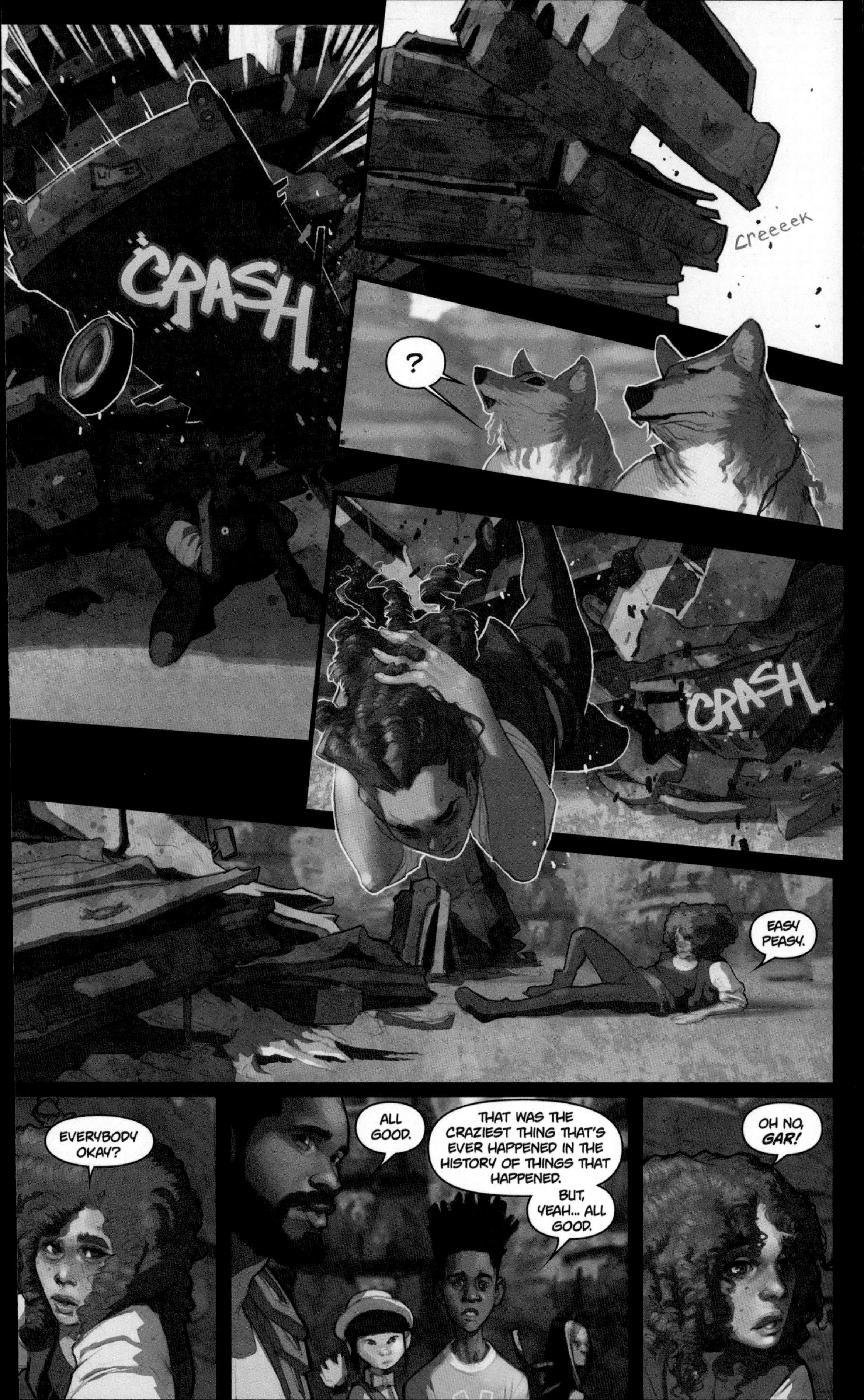
CRASH
Creeeek
?
CRASH
EASY PEASY.
EVERYBODY OKAY?
ALL GOOD.
THAT WAS THE CRAZIEST THING THAT'S EVER HAPPENED IN THE HISTORY OF THINGS THAT HAPPENED.
BUT, YEAH... ALL GOOD.
OH NO, GAR!

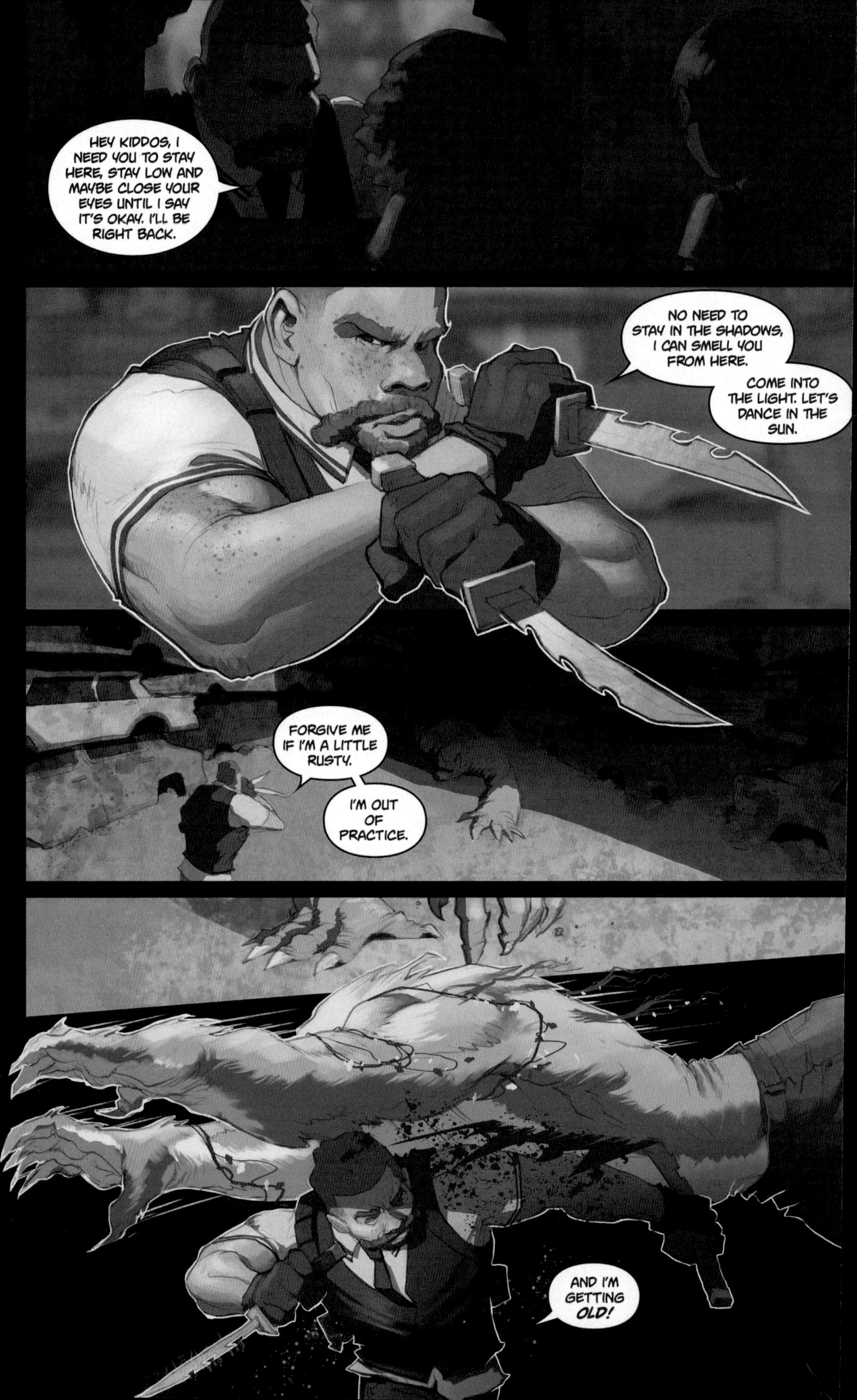
HEY KIDDOS, I NEED YOU TO STAY HERE, STAY LOW AND MAYBE CLOSE YOUR EYES UNTIL I SAY IT'S OKAY. I'LL BE RIGHT BACK.
NO NEED TO STAY IN THE SHADOWS, I CAN SMELL YOU FROM HERE.
COME INTO THE LIGHT. LET'S DANCE IN THE SUN.
FORGIVE ME IF I'M A LITTLE RUSTY.
I'M OUT OF PRACTICE.
AND I'M GETTING OLD!

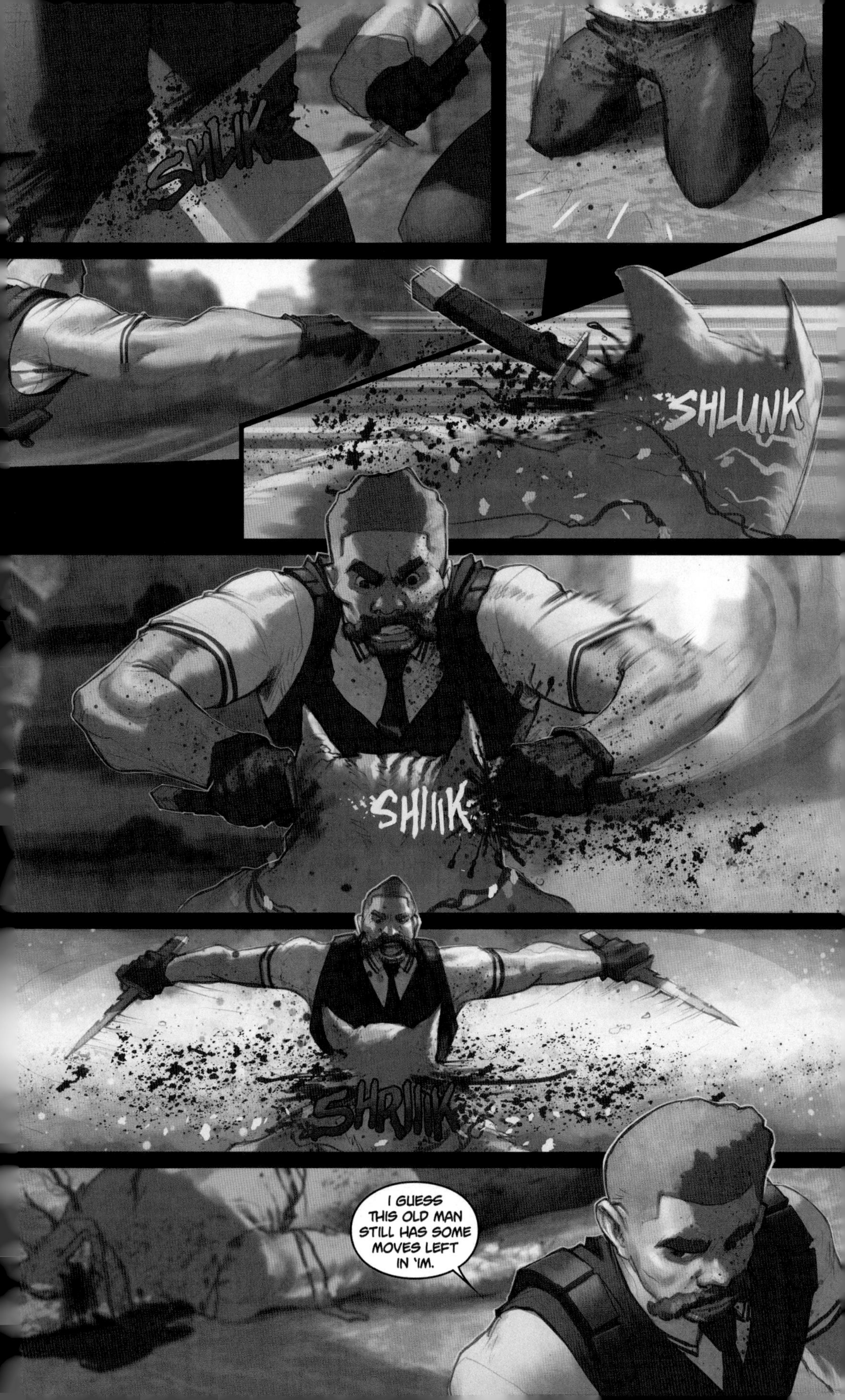
SHLIK
SHLUNK
SHIIIK
SHRIIIK
I GUESS THIS OLD MAN STILL HAS SOME MOVES LEFT IN 'IM.

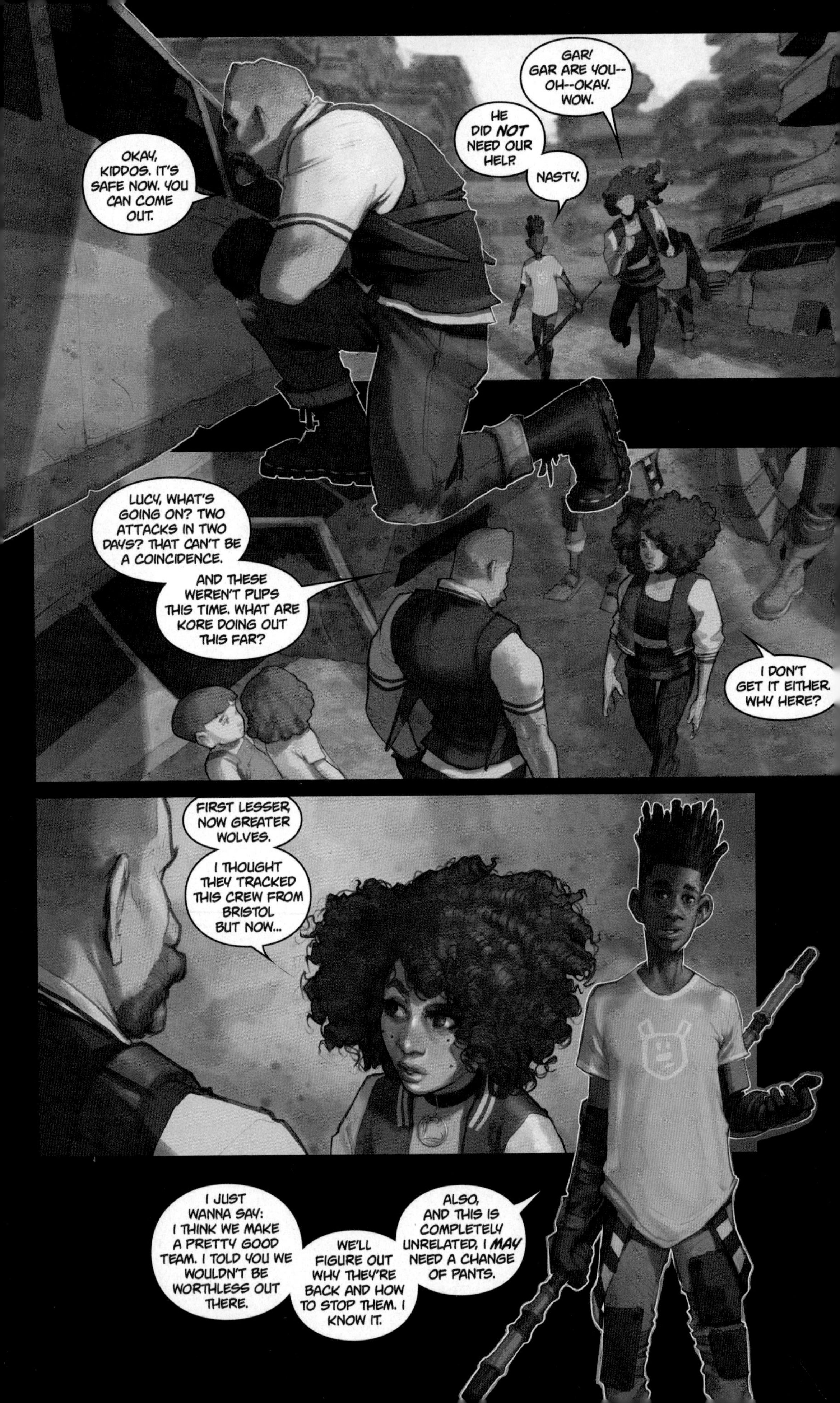
OKAY, KIDDOS. IT'S SAFE NOW. YOU CAN COME OUT.
GAR! GAR ARE YOU-- OH--OKAY. WOW.
HE DID NOT NEED OUR HELP.
NASTY.
LUCY, WHAT'S GOING ON? TWO ATTACKS IN TWO DAYS? THAT CAN'T BE A COINCIDENCE.
AND THESE WEREN'T PUPS THIS TIME. WHAT ARE KORE DOING OUT THIS FAR?
I DON'T GET IT EITHER. WHY HERE?
FIRST LESSER, NOW GREATER WOLVES.
I THOUGHT THEY TRACKED THIS CREW FROM BRISTOL BUT NOW...
I JUST WANNA SAY: I THINK WE MAKE A PRETTY GOOD TEAM. I TOLD YOU WE WOULDN'T BE WORTHLESS OUT THERE.
WE'LL FIGURE OUT WHY THEY'RE BACK AND HOW TO STOP THEM. I KNOW IT.
ALSO, AND THIS IS COMPLETELY UNRELATED, I MAY NEED A CHANGE OF PANTS.

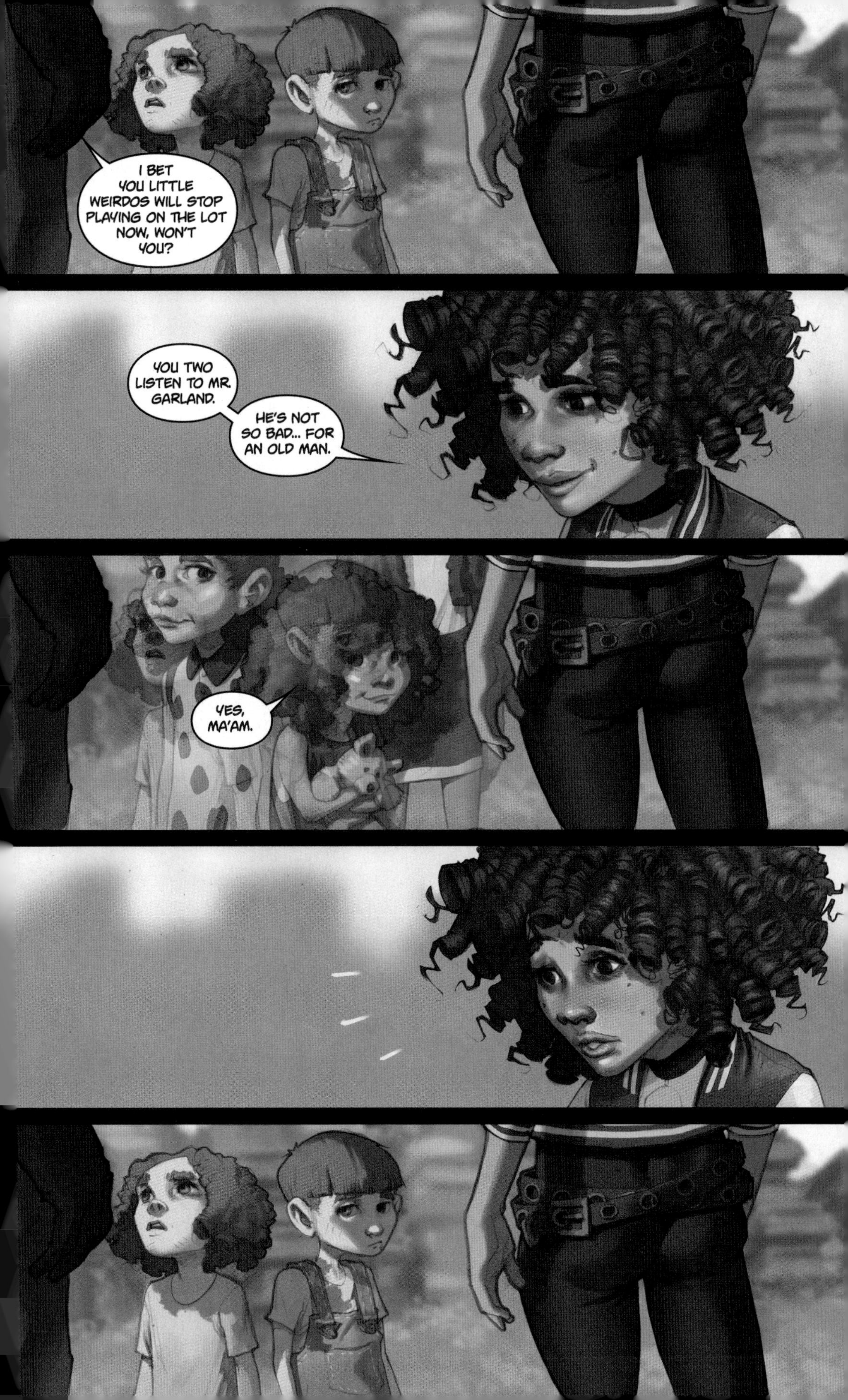
I BET YOU LITTLE WEIRDOS WILL STOP PLAYING ON THE LOT NOW, WON'T YOU?
YOU TWO LISTEN TO MR. GARLAND.
HE'S NOT SO BAD... FOR AN OLD MAN.
YES, MA'AM.

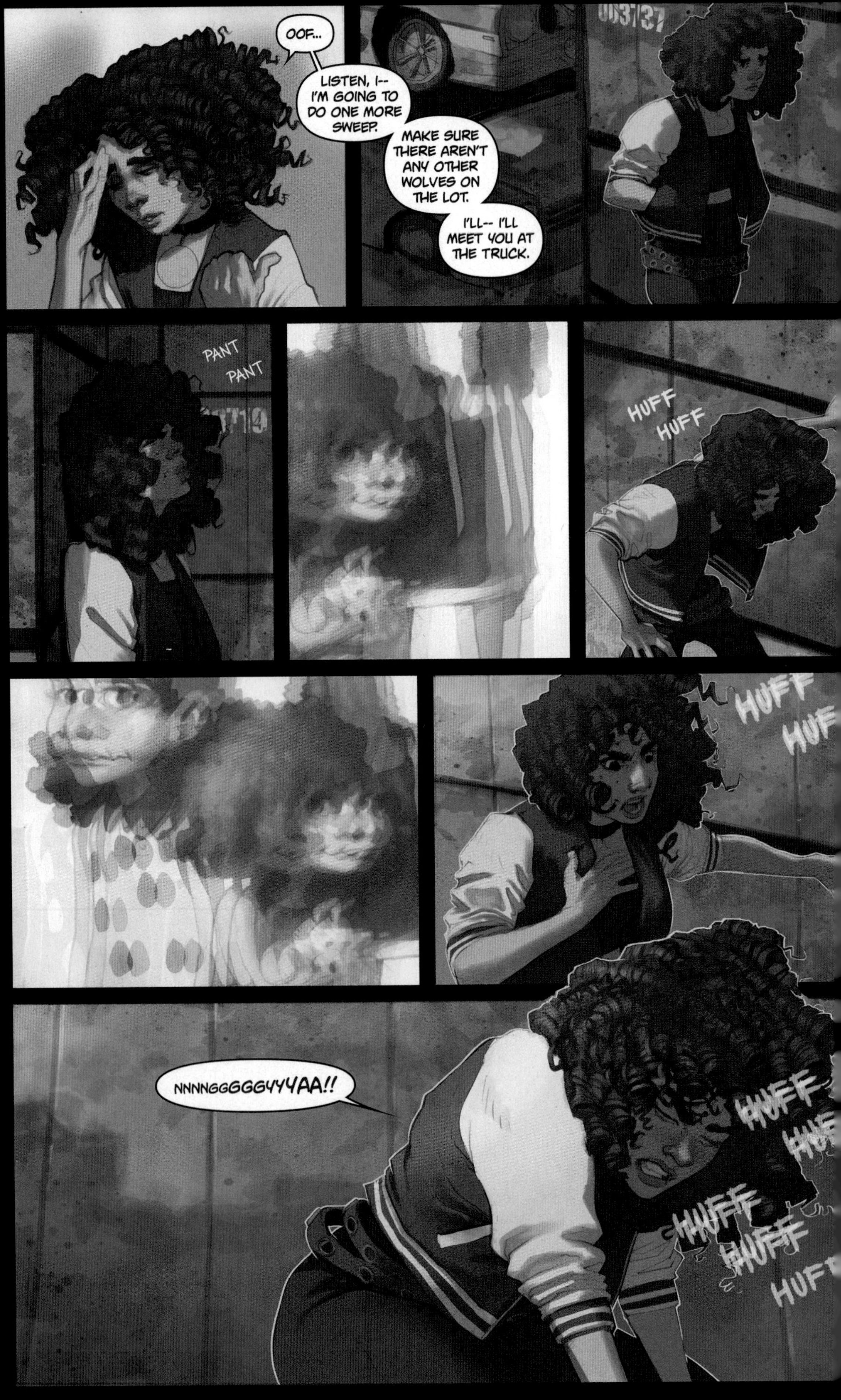
OOF...
LISTEN, I-- I'M GOING TO DO ONE MORE SWEEP.
MAKE SURE THERE AREN'T ANY OTHER WOLVES ON THE LOT.
I'LL-- I'LL MEET YOU AT THE TRUCK.
PANT PANT
HUFF HUFF
HUFF HUFF
NNNNGGGGGYYYAA!!
HUFF HUFF
HUFF HUFF HUFF

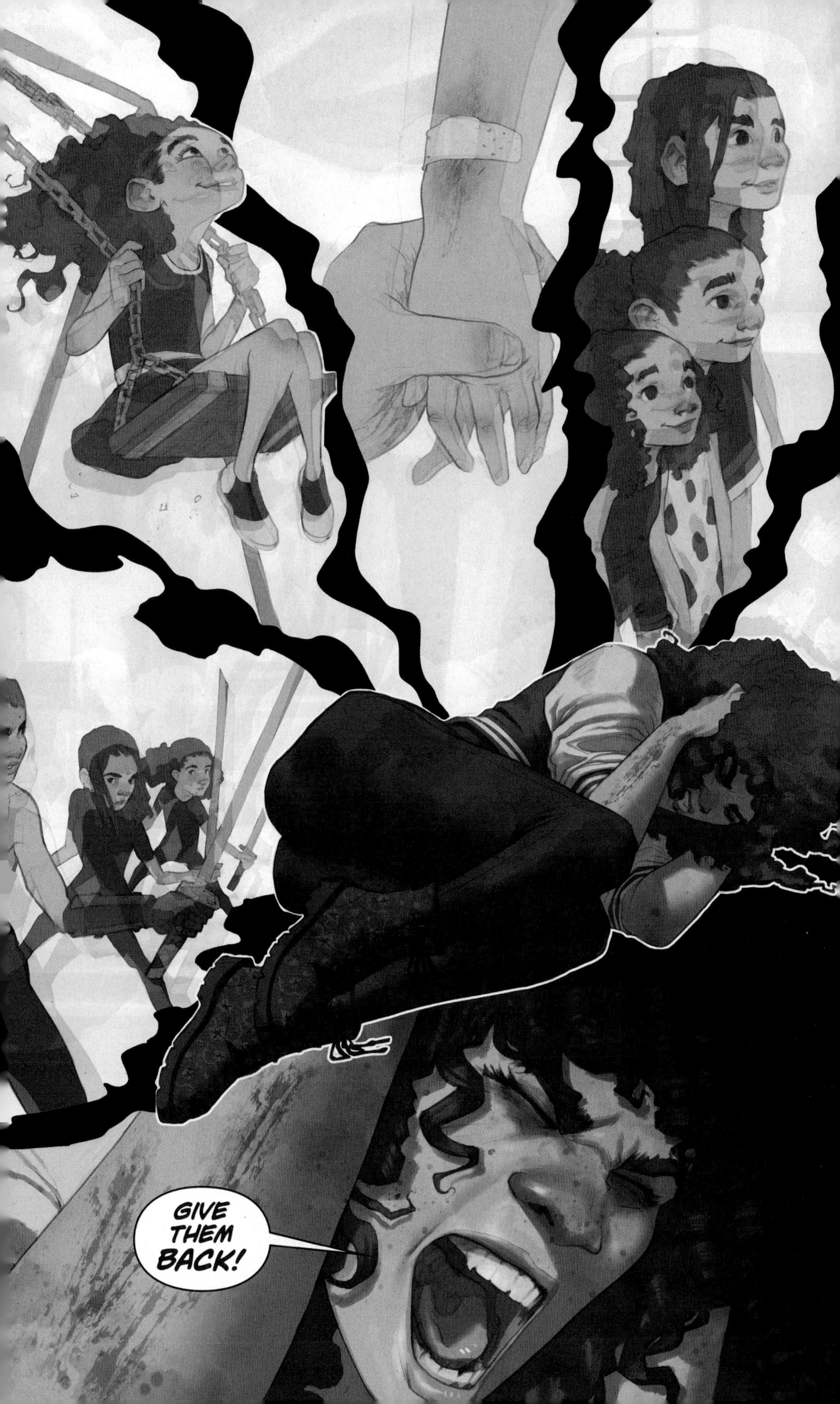
GIVE THEM BACK!

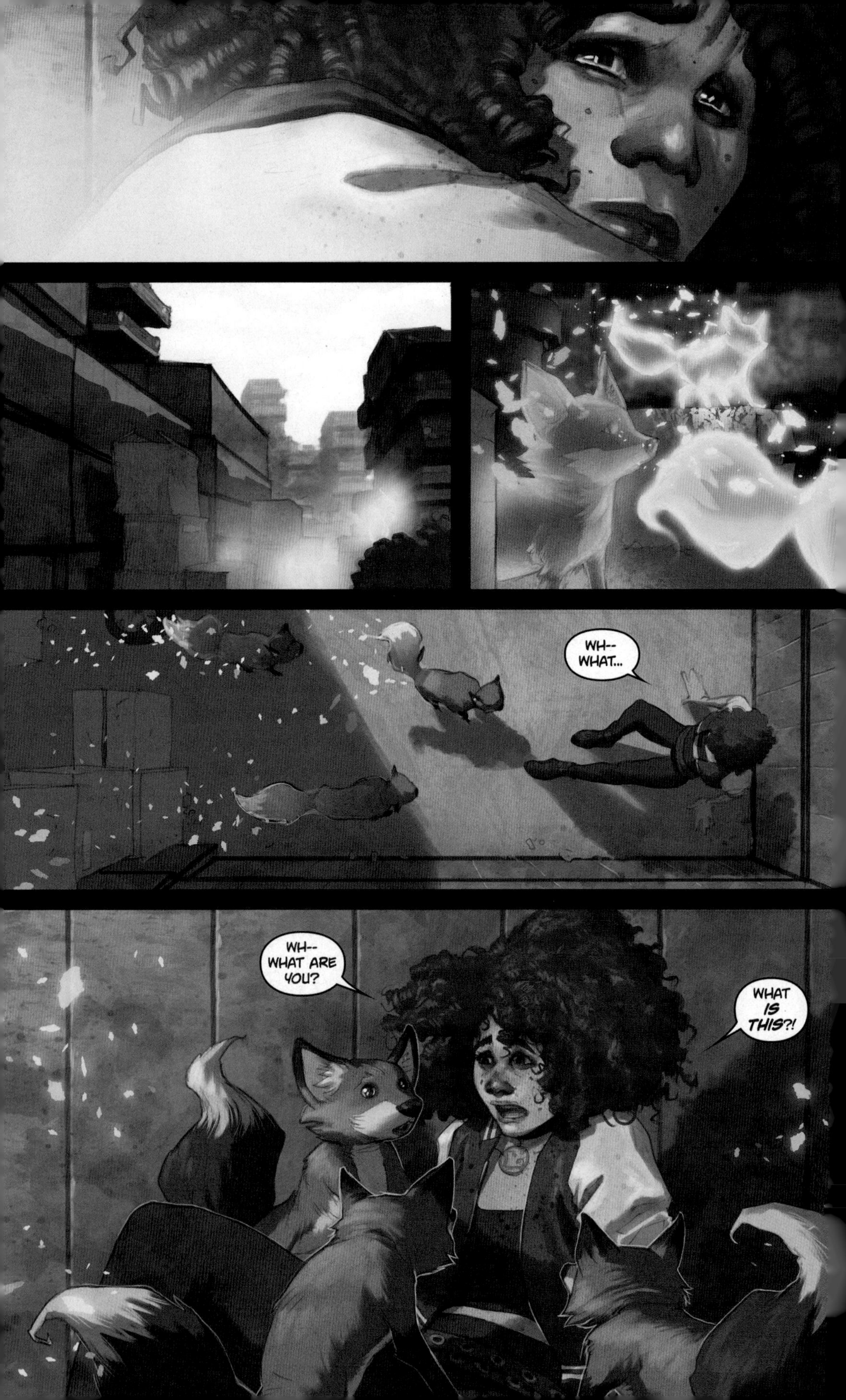
WH--
WHAT...
WH--
WHAT ARE
YOU?
WHAT
IS
THIS?!

CHAPTER THREE

"You were taken from me.
You were lost to me.
All was dark. All was silent.

Now, in this darkness, faintly,
I can hear you calling."

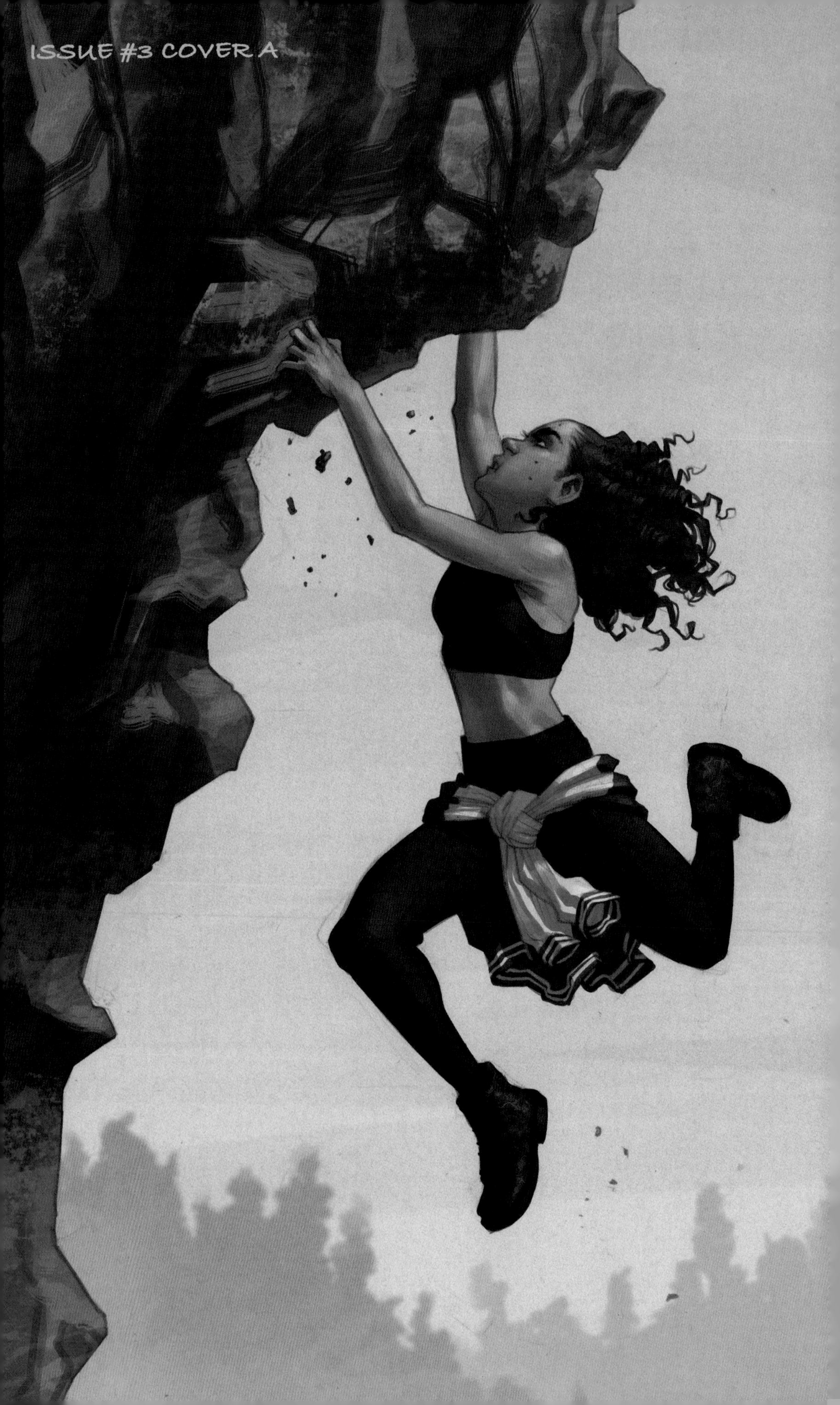
ISSUE #3 COVER A

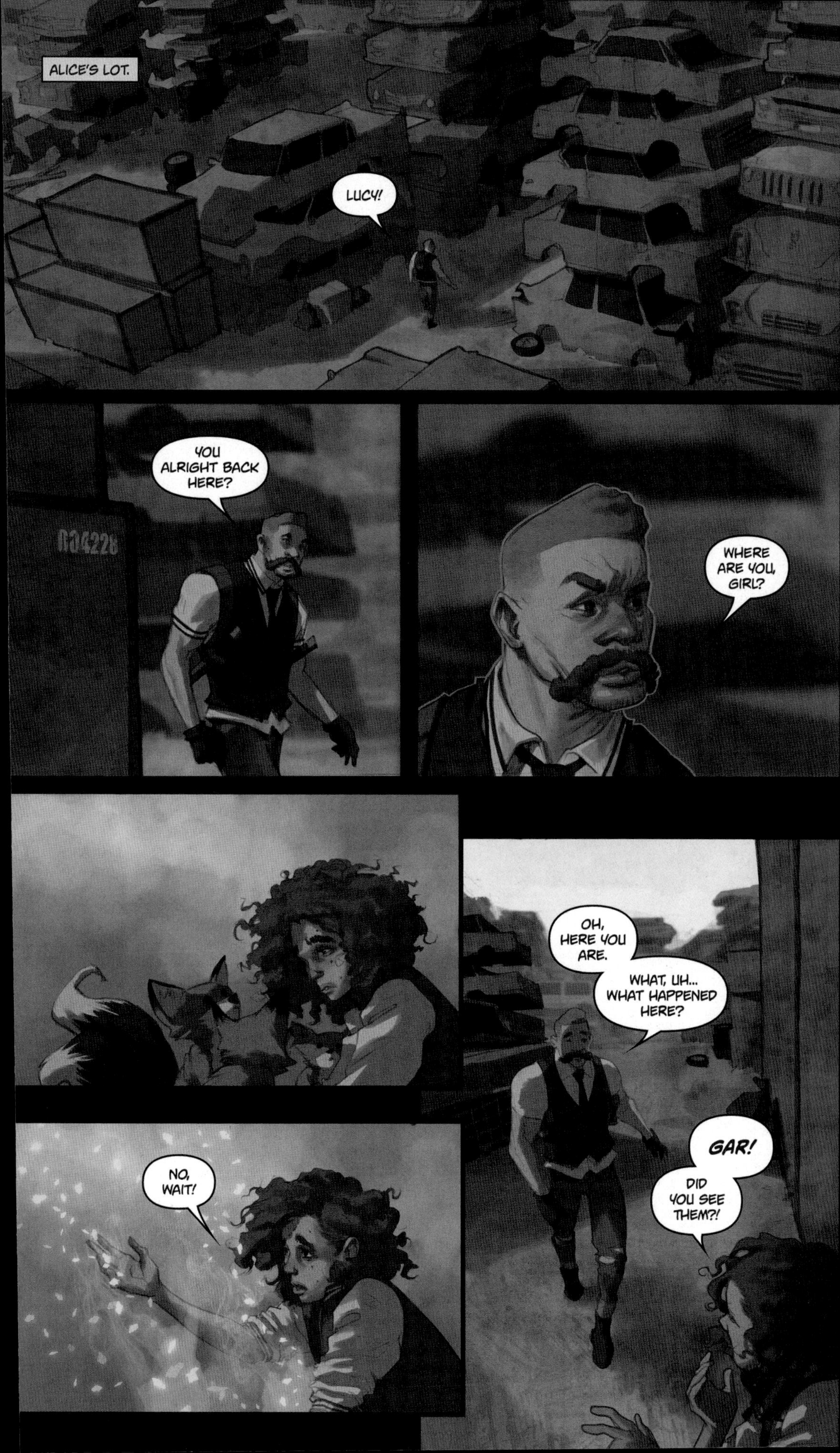
ALICE'S LOT.
LUCY!
YOU ALRIGHT BACK HERE?
WHERE ARE YOU, GIRL?
OH, HERE YOU ARE.
WHAT, UH... WHAT HAPPENED HERE?
NO, WAIT!
GAR!
DID YOU SEE THEM?!

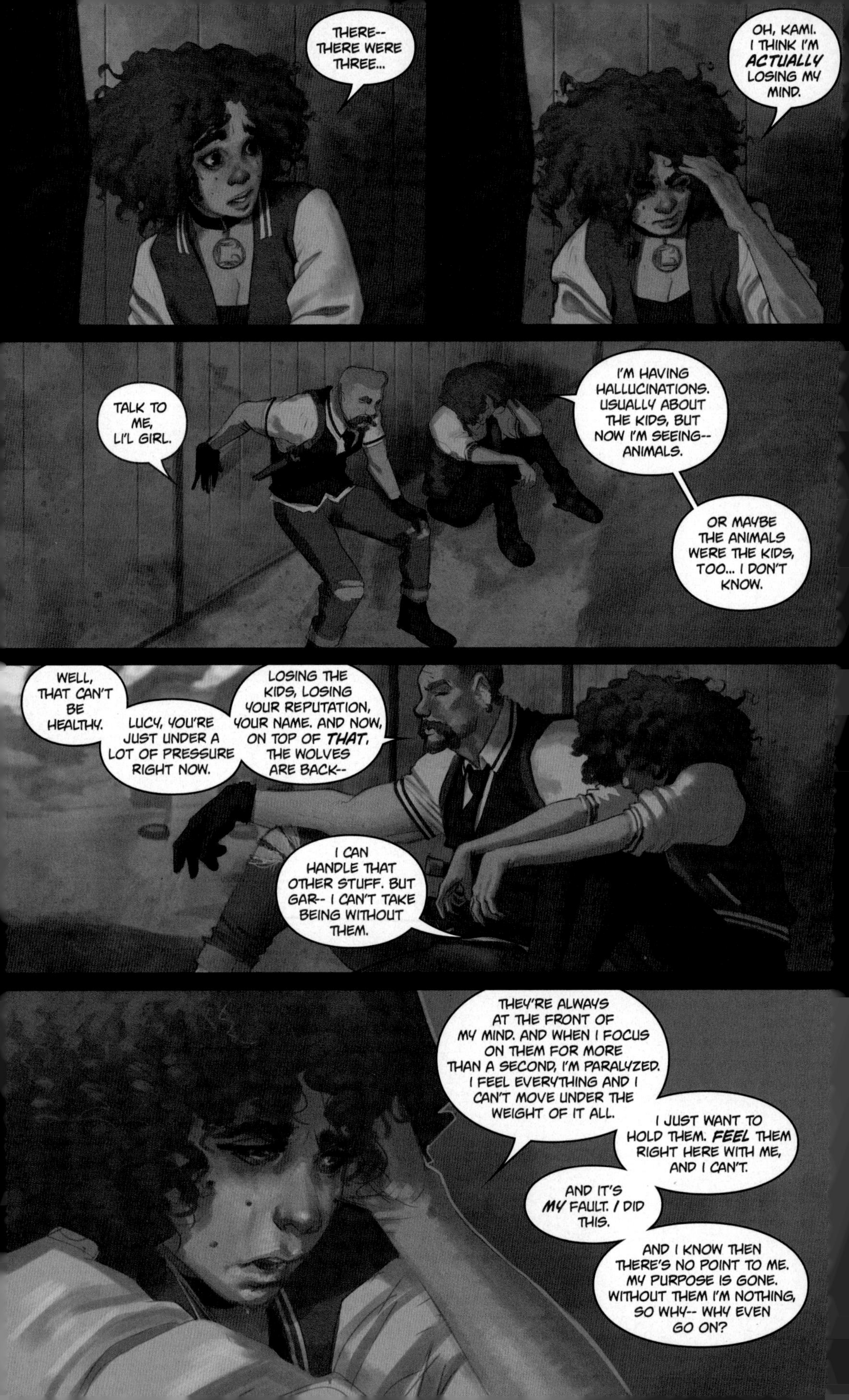
THERE-- THERE WERE THREE...
OH, KAMI. I THINK I'M *ACTUALLY* LOSING MY MIND.
TALK TO ME, LI'L GIRL.
I'M HAVING HALLUCINATIONS. USUALLY ABOUT THE KIDS, BUT NOW I'M SEEING-- ANIMALS.
OR MAYBE THE ANIMALS WERE THE KIDS, TOO... I DON'T KNOW.
WELL, THAT CAN'T BE HEALTHY.
LUCY, YOU'RE JUST UNDER A LOT OF PRESSURE RIGHT NOW.
LOSING THE KIDS, LOSING YOUR REPUTATION, YOUR NAME. AND NOW, ON TOP OF *THAT*, THE WOLVES ARE BACK--
I CAN HANDLE THAT OTHER STUFF. BUT GAR-- I CAN'T TAKE BEING WITHOUT THEM.
THEY'RE ALWAYS AT THE FRONT OF MY MIND. AND WHEN I FOCUS ON THEM FOR MORE THAN A SECOND, I'M PARALYZED. I FEEL EVERYTHING AND I CAN'T MOVE UNDER THE WEIGHT OF IT ALL.
I JUST WANT TO HOLD THEM. *FEEL* THEM RIGHT HERE WITH ME, AND I CAN'T.
AND IT'S *MY* FAULT. *I* DID THIS.
AND I KNOW THEN THERE'S NO POINT TO ME. MY PURPOSE IS GONE. WITHOUT THEM I'M NOTHING, SO WHY-- WHY EVEN GO ON?

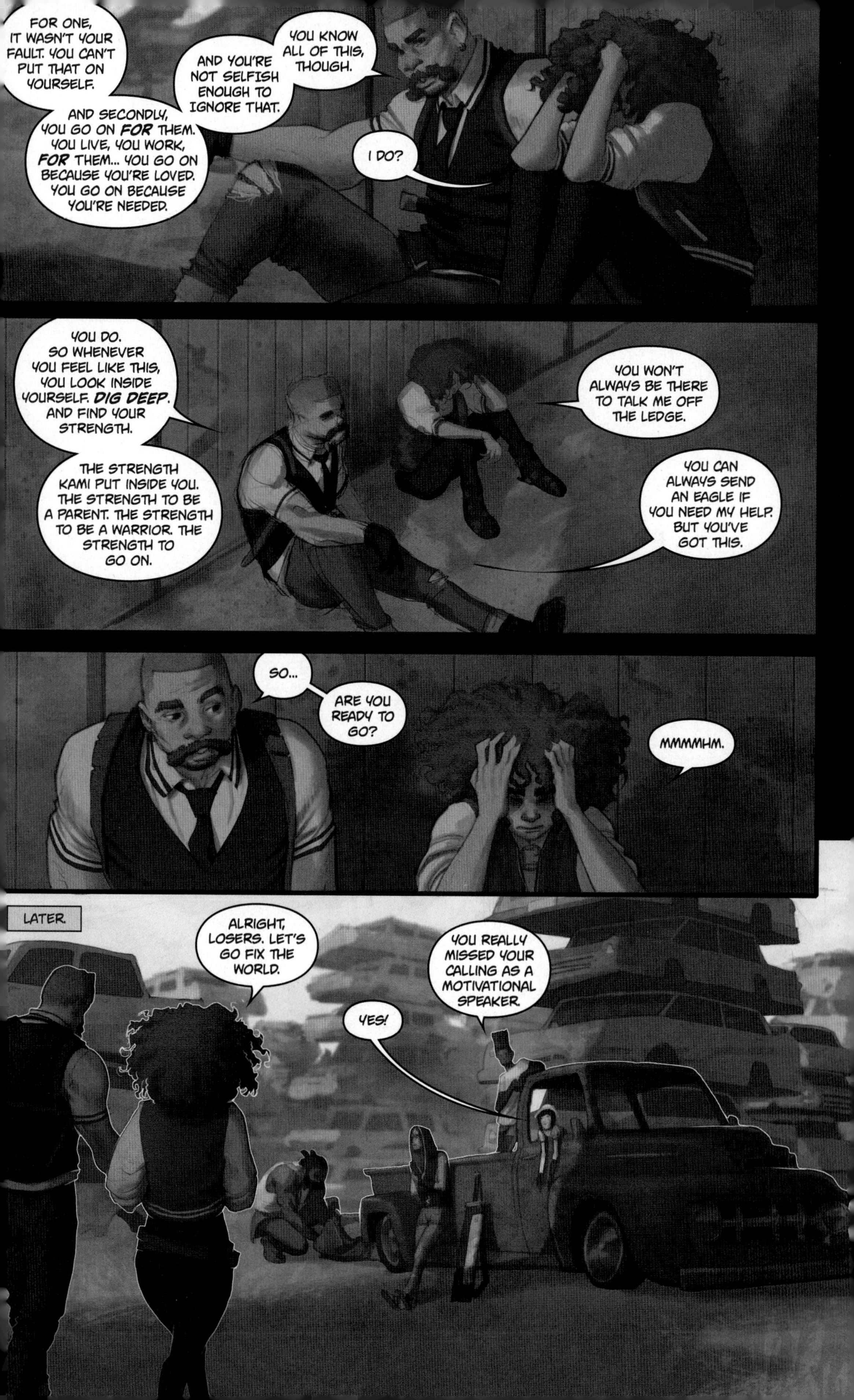
FOR ONE, IT WASN'T YOUR FAULT. YOU CAN'T PUT THAT ON YOURSELF.
AND YOU'RE NOT SELFISH ENOUGH TO IGNORE THAT.
YOU KNOW ALL OF THIS, THOUGH.
AND SECONDLY, YOU GO ON **FOR** THEM. YOU LIVE, YOU WORK, **FOR** THEM... YOU GO ON BECAUSE YOU'RE LOVED. YOU GO ON BECAUSE YOU'RE NEEDED.
I DO?
YOU DO. SO WHENEVER YOU FEEL LIKE THIS, YOU LOOK INSIDE YOURSELF. ***DIG DEEP***. AND FIND YOUR STRENGTH.
THE STRENGTH KAMI PUT INSIDE YOU. THE STRENGTH TO BE A PARENT. THE STRENGTH TO BE A WARRIOR. THE STRENGTH TO GO ON.
YOU WON'T ALWAYS BE THERE TO TALK ME OFF THE LEDGE.
YOU CAN ALWAYS SEND AN EAGLE IF YOU NEED MY HELP. BUT YOU'VE GOT THIS.
SO...
ARE YOU READY TO GO?
MMMMHM.
LATER.
ALRIGHT, LOSERS. LET'S GO FIX THE WORLD.
YOU REALLY MISSED YOUR CALLING AS A MOTIVATIONAL SPEAKER.
YES!

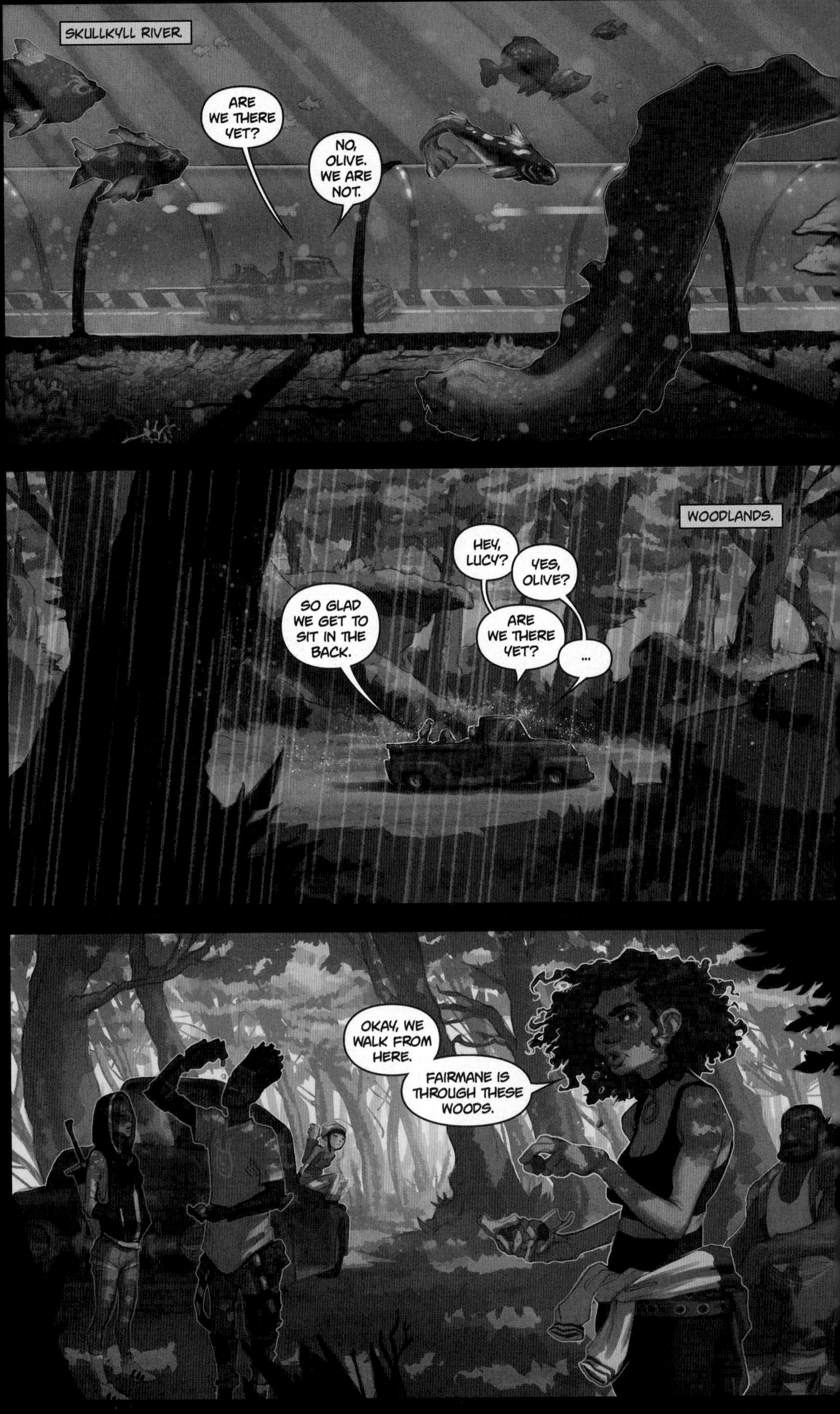
SKULLKYLL RIVER.
ARE WE THERE YET?
NO, OLIVE. WE ARE NOT.
WOODLANDS.
SO GLAD WE GET TO SIT IN THE BACK.
HEY, LUCY?
YES, OLIVE?
ARE WE THERE YET?
...
OKAY, WE WALK FROM HERE.
FAIRMANE IS THROUGH THESE WOODS.

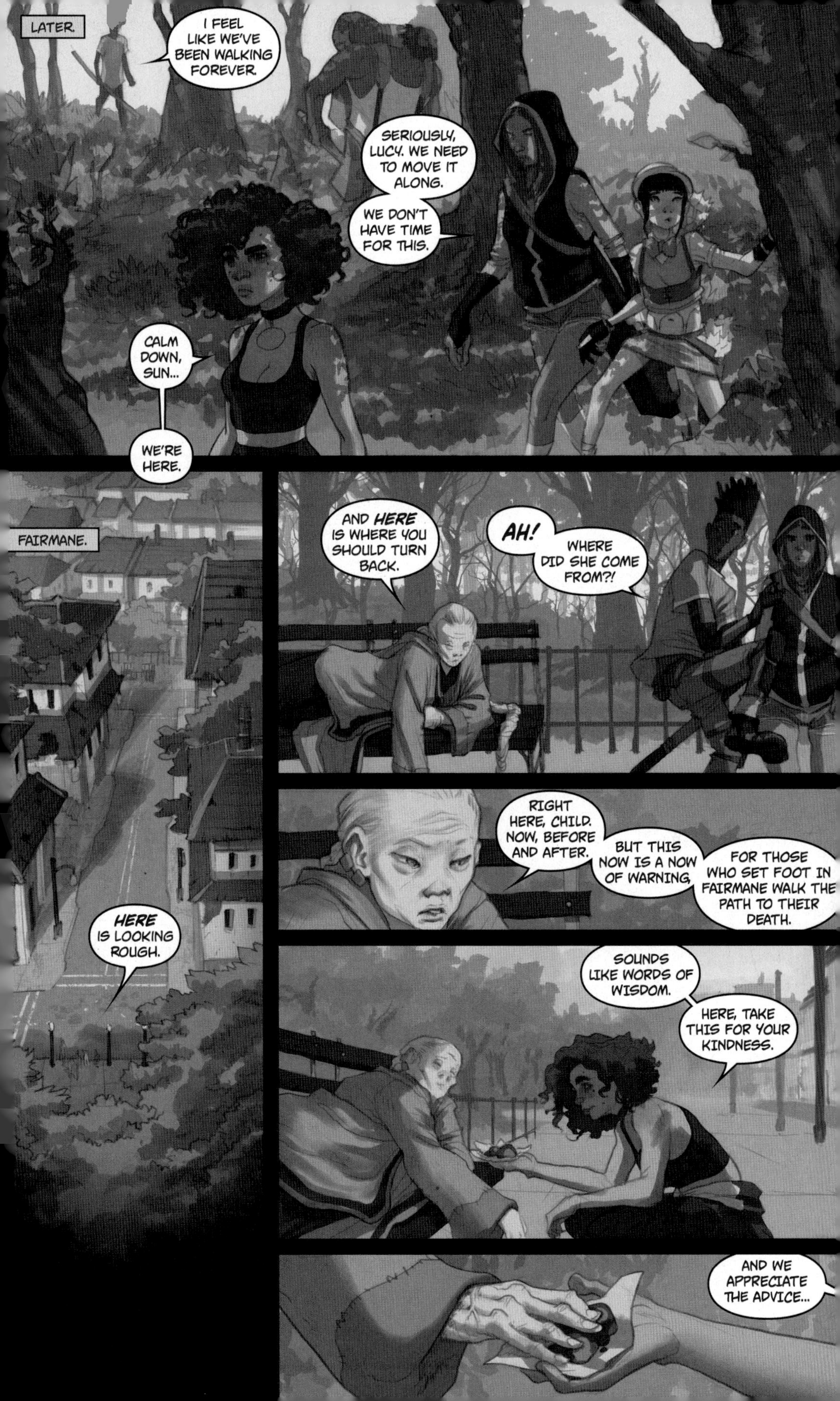
LATER.
I FEEL LIKE WE'VE BEEN WALKING FOREVER.
SERIOUSLY, LUCY. WE NEED TO MOVE IT ALONG.
WE DON'T HAVE TIME FOR THIS.
CALM DOWN, SUN...
WE'RE HERE.
FAIRMANE.
HERE IS LOOKING ROUGH.
AND HERE IS WHERE YOU SHOULD TURN BACK.
AH!
WHERE DID SHE COME FROM?!
RIGHT HERE, CHILD. NOW, BEFORE AND AFTER.
BUT THIS NOW IS A NOW OF WARNING,
FOR THOSE WHO SET FOOT IN FAIRMANE WALK THE PATH TO THEIR DEATH.
SOUNDS LIKE WORDS OF WISDOM.
HERE, TAKE THIS FOR YOUR KINDNESS.
AND WE APPRECIATE THE ADVICE...

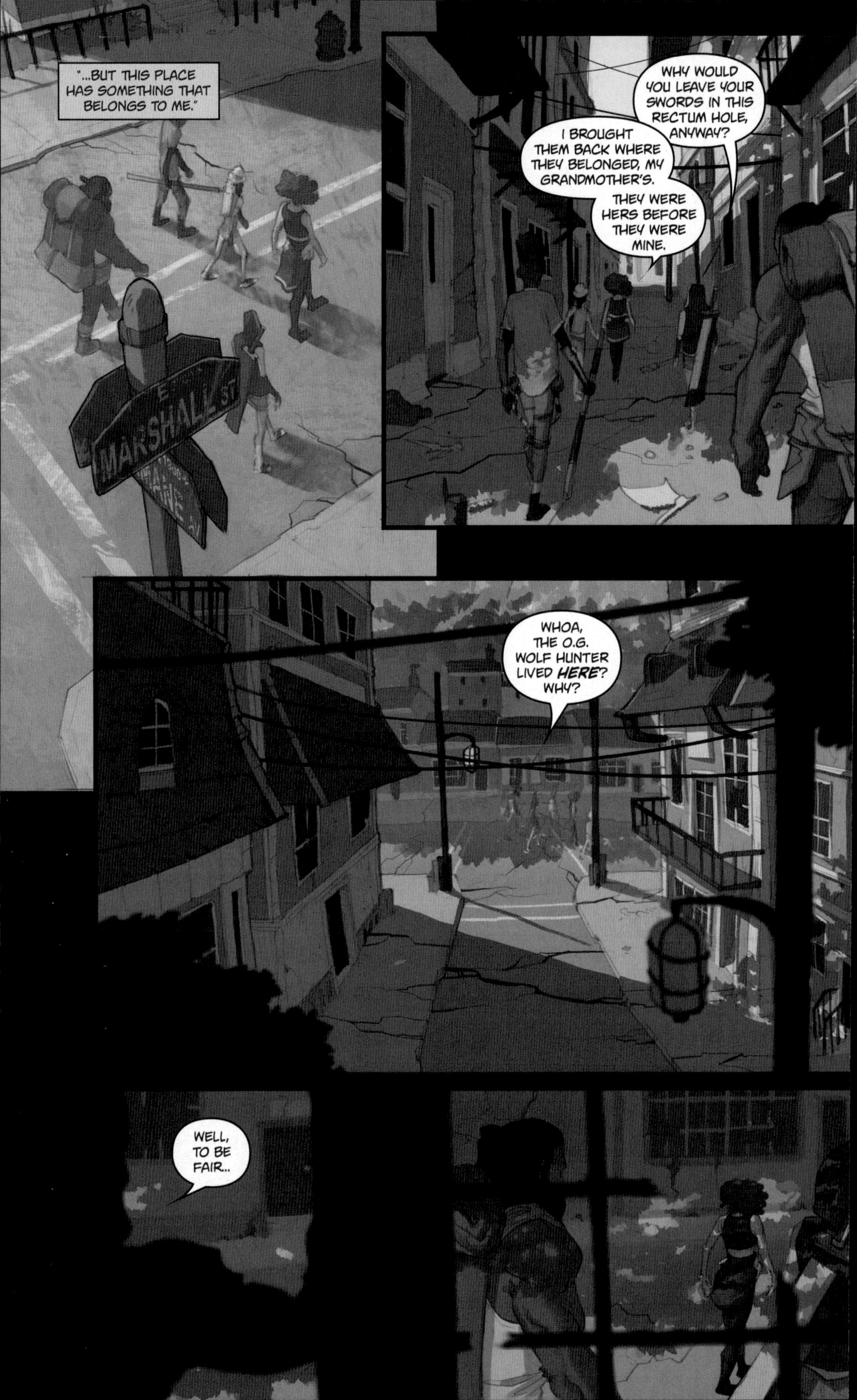
"...BUT THIS PLACE HAS SOMETHING THAT BELONGS TO ME."
E MARSHALL ST
WHY WOULD YOU LEAVE YOUR SWORDS IN THIS RECTUM HOLE, ANYWAY?
I BROUGHT THEM BACK WHERE THEY BELONGED, MY GRANDMOTHER'S.
THEY WERE HERS BEFORE THEY WERE MINE.
WHOA, THE O.G. WOLF HUNTER LIVED *HERE*? WHY?
WELL, TO BE FAIR...

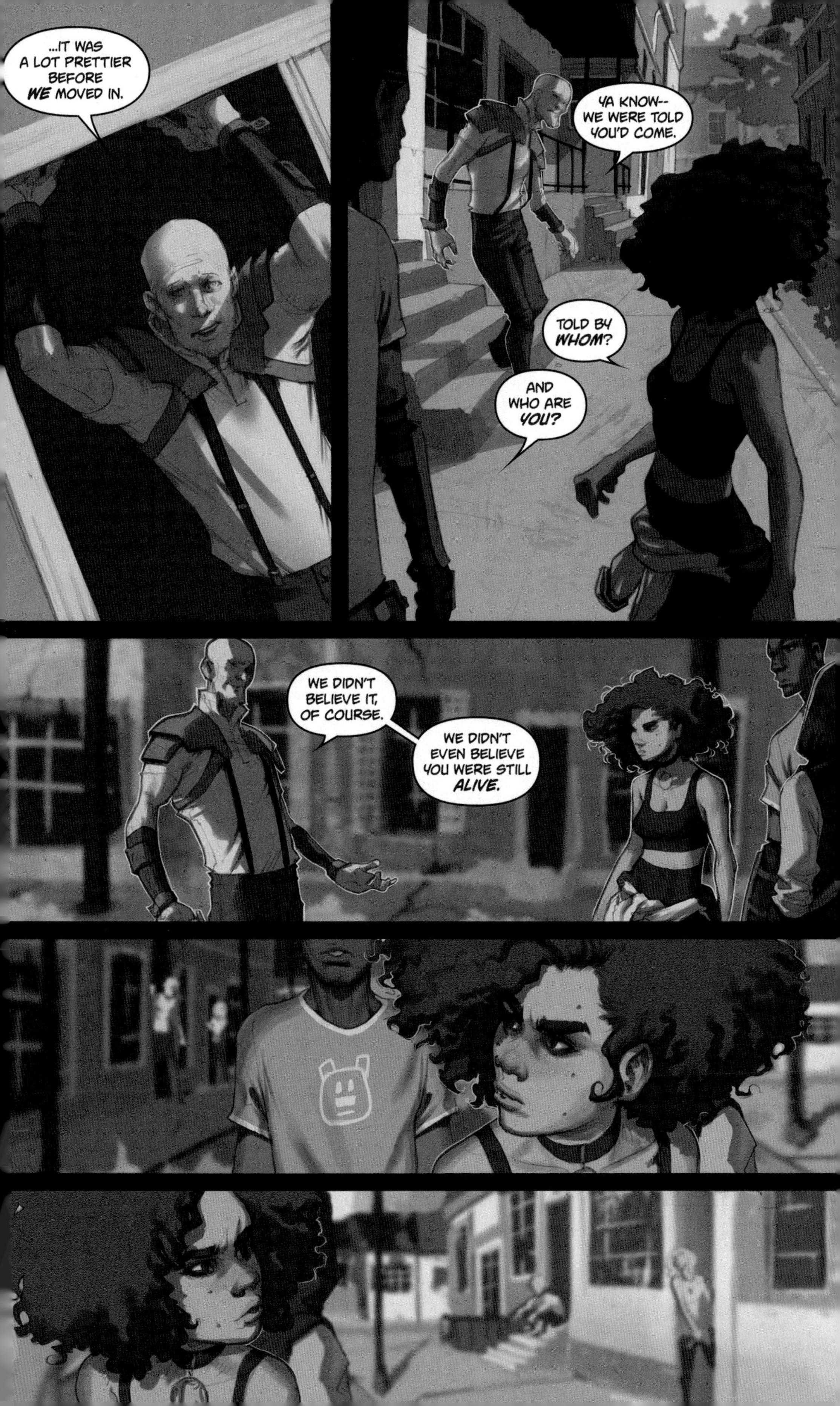
...IT WAS A LOT PRETTIER BEFORE *WE* MOVED IN.
YA KNOW-- WE WERE TOLD YOU'D COME.
TOLD BY *WHOM*?
AND WHO ARE *YOU*?
WE DIDN'T BELIEVE IT, OF COURSE.
WE DIDN'T EVEN BELIEVE YOU WERE STILL *ALIVE*.

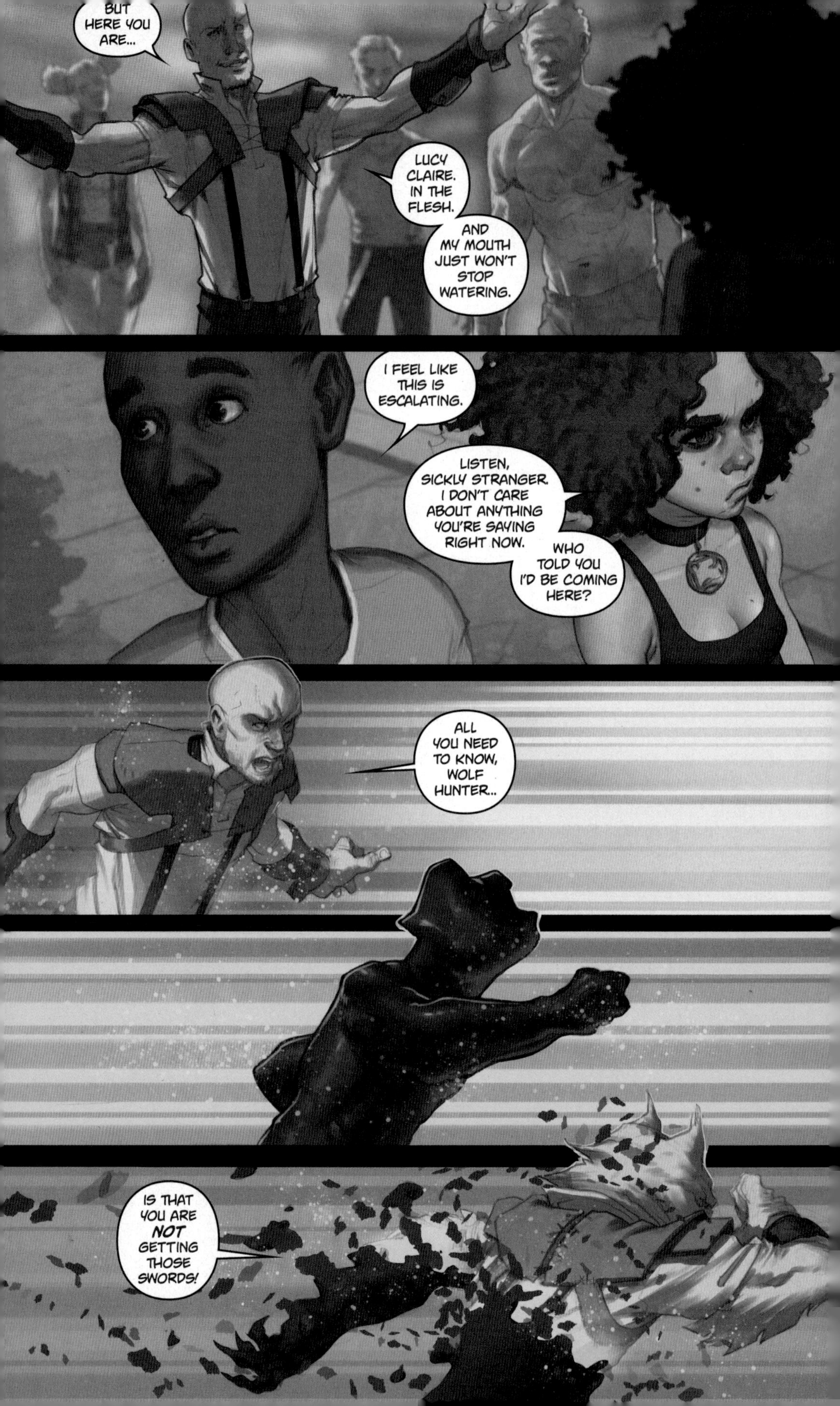
BUT HERE YOU ARE...
LUCY CLAIRE. IN THE FLESH.
AND MY MOUTH JUST WON'T STOP WATERING.
I FEEL LIKE THIS IS ESCALATING.
LISTEN, SICKLY STRANGER. I DON'T CARE ABOUT ANYTHING YOU'RE SAYING RIGHT NOW.
WHO TOLD YOU I'D BE COMING HERE?
ALL YOU NEED TO KNOW, WOLF HUNTER...
IS THAT YOU ARE *NOT* GETTING THOSE SWORDS!

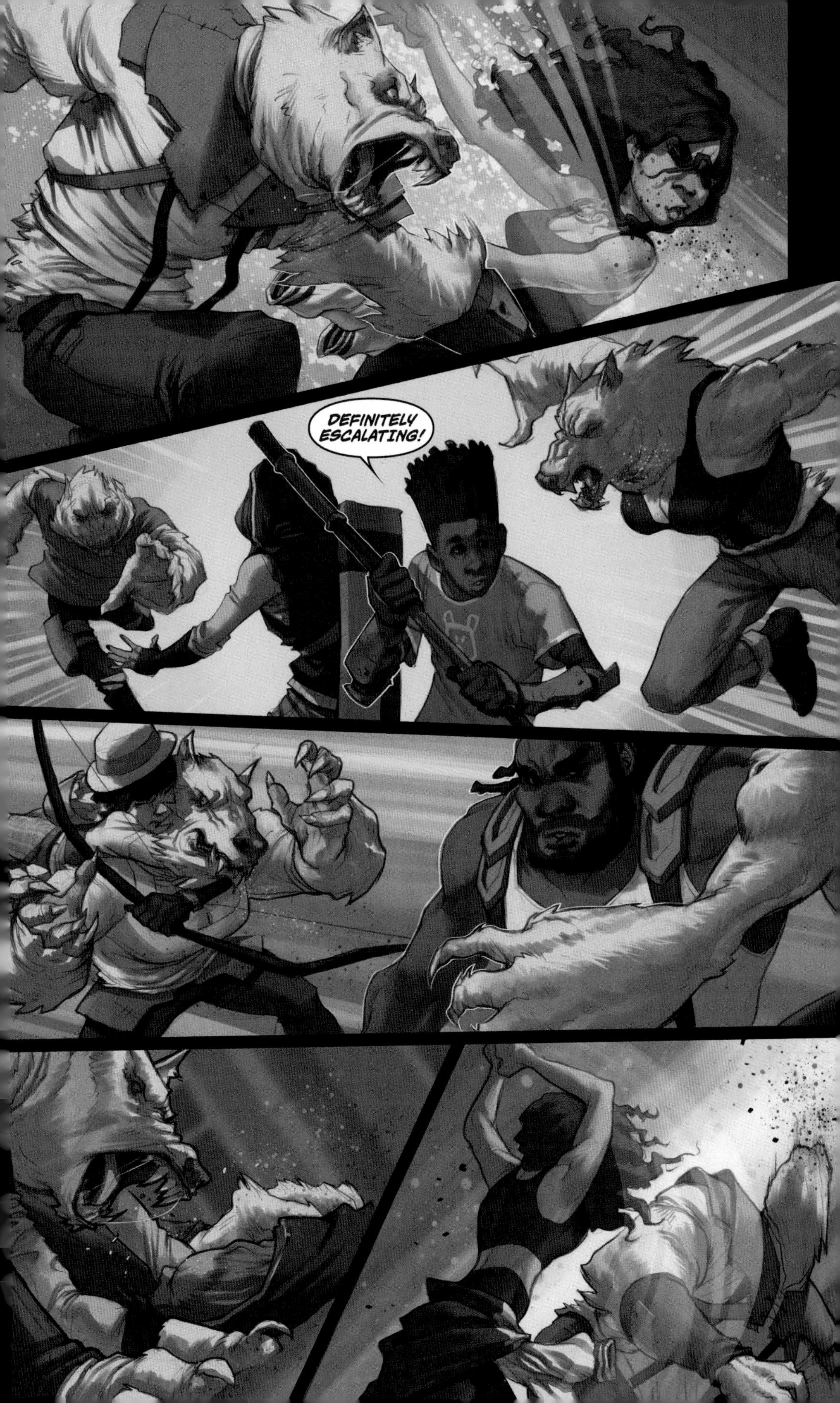
DEFINITELY ESCALATING!

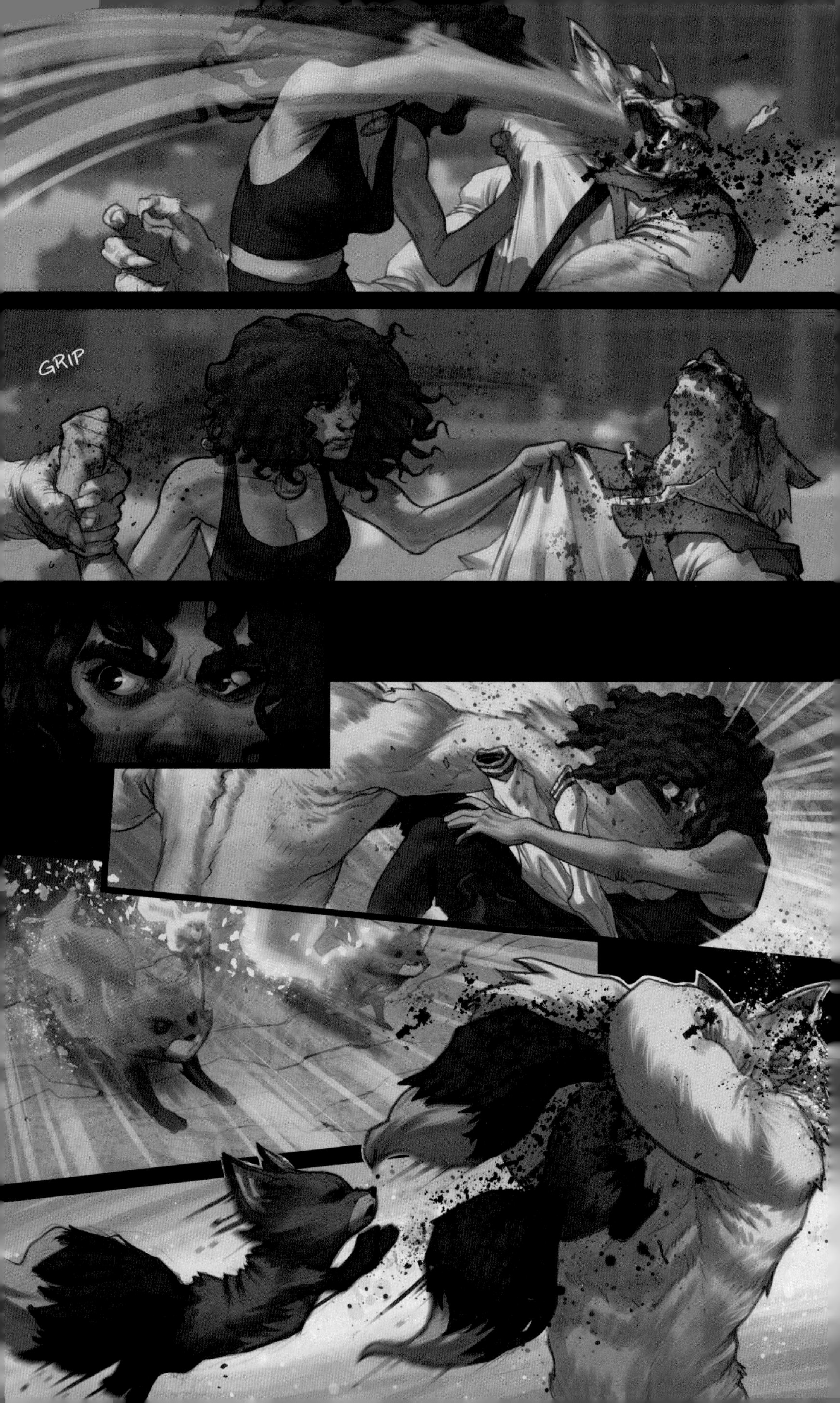
GRIP

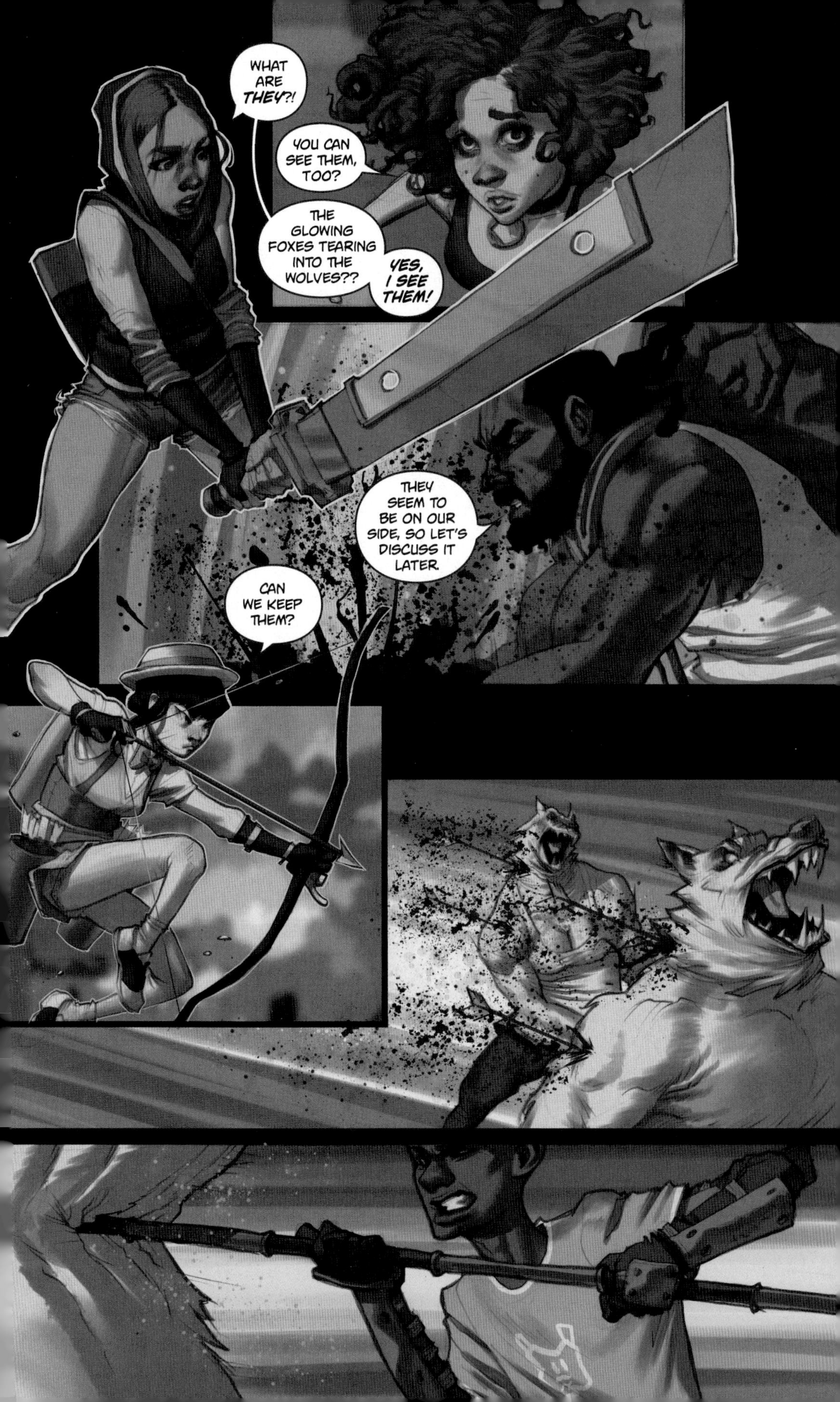
WHAT ARE *THEY*?!
YOU CAN SEE THEM, TOO?
THE GLOWING FOXES TEARING INTO THE WOLVES??
YES, I SEE THEM!
THEY SEEM TO BE ON OUR SIDE, SO LET'S DISCUSS IT LATER.
CAN WE KEEP THEM?

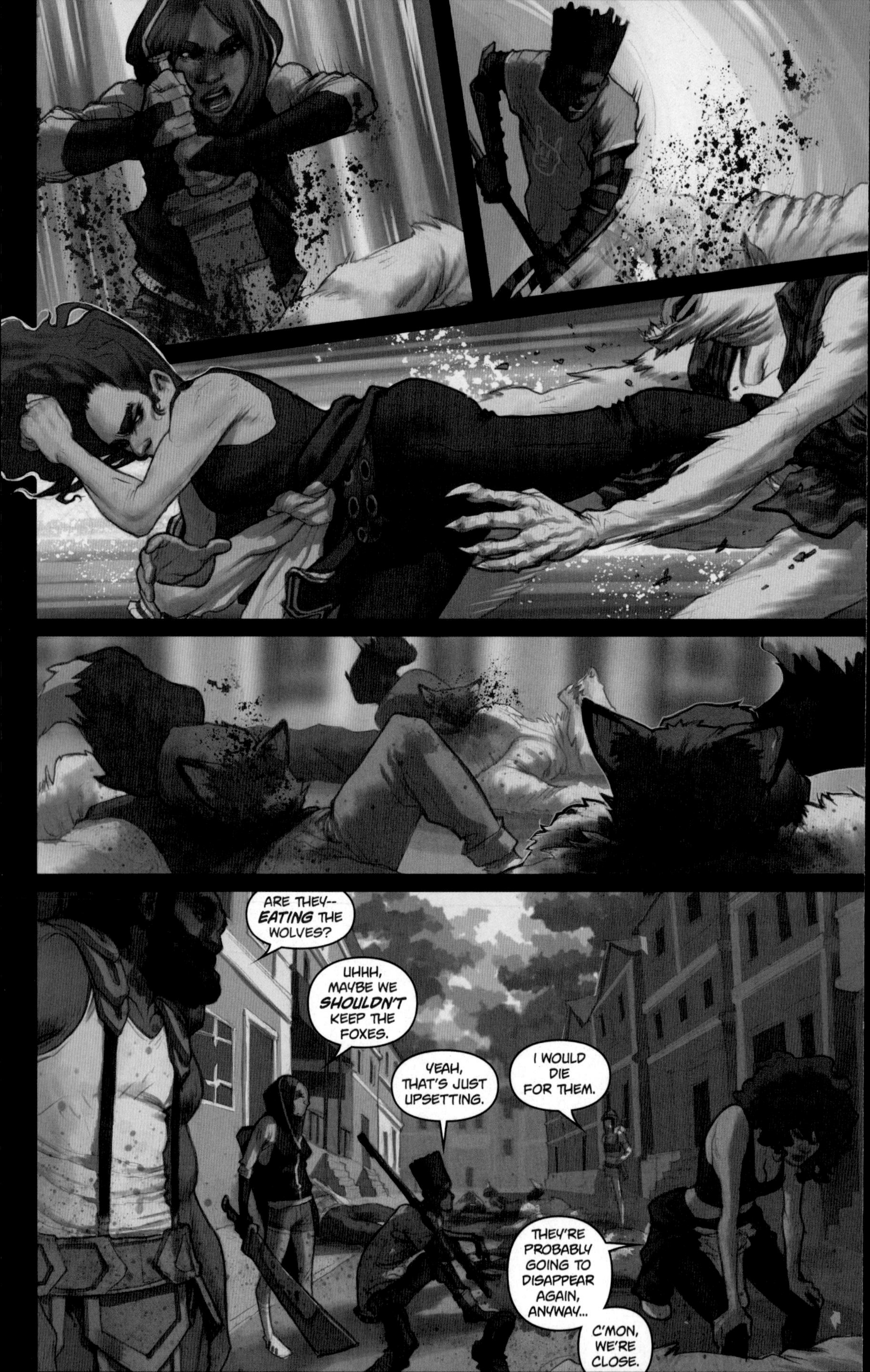
ARE THEY-- EATING THE WOLVES?
UHHH, MAYBE WE SHOULDN'T KEEP THE FOXES.
YEAH, THAT'S JUST UPSETTING.
I WOULD DIE FOR THEM.
THEY'RE PROBABLY GOING TO DISAPPEAR AGAIN, ANYWAY...
C'MON, WE'RE CLOSE.

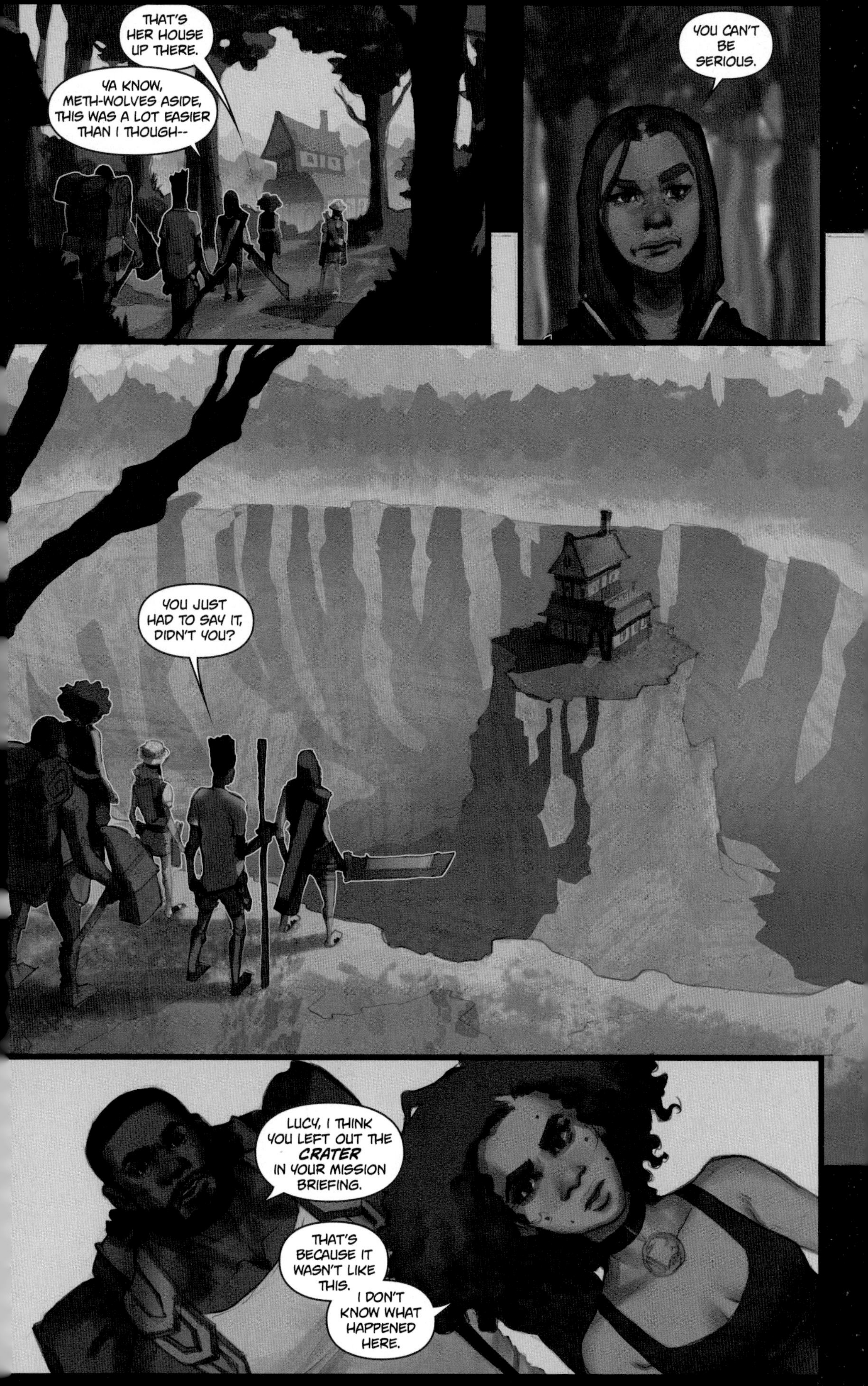
THAT'S HER HOUSE UP THERE.
YA KNOW, METH-WOLVES ASIDE, THIS WAS A LOT EASIER THAN I THOUGH--
YOU CAN'T BE SERIOUS.
YOU JUST HAD TO SAY IT, DIDN'T YOU?
LUCY, I THINK YOU LEFT OUT THE *CRATER* IN YOUR MISSION BRIEFING.
THAT'S BECAUSE IT WASN'T LIKE THIS.
I DON'T KNOW WHAT HAPPENED HERE.

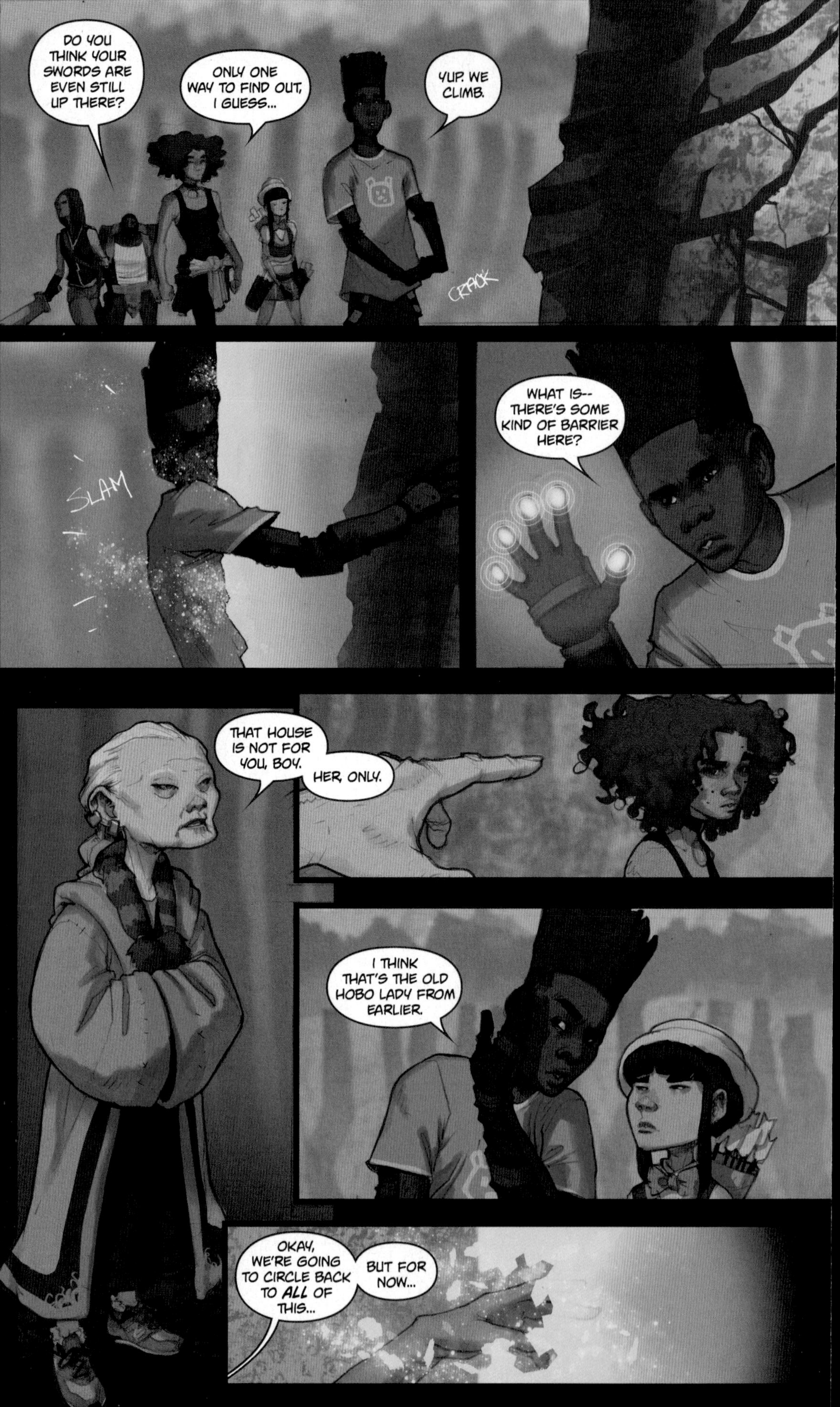
DO YOU THINK YOUR SWORDS ARE EVEN STILL UP THERE?
ONLY ONE WAY TO FIND OUT, I GUESS...
YUP. WE CLIMB.
CRACK
SLAM
WHAT IS-- THERE'S SOME KIND OF BARRIER HERE?
THAT HOUSE IS NOT FOR YOU, BOY.
HER, ONLY.
I THINK THAT'S THE OLD HOBO LADY FROM EARLIER.
OKAY, WE'RE GOING TO CIRCLE BACK TO ALL OF THIS...
BUT FOR NOW...

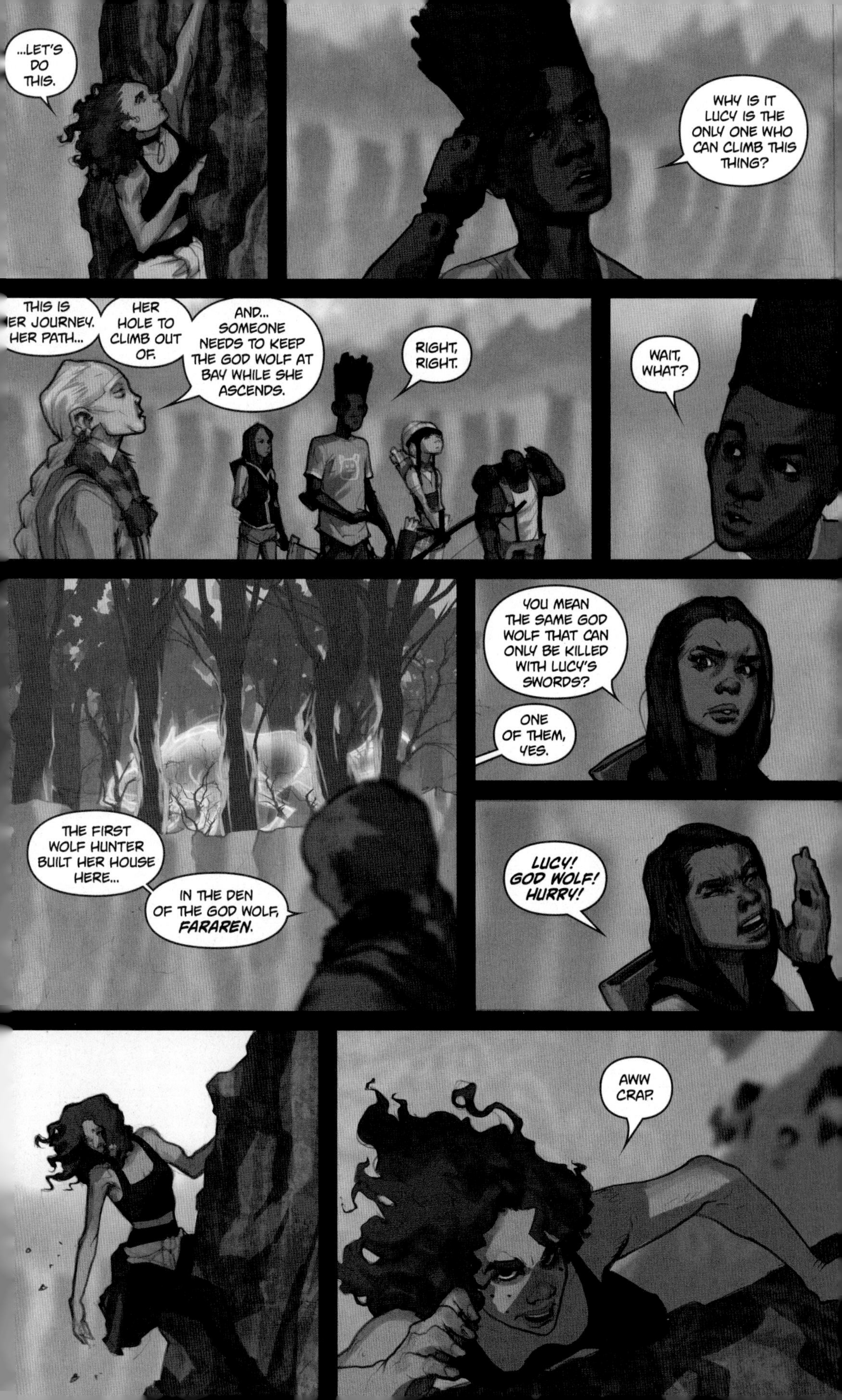

...LET'S DO THIS.
WHY IS IT LUCY IS THE ONLY ONE WHO CAN CLIMB THIS THING?
THIS IS ER JOURNEY. HER PATH...
HER HOLE TO CLIMB OUT OF.
AND... SOMEONE NEEDS TO KEEP THE GOD WOLF AT BAY WHILE SHE ASCENDS.
RIGHT, RIGHT.
WAIT, WHAT?
THE FIRST WOLF HUNTER BUILT HER HOUSE HERE...
IN THE DEN OF THE GOD WOLF, ***FARAREN***.
YOU MEAN THE SAME GOD WOLF THAT CAN ONLY BE KILLED WITH LUCY'S SWORDS?
ONE OF THEM, YES.
LUCY! GOD WOLF! HURRY!
AWW CRAP.

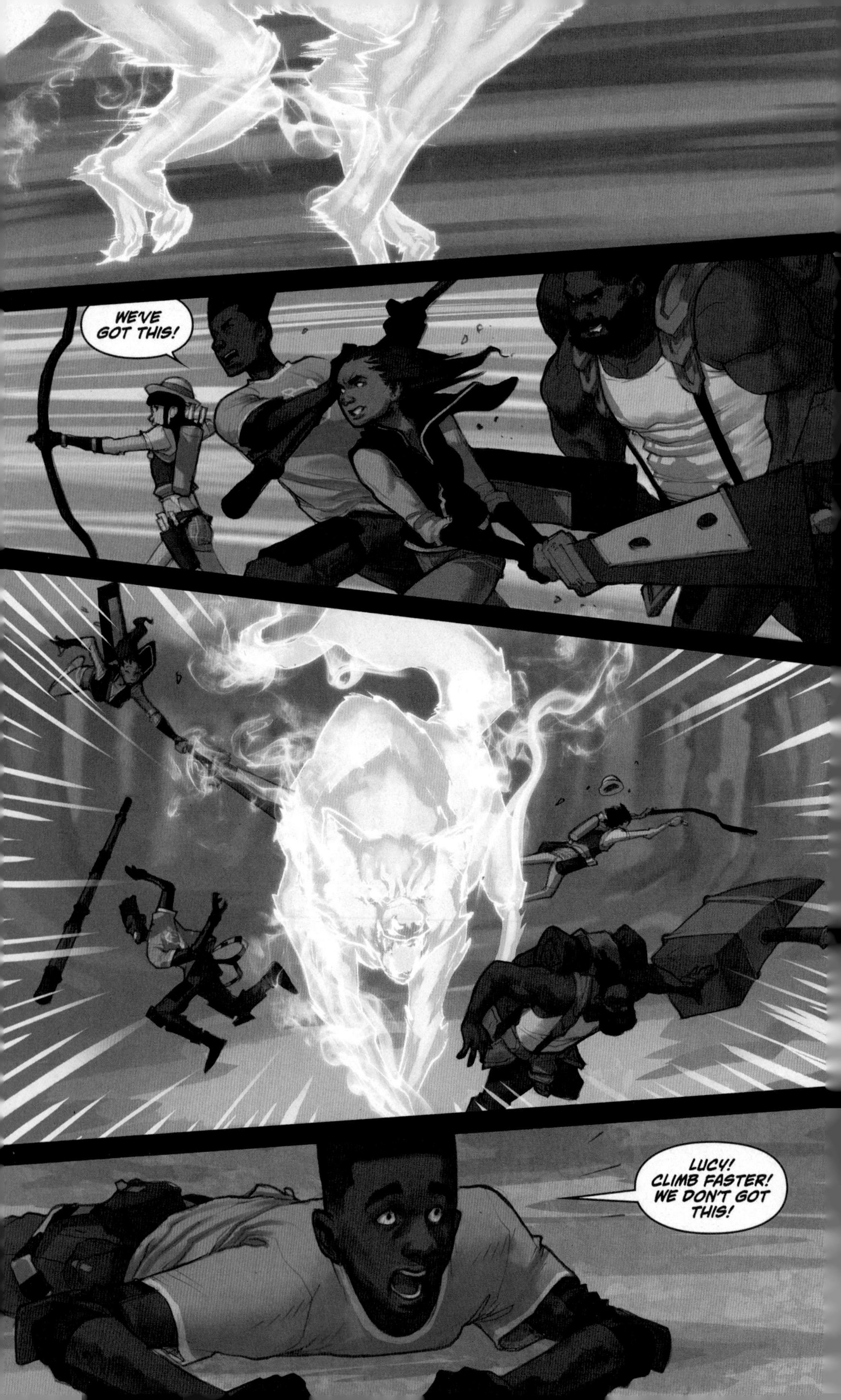
WE'VE GOT THIS!
LUCY! CLIMB FASTER! WE DON'T GOT THIS!

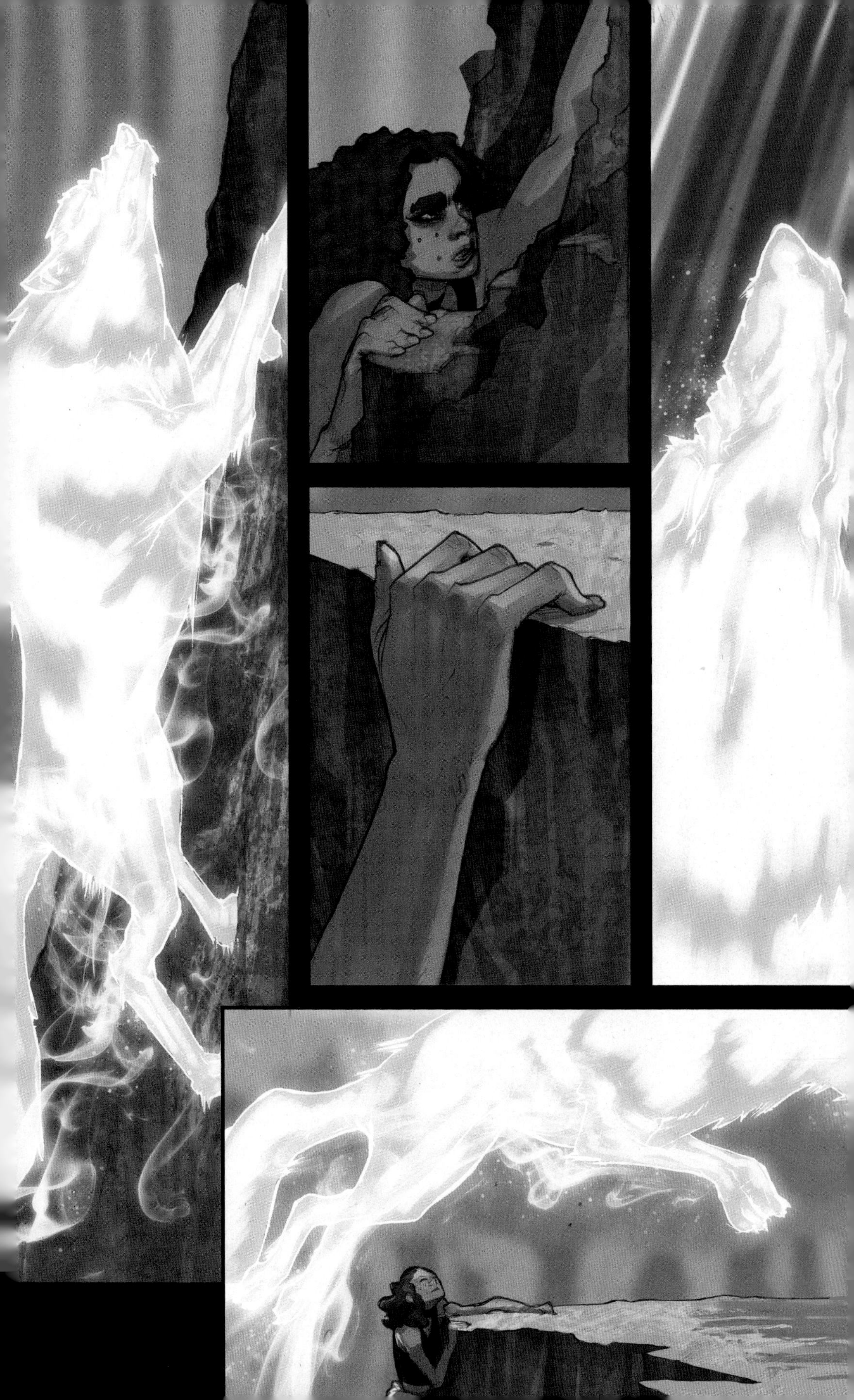

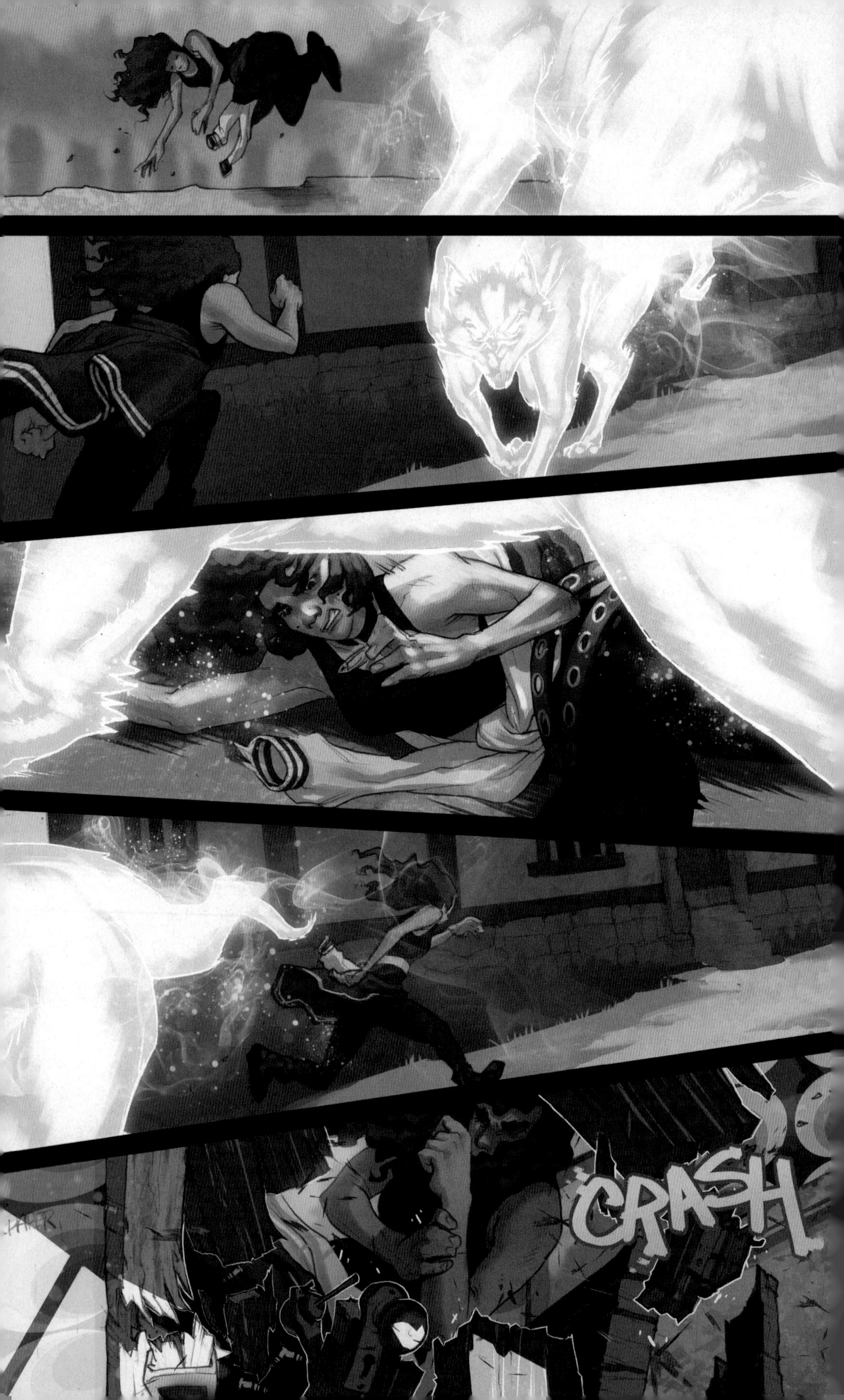
CRASH

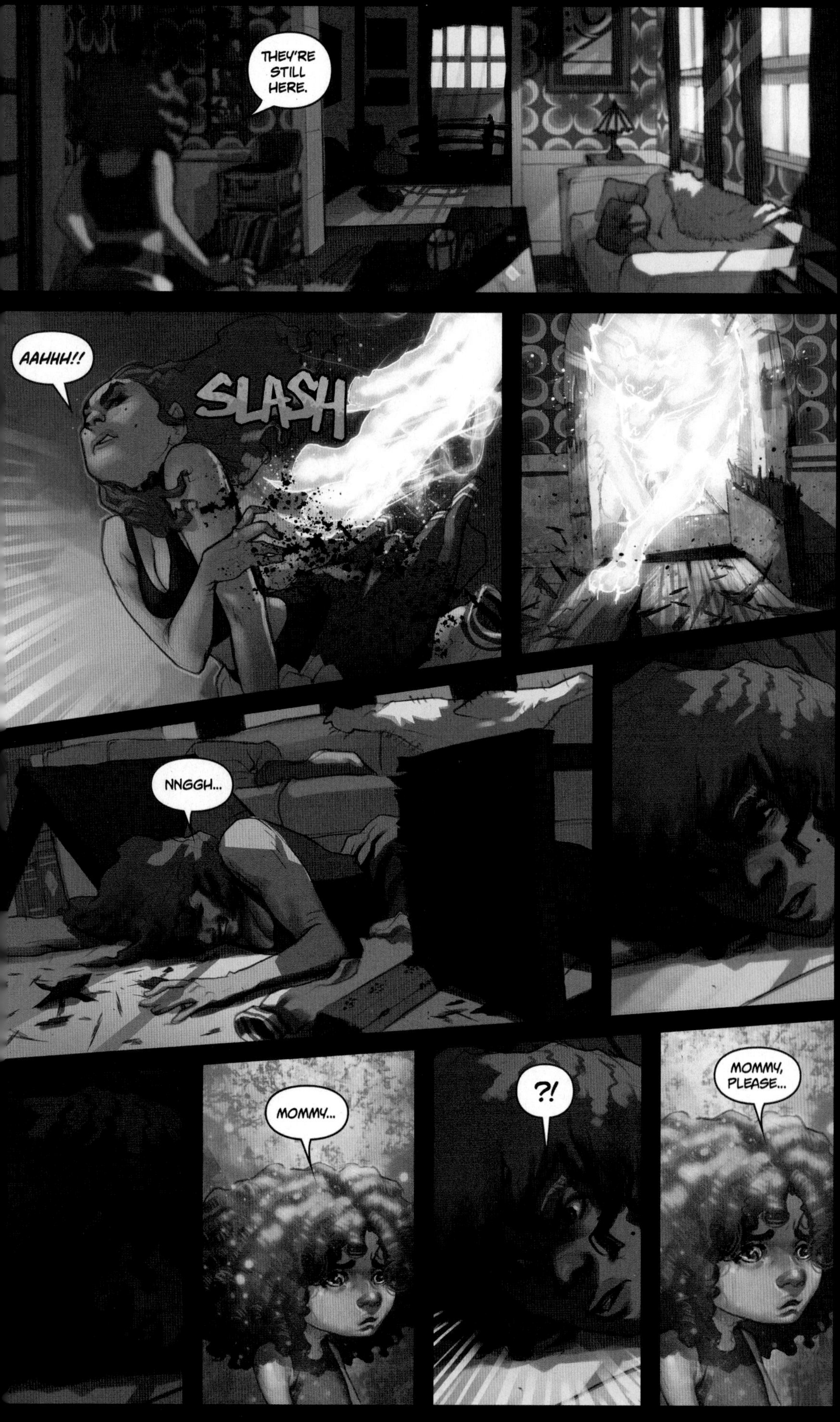

THEY'RE STILL HERE.
AAHHH!!
SLASH
NNGGH...
MOMMY...
?!
MOMMY, PLEASE...

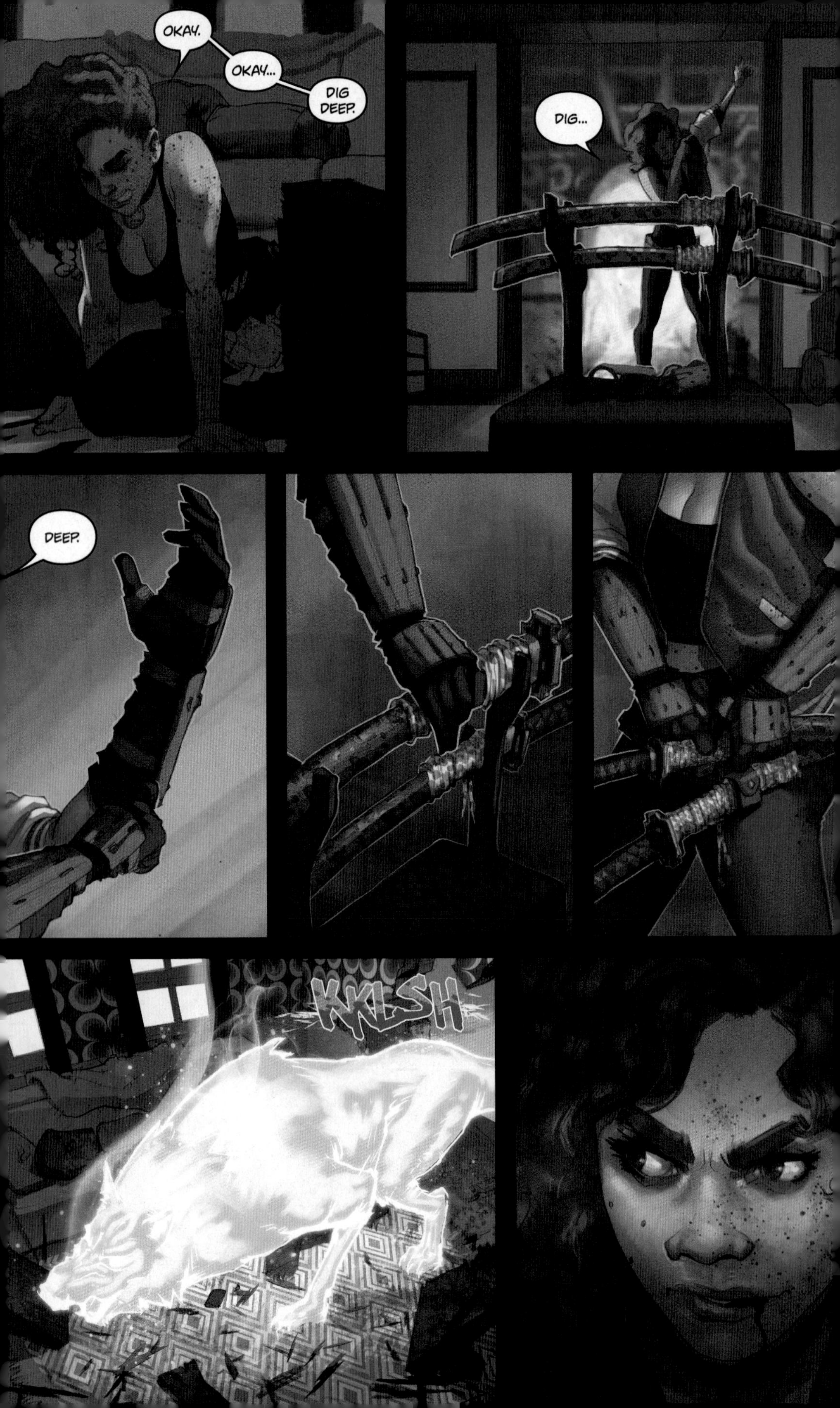
OKAY.
OKAY...
DIG DEEP.
DIG...
DEEP.
KKLSH

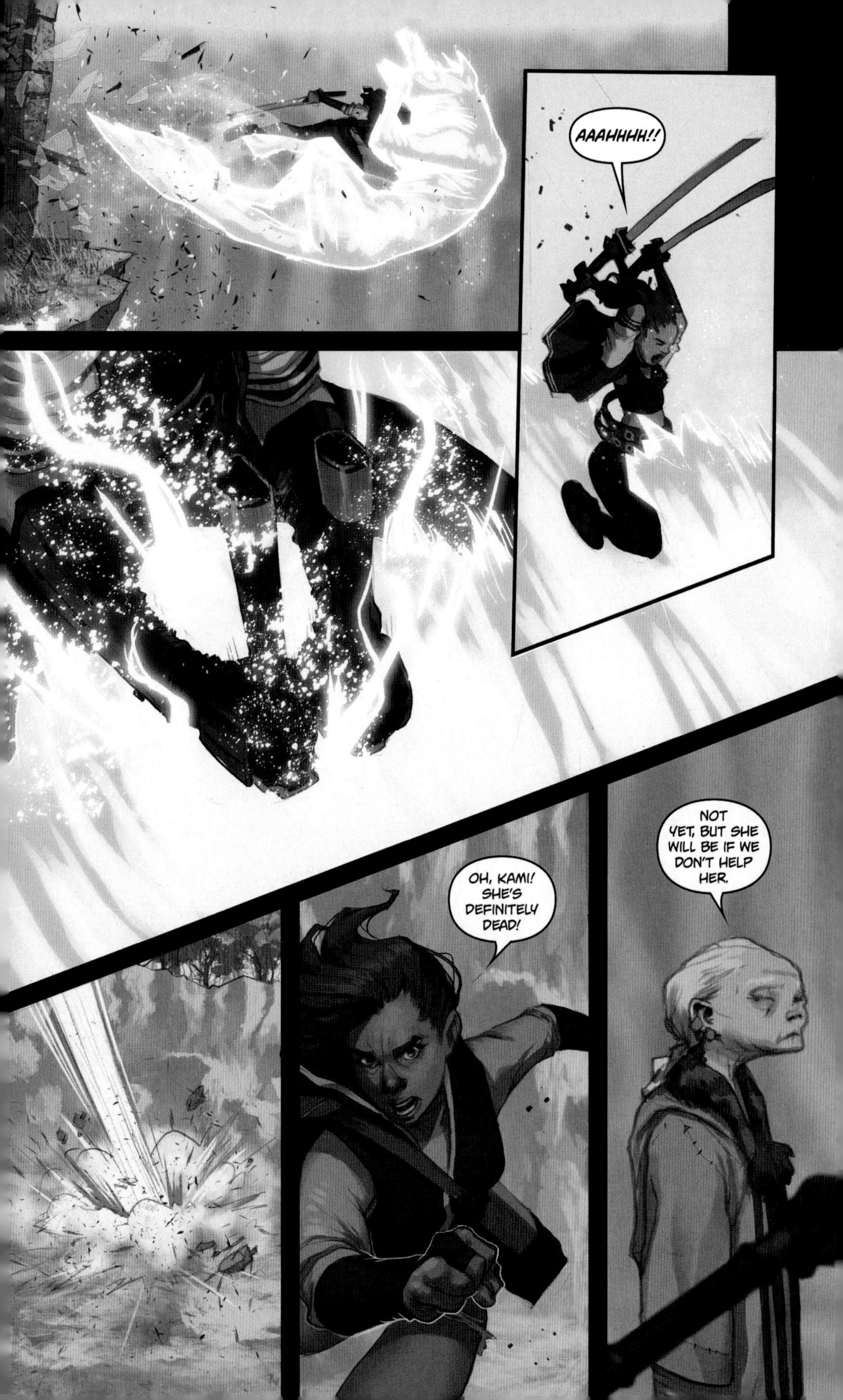
AAAHHHH!!
OH, KAMI! SHE'S DEFINITELY DEAD!
NOT YET, BUT SHE WILL BE IF WE DON'T HELP HER.

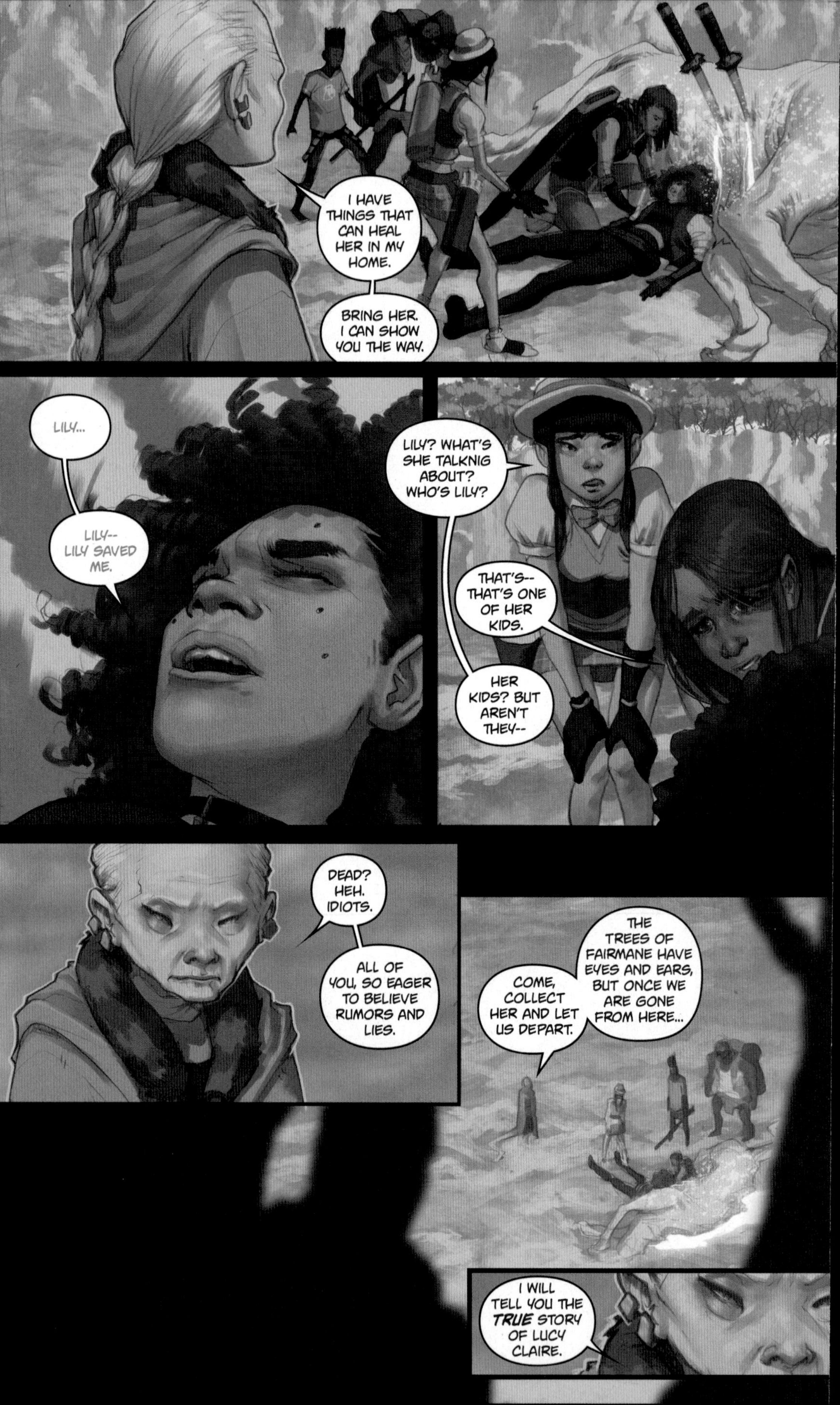
I HAVE THINGS THAT CAN HEAL HER IN MY HOME.
BRING HER. I CAN SHOW YOU THE WAY.
LILY...
LILY-- LILY SAVED ME.
LILY? WHAT'S SHE TALKNIG ABOUT? WHO'S LILY?
THAT'S-- THAT'S ONE OF HER KIDS.
HER KIDS? BUT AREN'T THEY--
DEAD? HEH. IDIOTS.
ALL OF YOU, SO EAGER TO BELIEVE RUMORS AND LIES.
COME, COLLECT HER AND LET US DEPART.
THE TREES OF FAIRMANE HAVE EYES AND EARS, BUT ONCE WE ARE GONE FROM HERE...
I WILL TELL YOU THE TRUE STORY OF LUCY CLAIRE.

CHAPTER FOUR

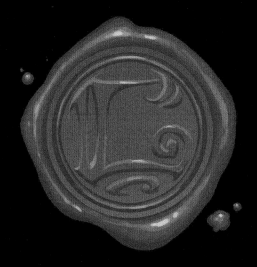

"TO DEPART FROM you IS TO HURT you,
TO PURSUE you IS TO HURT you MORE.

I PURSUE you BECAUSE I LOVE you,
I DEPART FROM you BECAUSE I LOVE you MORE."

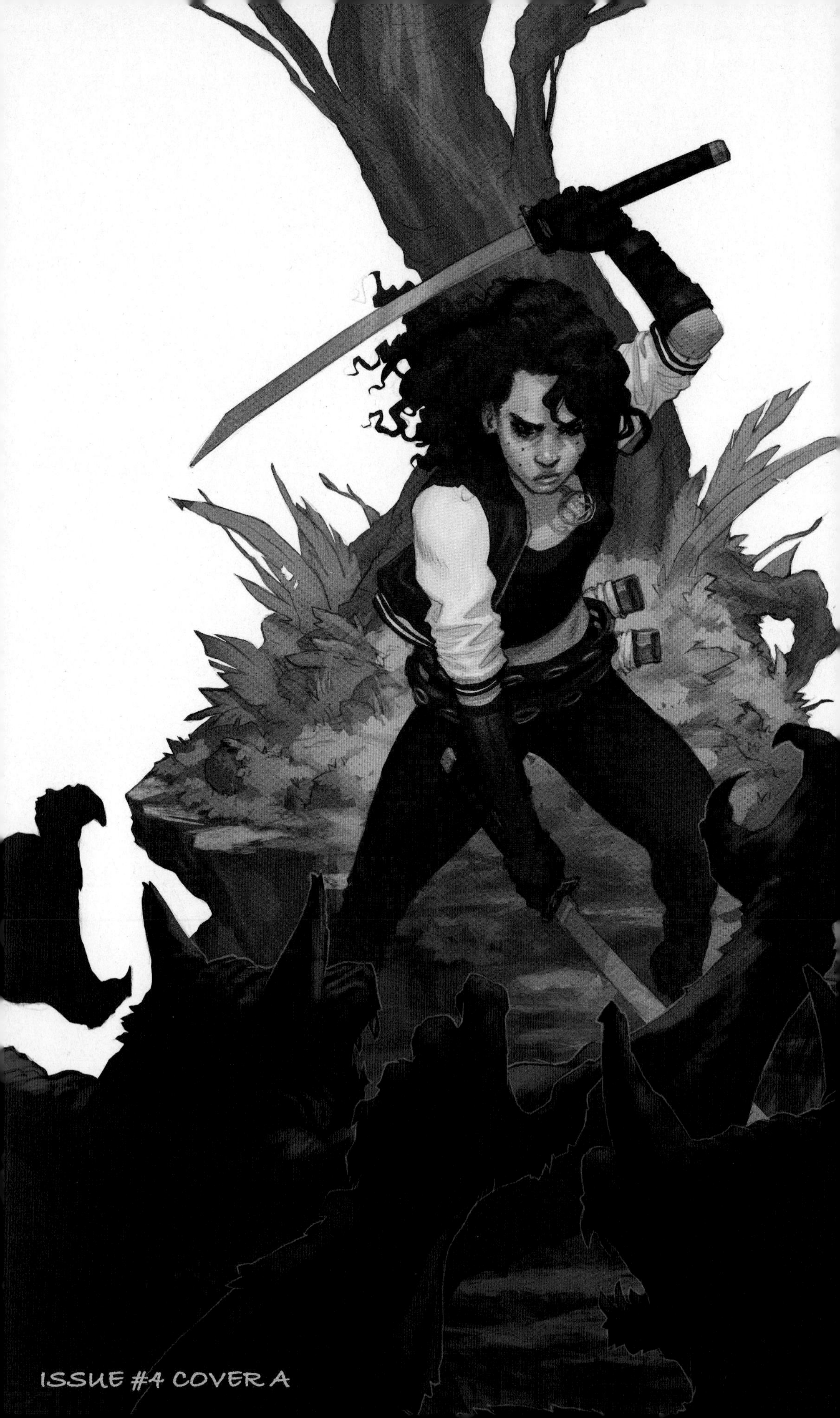

ISSUE #4 COVER A

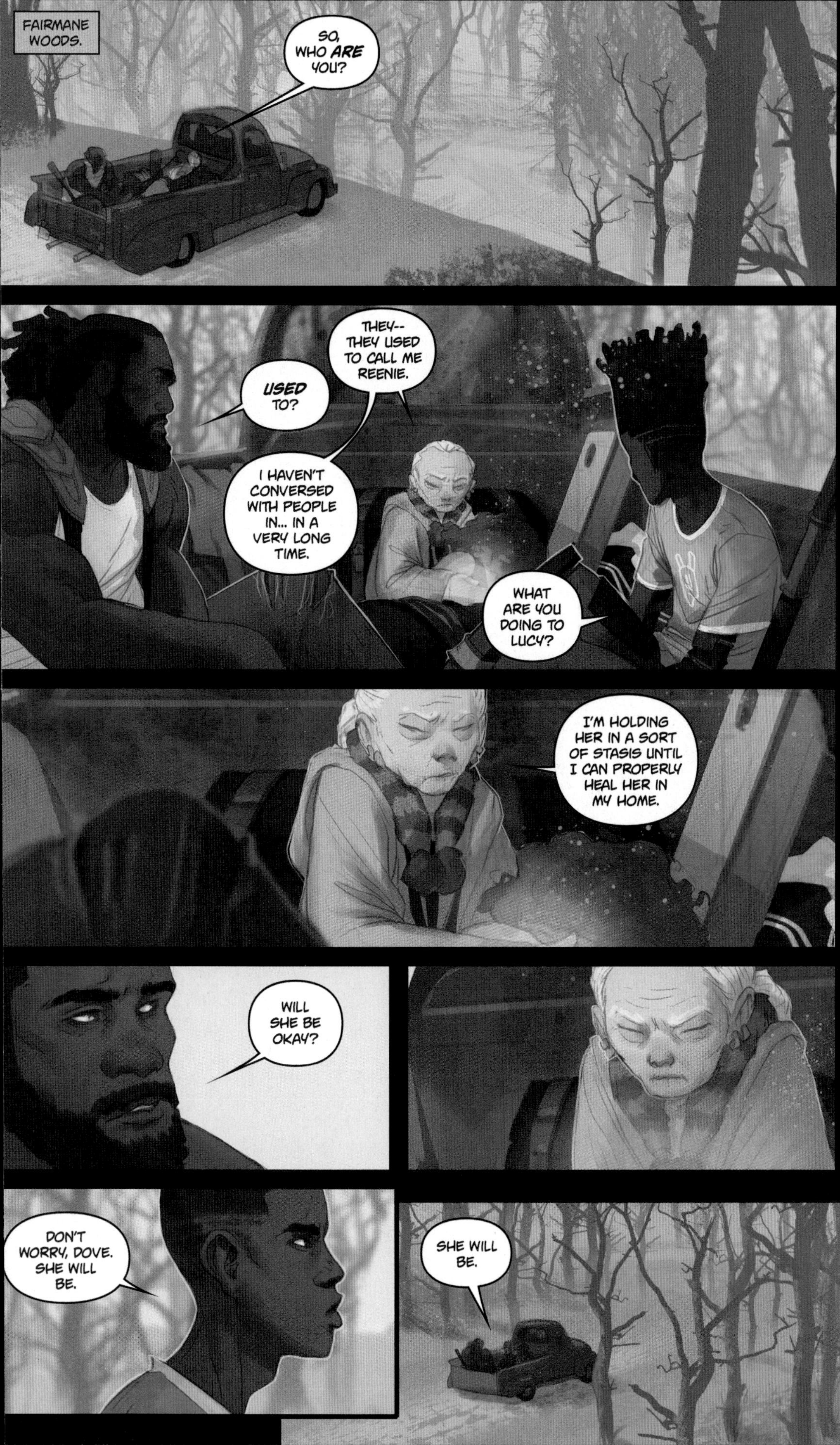
FAIRMANE WOODS.
SO, WHO ARE YOU?
THEY-- THEY USED TO CALL ME REENIE.
USED TO?
I HAVEN'T CONVERSED WITH PEOPLE IN... IN A VERY LONG TIME.
WHAT ARE YOU DOING TO LUCY?
I'M HOLDING HER IN A SORT OF STASIS UNTIL I CAN PROPERLY HEAL HER IN MY HOME.
WILL SHE BE OKAY?
DON'T WORRY, DOVE. SHE WILL BE.
SHE WILL BE.

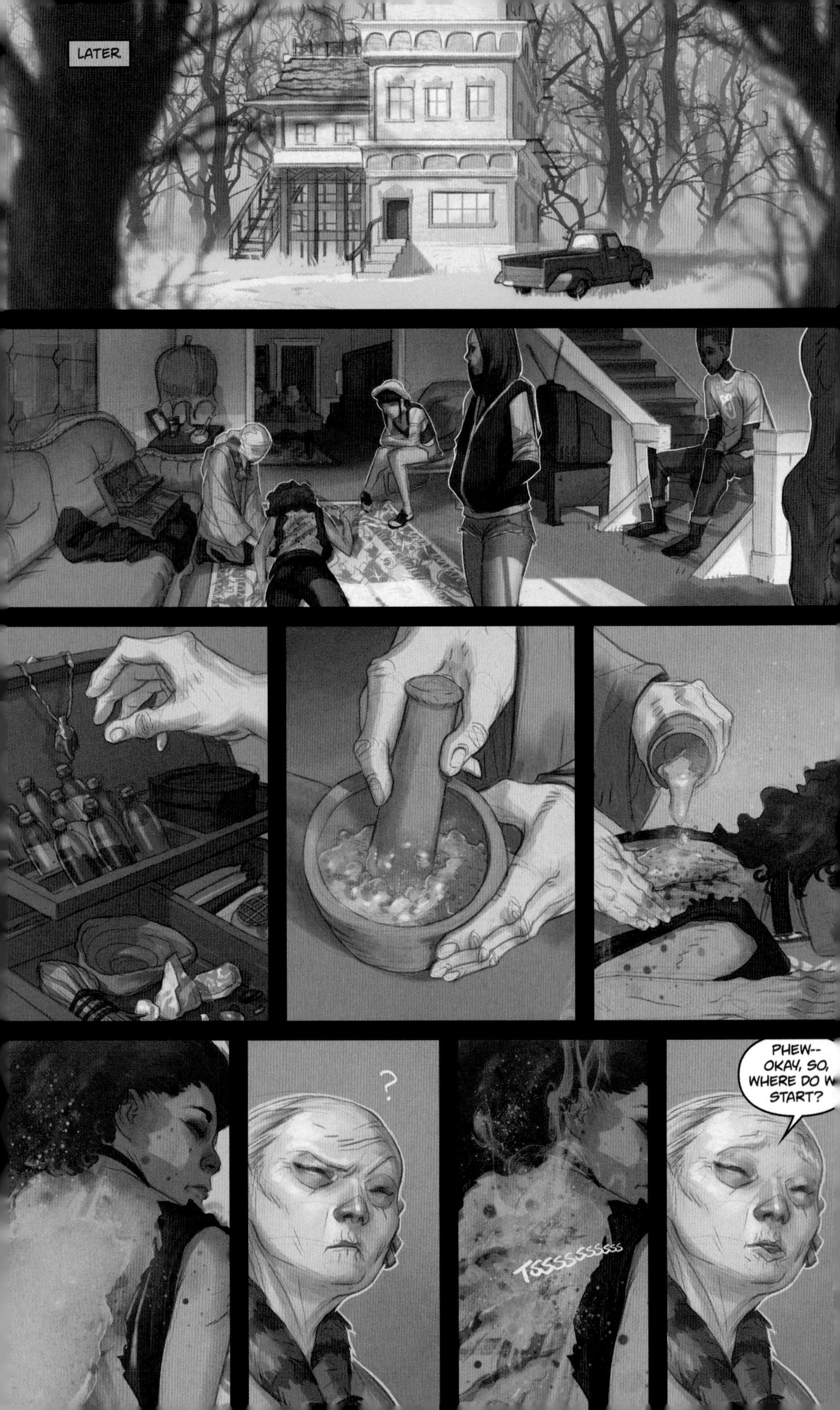
LATER.
?
TSSSSSSSSS
PHEW--
OKAY, SO,
WHERE DO W
START?

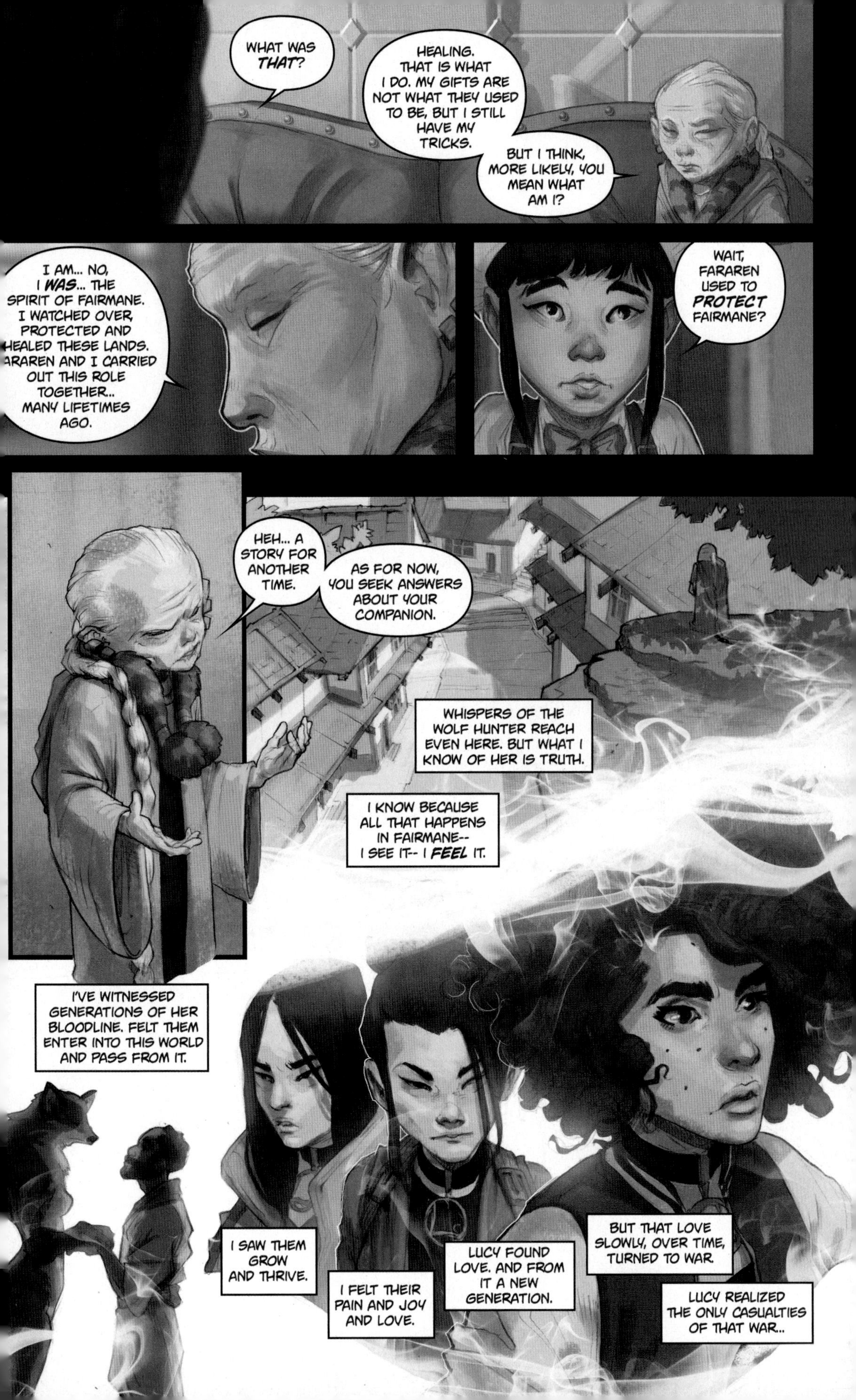
WHAT WAS THAT?
HEALING. THAT IS WHAT I DO. MY GIFTS ARE NOT WHAT THEY USED TO BE, BUT I STILL HAVE MY TRICKS.
BUT I THINK, MORE LIKELY, YOU MEAN WHAT AM I?
I AM... NO, I WAS... THE SPIRIT OF FAIRMANE. I WATCHED OVER, PROTECTED AND HEALED THESE LANDS. FARAREN AND I CARRIED OUT THIS ROLE TOGETHER... MANY LIFETIMES AGO.
WAIT, FARAREN USED TO PROTECT FAIRMANE?
HEH... A STORY FOR ANOTHER TIME.
AS FOR NOW, YOU SEEK ANSWERS ABOUT YOUR COMPANION.
WHISPERS OF THE WOLF HUNTER REACH EVEN HERE. BUT WHAT I KNOW OF HER IS TRUTH.
I KNOW BECAUSE ALL THAT HAPPENS IN FAIRMANE-- I SEE IT-- I FEEL IT.
I'VE WITNESSED GENERATIONS OF HER BLOODLINE. FELT THEM ENTER INTO THIS WORLD AND PASS FROM IT.
I SAW THEM GROW AND THRIVE.
I FELT THEIR PAIN AND JOY AND LOVE.
LUCY FOUND LOVE. AND FROM IT A NEW GENERATION.
BUT THAT LOVE SLOWLY, OVER TIME, TURNED TO WAR.
LUCY REALIZED THE ONLY CASUALTIES OF THAT WAR...

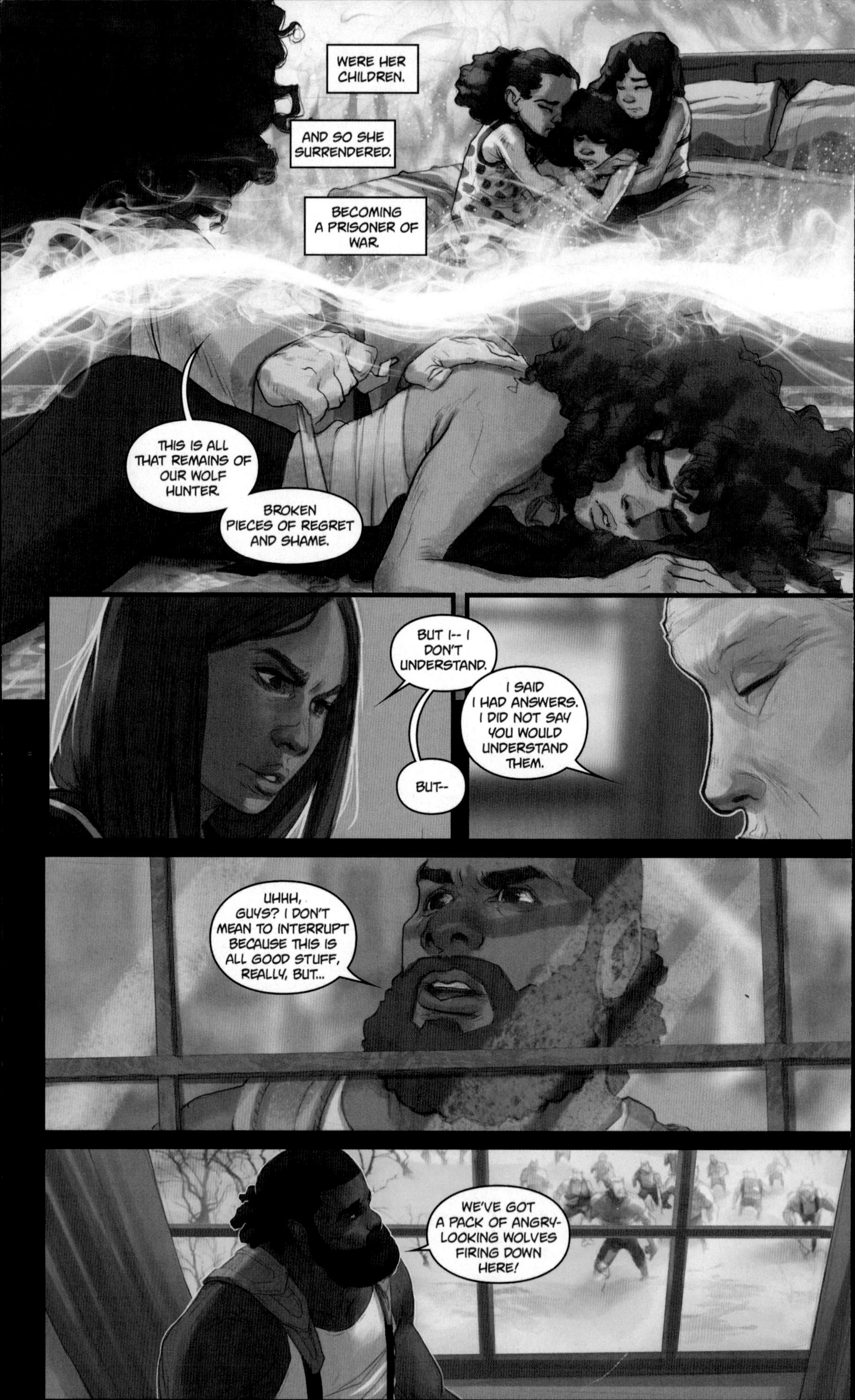
WERE HER CHILDREN.
AND SO SHE SURRENDERED.
BECOMING A PRISONER OF WAR.
THIS IS ALL THAT REMAINS OF OUR WOLF HUNTER.
BROKEN PIECES OF REGRET AND SHAME.
BUT I-- I DON'T UNDERSTAND.
I SAID I HAD ANSWERS. I DID NOT SAY YOU WOULD UNDERSTAND THEM.
BUT--
UHHH, GUYS? I DON'T MEAN TO INTERRUPT BECAUSE THIS IS ALL GOOD STUFF, REALLY, BUT...
WE'VE GOT A PACK OF ANGRY-LOOKING WOLVES FIRING DOWN HERE!

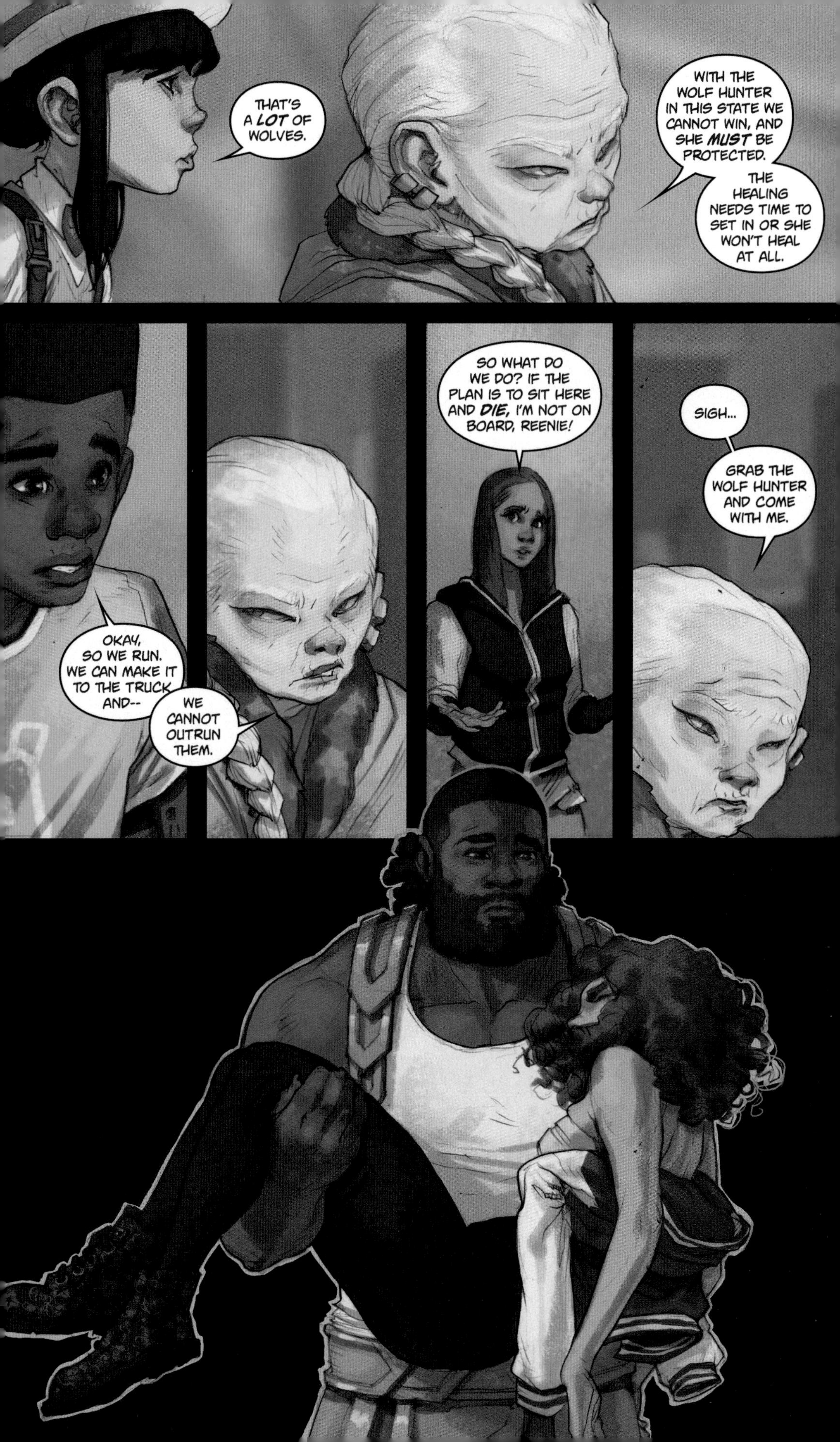
THAT'S A LOT OF WOLVES.
WITH THE WOLF HUNTER IN THIS STATE WE CANNOT WIN, AND SHE MUST BE PROTECTED.
THE HEALING NEEDS TIME TO SET IN OR SHE WON'T HEAL AT ALL.
OKAY, SO WE RUN. WE CAN MAKE IT TO THE TRUCK AND--
WE CANNOT OUTRUN THEM.
SO WHAT DO WE DO? IF THE PLAN IS TO SIT HERE AND DIE, I'M NOT ON BOARD, REENIE!
SIGH...
GRAB THE WOLF HUNTER AND COME WITH ME.

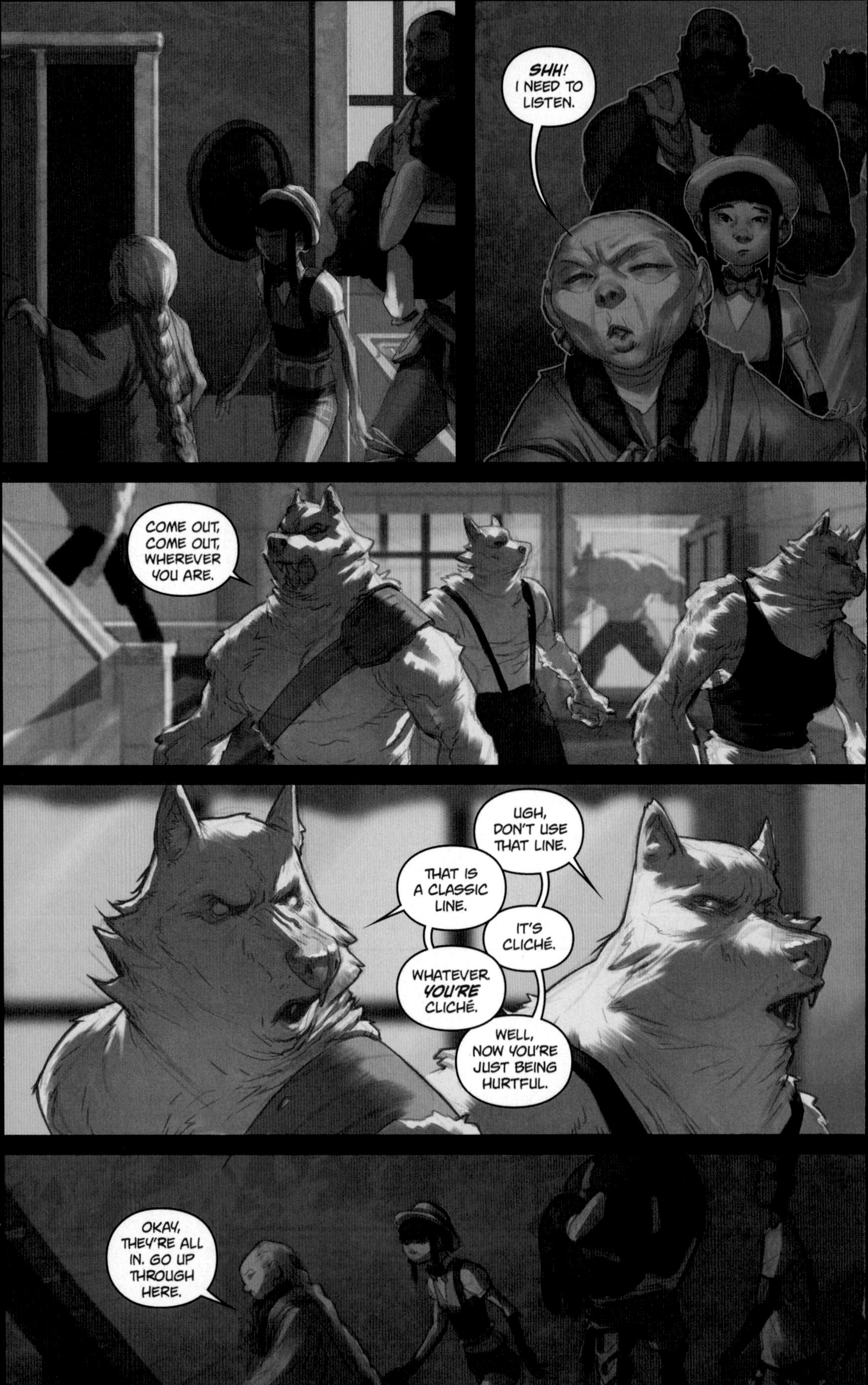
SHH! I NEED TO LISTEN.
COME OUT, COME OUT, WHEREVER YOU ARE.
UGH, DON'T USE THAT LINE.
THAT IS A CLASSIC LINE.
IT'S CLICHÉ.
WHATEVER. YOU'RE CLICHÉ.
WELL, NOW YOU'RE JUST BEING HURTFUL.
OKAY, THEY'RE ALL IN. GO UP THROUGH HERE.

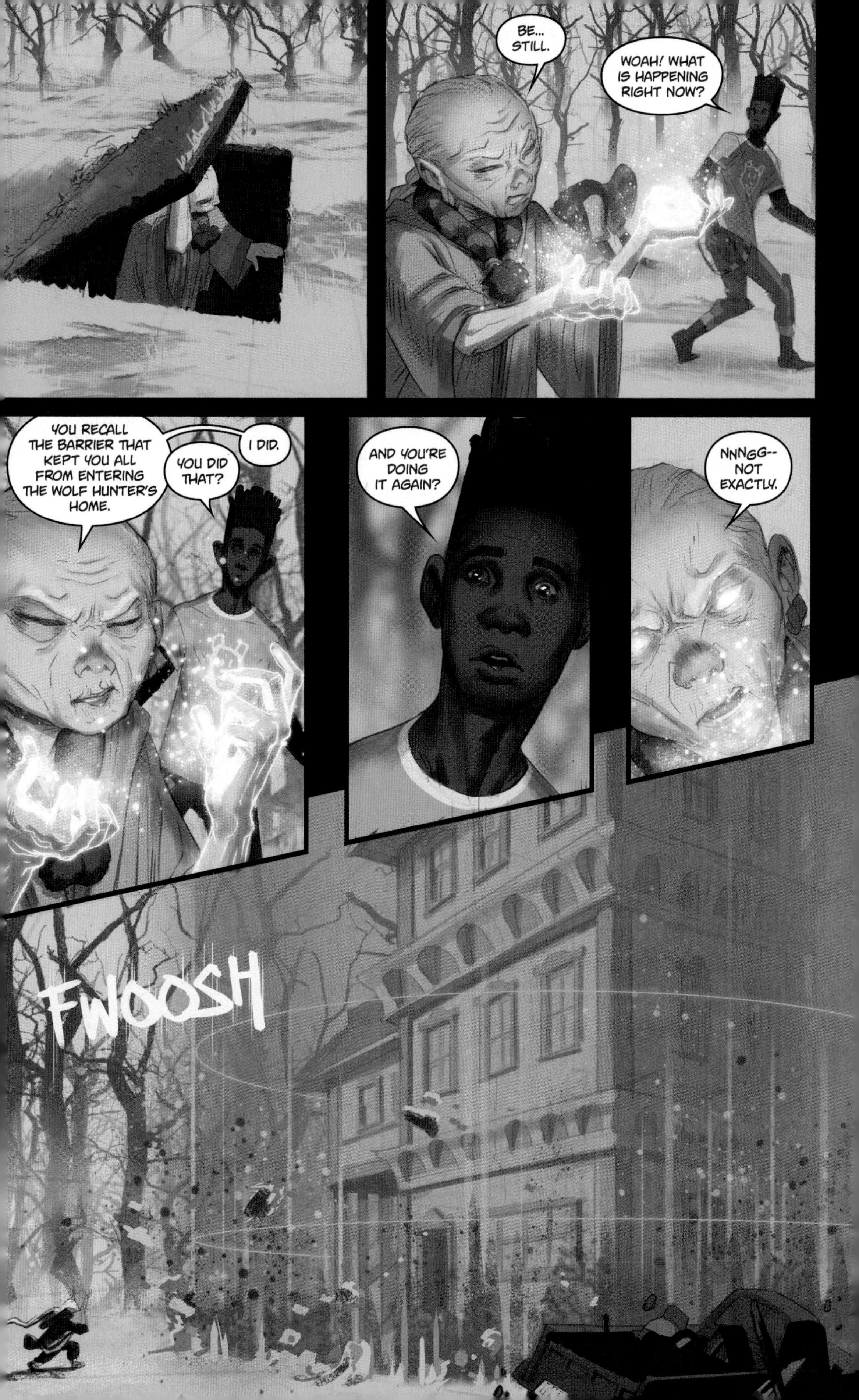
BE... STILL.
WOAH! WHAT IS HAPPENING RIGHT NOW?
YOU RECALL THE BARRIER THAT KEPT YOU ALL FROM ENTERING THE WOLF HUNTER'S HOME.
I DID.
YOU DID THAT?
AND YOU'RE DOING IT AGAIN?
NNNGG-- NOT EXACTLY.
FWOOSH

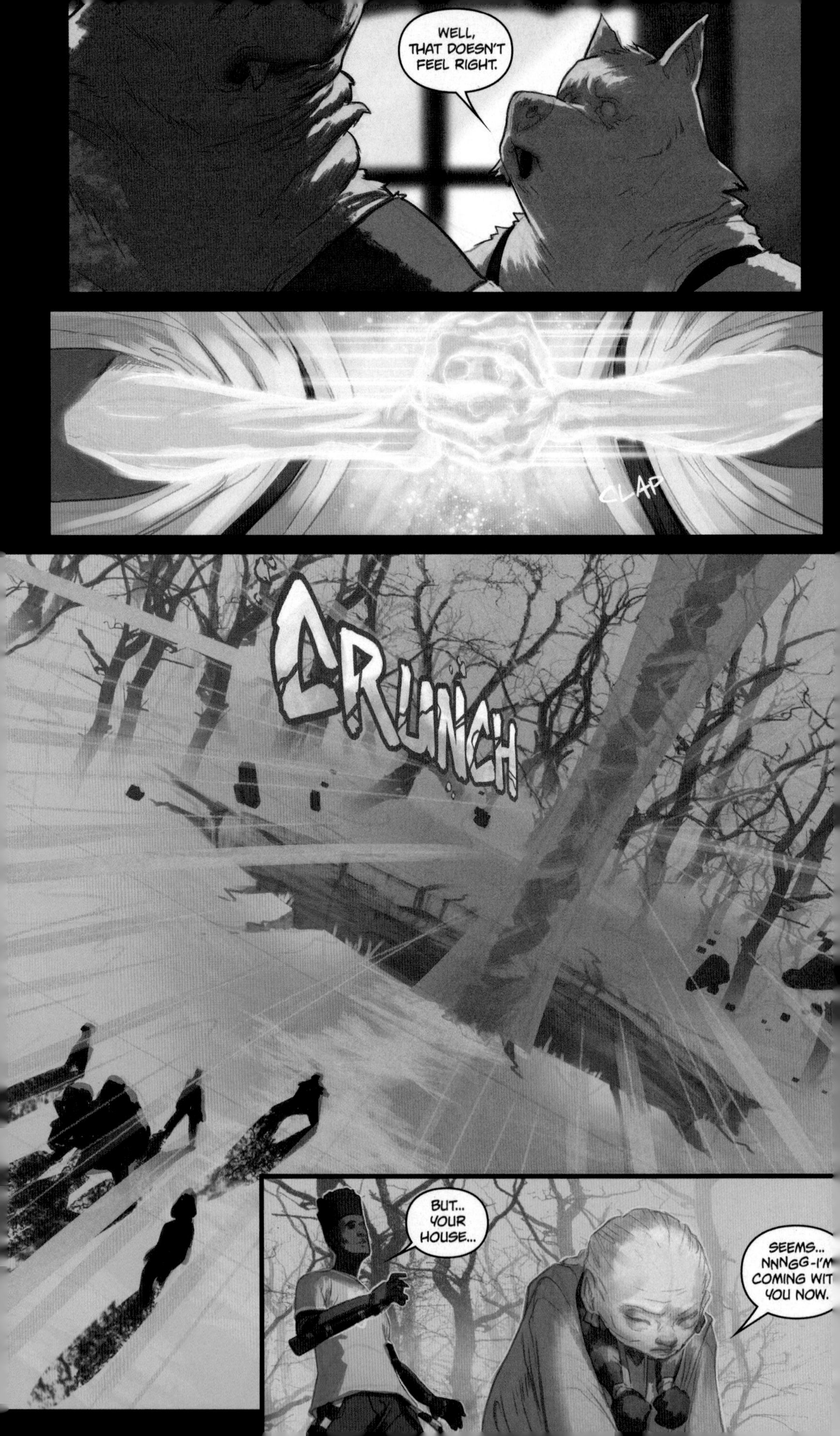
WELL, THAT DOESN'T FEEL RIGHT.
CLAP
CRUNCH
BUT... YOUR HOUSE...
SEEMS... NNNGG-I'M COMING WIT YOU NOW.

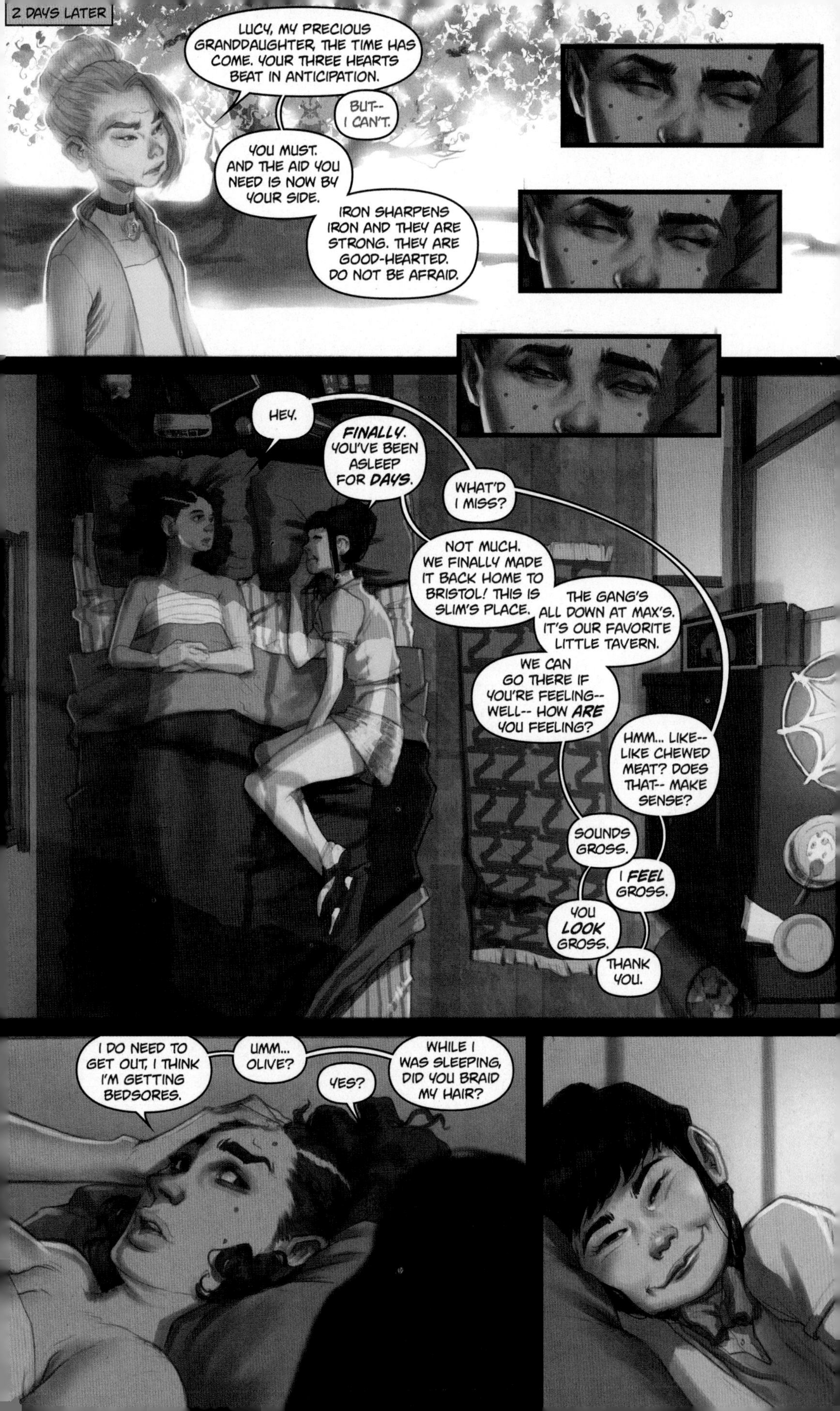

2 DAYS LATER
LUCY, MY PRECIOUS GRANDDAUGHTER, THE TIME HAS COME. YOUR THREE HEARTS BEAT IN ANTICIPATION.
BUT-- I CAN'T.
YOU MUST. AND THE AID YOU NEED IS NOW BY YOUR SIDE.
IRON SHARPENS IRON AND THEY ARE STRONG. THEY ARE GOOD-HEARTED. DO NOT BE AFRAID.
HEY.
FINALLY. YOU'VE BEEN ASLEEP FOR DAYS.
WHAT'D I MISS?
NOT MUCH. WE FINALLY MADE IT BACK HOME TO BRISTOL! THIS IS SLIM'S PLACE.
THE GANG'S ALL DOWN AT MAX'S. IT'S OUR FAVORITE LITTLE TAVERN.
WE CAN GO THERE IF YOU'RE FEELING-- WELL-- HOW ARE YOU FEELING?
HMM... LIKE-- LIKE CHEWED MEAT? DOES THAT-- MAKE SENSE?
SOUNDS GROSS.
I FEEL GROSS.
YOU LOOK GROSS.
THANK YOU.
I DO NEED TO GET OUT, I THINK I'M GETTING BEDSORES.
UMM... OLIVE?
YES?
WHILE I WAS SLEEPING, DID YOU BRAID MY HAIR?

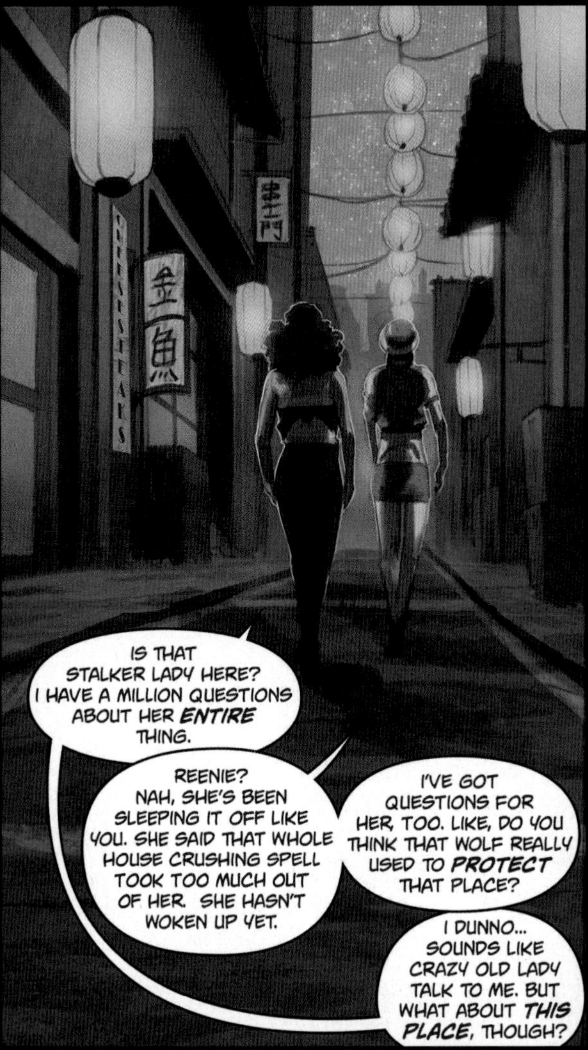
金魚
IS THAT STALKER LADY HERE? I HAVE A MILLION QUESTIONS ABOUT HER ***ENTIRE*** THING.
REENIE? NAH, SHE'S BEEN SLEEPING IT OFF LIKE YOU. SHE SAID THAT WHOLE HOUSE CRUSHING SPELL TOOK TOO MUCH OUT OF HER. SHE HASN'T WOKEN UP YET.
I'VE GOT QUESTIONS FOR HER, TOO. LIKE, DO YOU THINK THAT WOLF REALLY USED TO ***PROTECT*** THAT PLACE?
I DUNNO... SOUNDS LIKE CRAZY OLD LADY TALK TO ME. BUT WHAT ABOUT ***THIS PLACE***, THOUGH?

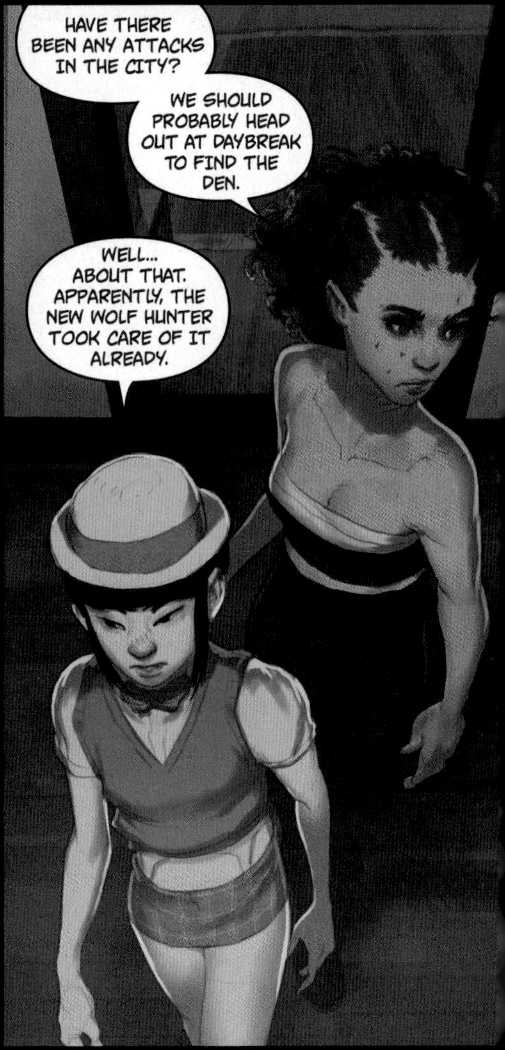
HAVE THERE BEEN ANY ATTACKS IN THE CITY?
WE SHOULD PROBABLY HEAD OUT AT DAYBREAK TO FIND THE DEN.
WELL... ABOUT THAT. APPARENTLY, THE NEW WOLF HUNTER TOOK CARE OF IT ALREADY.

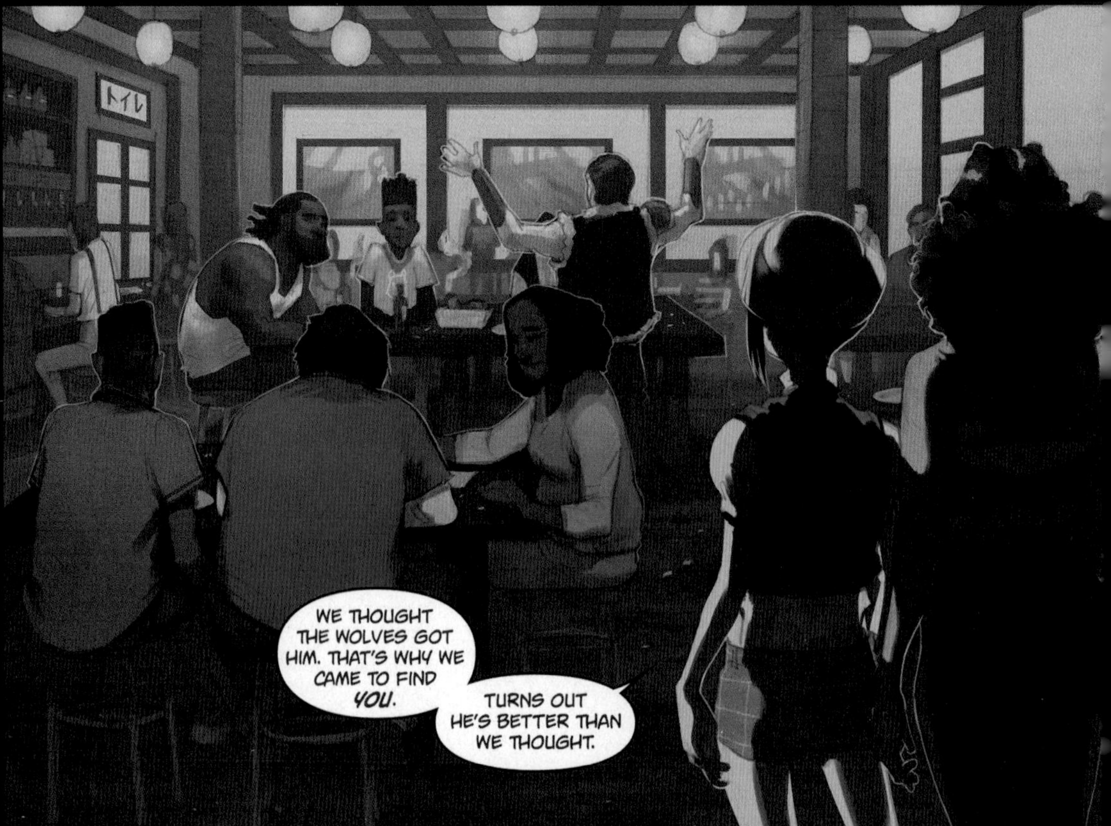
トイレ
WE THOUGHT THE WOLVES GOT HIM. THAT'S WHY WE CAME TO FIND ***YOU***.
TURNS OUT HE'S BETTER THAN WE THOUGHT.

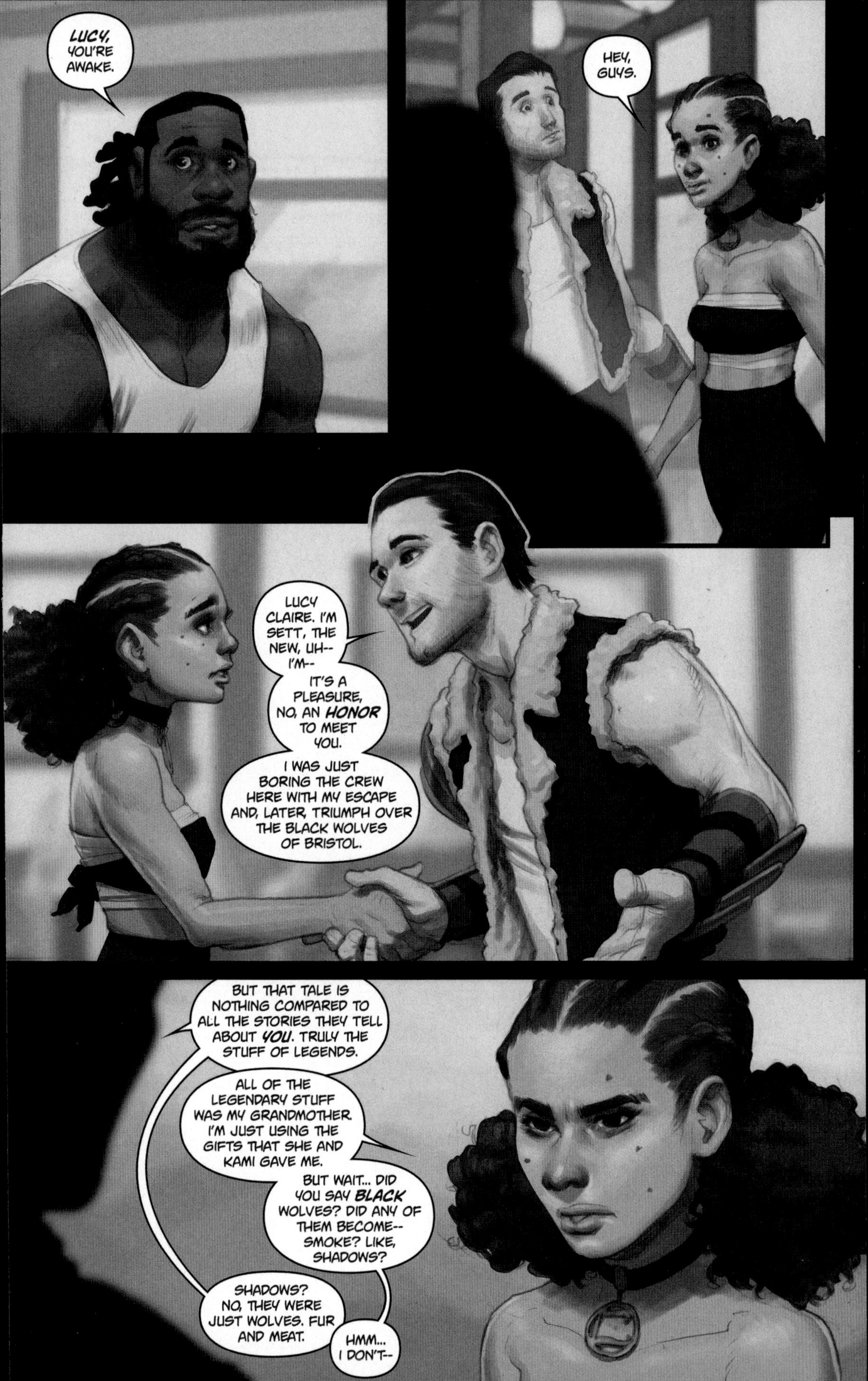
LUCY, YOU'RE AWAKE.
HEY, GUYS.
LUCY CLAIRE. I'M SETT, THE NEW, UH-- I'M--
IT'S A PLEASURE, NO, AN HONOR TO MEET YOU.
I WAS JUST BORING THE CREW HERE WITH MY ESCAPE AND, LATER, TRIUMPH OVER THE BLACK WOLVES OF BRISTOL.
BUT THAT TALE IS NOTHING COMPARED TO ALL THE STORIES THEY TELL ABOUT YOU. TRULY THE STUFF OF LEGENDS.
ALL OF THE LEGENDARY STUFF WAS MY GRANDMOTHER. I'M JUST USING THE GIFTS THAT SHE AND KAMI GAVE ME.
BUT WAIT... DID YOU SAY BLACK WOLVES? DID ANY OF THEM BECOME-- SMOKE? LIKE, SHADOWS?
SHADOWS? NO, THEY WERE JUST WOLVES. FUR AND MEAT.
HMM... I DON'T--

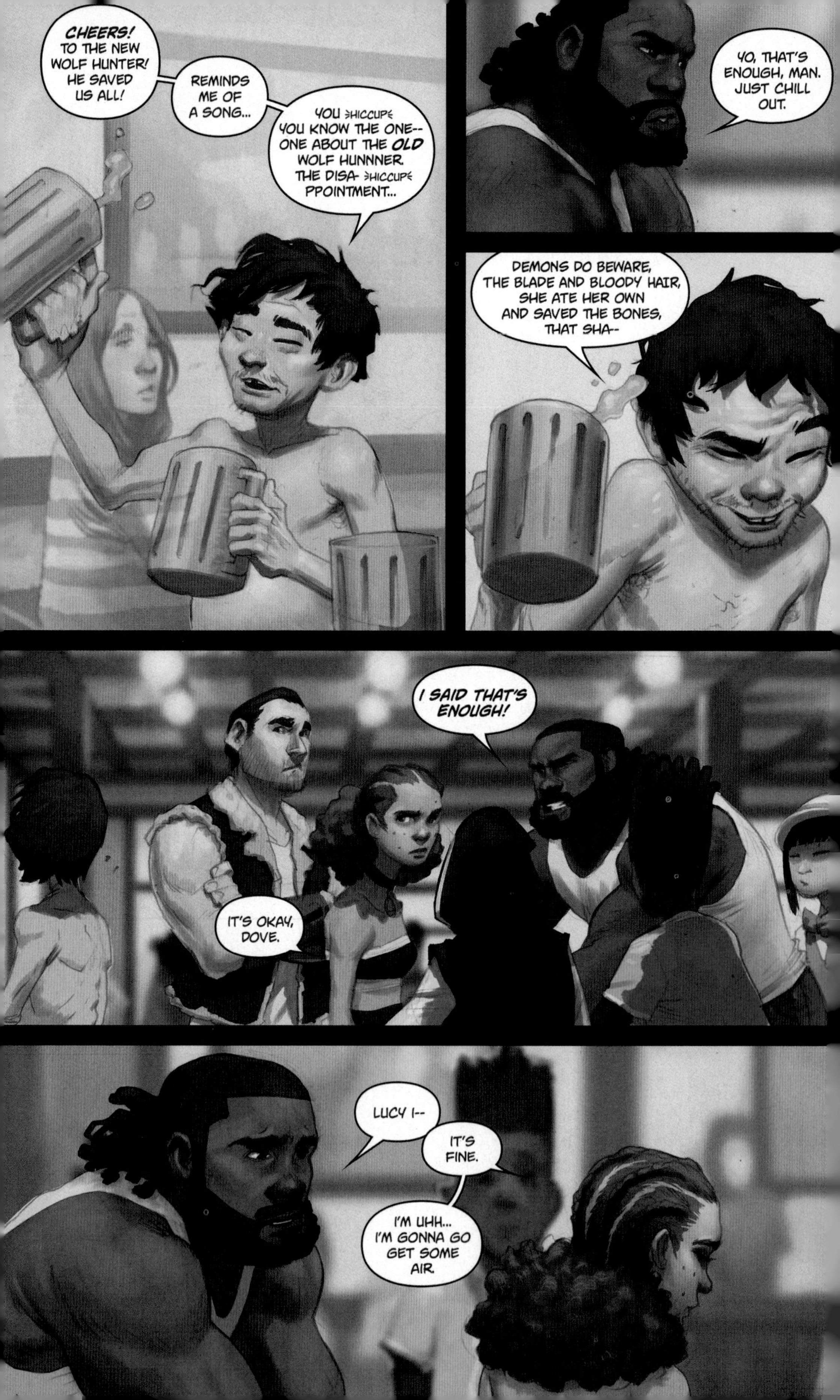
CHEERS! TO THE NEW WOLF HUNTER! HE SAVED US ALL!
REMINDS ME OF A SONG...
YOU ≯HICCUP≼ YOU KNOW THE ONE-- ONE ABOUT THE OLD WOLF HUNNNER. THE DISA- ≯HICCUP≼ PPOINTMENT...
YO, THAT'S ENOUGH, MAN. JUST CHILL OUT.
DEMONS DO BEWARE, THE BLADE AND BLOODY HAIR, SHE ATE HER OWN AND SAVED THE BONES, THAT SHA--
I SAID THAT'S ENOUGH!
IT'S OKAY, DOVE.
LUCY I--
IT'S FINE.
I'M UHH... I'M GONNA GO GET SOME AIR.

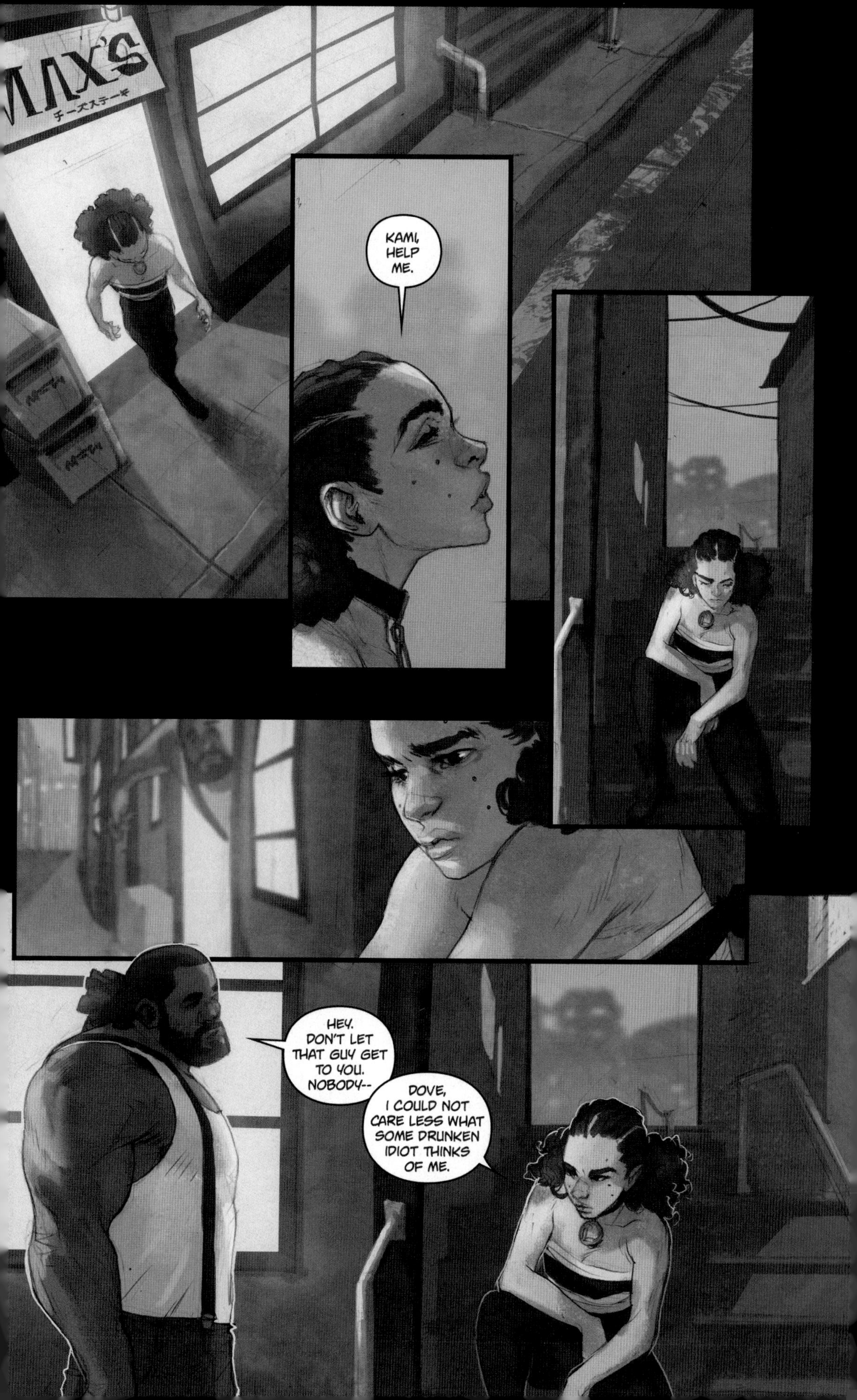

MAX'S
チーズステーキ
KAMI, HELP ME.
HEY. DON'T LET THAT GUY GET TO YOU. NOBODY--
DOVE, I COULD NOT CARE LESS WHAT SOME DRUNKEN IDIOT THINKS OF ME.

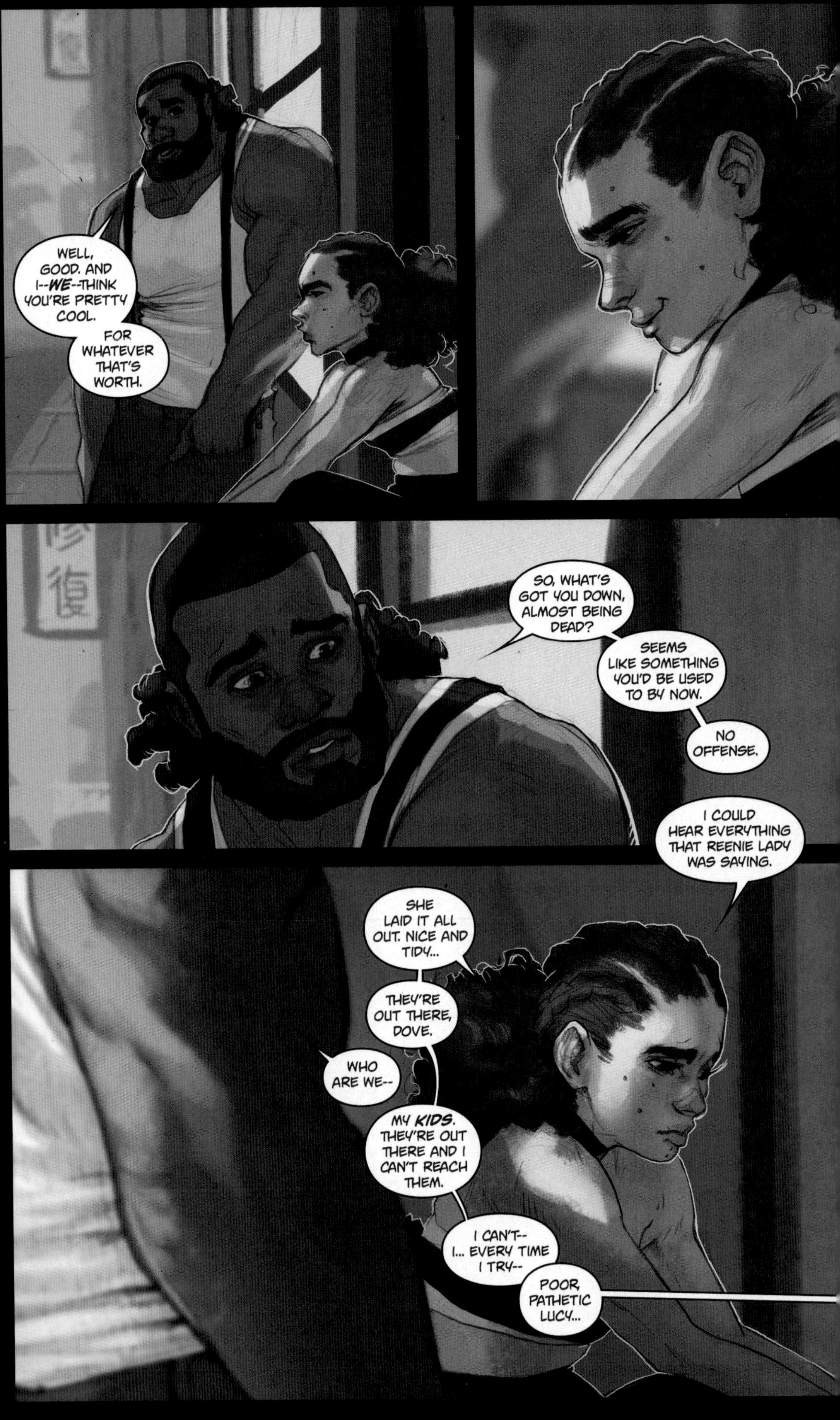
WELL, GOOD. AND I--*WE*--THINK YOU'RE PRETTY COOL.
FOR WHATEVER THAT'S WORTH.
SO, WHAT'S GOT YOU DOWN, ALMOST BEING DEAD?
SEEMS LIKE SOMETHING YOU'D BE USED TO BY NOW.
NO OFFENSE.
I COULD HEAR EVERYTHING THAT REENIE LADY WAS SAYING.
SHE LAID IT ALL OUT. NICE AND TIDY...
THEY'RE OUT THERE, DOVE.
WHO ARE WE--
MY *KIDS*. THEY'RE OUT THERE AND I CAN'T REACH THEM.
I CAN'T-- I... EVERY TIME I TRY--
POOR, PATHETIC LUCY...

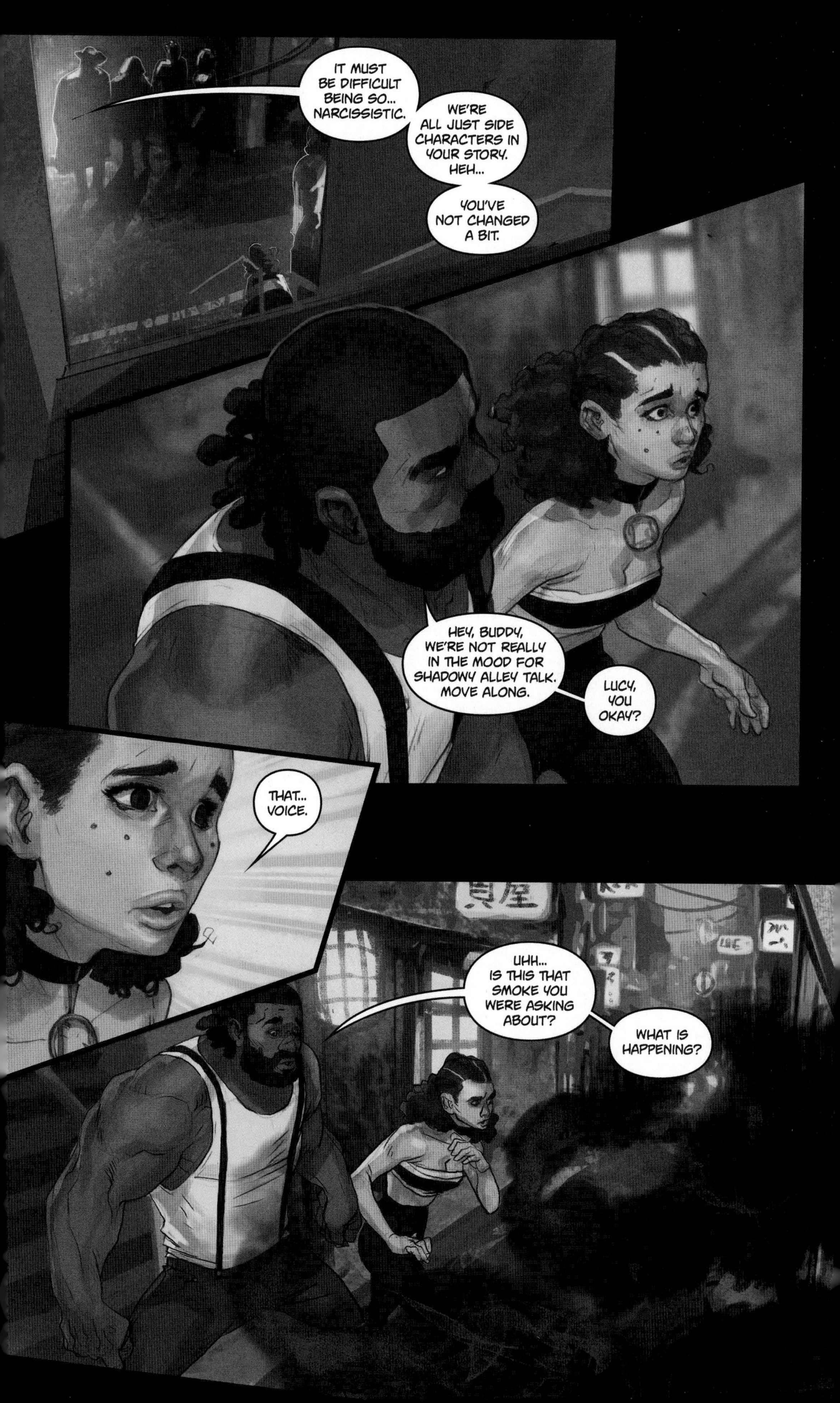
IT MUST BE DIFFICULT BEING SO... NARCISSISTIC.
WE'RE ALL JUST SIDE CHARACTERS IN YOUR STORY. HEH...
YOU'VE NOT CHANGED A BIT.
HEY, BUDDY, WE'RE NOT REALLY IN THE MOOD FOR SHADOWY ALLEY TALK. MOVE ALONG.
LUCY, YOU OKAY?
THAT... VOICE.
UHH... IS THIS THAT SMOKE YOU WERE ASKING ABOUT?
WHAT IS HAPPENING?

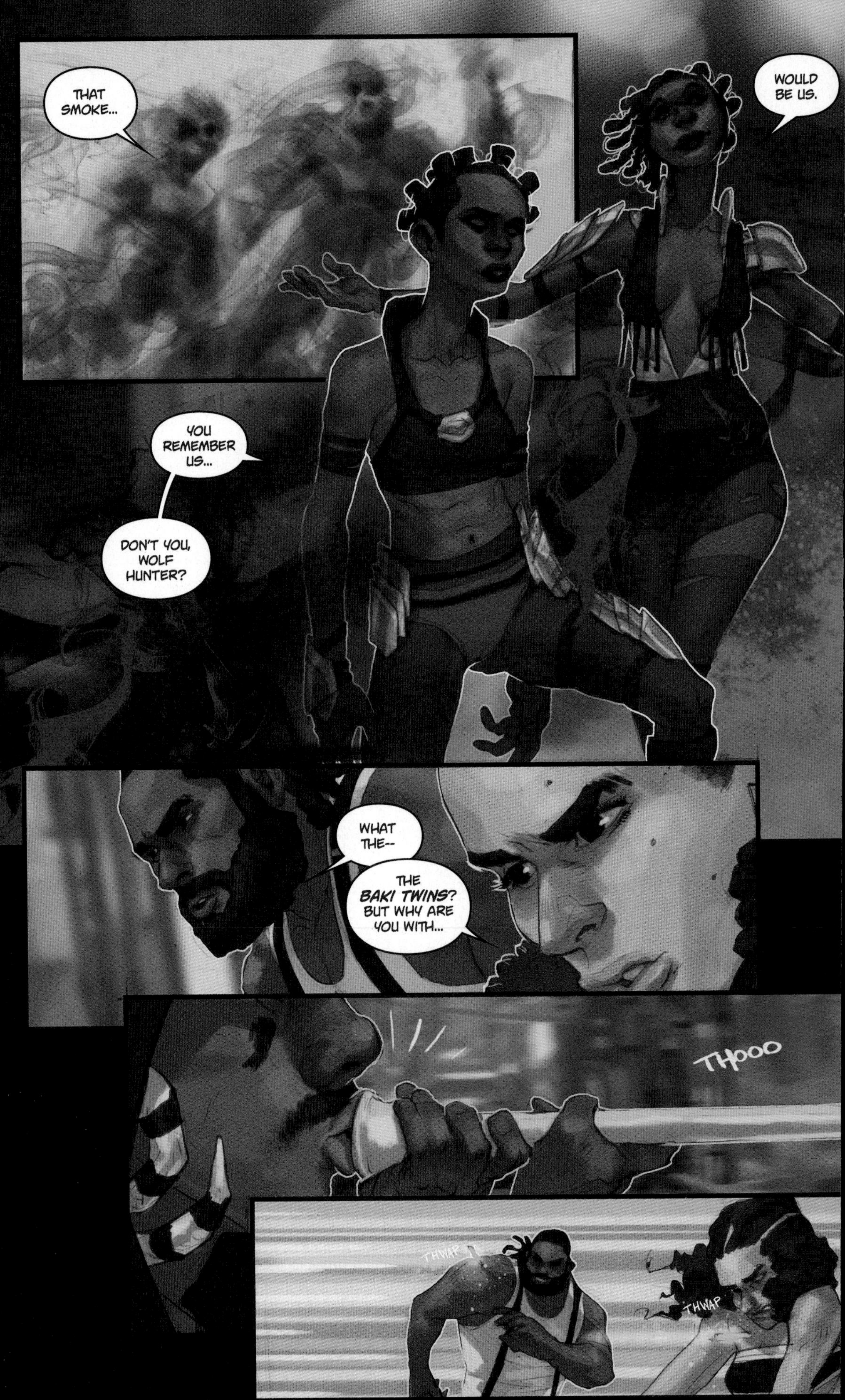
THAT SMOKE...
WOULD BE US.
YOU REMEMBER US...
DON'T YOU, WOLF HUNTER?
WHAT THE--
THE BAKI TWINS? BUT WHY ARE YOU WITH...
THOOO
THWAP
THWAP

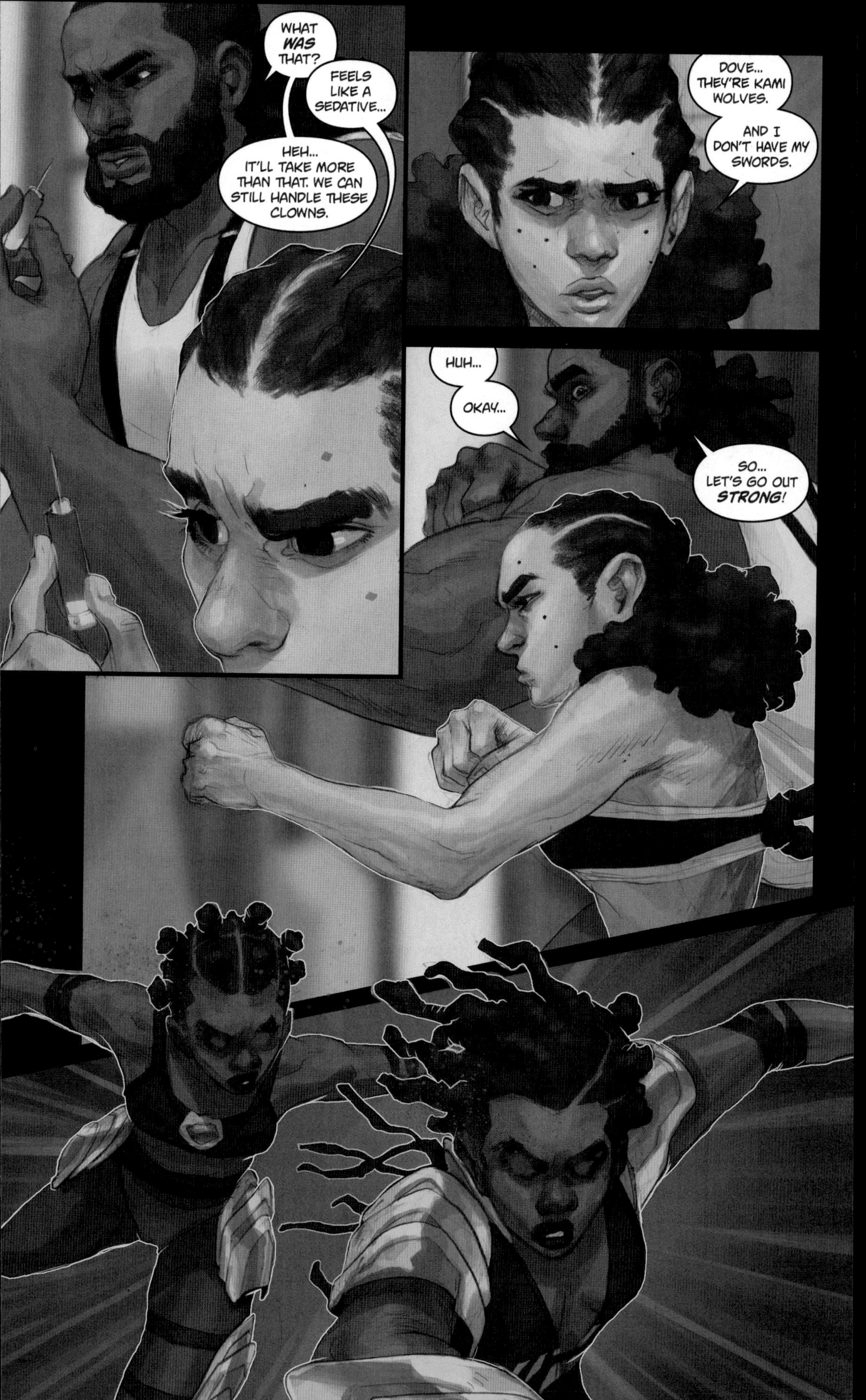
WHAT **WAS** THAT?
FEELS LIKE A SEDATIVE...
HEH... IT'LL TAKE MORE THAN THAT. WE CAN STILL HANDLE THESE CLOWNS.
DOVE... THEY'RE KAMI WOLVES.
AND I DON'T HAVE MY SWORDS.
HUH...
OKAY...
SO... LET'S GO OUT **STRONG**!

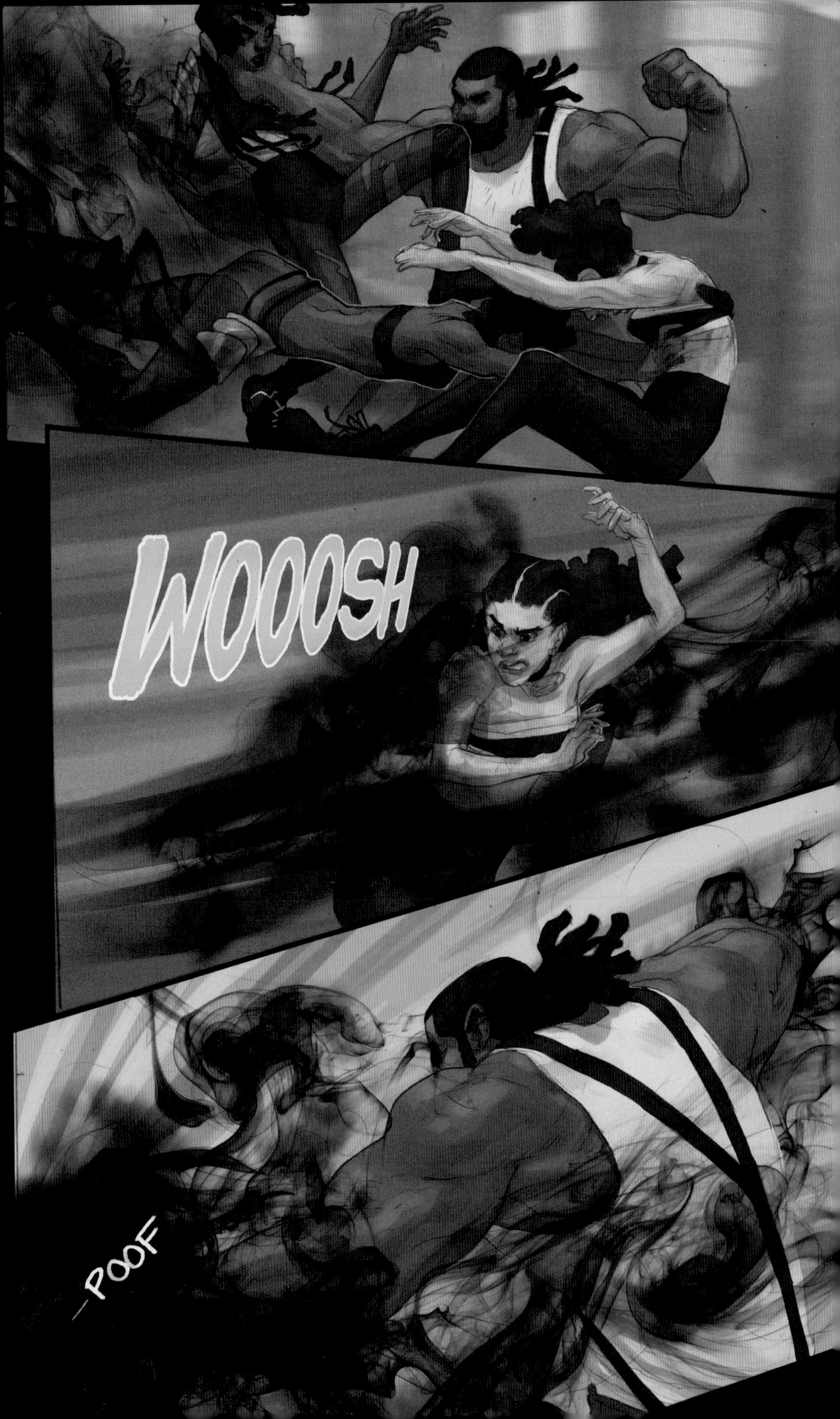

WOOOSH
POOF

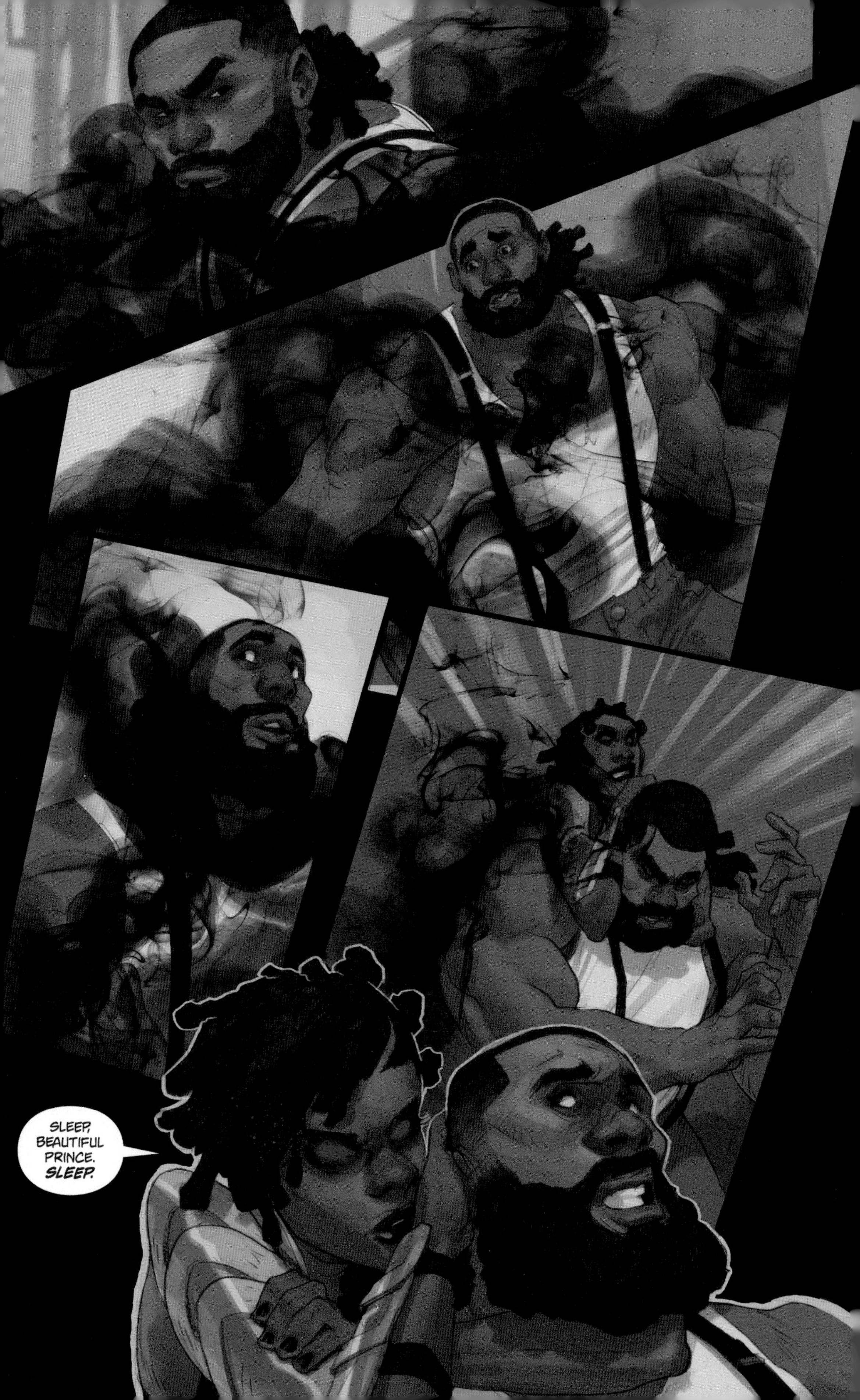
SLEEP, BEAUTIFUL PRINCE. *SLEEP.*

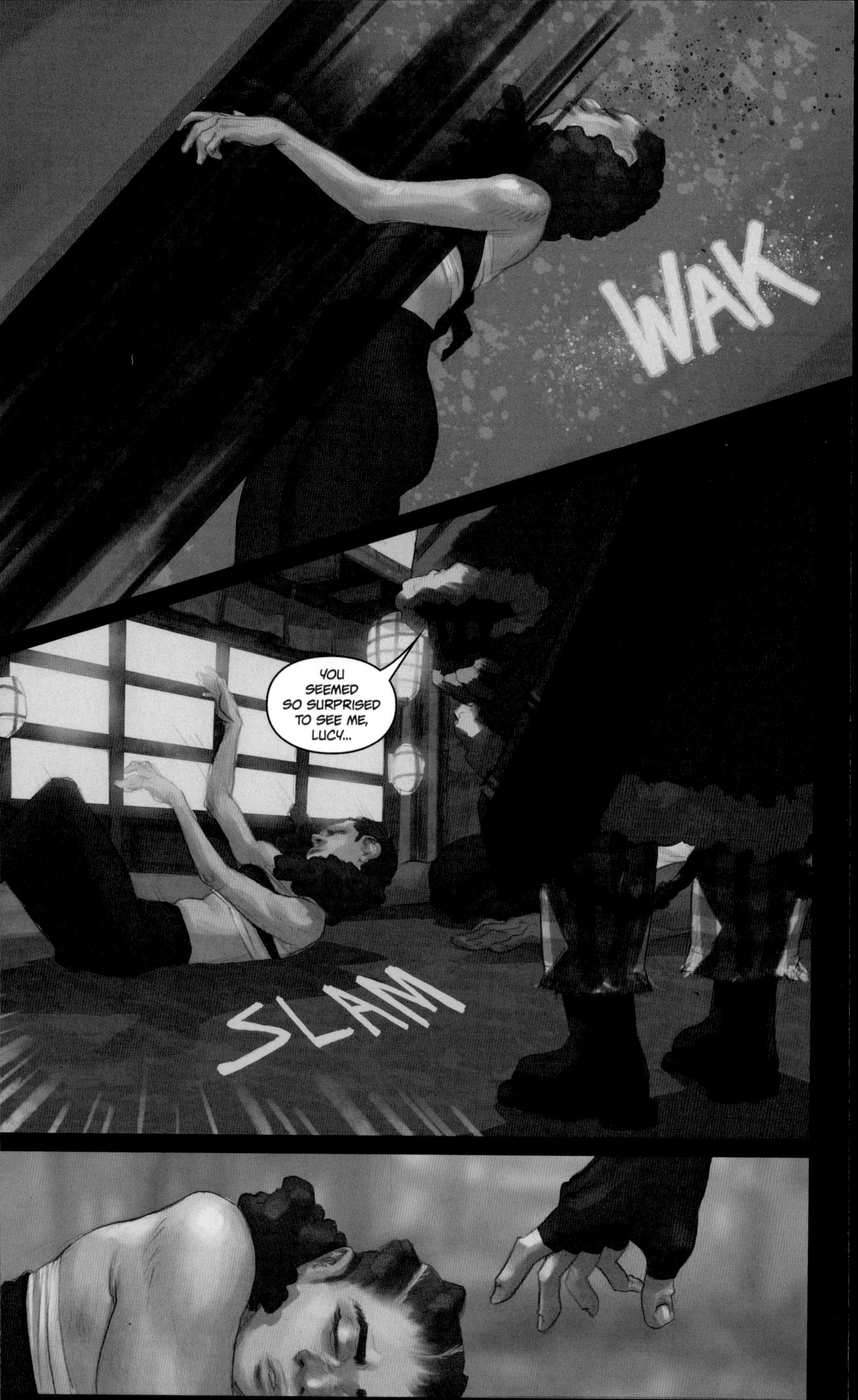
WAK
YOU SEEMED SO SURPRISED TO SEE ME, LUCY...
SLAM

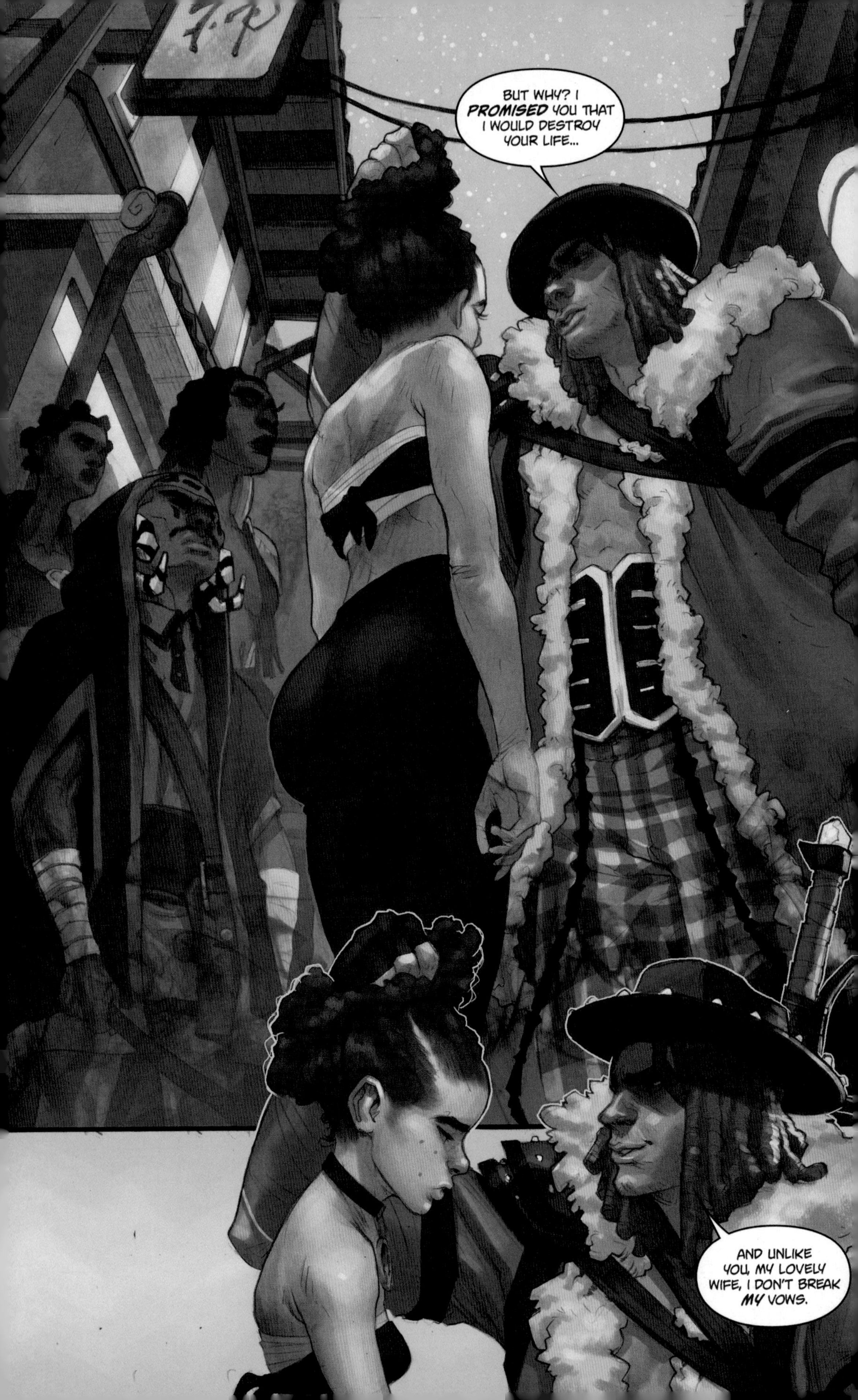
BUT WHY? I PROMISED YOU THAT I WOULD DESTROY YOUR LIFE...
AND UNLIKE YOU, MY LOVELY WIFE, I DON'T BREAK MY VOWS.

CHAPTER FIVE

"My CHEST IS HEAVY.
I CAN'T BREATHE.
I CAN'T STOP MY TEARS.

I CAN'T STOP MY ANGUISH
WHENEVER I THINK OF YOU,
AND I'M NEVER THINKING OF ANYTHING ELSE."

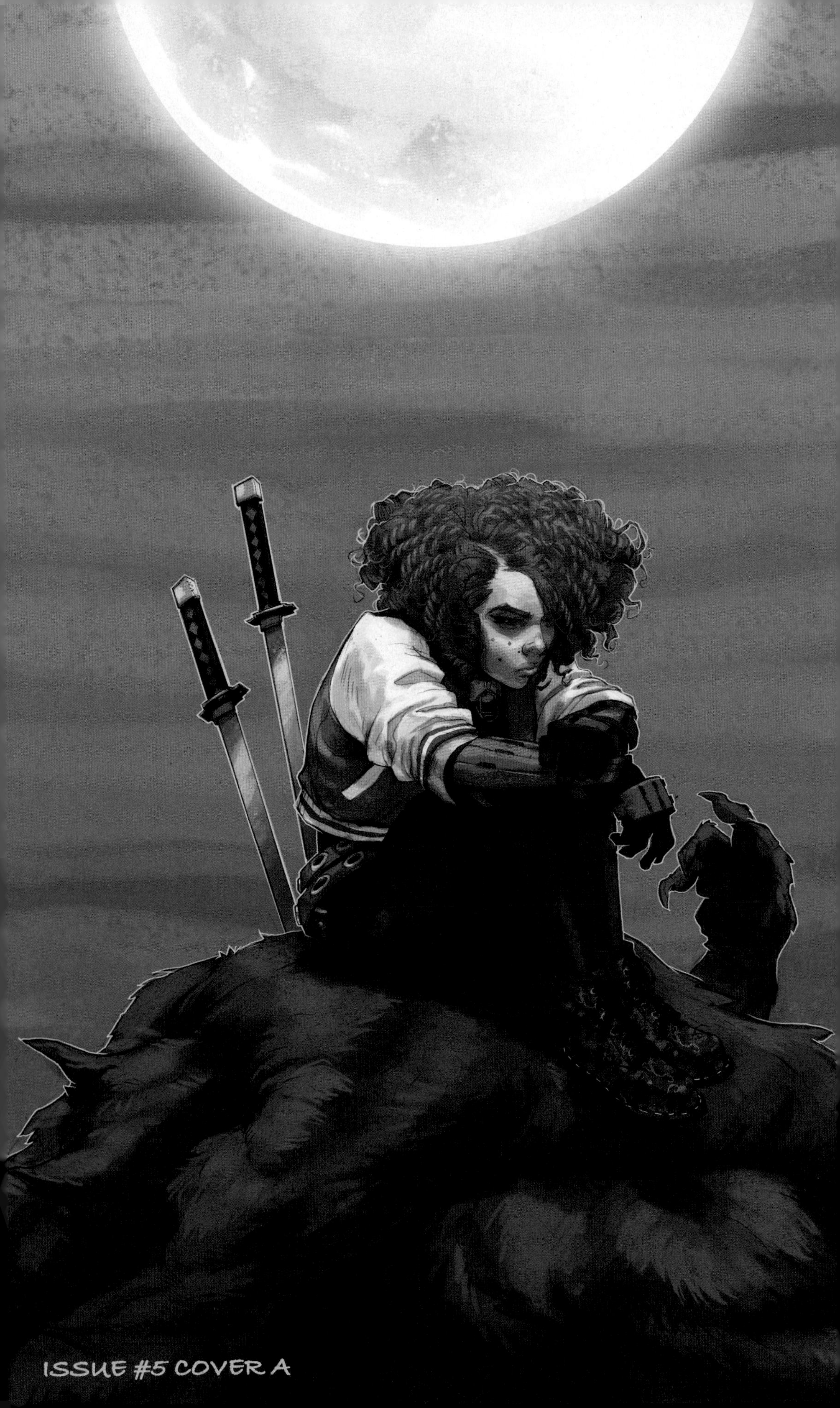

ISSUE #5 COVER A

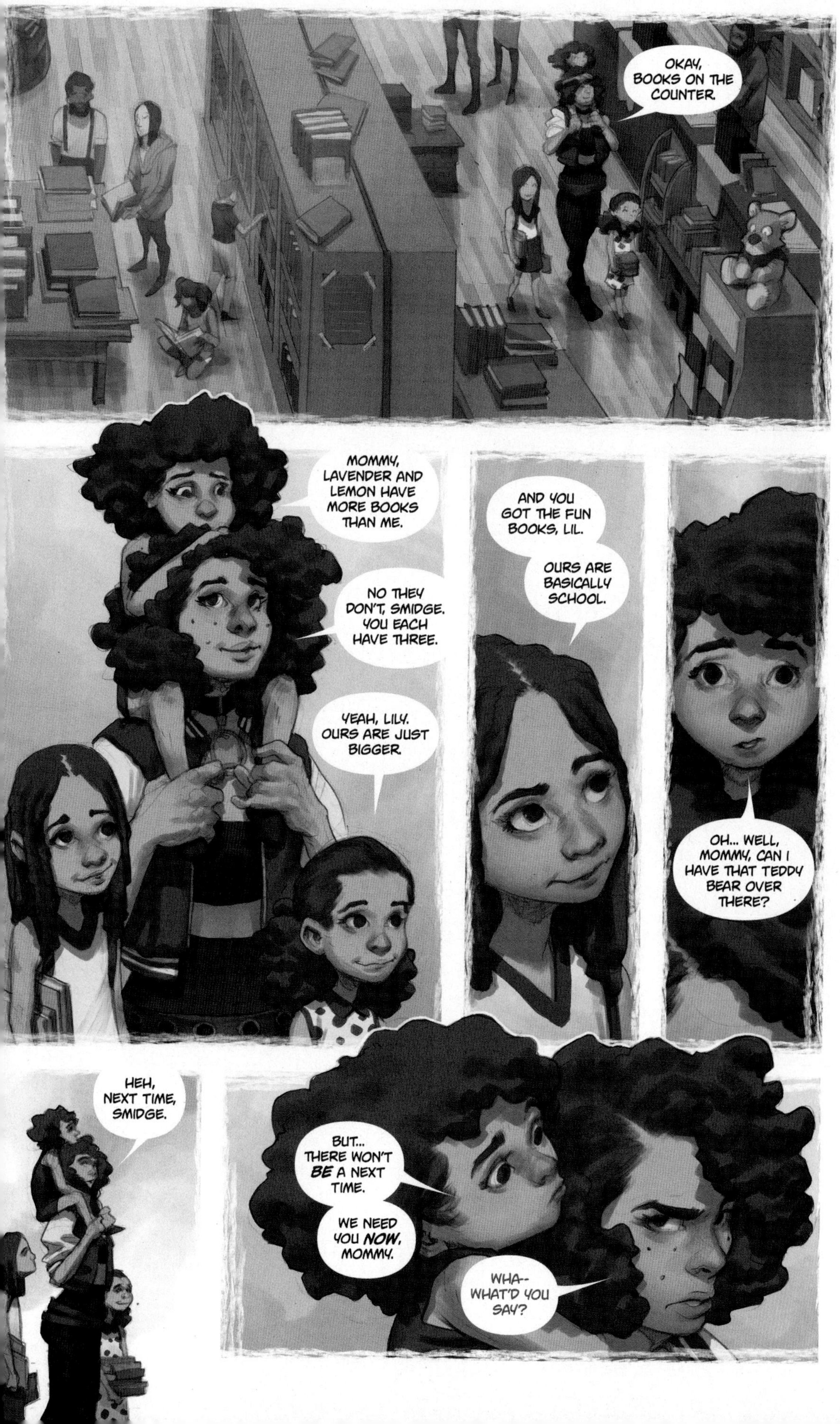
OKAY, BOOKS ON THE COUNTER.
MOMMY, LAVENDER AND LEMON HAVE MORE BOOKS THAN ME.
NO THEY DON'T, SMIDGE. YOU EACH HAVE THREE.
YEAH, LILY. OURS ARE JUST BIGGER.
AND YOU GOT THE FUN BOOKS, LIL.
OURS ARE BASICALLY SCHOOL.
OH... WELL, MOMMY, CAN I HAVE THAT TEDDY BEAR OVER THERE?
HEH, NEXT TIME, SMIDGE.
BUT... THERE WON'T *BE* A NEXT TIME.
WE NEED YOU *NOW*, MOMMY.
WHA-- WHAT'D YOU SAY?

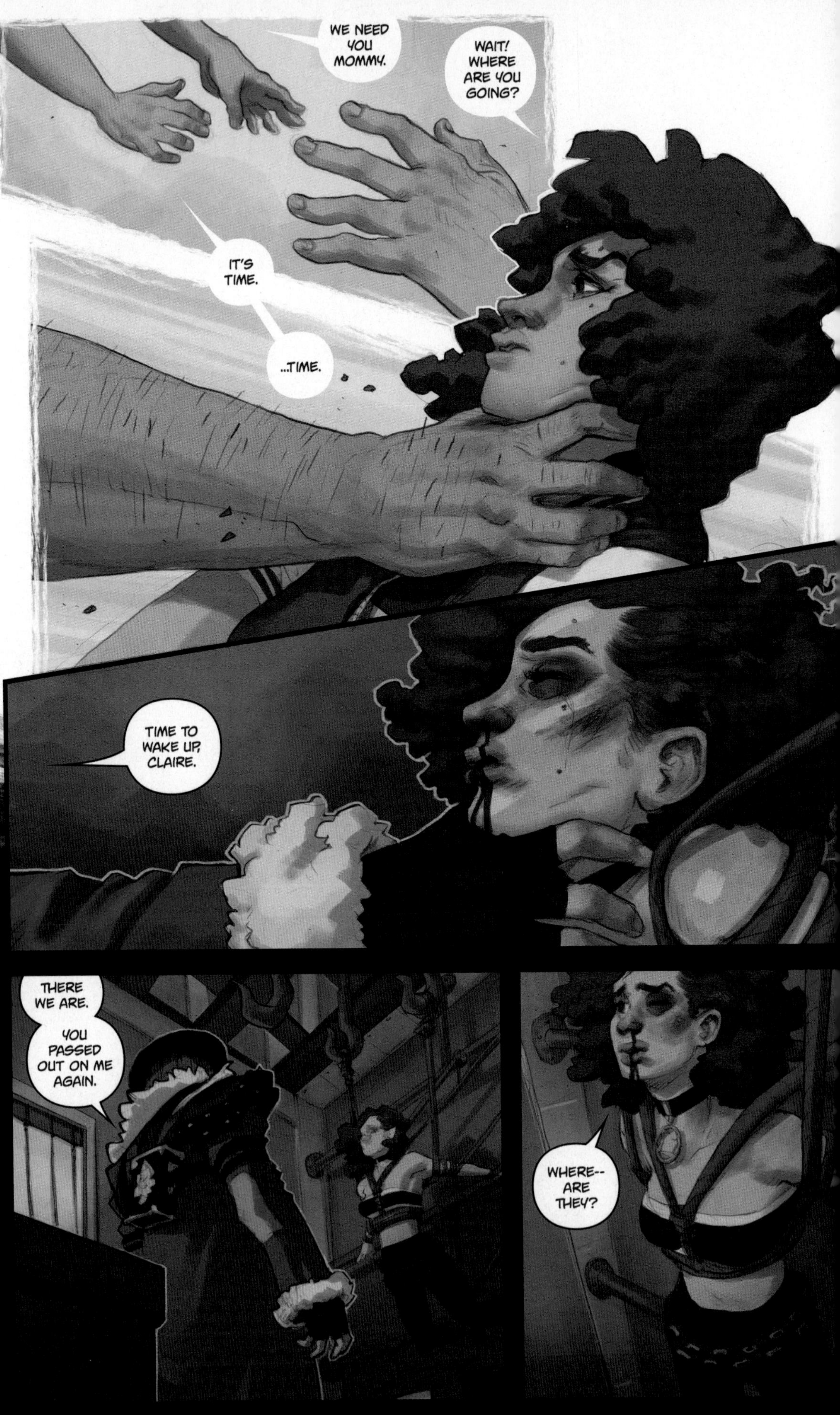
WE NEED YOU MOMMY.
WAIT! WHERE ARE YOU GOING?
IT'S TIME.
...TIME.
TIME TO WAKE UP, CLAIRE.
THERE WE ARE.
YOU PASSED OUT ON ME AGAIN.
WHERE-- ARE THEY?

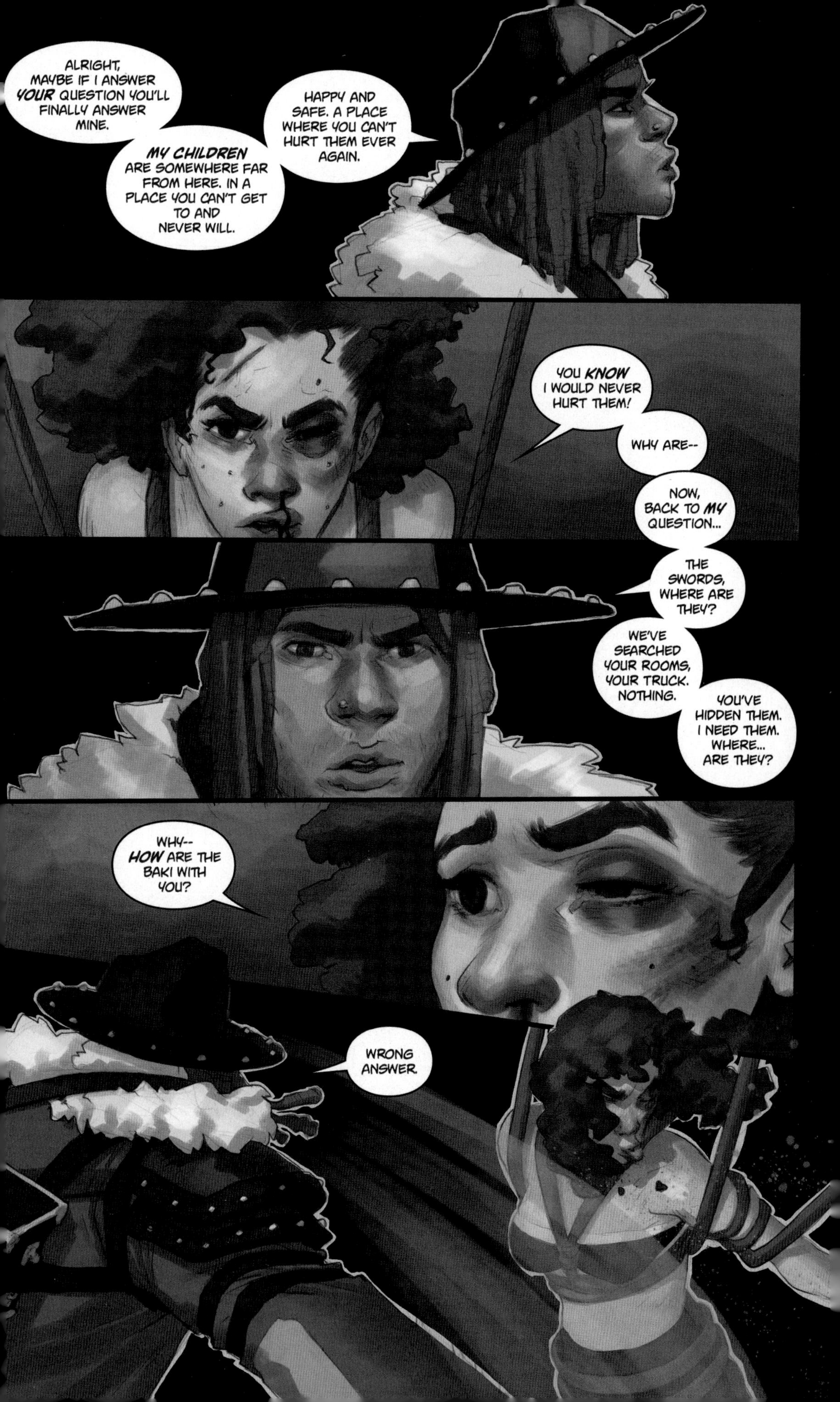
ALRIGHT, MAYBE IF I ANSWER **YOUR** QUESTION YOU'LL FINALLY ANSWER MINE.
MY CHILDREN ARE SOMEWHERE FAR FROM HERE. IN A PLACE YOU CAN'T GET TO AND NEVER WILL.
HAPPY AND SAFE. A PLACE WHERE YOU CAN'T HURT THEM EVER AGAIN.
YOU **KNOW** I WOULD NEVER HURT THEM!
WHY ARE--
NOW, BACK TO **MY** QUESTION...
THE SWORDS, WHERE ARE THEY?
WE'VE SEARCHED YOUR ROOMS, YOUR TRUCK. NOTHING.
YOU'VE HIDDEN THEM. I NEED THEM. WHERE... ARE THEY?
WHY-- **HOW** ARE THE BAKI WITH YOU?
WRONG ANSWER.

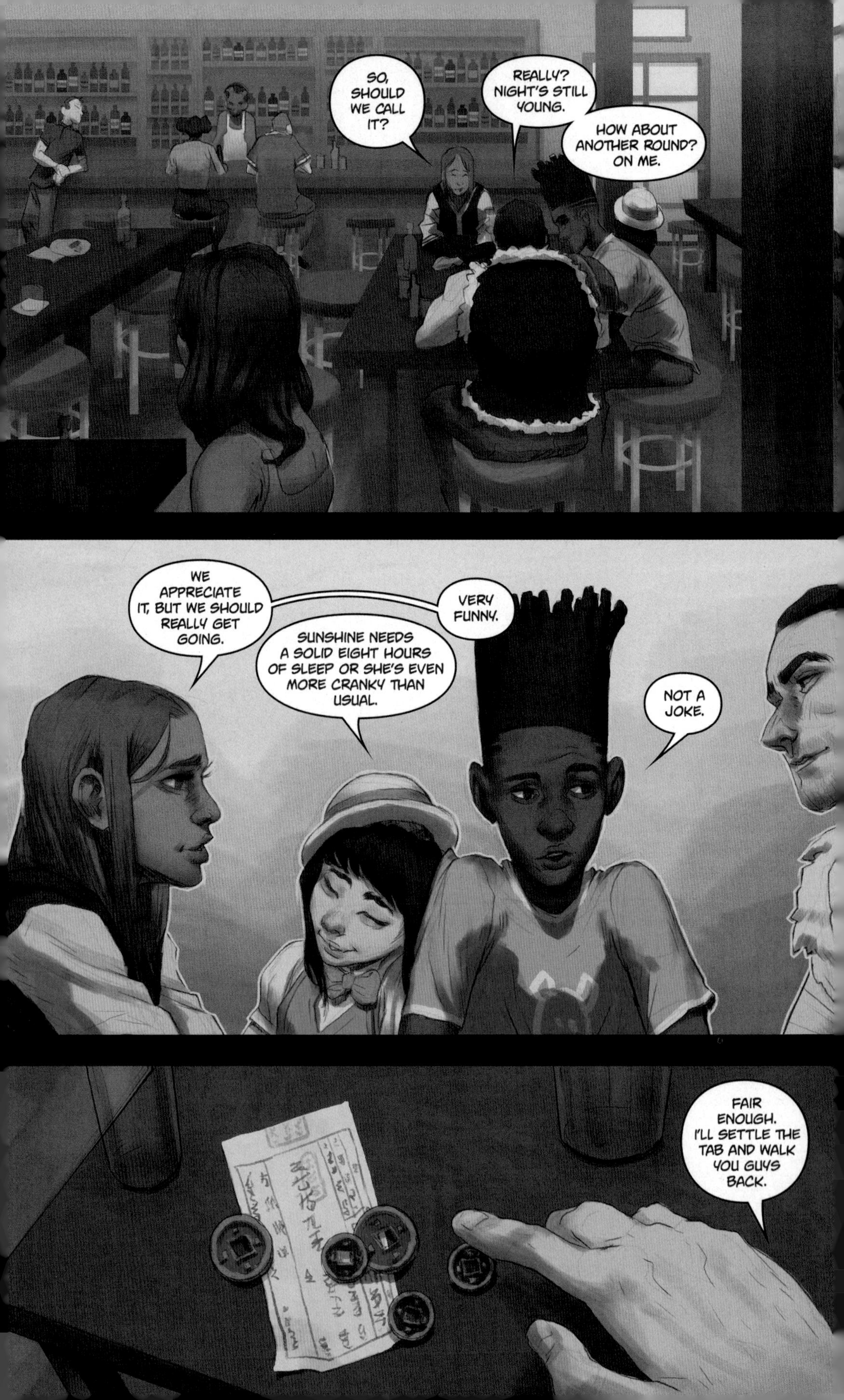
SO, SHOULD WE CALL IT?
REALLY? NIGHT'S STILL YOUNG.
HOW ABOUT ANOTHER ROUND? ON ME.
WE APPRECIATE IT, BUT WE SHOULD REALLY GET GOING.
VERY FUNNY.
SUNSHINE NEEDS A SOLID EIGHT HOURS OF SLEEP OR SHE'S EVEN MORE CRANKY THAN USUAL.
NOT A JOKE.
FAIR ENOUGH. I'LL SETTLE THE TAB AND WALK YOU GUYS BACK.

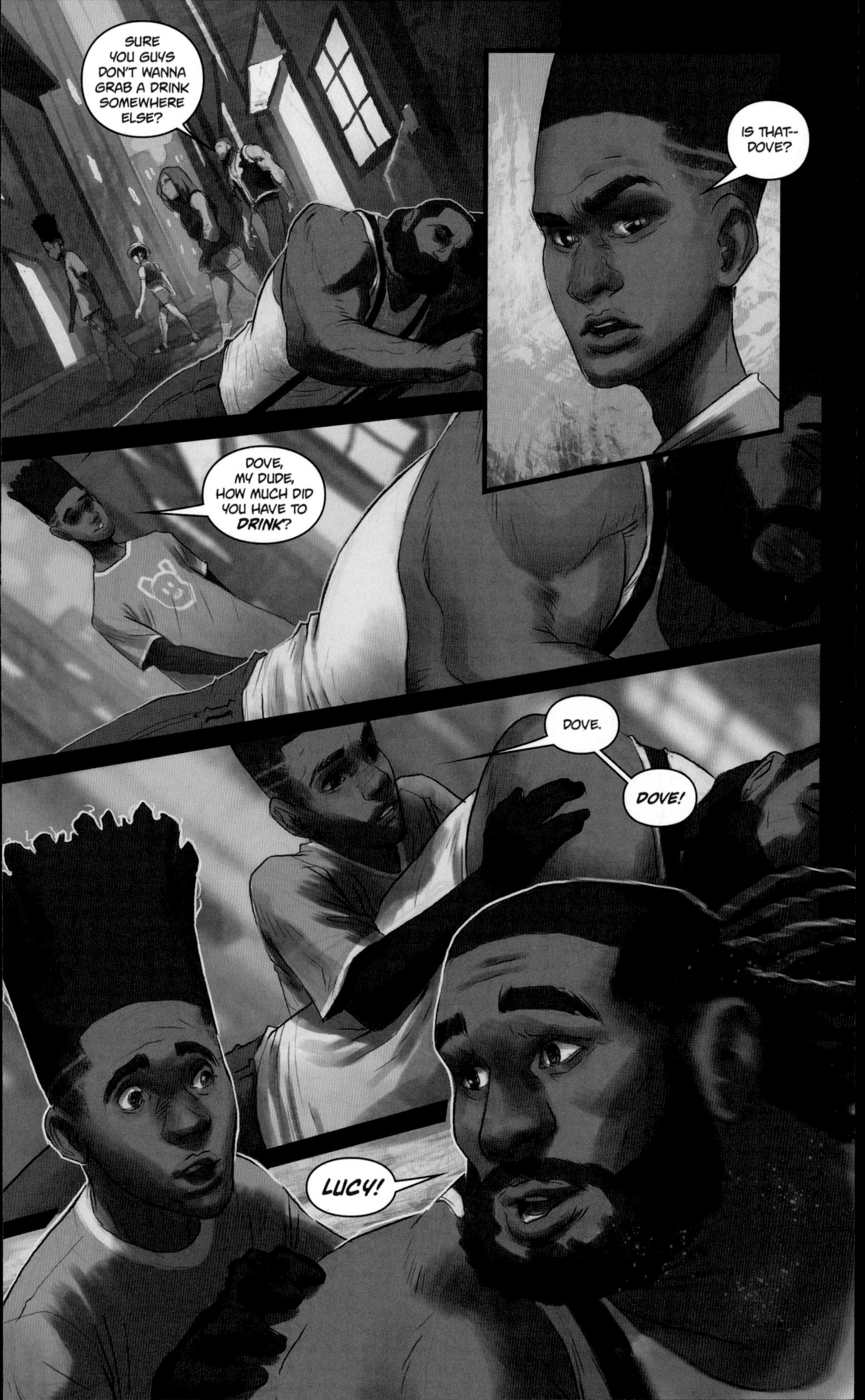
SURE YOU GUYS DON'T WANNA GRAB A DRINK SOMEWHERE ELSE?
IS THAT-- DOVE?
DOVE, MY DUDE, HOW MUCH DID YOU HAVE TO DRINK?
DOVE.
DOVE!
LUCY!

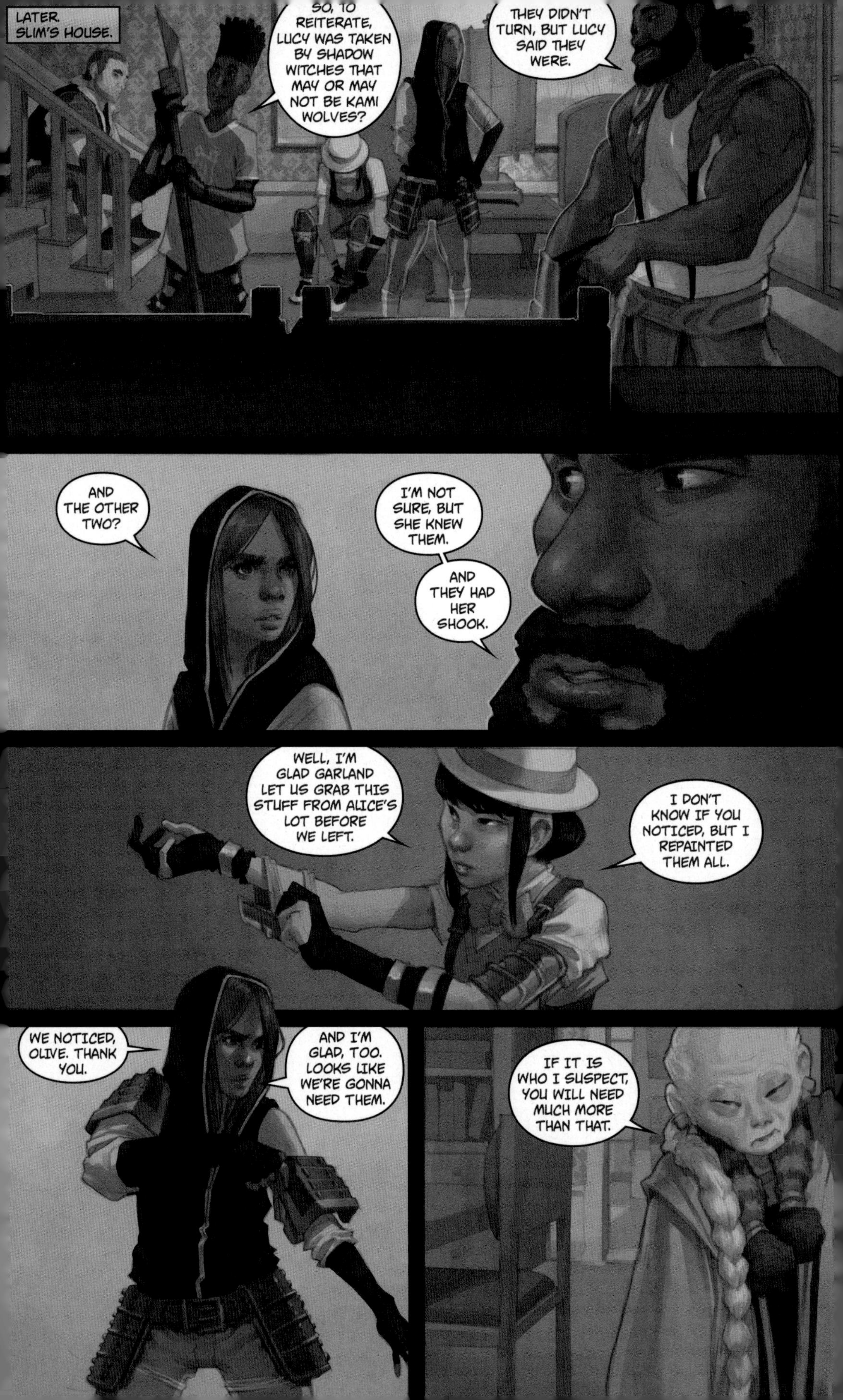
LATER. SLIM'S HOUSE.
SO, TO REITERATE, LUCY WAS TAKEN BY SHADOW WITCHES THAT MAY OR MAY NOT BE KAMI WOLVES?
THEY DIDN'T TURN, BUT LUCY SAID THEY WERE.
AND THE OTHER TWO?
I'M NOT SURE, BUT SHE KNEW THEM.
AND THEY HAD HER SHOOK.
WELL, I'M GLAD GARLAND LET US GRAB THIS STUFF FROM ALICE'S LOT BEFORE WE LEFT.
I DON'T KNOW IF YOU NOTICED, BUT I REPAINTED THEM ALL.
WE NOTICED, OLIVE. THANK YOU.
AND I'M GLAD, TOO. LOOKS LIKE WE'RE GONNA NEED THEM.
IF IT IS WHO I SUSPECT, YOU WILL NEED MUCH MORE THAN THAT.

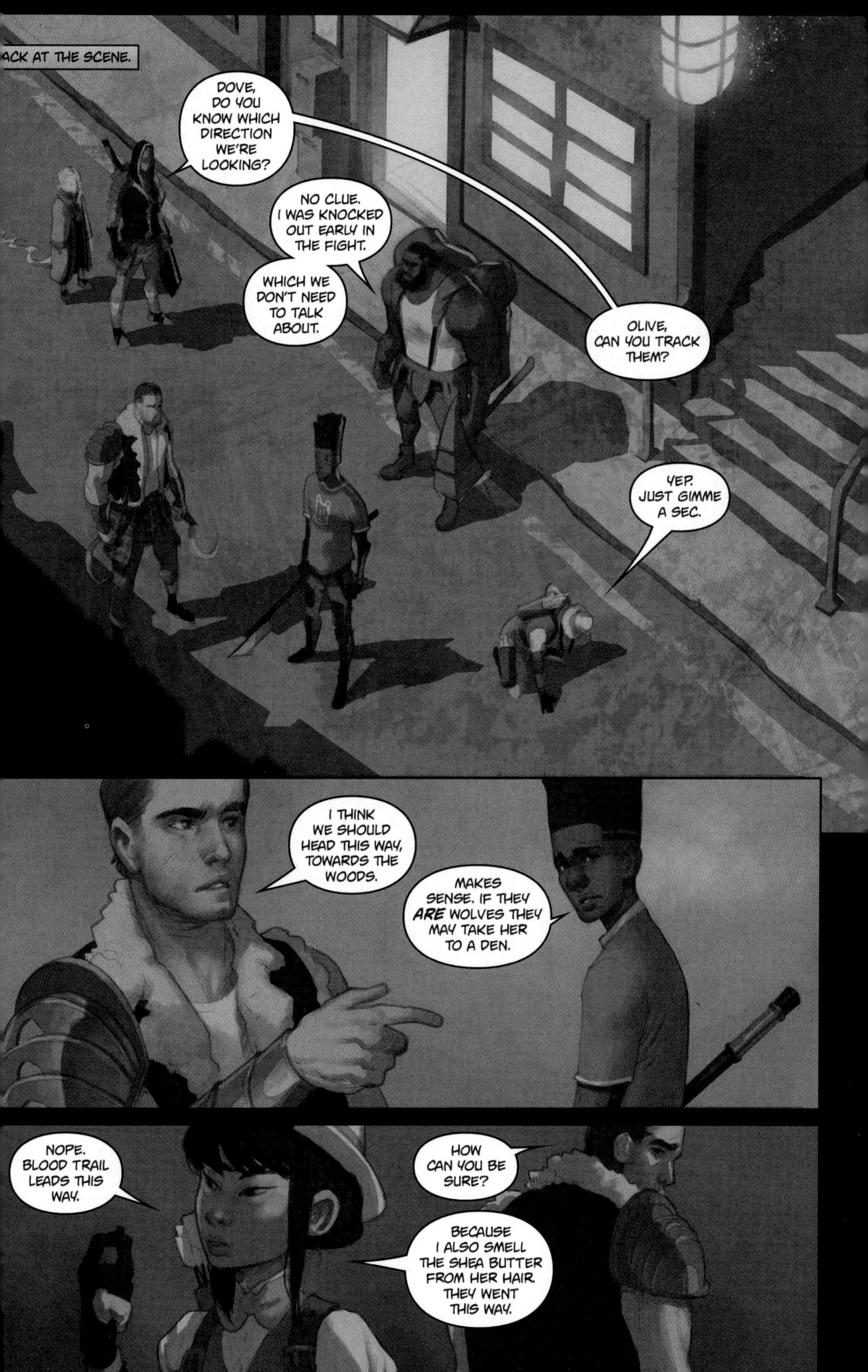

ACK AT THE SCENE.
DOVE, DO YOU KNOW WHICH DIRECTION WE'RE LOOKING?
NO CLUE. I WAS KNOCKED OUT EARLY IN THE FIGHT.
WHICH WE DON'T NEED TO TALK ABOUT.
OLIVE, CAN YOU TRACK THEM?
YEP. JUST GIMME A SEC.
I THINK WE SHOULD HEAD THIS WAY, TOWARDS THE WOODS.
MAKES SENSE. IF THEY *ARE* WOLVES THEY MAY TAKE HER TO A DEN.
NOPE. BLOOD TRAIL LEADS THIS WAY.
HOW CAN YOU BE SURE?
BECAUSE I ALSO SMELL THE SHEA BUTTER FROM HER HAIR. THEY WENT THIS WAY.

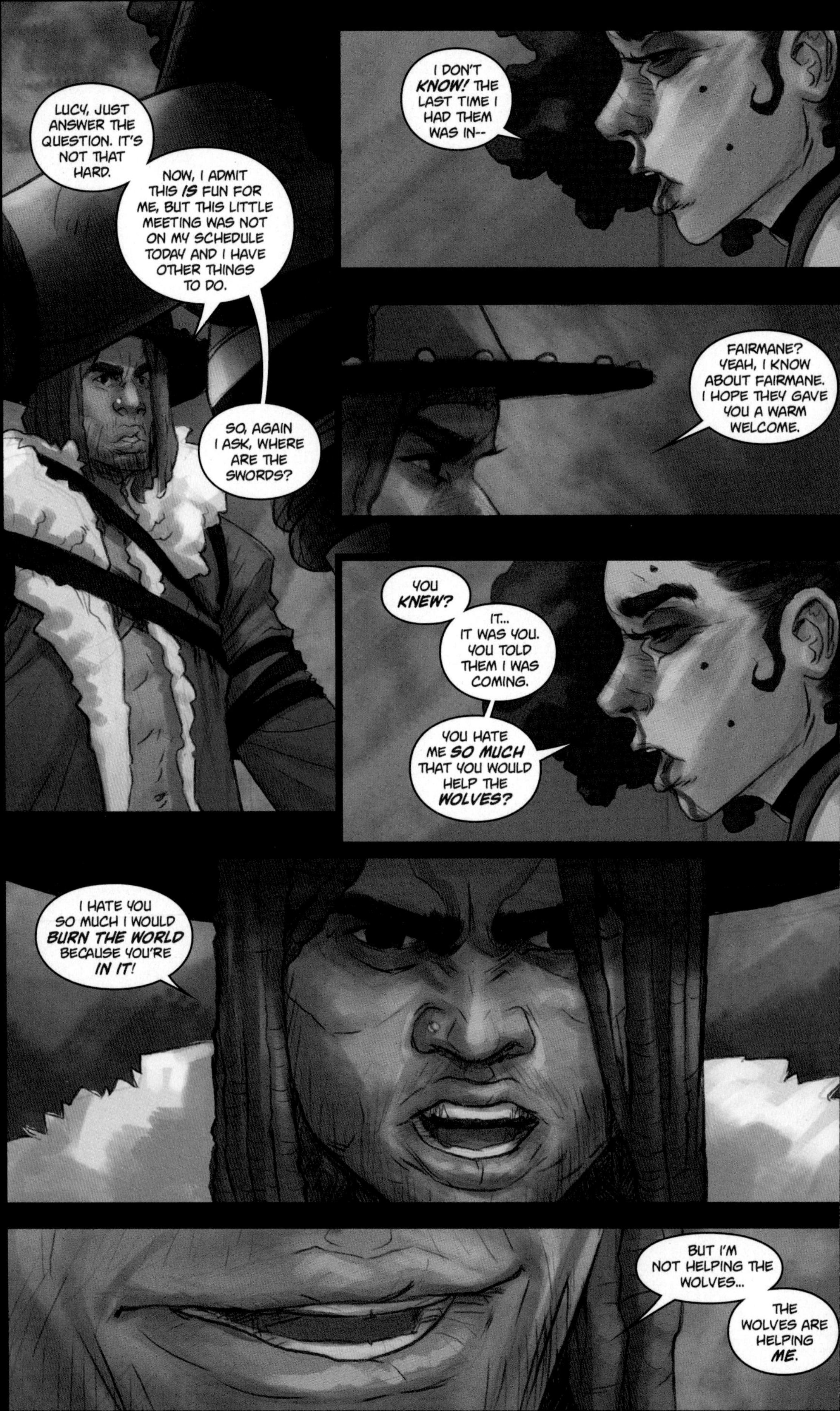
LUCY, JUST ANSWER THE QUESTION. IT'S NOT THAT HARD.
NOW, I ADMIT THIS **IS** FUN FOR ME, BUT THIS LITTLE MEETING WAS NOT ON MY SCHEDULE TODAY AND I HAVE OTHER THINGS TO DO.
SO, AGAIN I ASK, WHERE ARE THE SWORDS?
I DON'T **KNOW!** THE LAST TIME I HAD THEM WAS IN--
FAIRMANE? YEAH, I KNOW ABOUT FAIRMANE. I HOPE THEY GAVE YOU A WARM WELCOME.
YOU **KNEW?**
IT... IT WAS YOU. YOU TOLD THEM I WAS COMING.
YOU HATE ME **SO MUCH** THAT YOU WOULD HELP THE **WOLVES?**
I HATE YOU SO MUCH I WOULD **BURN THE WORLD** BECAUSE YOU'RE **IN IT!**
BUT I'M NOT HELPING THE WOLVES...
THE WOLVES ARE HELPING **ME.**

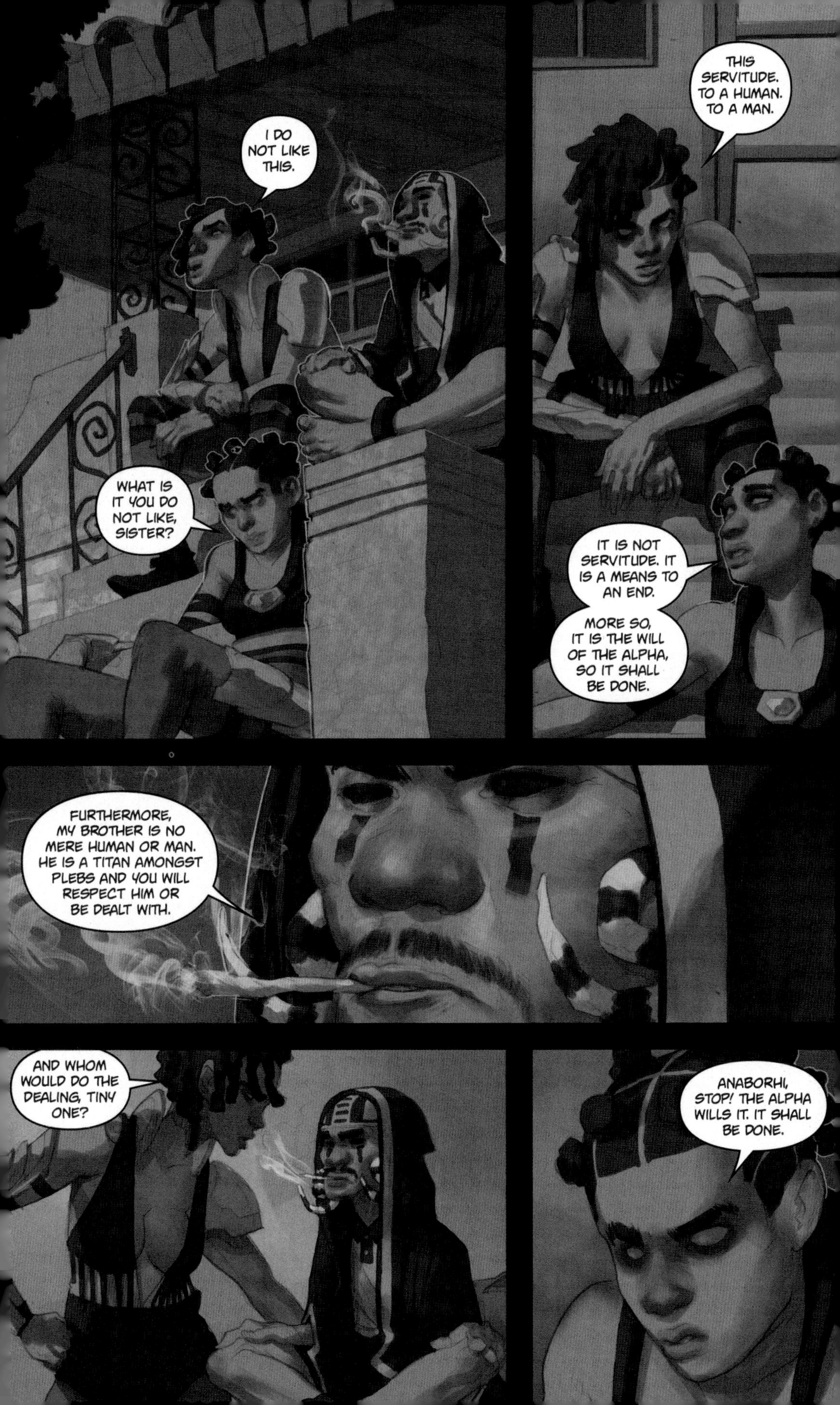

I DO NOT LIKE THIS.
WHAT IS IT YOU DO NOT LIKE, SISTER?
THIS SERVITUDE. TO A HUMAN. TO A MAN.
IT IS NOT SERVITUDE. IT IS A MEANS TO AN END.
MORE SO, IT IS THE WILL OF THE ALPHA, SO IT SHALL BE DONE.
FURTHERMORE, MY BROTHER IS NO MERE HUMAN OR MAN. HE IS A TITAN AMONGST PLEBS AND YOU WILL RESPECT HIM OR BE DEALT WITH.
AND WHOM WOULD DO THE DEALING, TINY ONE?
ANABORHI, STOP! THE ALPHA WILLS IT. IT SHALL BE DONE.

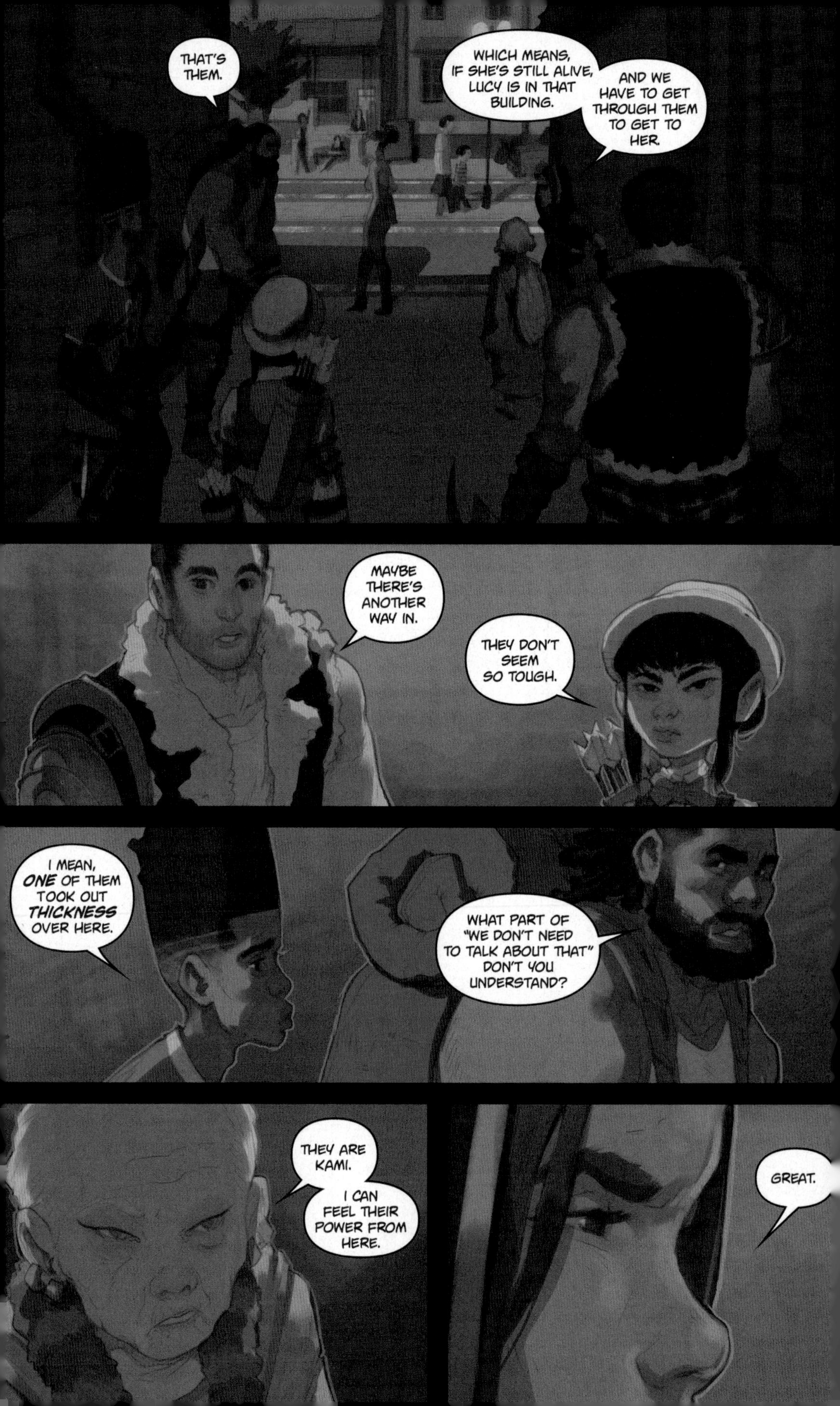
THAT'S THEM.
WHICH MEANS, IF SHE'S STILL ALIVE, LUCY IS IN THAT BUILDING.
AND WE HAVE TO GET THROUGH THEM TO GET TO HER.
MAYBE THERE'S ANOTHER WAY IN.
THEY DON'T SEEM SO TOUGH.
I MEAN, ONE OF THEM TOOK OUT THICKNESS OVER HERE.
WHAT PART OF "WE DON'T NEED TO TALK ABOUT THAT" DON'T YOU UNDERSTAND?
THEY ARE KAMI.
I CAN FEEL THEIR POWER FROM HERE.
GREAT.

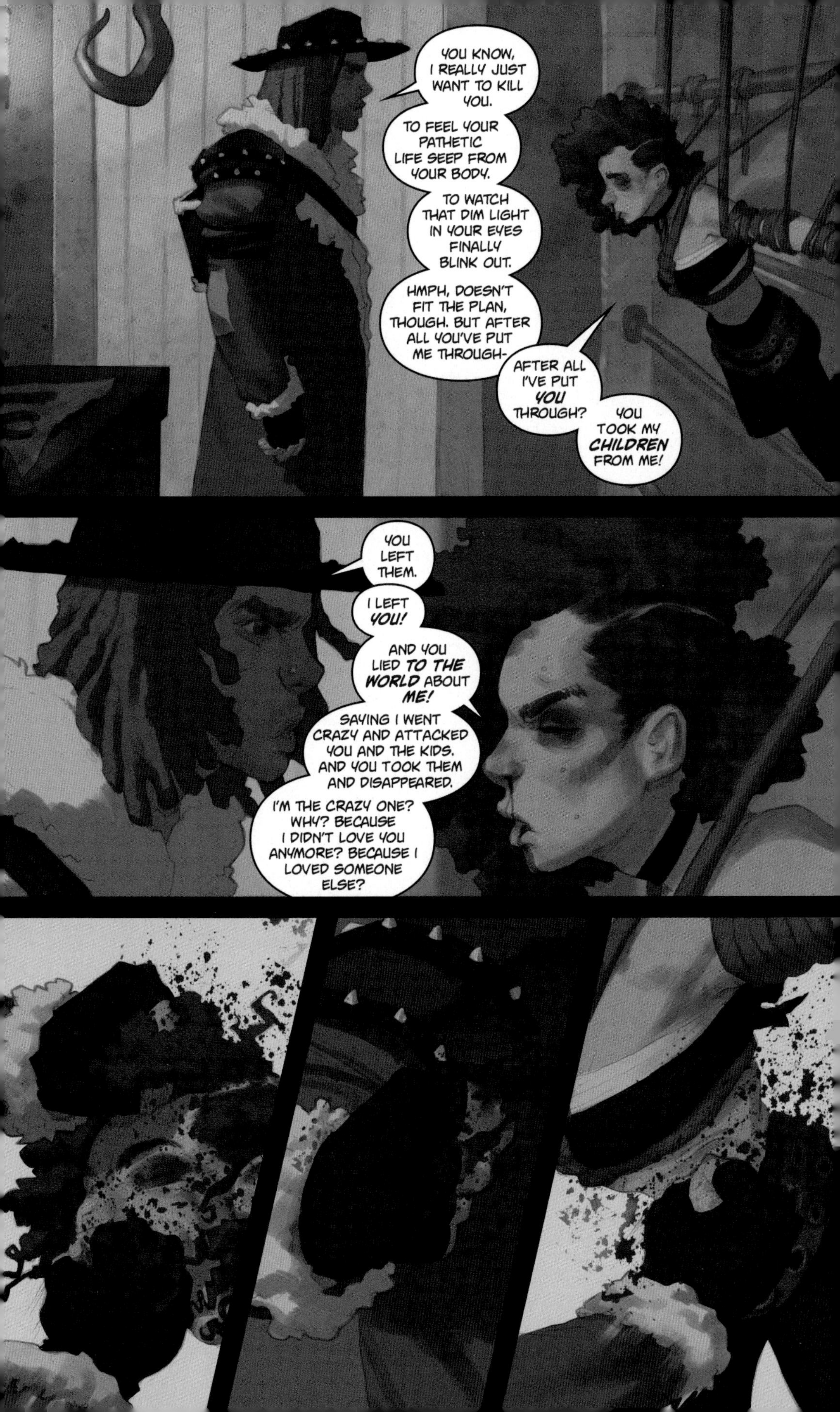
YOU KNOW, I REALLY JUST WANT TO KILL YOU.
TO FEEL YOUR PATHETIC LIFE SEEP FROM YOUR BODY.
TO WATCH THAT DIM LIGHT IN YOUR EYES FINALLY BLINK OUT.
HMPH, DOESN'T FIT THE PLAN, THOUGH. BUT AFTER ALL YOU'VE PUT ME THROUGH-
AFTER ALL I'VE PUT ***YOU*** THROUGH?
YOU TOOK MY ***CHILDREN*** FROM ME!
YOU LEFT THEM.
I LEFT ***YOU!***
AND YOU LIED ***TO THE WORLD*** ABOUT ***ME!***
SAYING I WENT CRAZY AND ATTACKED YOU AND THE KIDS. AND YOU TOOK THEM AND DISAPPEARED.
I'M THE CRAZY ONE? WHY? BECAUSE I DIDN'T LOVE YOU ANYMORE? BECAUSE I LOVED SOMEONE ELSE?

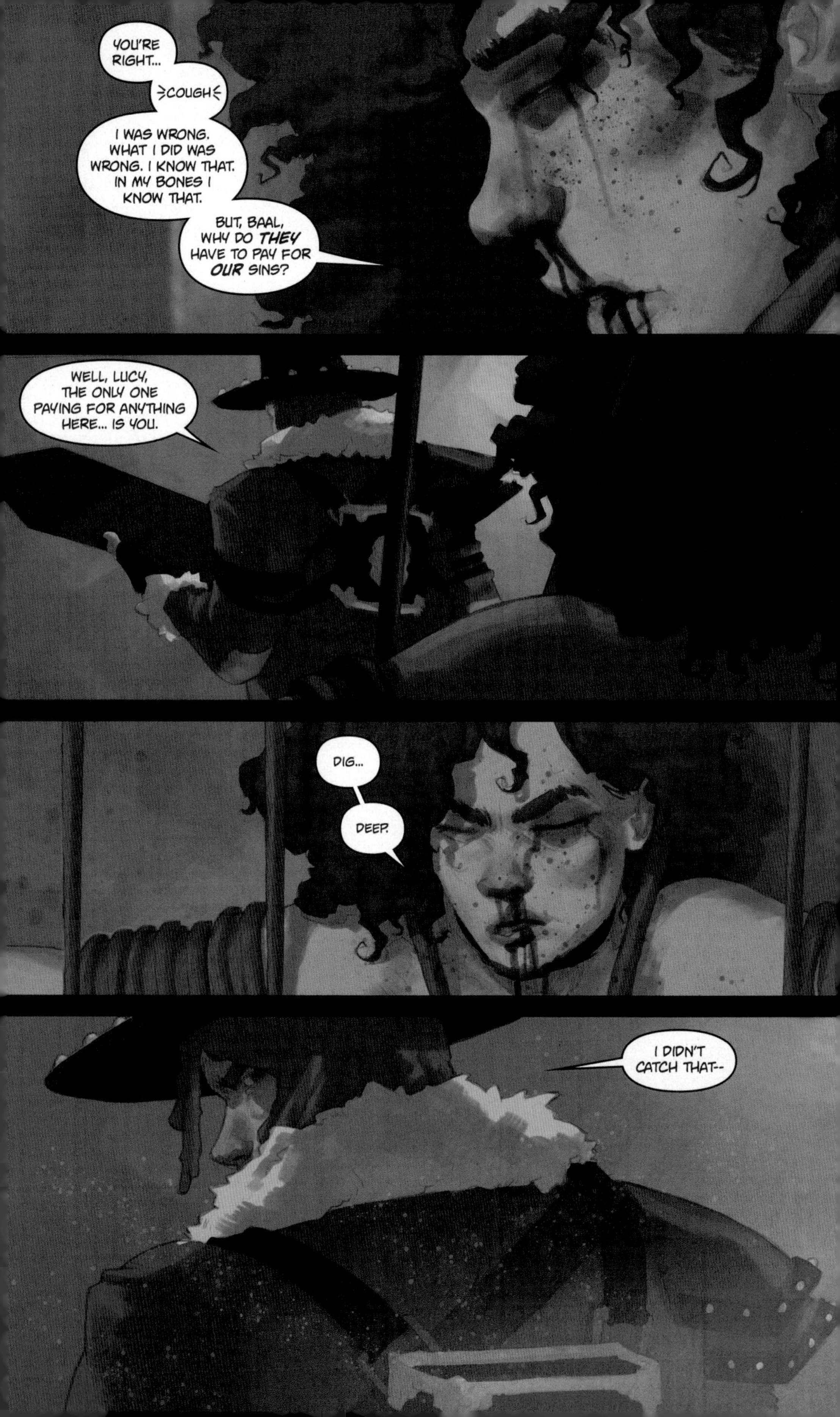
YOU'RE RIGHT...
>COUGH<
I WAS WRONG. WHAT I DID WAS WRONG. I KNOW THAT. IN MY BONES I KNOW THAT.
BUT, BAAL, WHY DO *THEY* HAVE TO PAY FOR *OUR* SINS?
WELL, LUCY, THE ONLY ONE PAYING FOR ANYTHING HERE... IS YOU.
DIG...
DEEP.
I DIDN'T CATCH THAT--

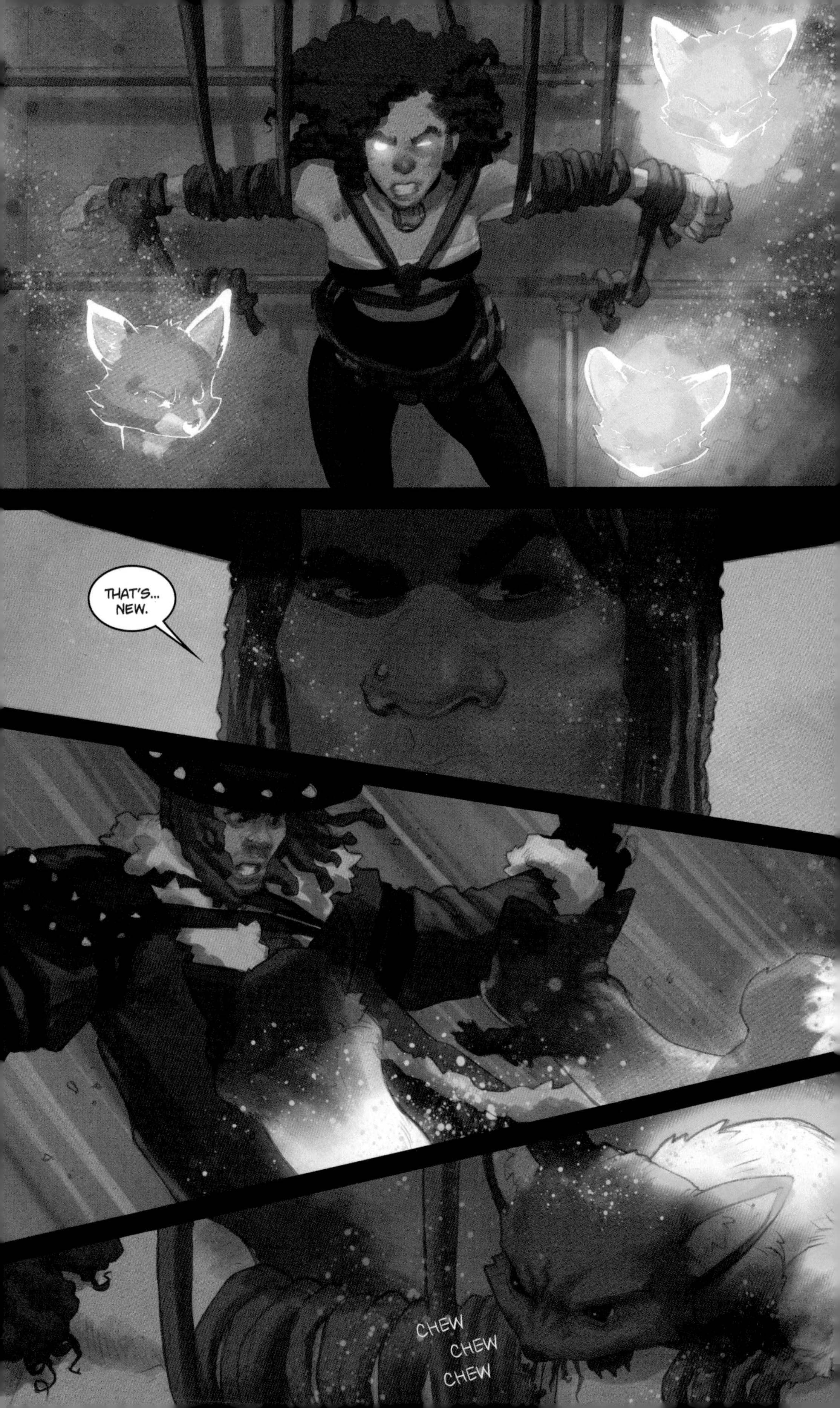
THAT'S... NEW.
CHEW
CHEW
CHEW

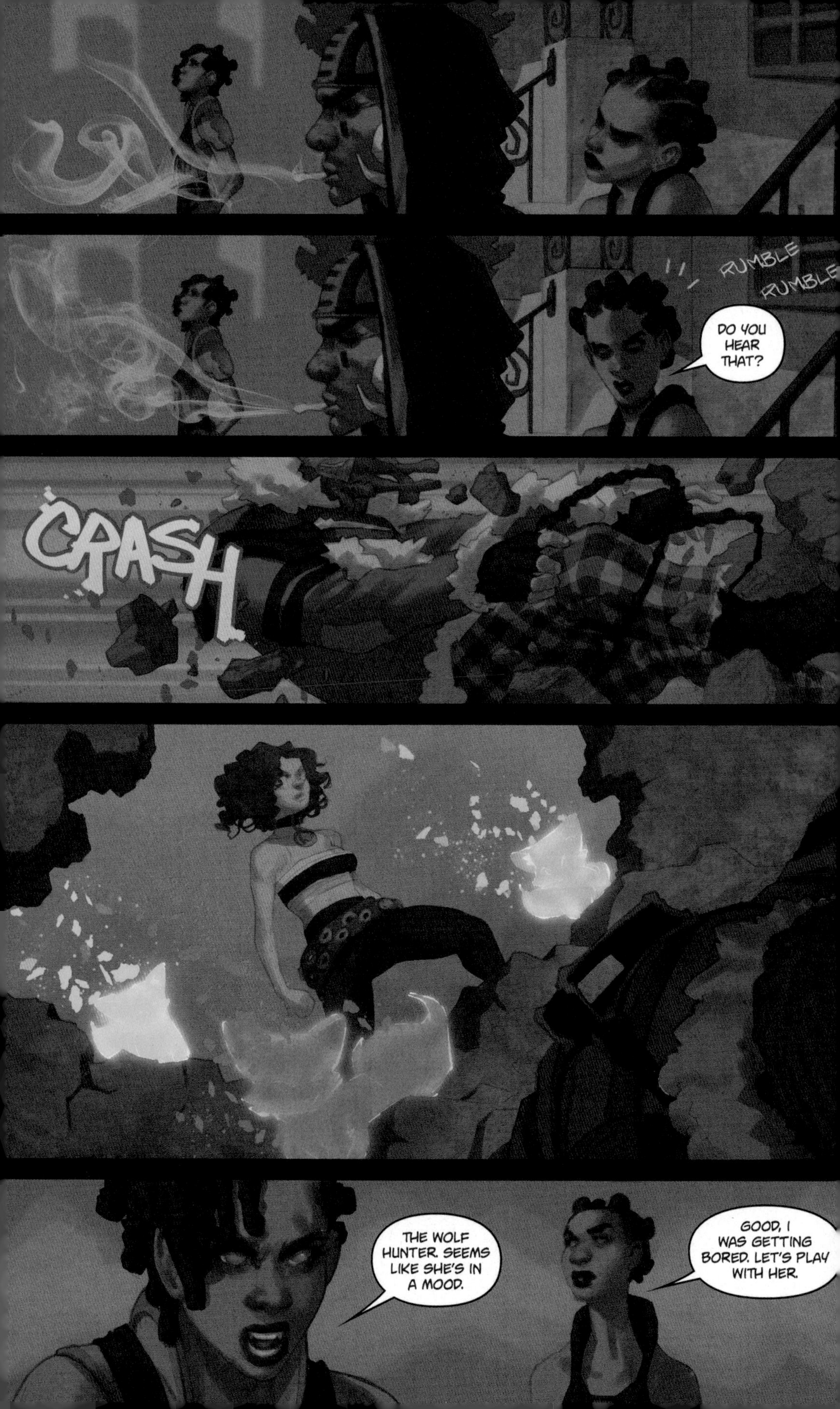
RUMBLE
RUMBLE
DO YOU HEAR THAT?
CRASH
THE WOLF HUNTER. SEEMS LIKE SHE'S IN A MOOD.
GOOD, I WAS GETTING BORED. LET'S PLAY WITH HER.

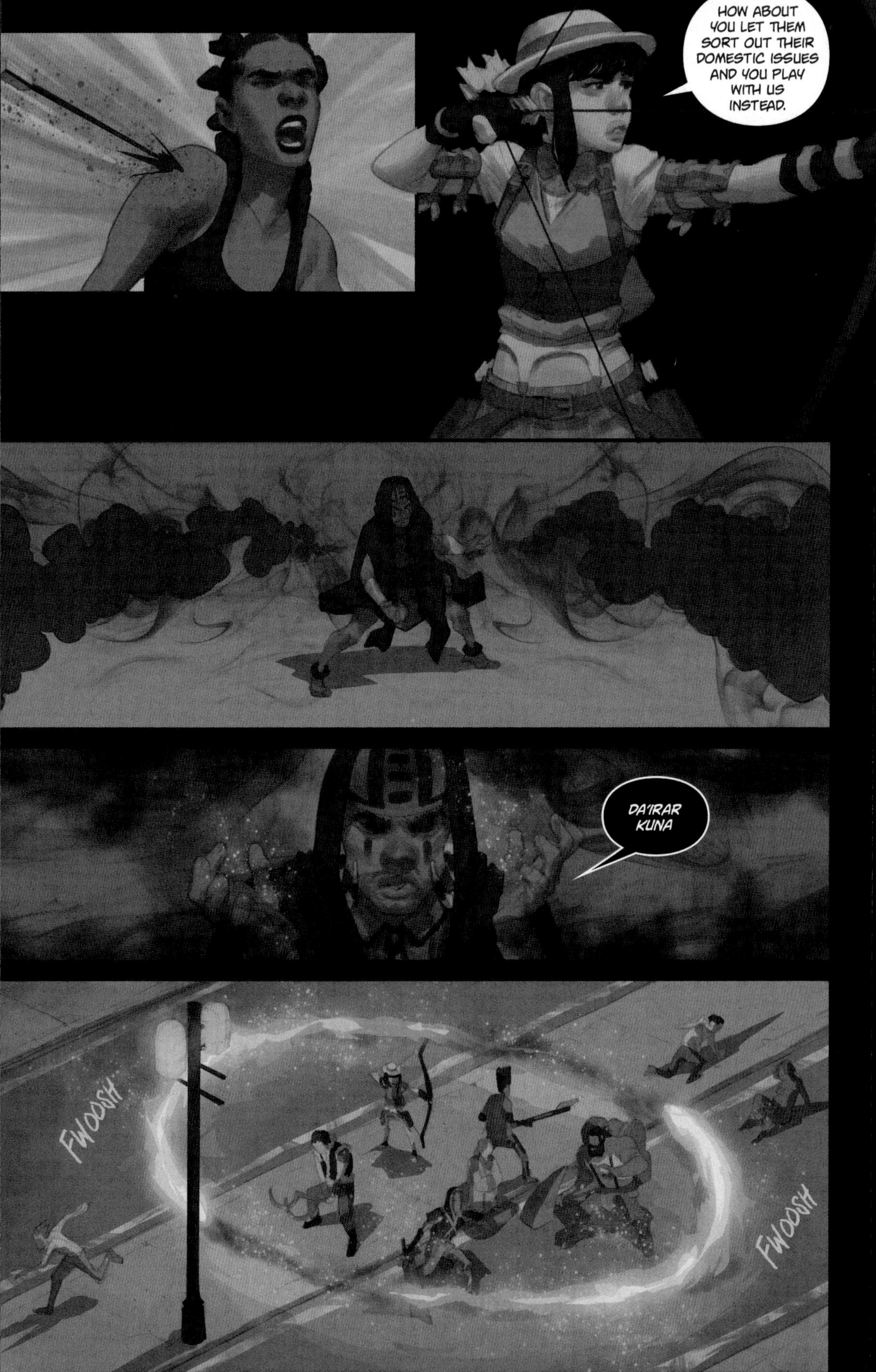
HOW ABOUT YOU LET THEM SORT OUT THEIR DOMESTIC ISSUES AND YOU PLAY WITH US INSTEAD.
DA'IRAR KUNA
FWOOSH
FWOOSH

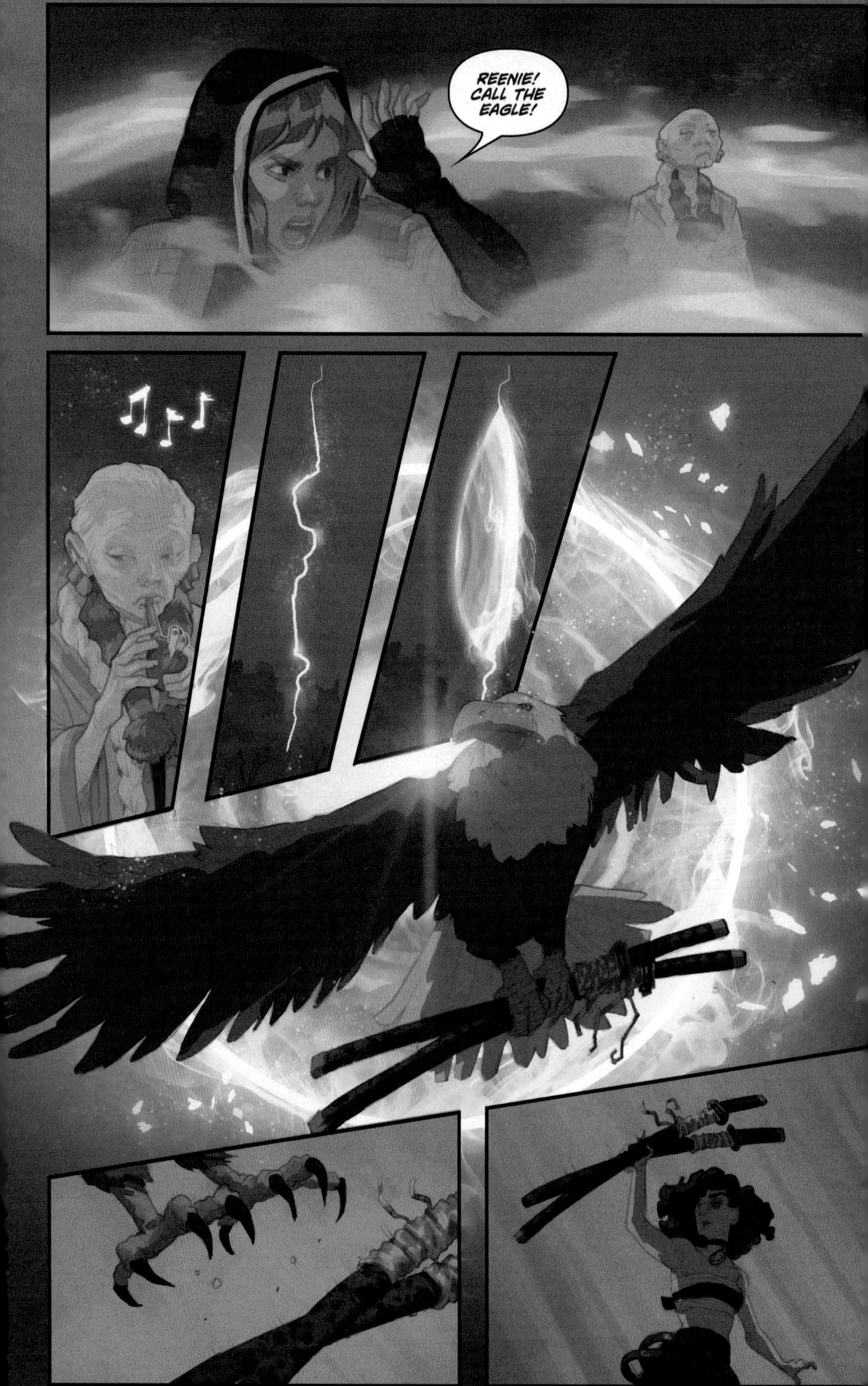
REENIE! CALL THE EAGLE!

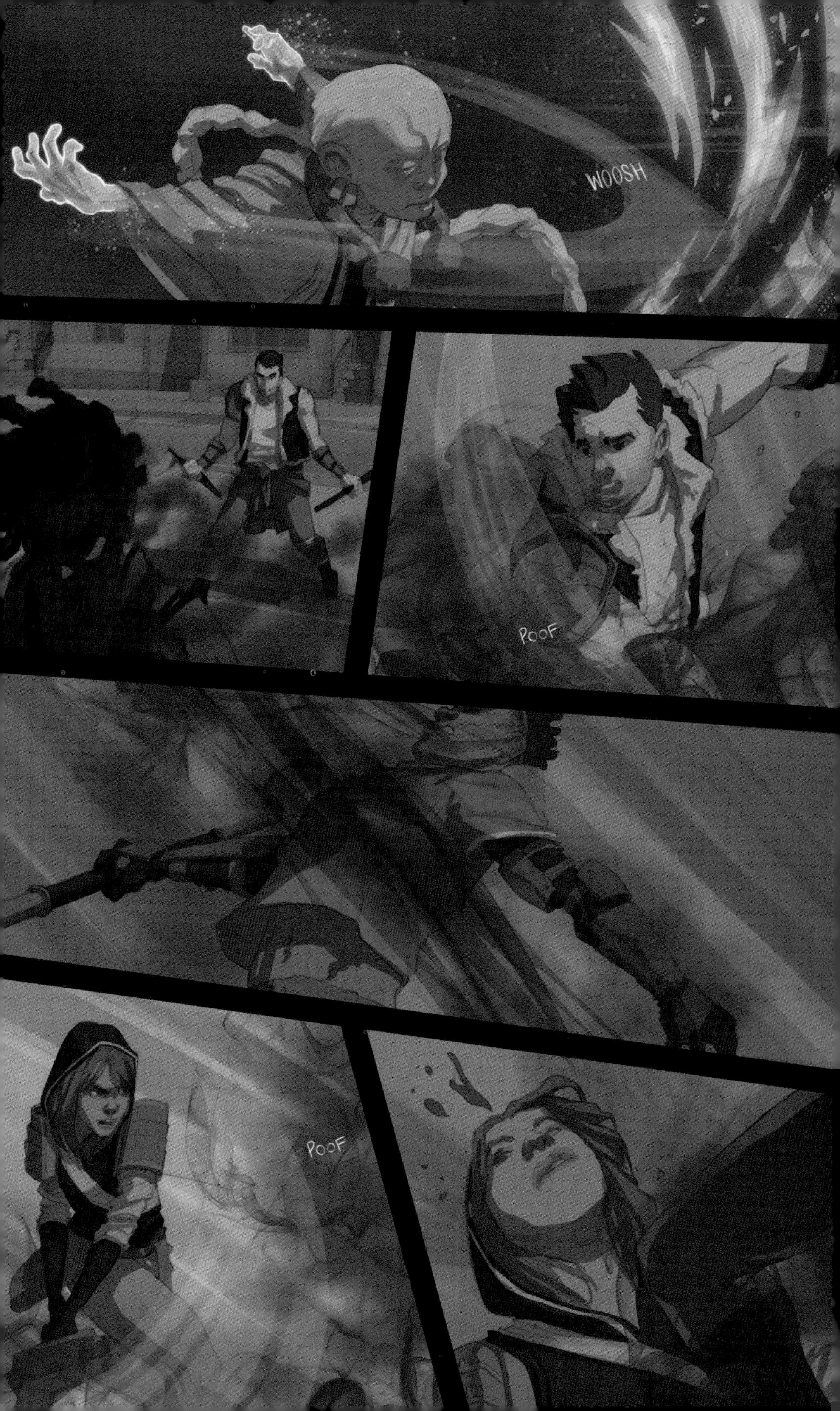
WOOSH
POOF
POOF

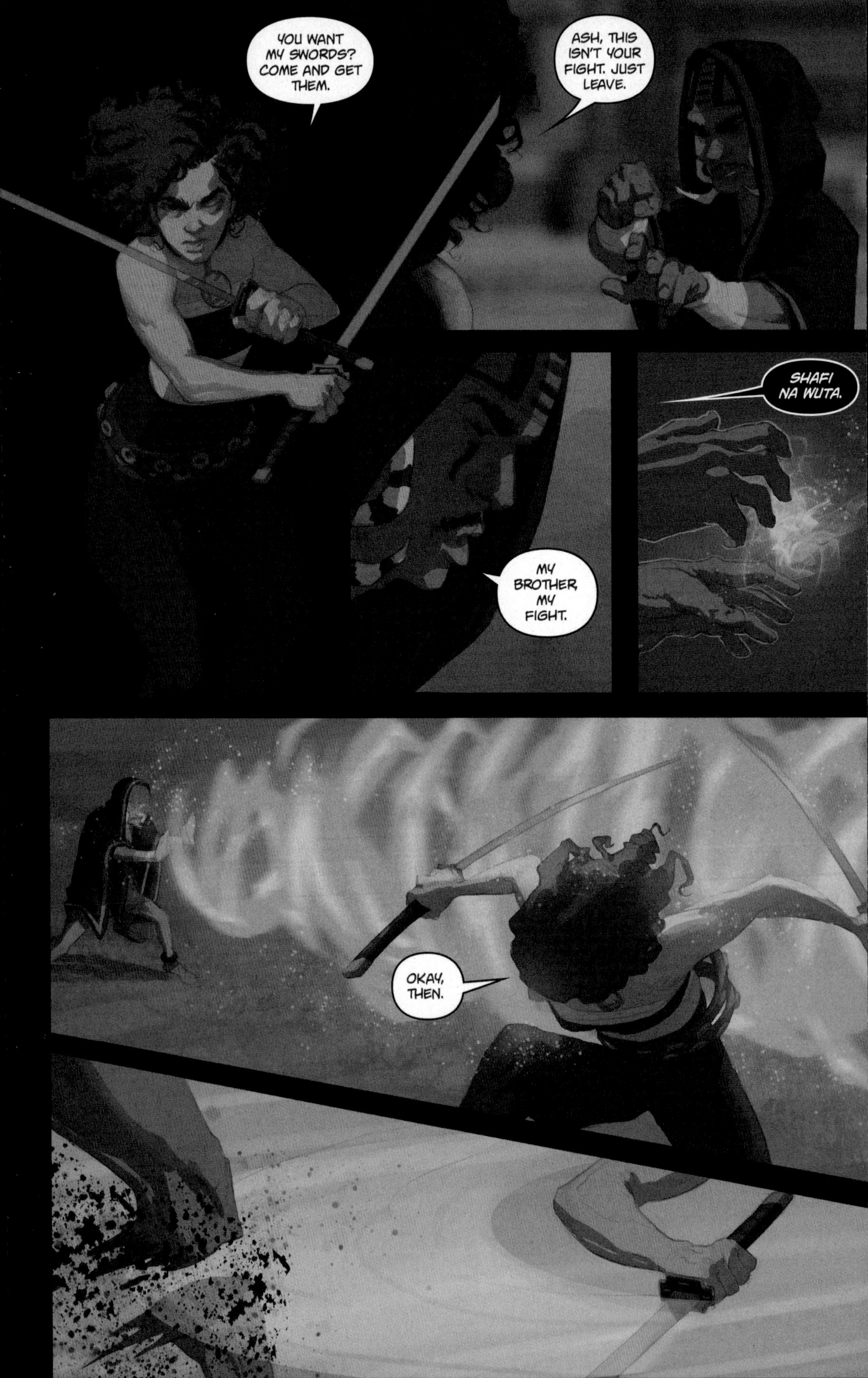

YOU WANT MY SWORDS? COME AND GET THEM.
ASH, THIS ISN'T YOUR FIGHT. JUST LEAVE.
MY BROTHER, MY FIGHT.
SHAFI NA WUTA.
OKAY, THEN.

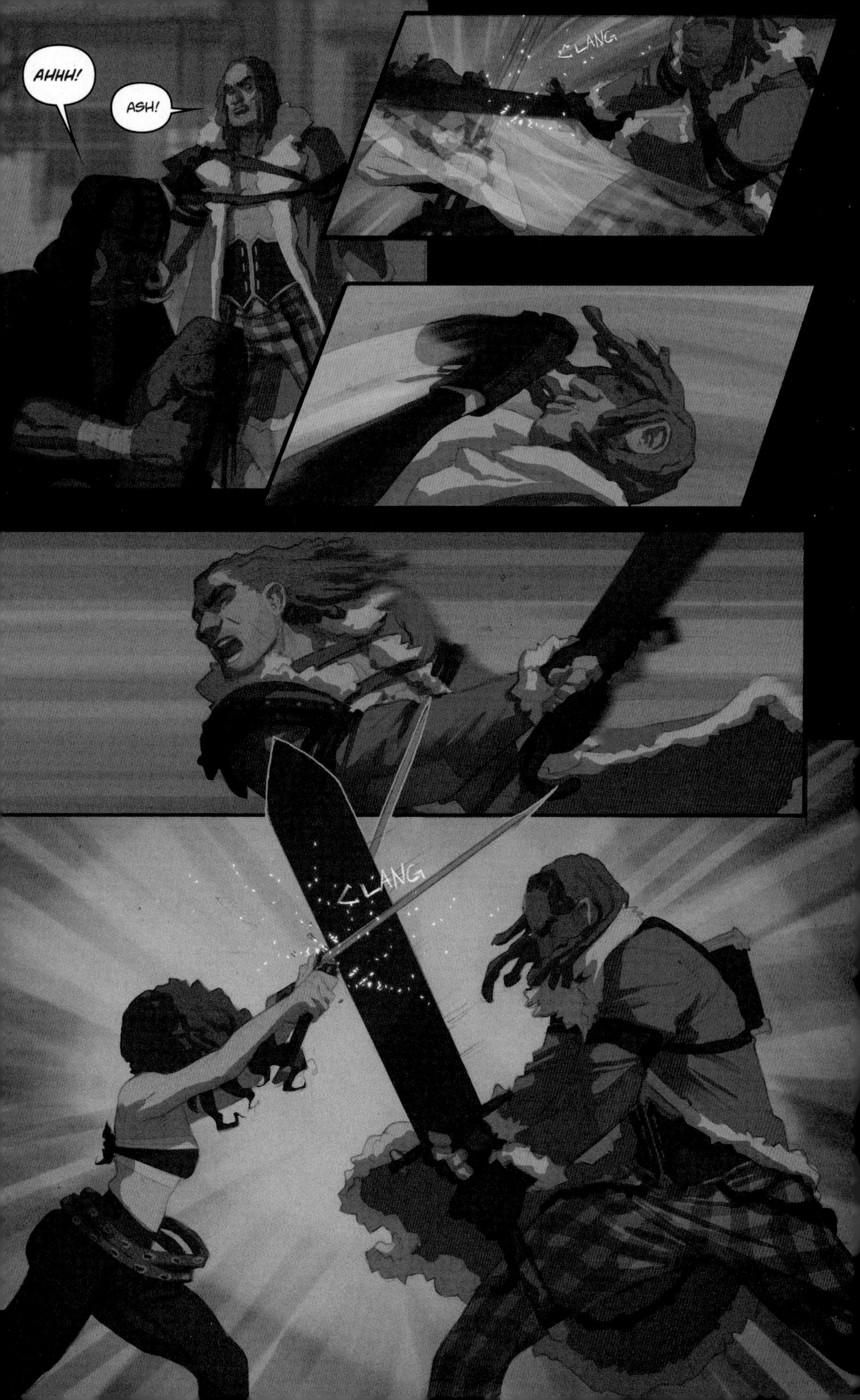
AHHH!
ASH!
CLANG
CLANG

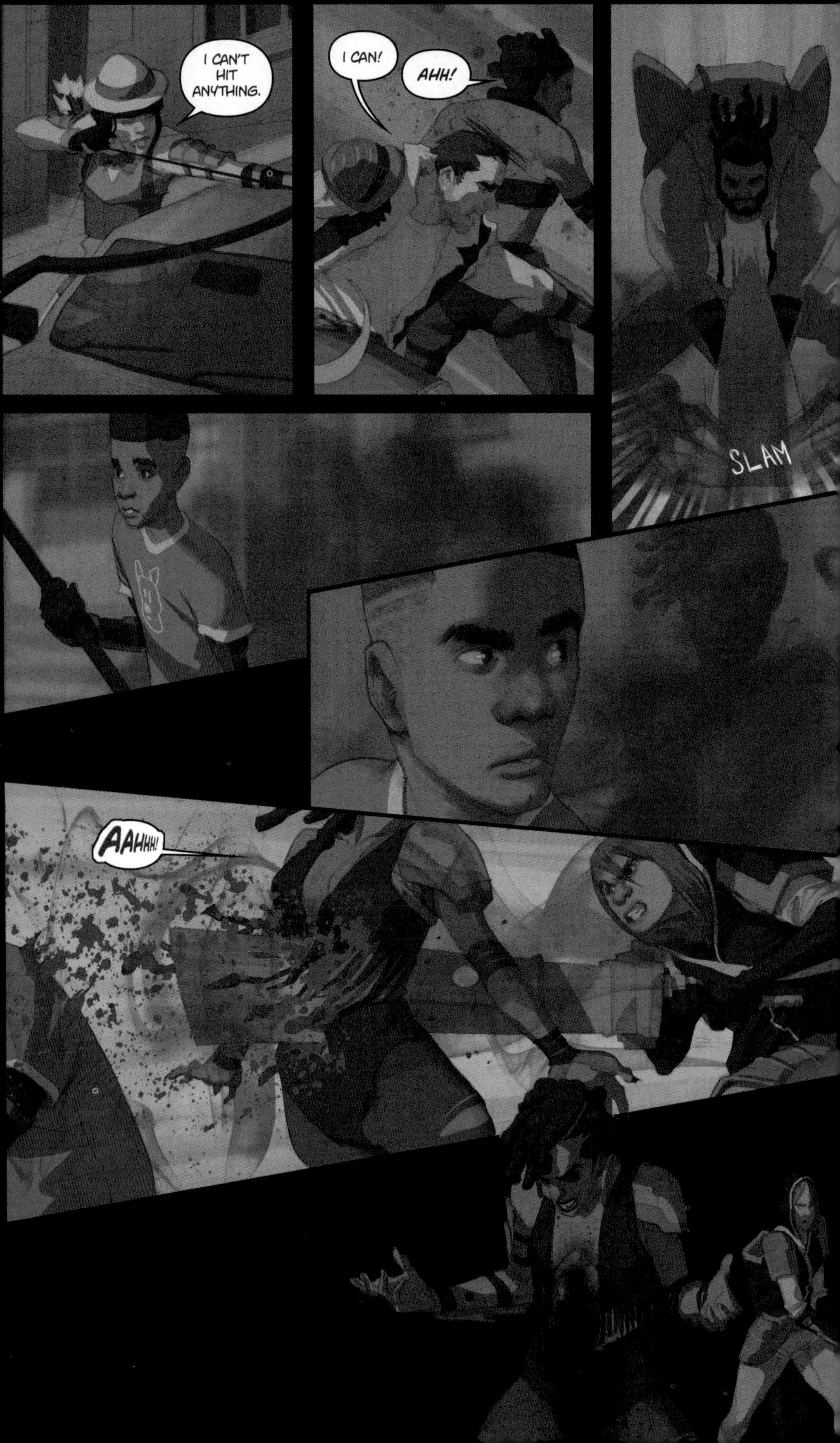

I CAN'T HIT ANYTHING.
I CAN!
AHH!
SLAM
AAHHH!

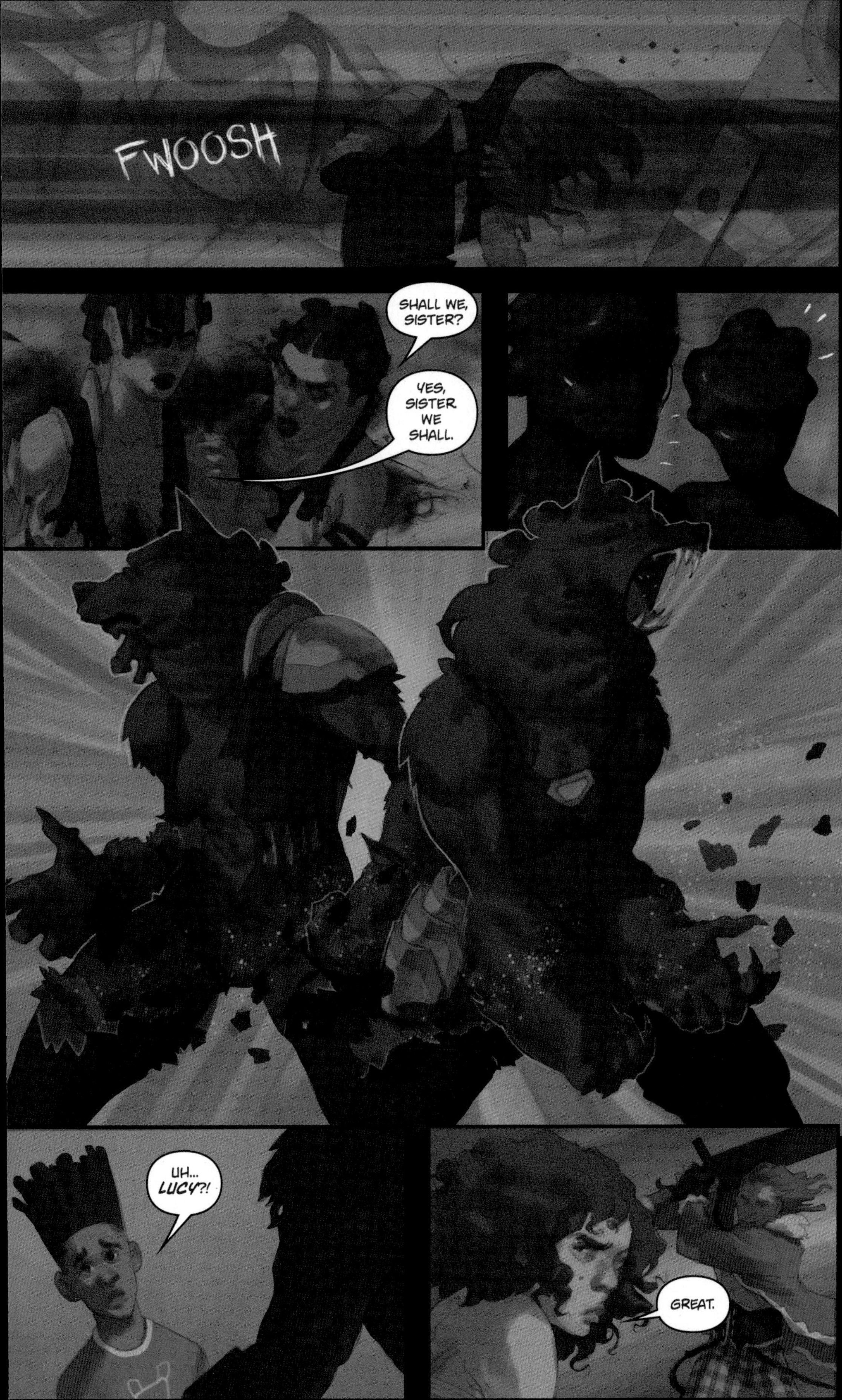
FWOOSH
SHALL WE, SISTER?
YES, SISTER WE SHALL.
UH... LUCY?!
GREAT.

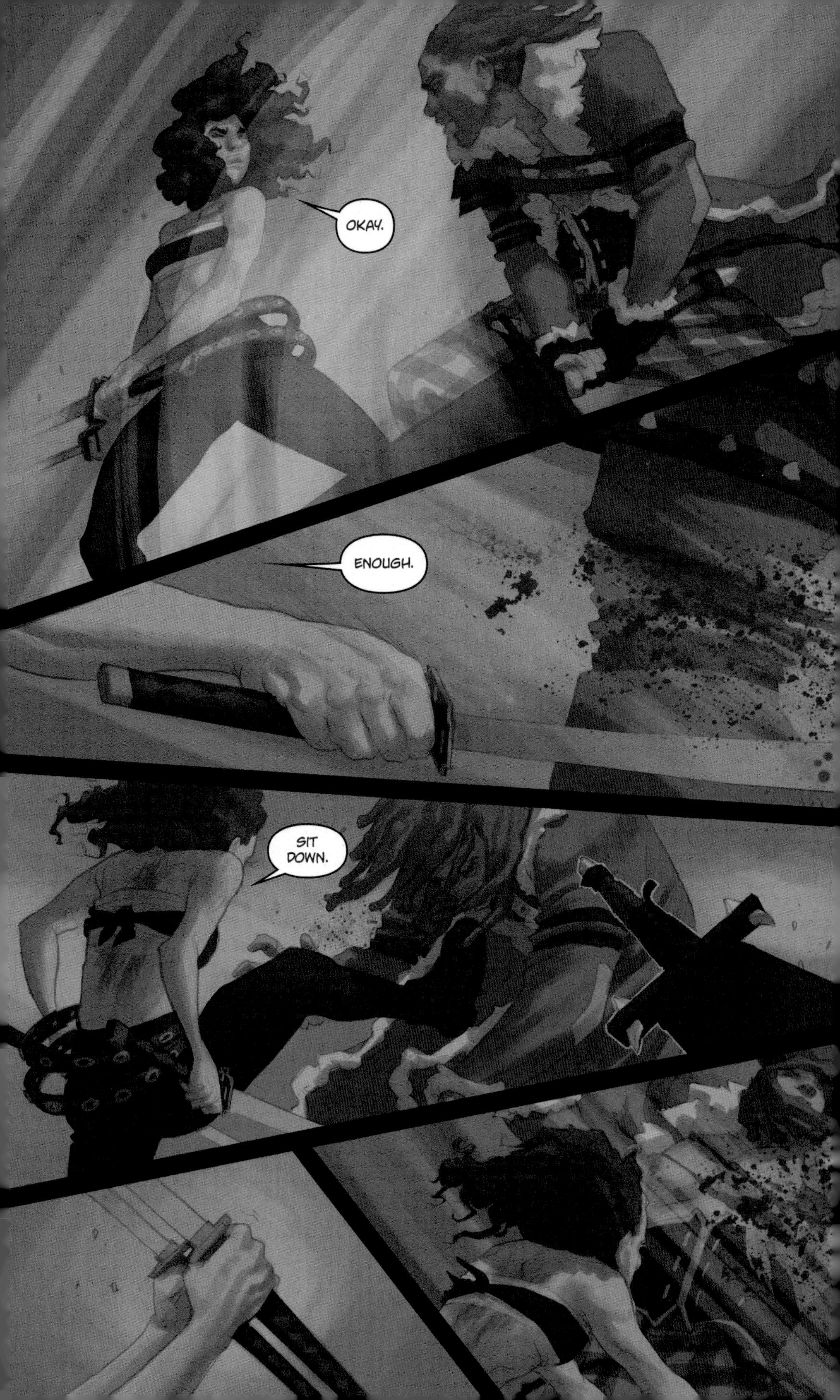
OKAY.
ENOUGH.
SIT DOWN.

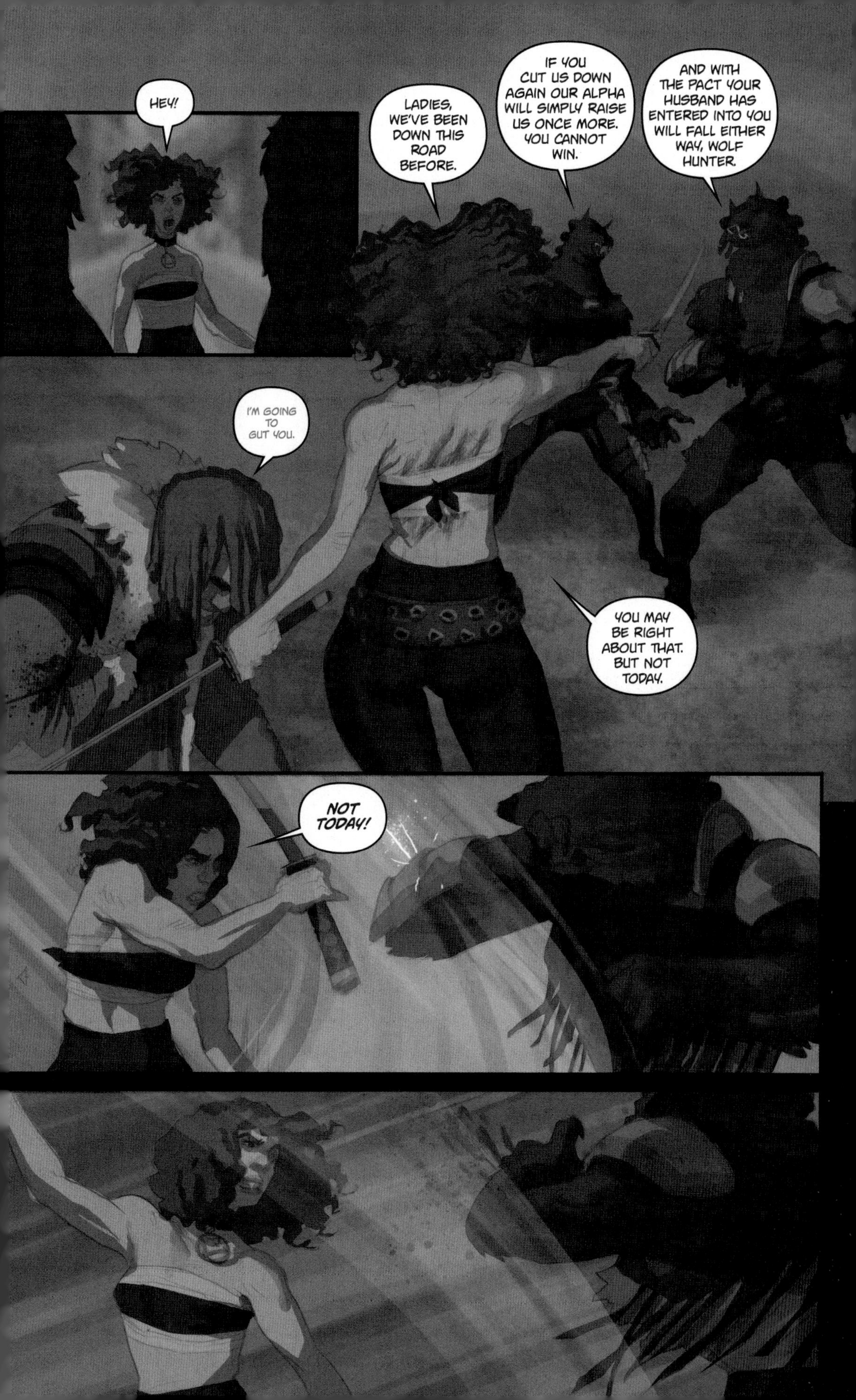
HEY!
LADIES, WE'VE BEEN DOWN THIS ROAD BEFORE.
IF YOU CUT US DOWN AGAIN OUR ALPHA WILL SIMPLY RAISE US ONCE MORE. YOU CANNOT WIN.
AND WITH THE PACT YOUR HUSBAND HAS ENTERED INTO YOU WILL FALL EITHER WAY, WOLF HUNTER.
I'M GOING TO GUT YOU.
YOU MAY BE RIGHT ABOUT THAT. BUT NOT TODAY.
NOT TODAY!

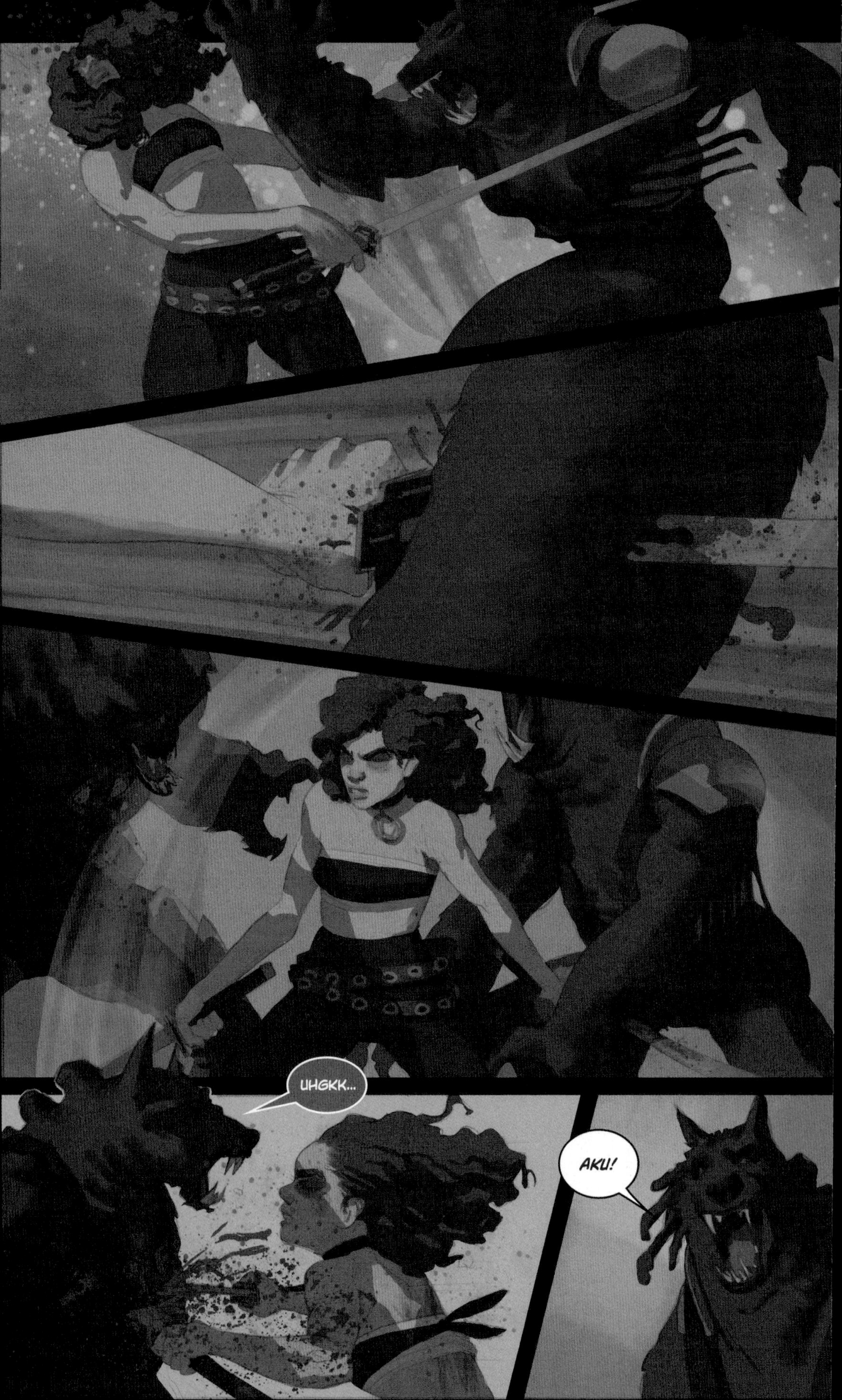
UHGKK...
AKU!

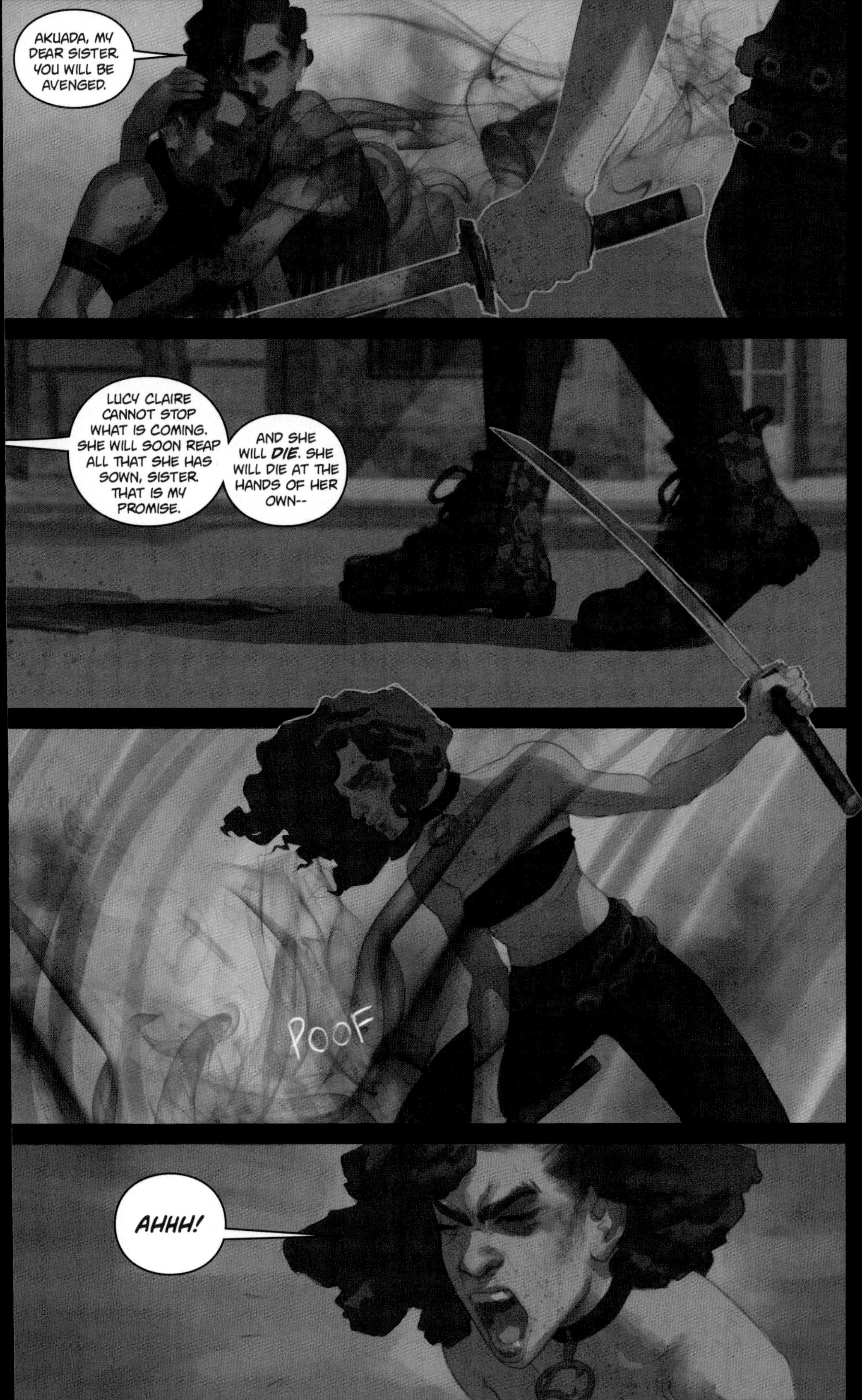
AKUADA, MY DEAR SISTER. YOU WILL BE AVENGED.
LUCY CLAIRE CANNOT STOP WHAT IS COMING. SHE WILL SOON REAP ALL THAT SHE HAS SOWN, SISTER. THAT IS MY PROMISE.
AND SHE WILL *DIE*. SHE WILL DIE AT THE HANDS OF HER OWN--
POOF
AHHH!

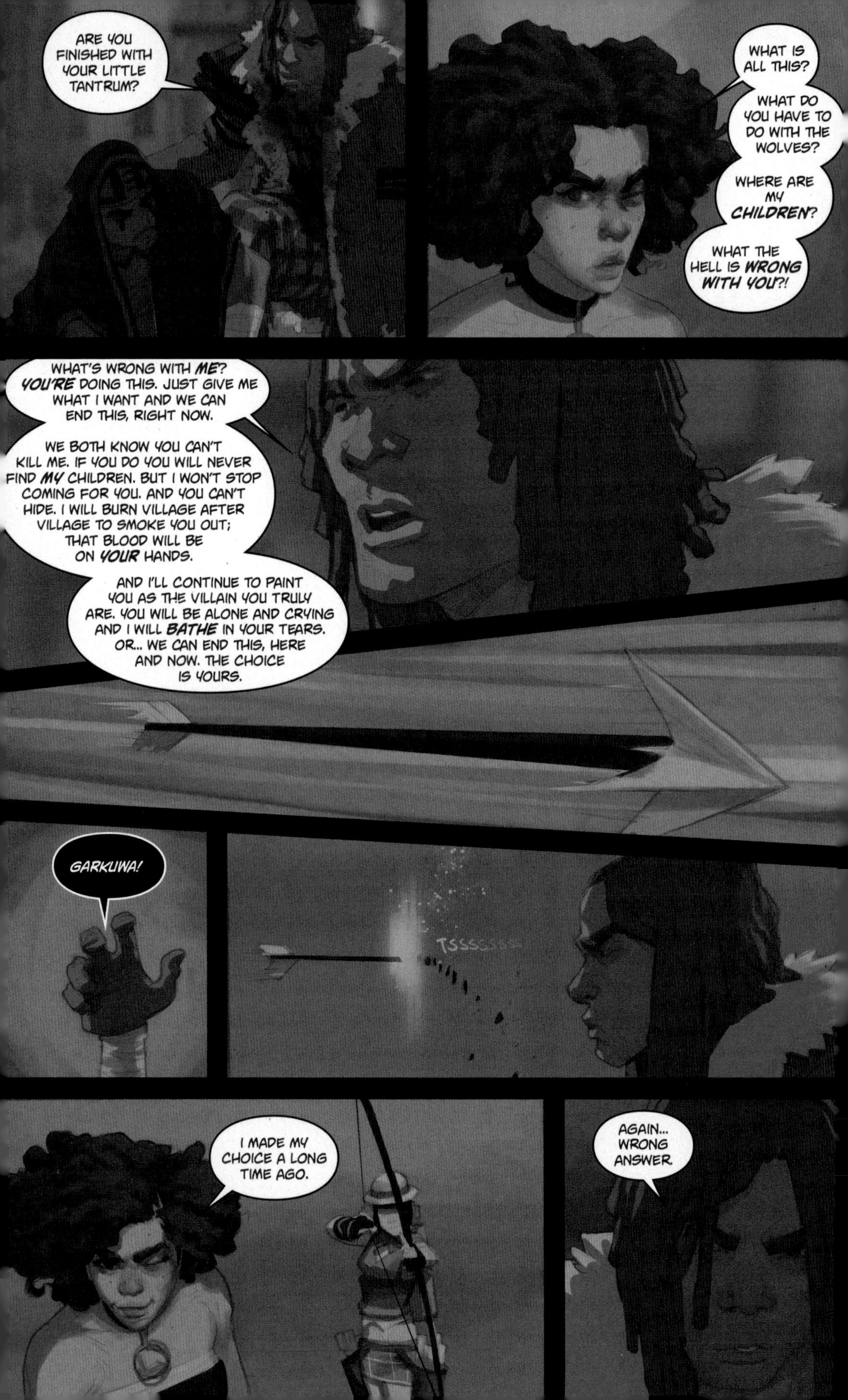
ARE YOU FINISHED WITH YOUR LITTLE TANTRUM?
WHAT IS ALL THIS?
WHAT DO YOU HAVE TO DO WITH THE WOLVES?
WHERE ARE MY CHILDREN?
WHAT THE HELL IS WRONG WITH YOU?!
WHAT'S WRONG WITH ME? YOU'RE DOING THIS. JUST GIVE ME WHAT I WANT AND WE CAN END THIS, RIGHT NOW.
WE BOTH KNOW YOU CAN'T KILL ME. IF YOU DO YOU WILL NEVER FIND MY CHILDREN. BUT I WON'T STOP COMING FOR YOU. AND YOU CAN'T HIDE. I WILL BURN VILLAGE AFTER VILLAGE TO SMOKE YOU OUT; THAT BLOOD WILL BE ON YOUR HANDS.
AND I'LL CONTINUE TO PAINT YOU AS THE VILLAIN YOU TRULY ARE. YOU WILL BE ALONE AND CRYING AND I WILL BATHE IN YOUR TEARS. OR... WE CAN END THIS, HERE AND NOW. THE CHOICE IS YOURS.
GARKUWA!
TSSSSSSS
I MADE MY CHOICE A LONG TIME AGO.
AGAIN... WRONG ANSWER.

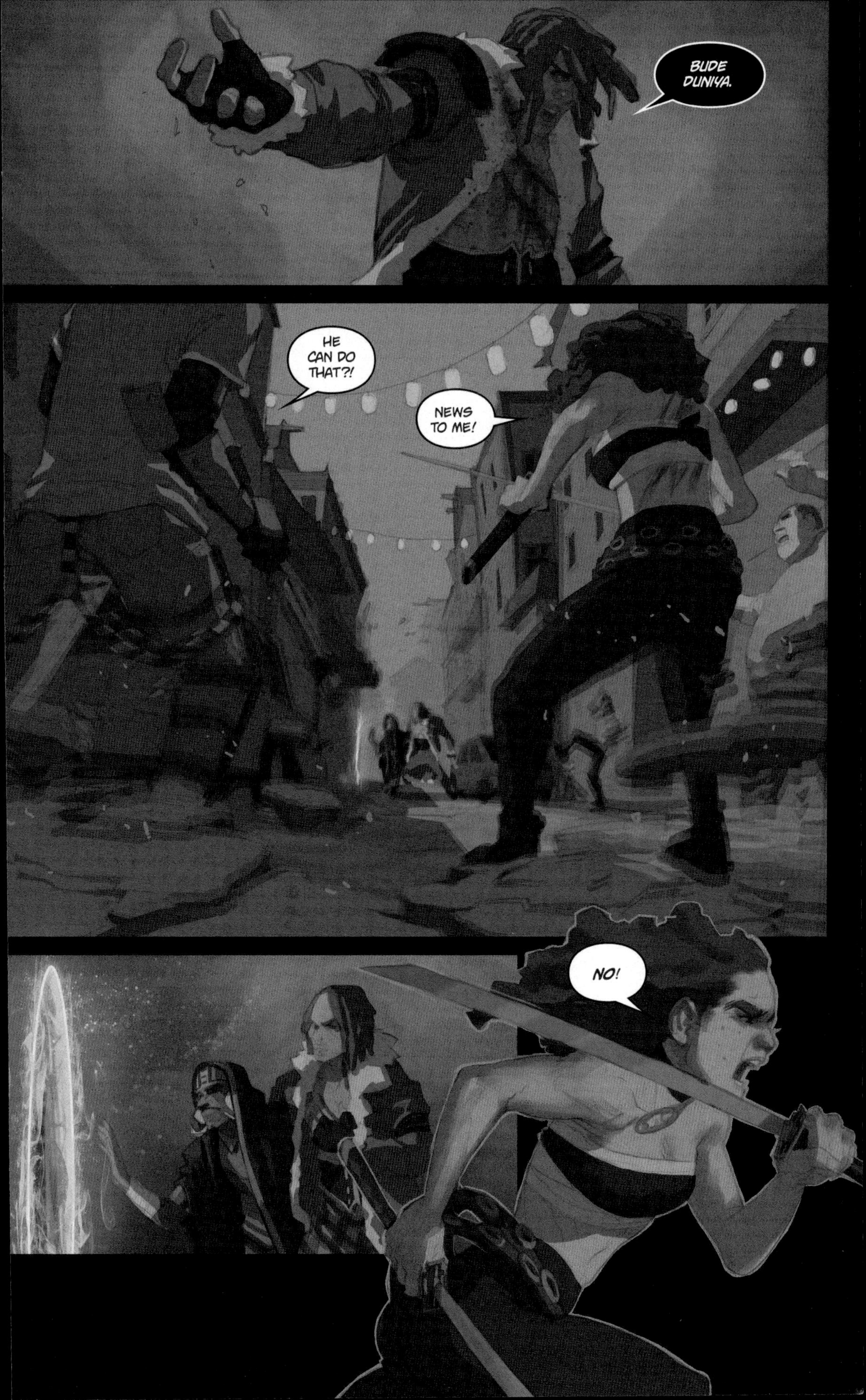
BUDE DUNIYA.
HE CAN DO THAT?!
NEWS TO ME!
NO!

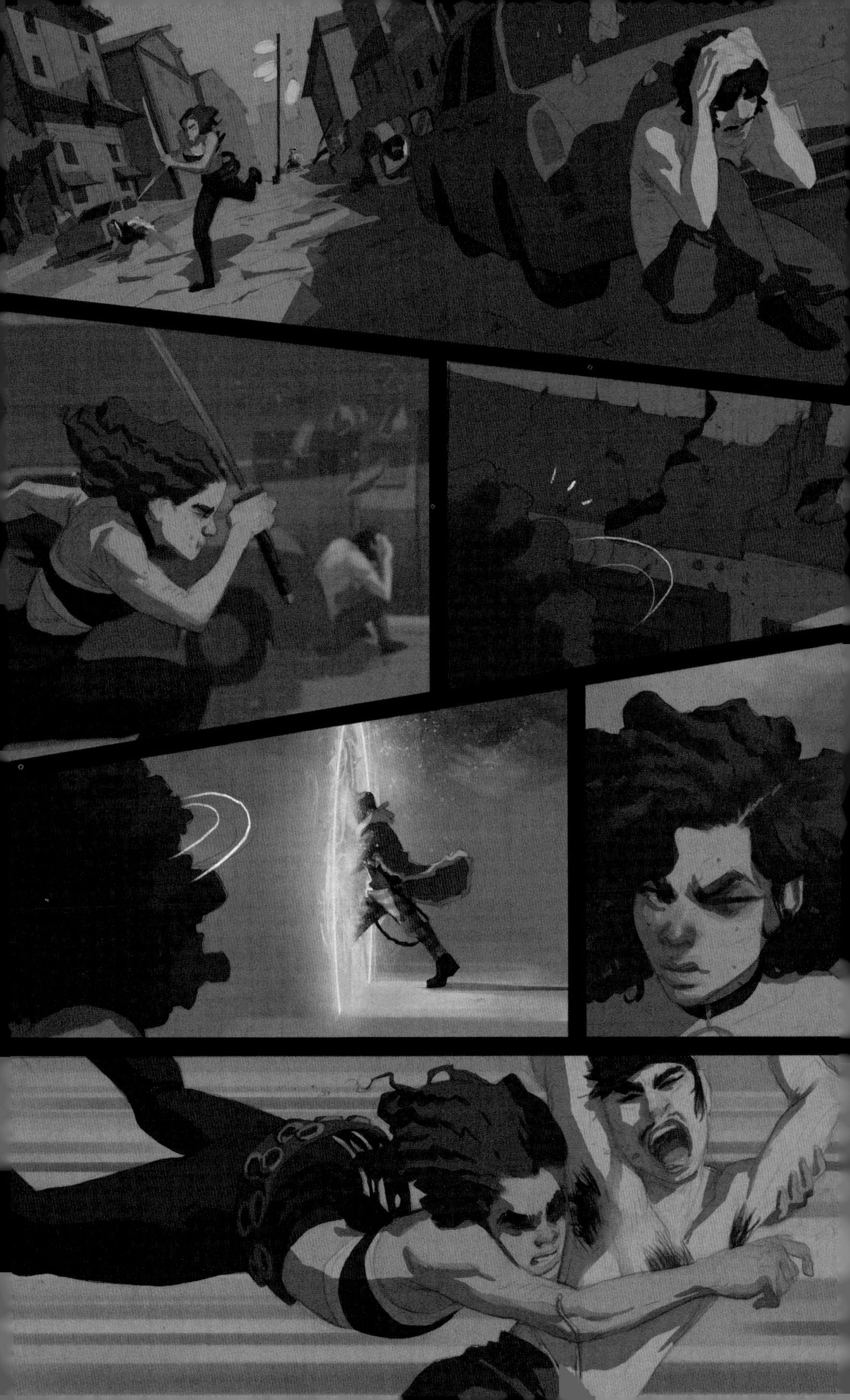

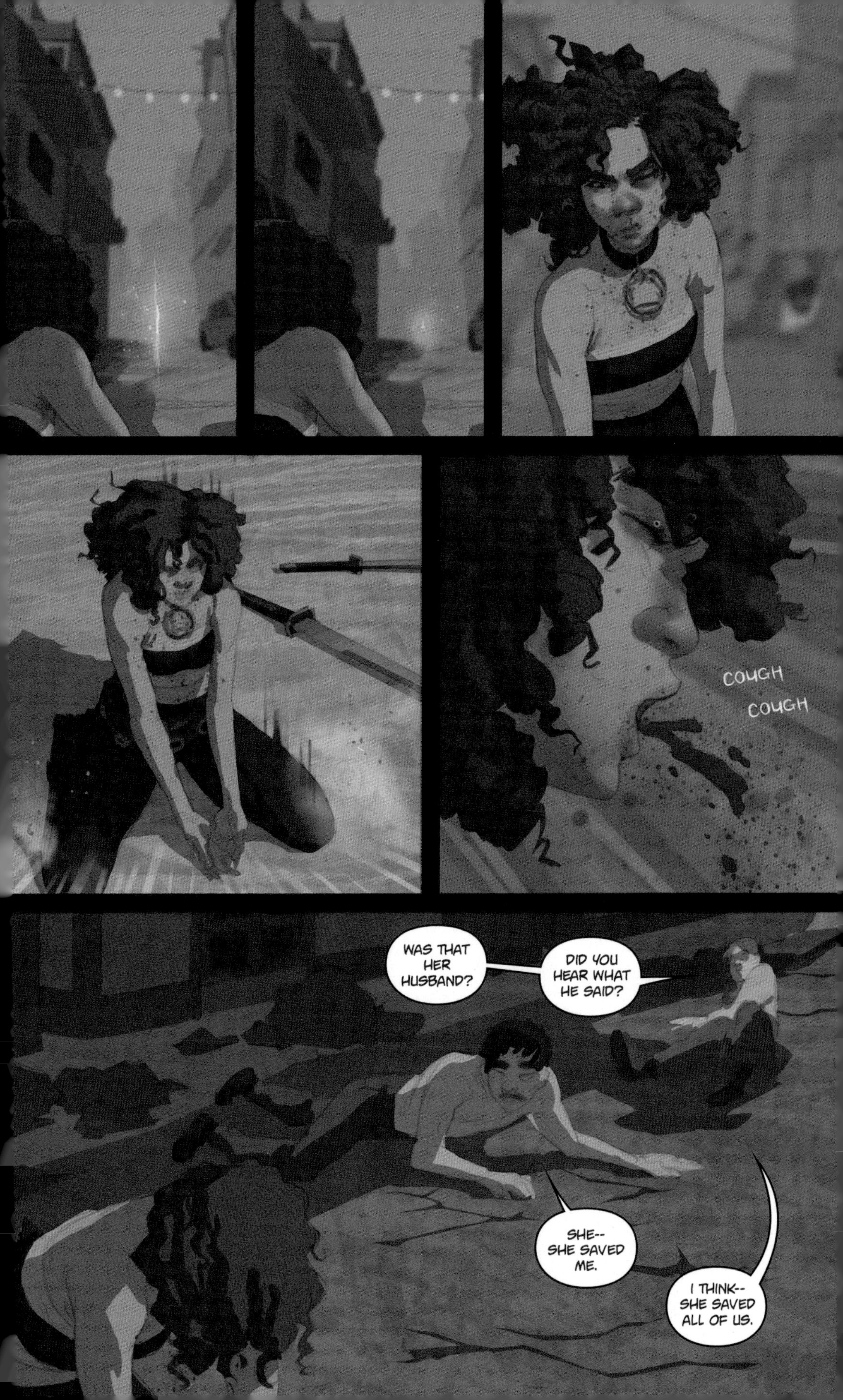
COUGH
COUGH
WAS THAT HER HUSBAND?
DID YOU HEAR WHAT HE SAID?
SHE-- SHE SAVED ME.
I THINK-- SHE SAVED ALL OF US.

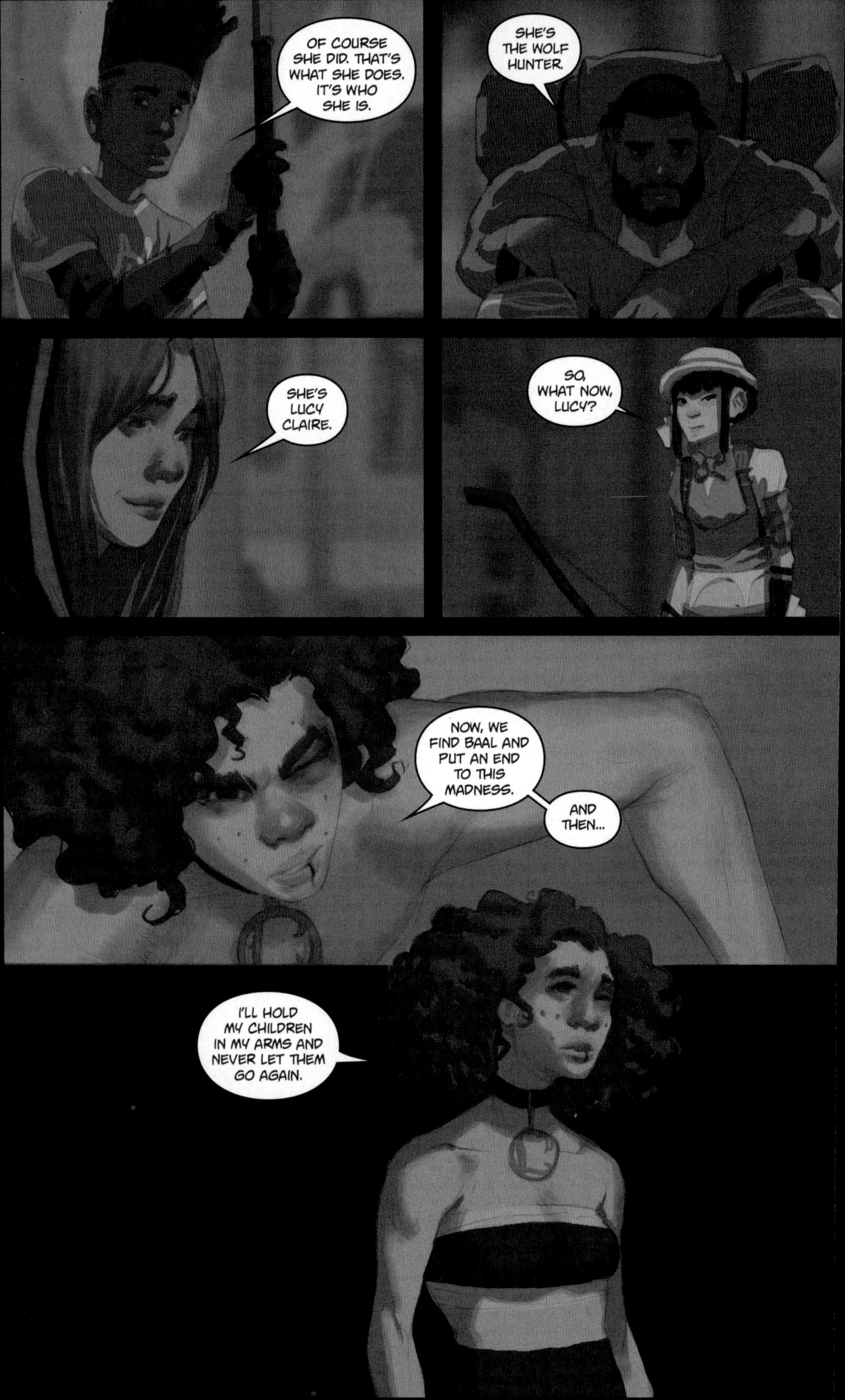
OF COURSE SHE DID. THAT'S WHAT SHE DOES. IT'S WHO SHE IS.
SHE'S THE WOLF HUNTER.
SHE'S LUCY CLAIRE.
SO, WHAT NOW, LUCY?
NOW, WE FIND BAAL AND PUT AN END TO THIS MADNESS.
AND THEN...
I'LL HOLD MY CHILDREN IN MY ARMS AND NEVER LET THEM GO AGAIN.

EXTRAS

B Covers
Unused Covers
Sketchbook

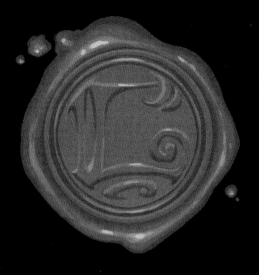

ISSUE #1 COVER B

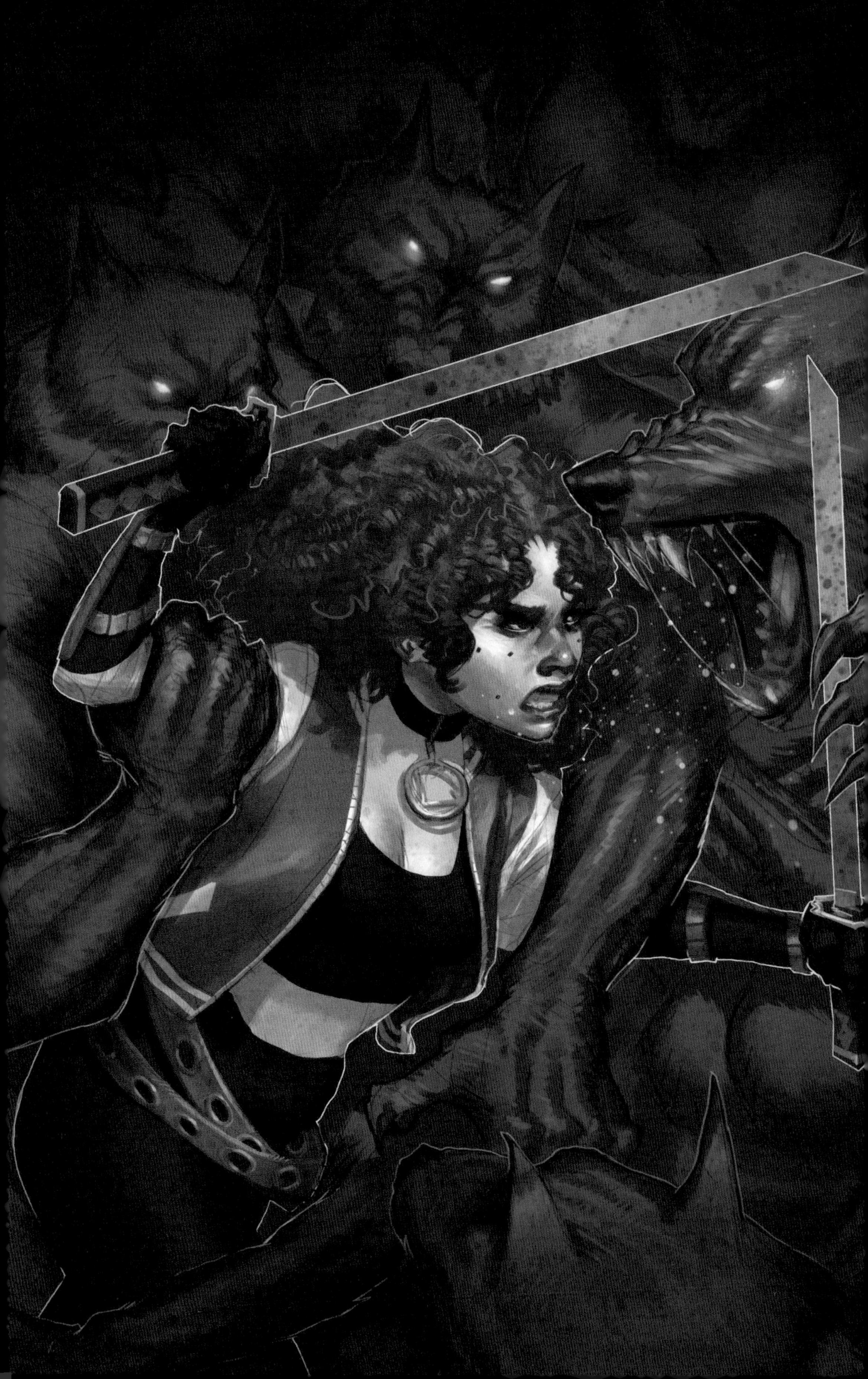

ISSUE #2 COVER B

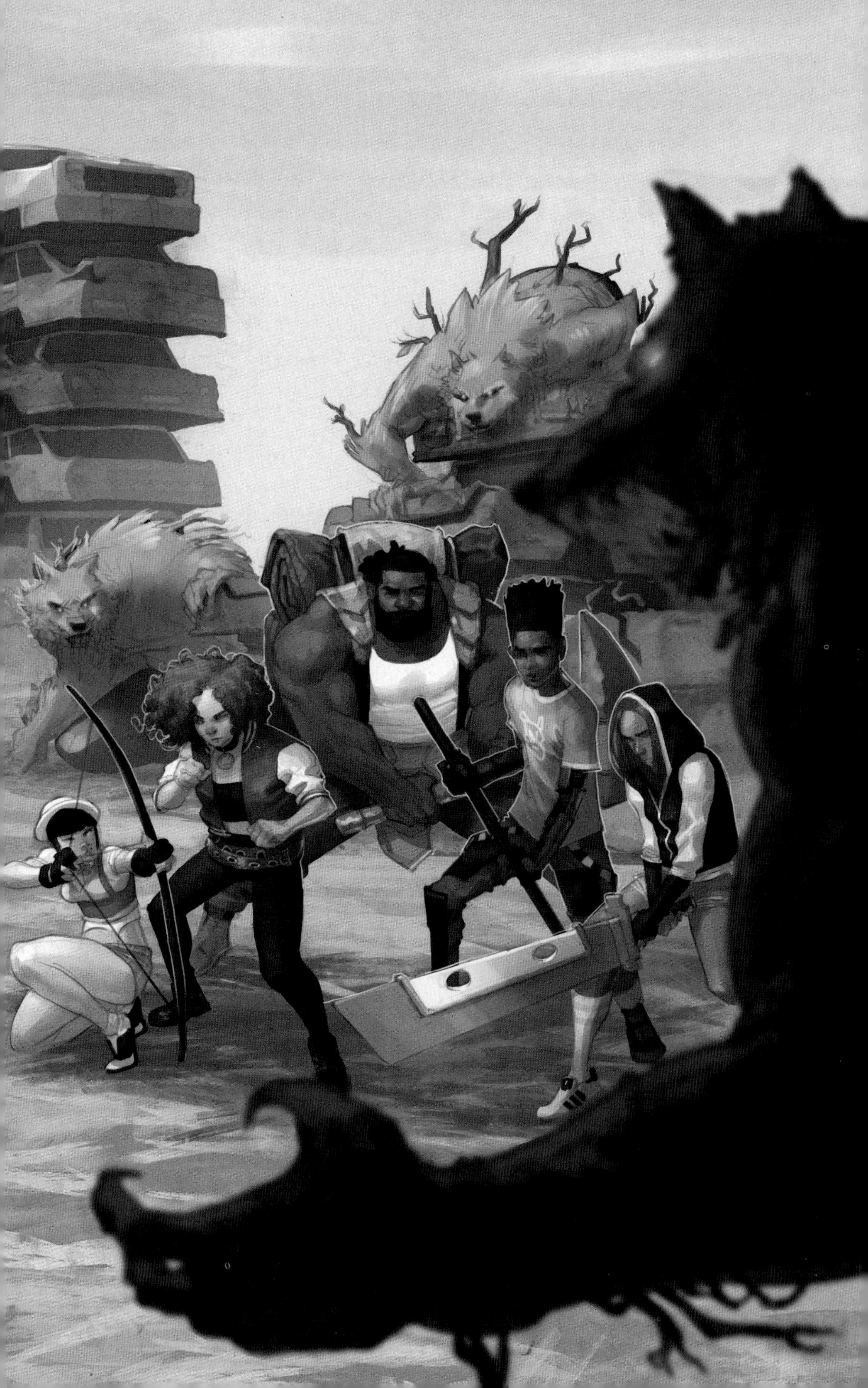

ISSUE #3 COVER B

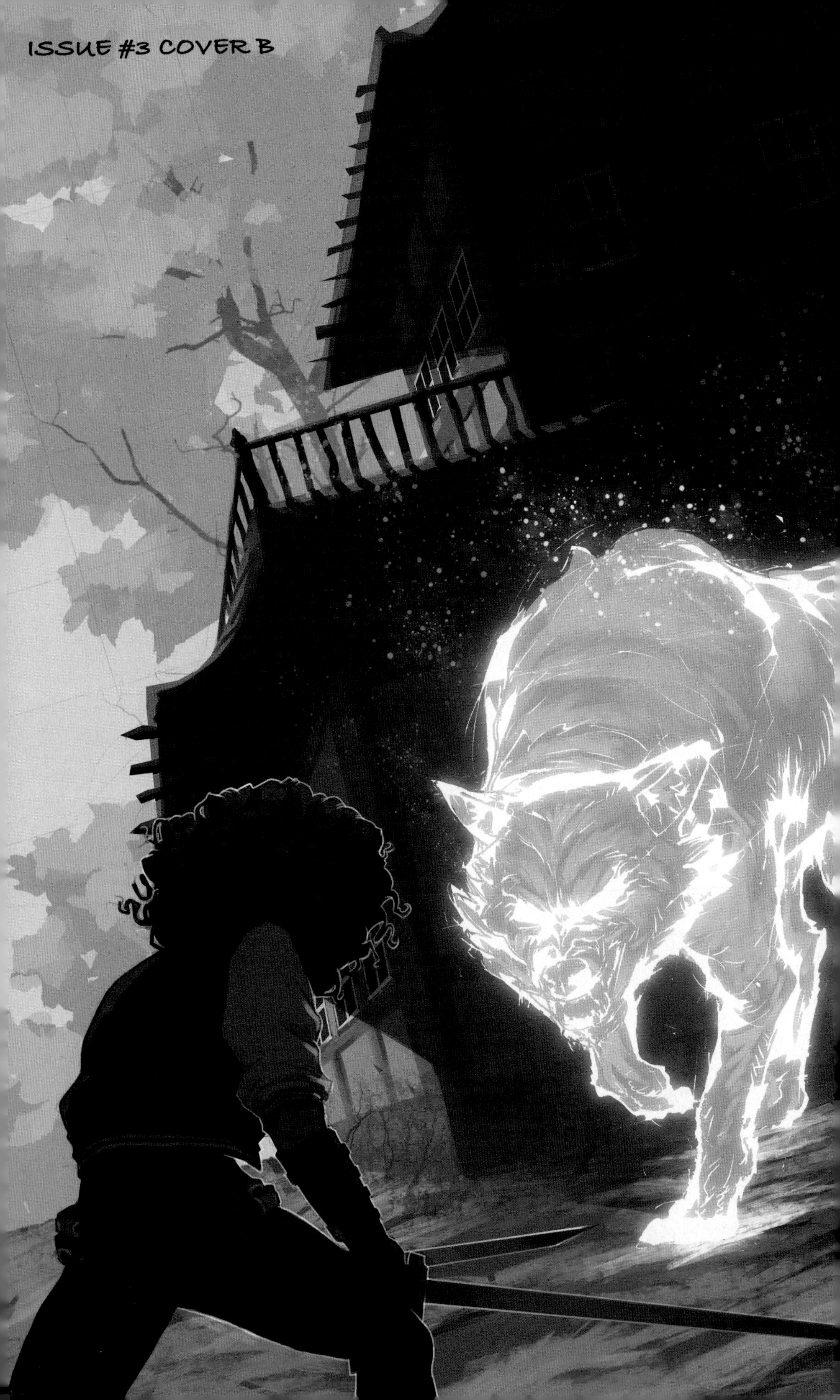

ISSUE #4 COVER B

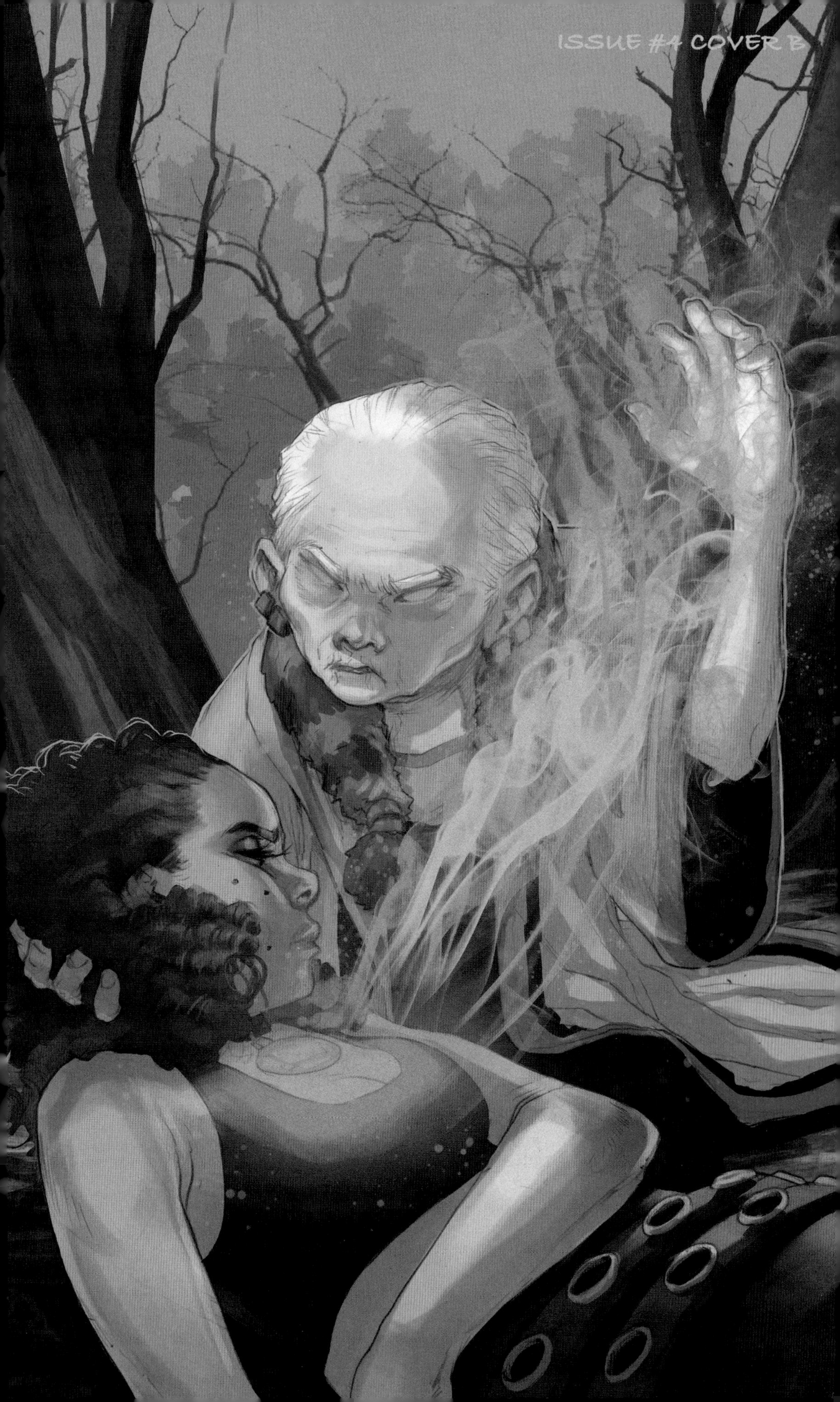

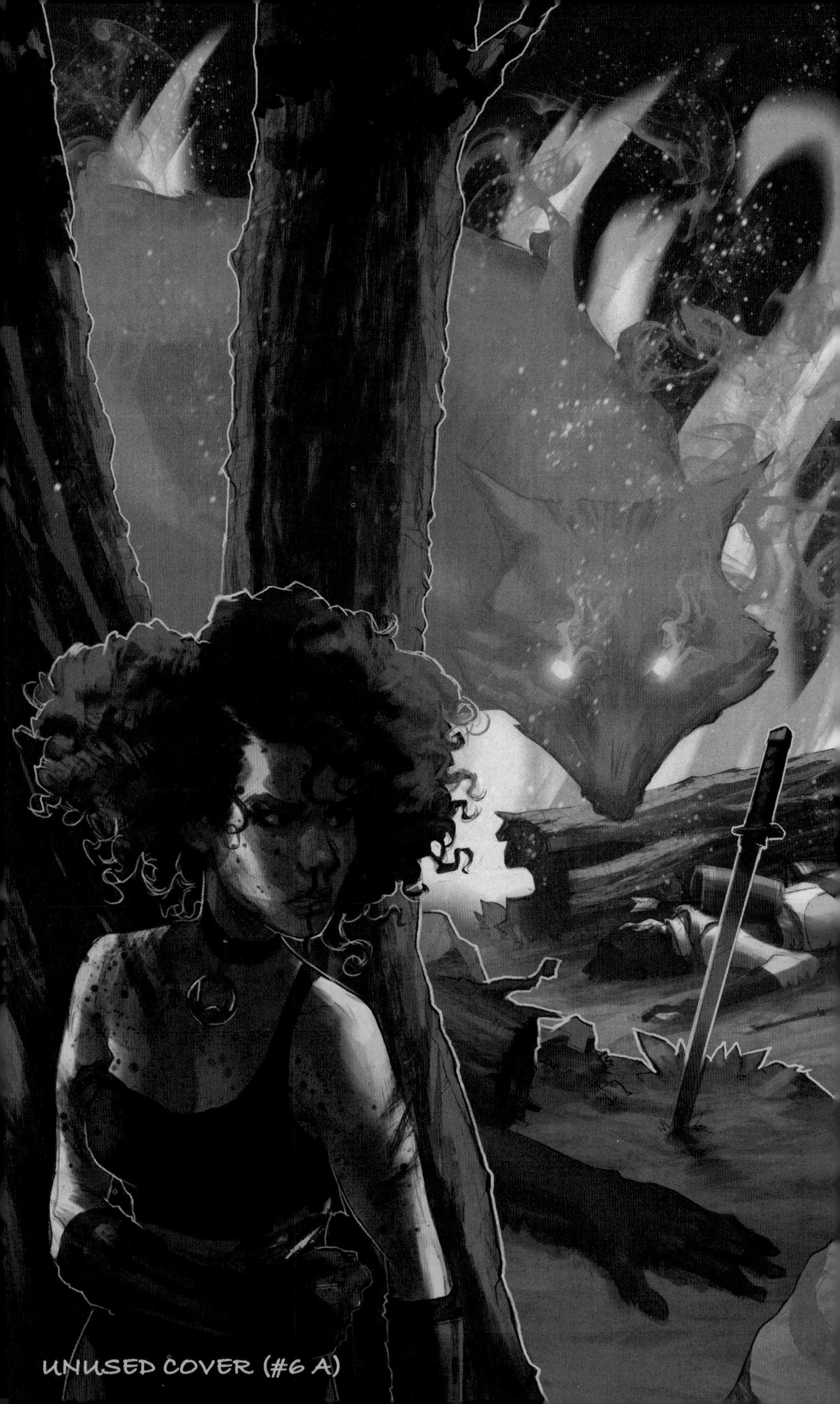

UNUSED COVER (#6 A)

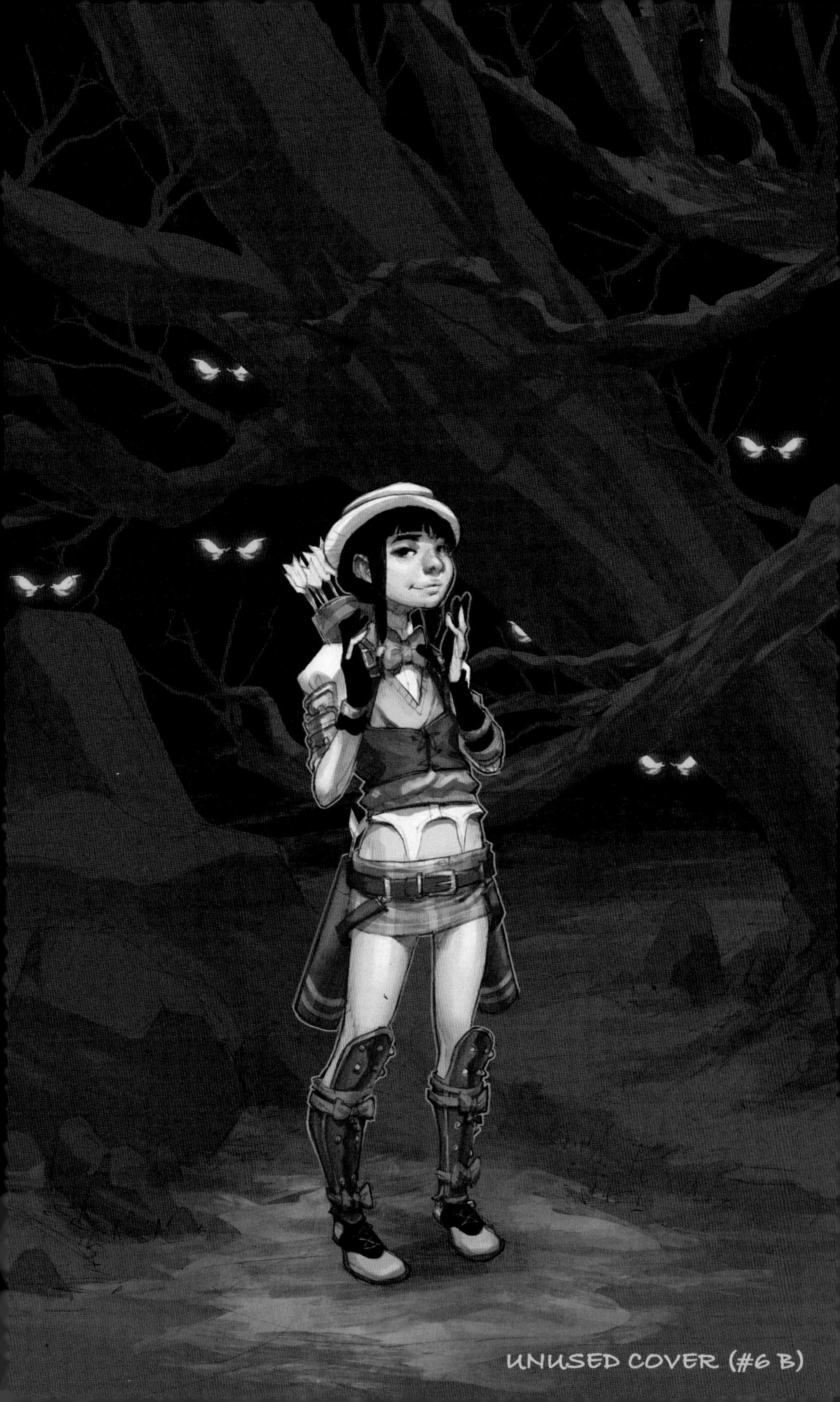

UNUSED COVER (#6 B)

LUCY CLAIRE REDEMPTION

SKETCHBOOK

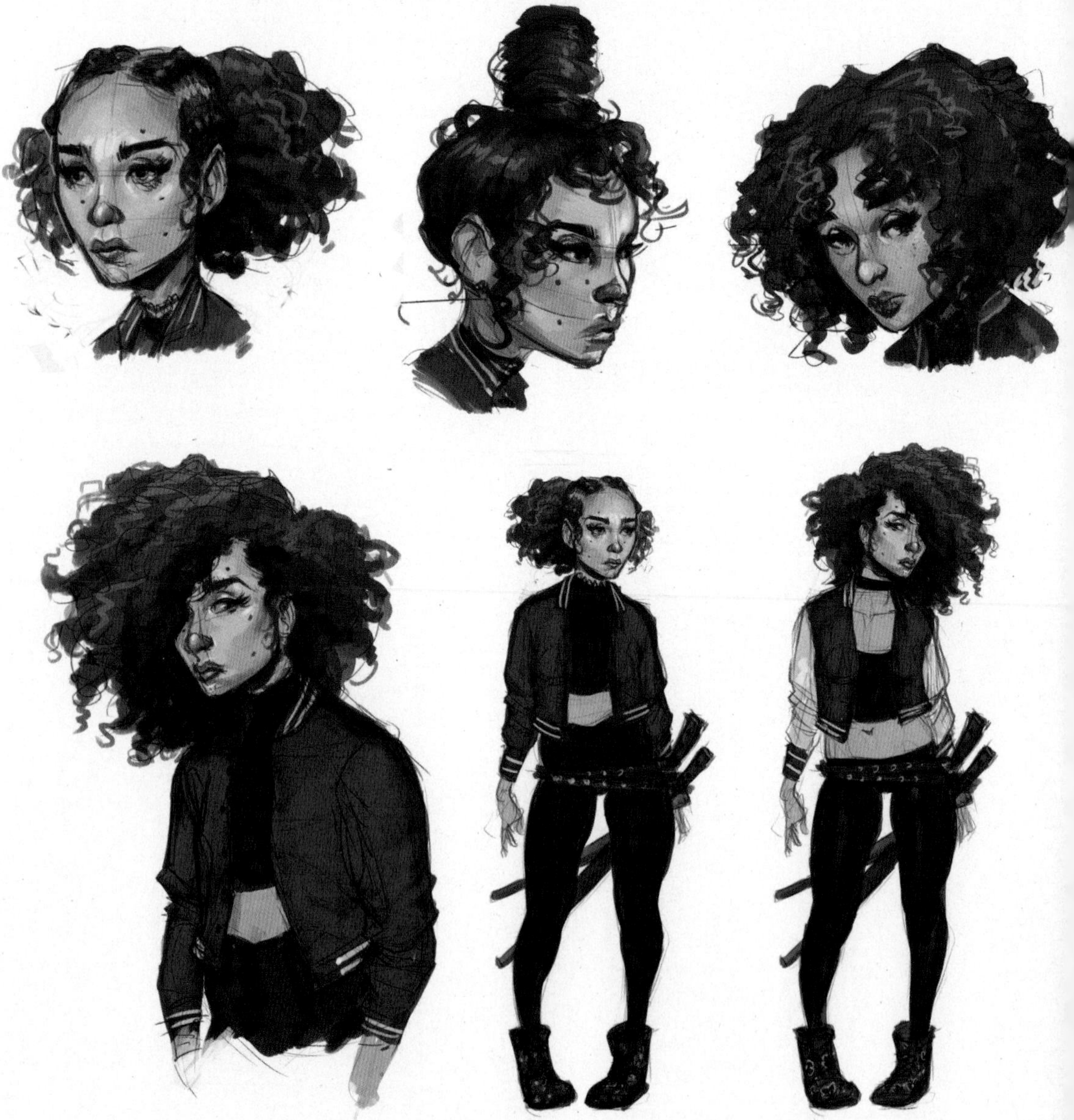

EARLY CHARACTER DESIGNS FOR OUR MAIN PROTAGONIST - LUCY CLAIRE

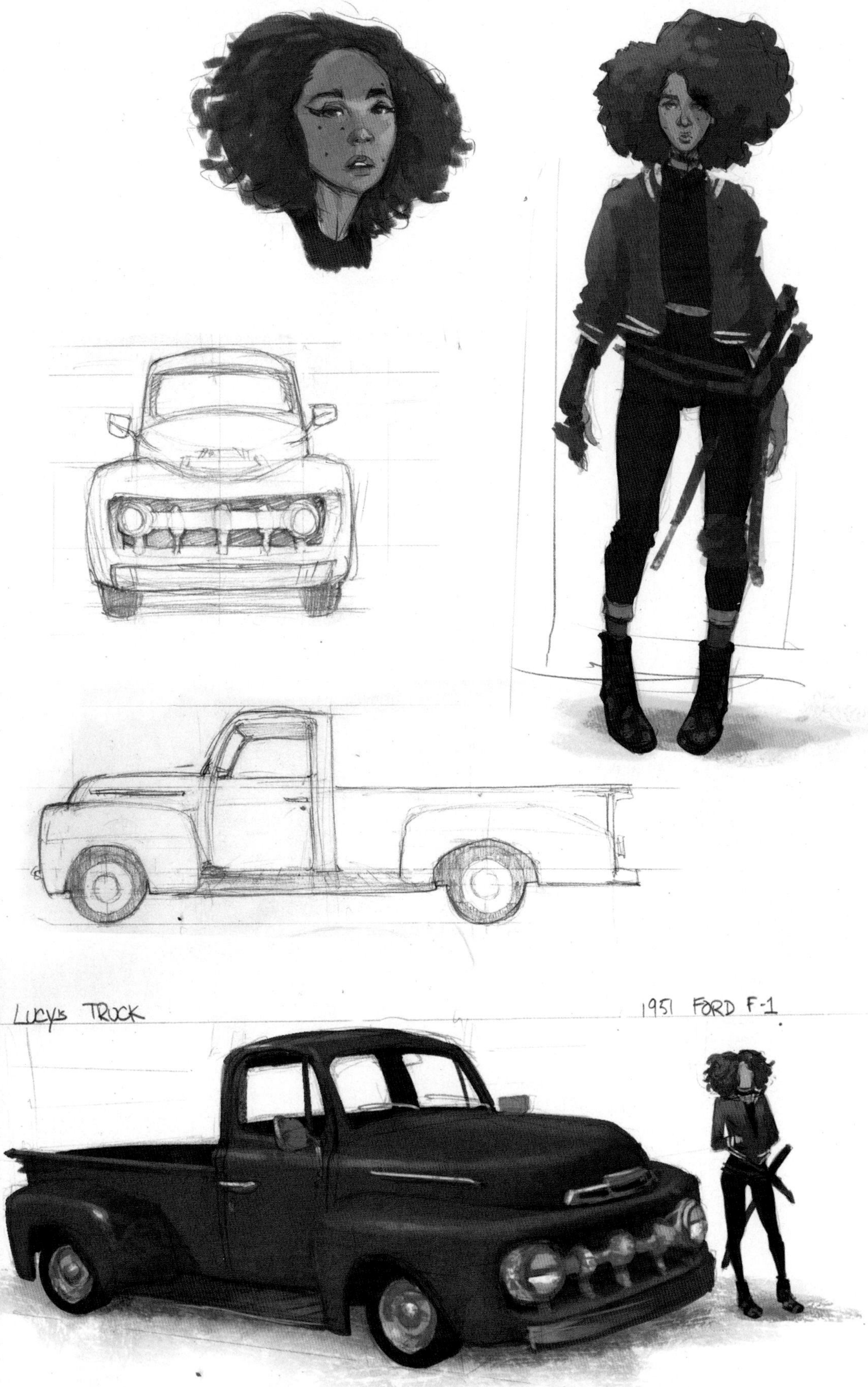
Lucy's TRUCK
1951 FORD F-1

LUCY CONCEPTS AND EARLY DESIGNS FOR THE WOLF HUNTER'S TRUCK

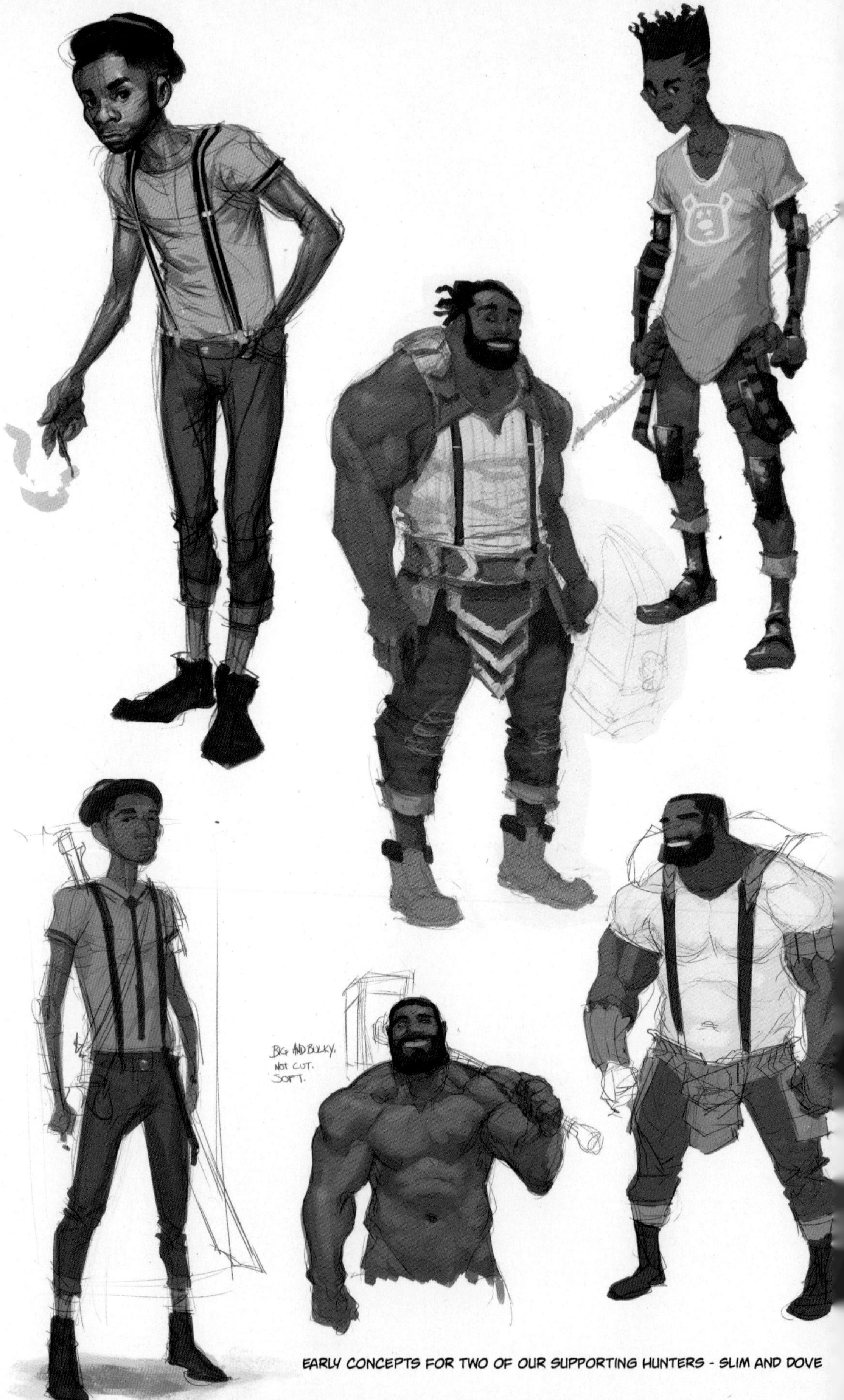
BIG AND BULKY.
NOT CUT.
SOFT.

EARLY CONCEPTS FOR TWO OF OUR SUPPORTING HUNTERS - SLIM AND DOVE

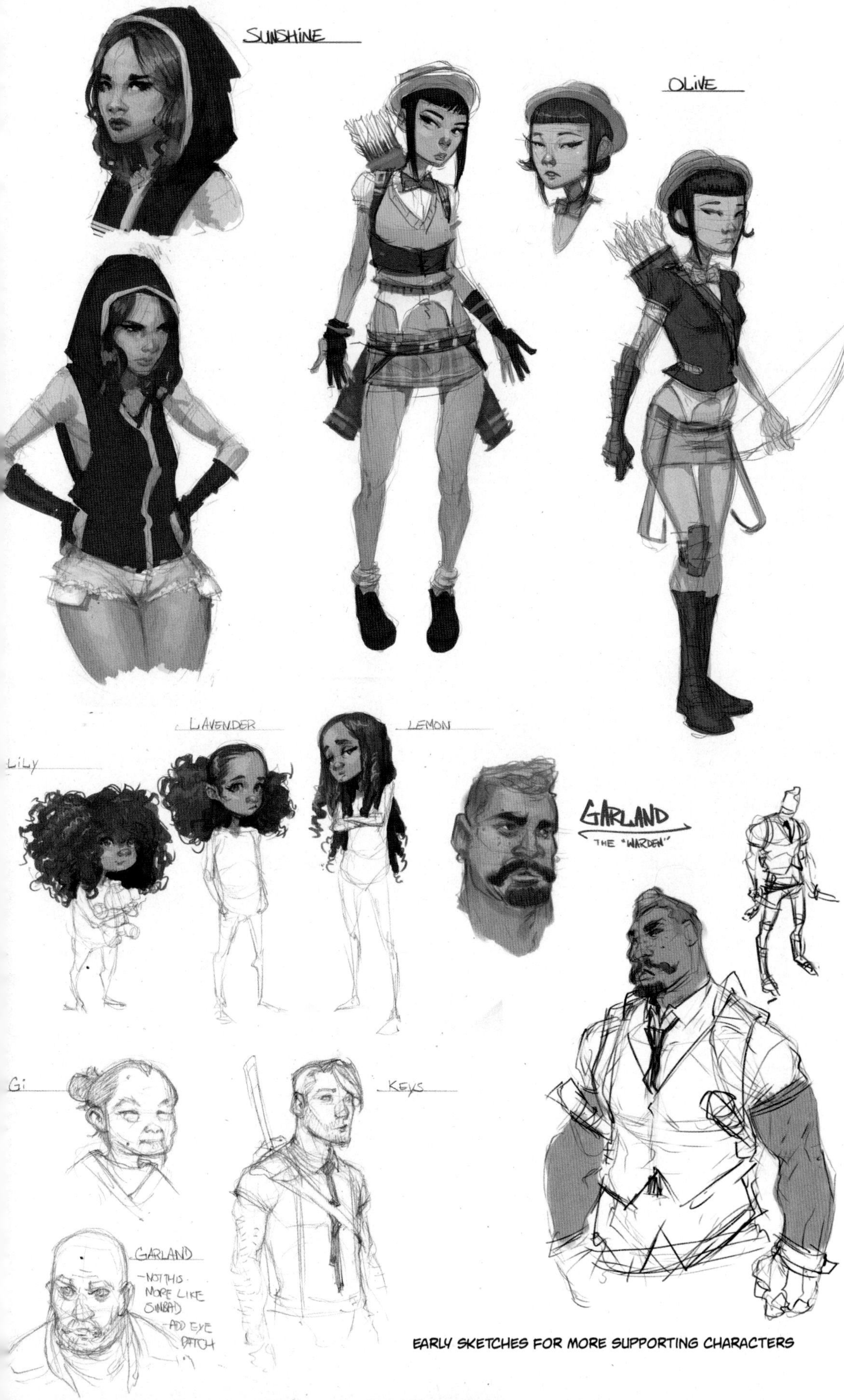
SUNSHINE
OLIVE
LAVENDER
LEMON
LILY
GARLAND
THE "WARDEN"
GI
KEYS
GARLAND
-NOT THIS
MORE LIKE
SINBAD
-ADD EYE
PATCH

EARLY SKETCHES FOR MORE SUPPORTING CHARACTERS

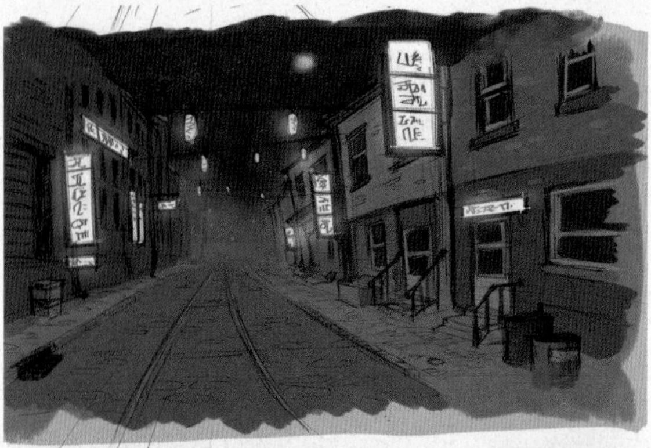

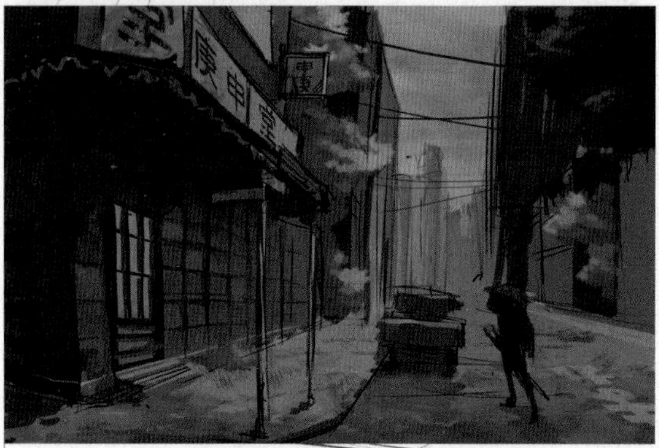

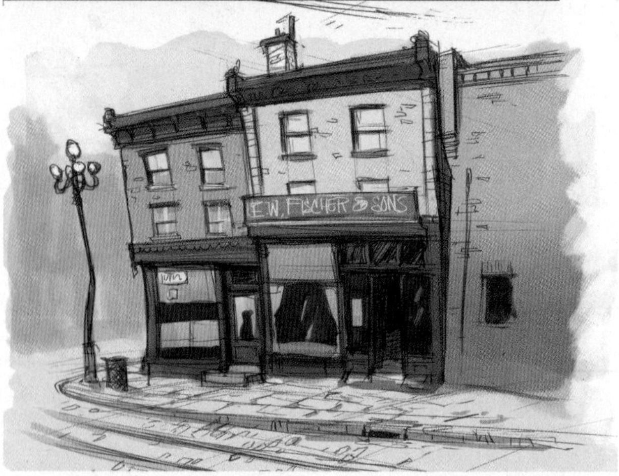
E.W. FISCHER & SONS

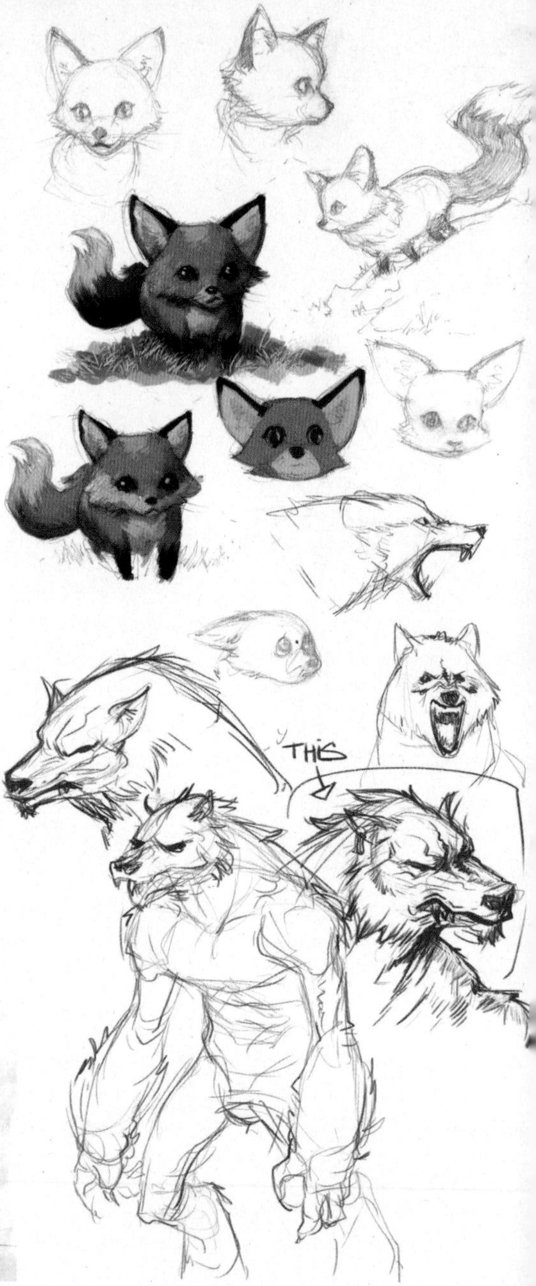
THIS

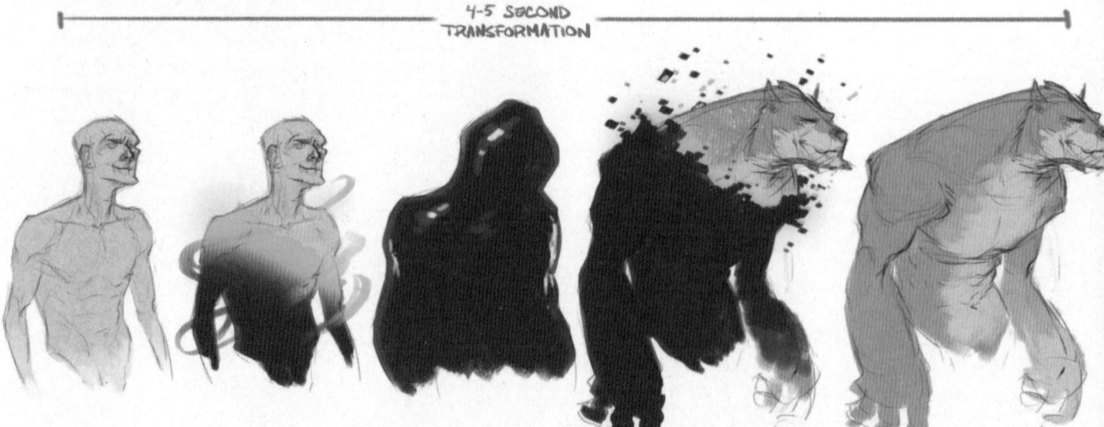
4-5 SECOND TRANSFORMATION

ENVIRONMENTAL DESIGNS AS WELL AS CREATURE CONCEPTS AND WOLF TRANSFORMATION